UNSUSPECTING, WE STEPPED INTO PROTEUS STATION.

I maneuvered us through the crowd to our desk and smiled at the female Filly seated there. From the hovering presence of a much older male Filly behind her, I guessed this was probably her first day on the job and he was there to vet her performance. "I greet you," I said, offering my hand to the reader to confirm my identity. "You have a very efficient—"

"Mr. Frank Compton?" the older Filly interrupted as he strode up to the desk.

"Yes," I confirmed. "My bags are those two over—"

"I am *Chinzro* Hchchu, assistant director of *Kuzyatru* Station," he interrupted, raising his hand like the Pope delivering a blessing. In response, three tall Fillies wearing gray and black jumpsuits, who had been loitering behind the row of desks to either side of us, started forward.

"Is there a problem?" I asked carefully, watching the approaching Fillies out of the corner of my eye. In my pocket, I could feel the *kwi* tingling as Bayta activated it.

"A very serious problem," Hchchu said sternly. "You are under arrest." He paused dramatically. "For murder."

"Packed with intrigue and action—and with questions of who is really on the side of whom up to the last chapter—this is must reading for all who liked the previous Quadrail novels."   —*Booklist*

Turn the page for more raves.

Praise for *Judgment at Proteus*

"For those who like shoot 'em up, blow 'em up, smash 'em up, blast 'em to atoms space opera, *Judgment at Proteus* by Hugo-winning Timothy Zahn, who has written plenty of authorized Star Wars™ novels, can't be beaten."   —*AmoXcalli*

"Zahn is not loath to spring traps, create setups, and twist things around. I want to go back to the beginning of the series and read it all the way through in one sitting!"   —*KD Did It*

"The latest action-packed Quadrail space adventure (see *The Domino Pattern*) is an exciting science fiction thriller filled with twists."   —*Midwest Book Review*

———————————

. . . and Praise for the Quadrail Series

"Years ago, Timothy Zahn leaped out of my slush pile: one of the first new writers to rivet my attention so thoroughly I almost missed my train. Since then he's grown impressively and remains one of science fiction's best practitioners of solid imagining and storytelling."
                              —Stanley Schmidt, *Analog Magazine*

"Tim Zahn is a master of tactics and puts his own edge on complex hard-SF thrillers. His original work is sure to please his legions of Star Wars™ fans."
                              —Kevin J. Anderson,
                              New York Times bestselling coauthor of
                              Dune: The Battle of Corrin

"Timothy Zahn takes a boldly anachronistic approach to space travel. . . . Once you accept the trains and go along for the ride, *Night Train to Rigel* is a fun trip to the end of the line."   —*The Denver Post*

BOOKS BY TIMOTHY ZAHN

*Denotes a Tor Book

Judgment at Proteus

Timothy Zahn

A TOM DOHERTY ASSOCIATES BOOK | NEW YORK

This is a work of fiction. All of the characters, organizations, and events portrayed in this novel are either products of the author's imagination or are used fictitiously.

JUDGMENT AT PROTEUS

Copyright © 2012 by Timothy Zahn

All rights reserved.

Edited by James Frenkel

A Tor Book
Published by Tom Doherty Associates, LLC
175 Fifth Avenue
New York, NY 10010

www.tor-forge.com

Tor® is a registered trademark of Tom Doherty Associates, LLC.

ISBN 978-0-7653-6194-3

Tor books may be purchsed for educational, business, or promotional use. For information on bulk purchases, please contact Macmillan Corporate and Premium Sales Deportment at 1-800-221-7945 extension 5442 or write specialmarkets@macmillan.com.

First Edition: June 2012
First Mass Market Edition: May 2013

Printed in the United States of America

0 9 8 7 6 5 4 3 2 1

For Corwin
For all his help in guiding
the Quadrail series safely into station

Judgment at Proteus

ONE :

The Filiaelian facing me was a bit bigger than most of those of his species, a couple of centimeters taller than I was and about ten kilos heavier. There was a sheen of sweat on his long, horse-like face, and the dark eyes boring out at me had a deadly carnest expression to them.

The expression, and the face, shook briefly as the hand gripping my throat slammed my head and back hard against the display window of my first-class Quad-rail compartment.

From my right came a muffled gasp, and my eyes flicked in that direction. Bayta, my companion and partner in this quiet war I'd joined nearly two years ago, was standing across the room watching us, her eyes wide, one hand gripping the edge of the partially open divider that separated the halves of our double compartment.

I shifted my attention back to the long Filly face bare centimeters from my own. *Logra* Emikai had once been a cop, genetically engineered for loyalty to the rulers of his species. He had probably also been engineered for strength, agility, and God only knew what else.

The hand around my throat tightened a little. "Well, Mr. Compton?" he asked softly.

His other hand was wrapped around my right biceps, effectively putting that arm out of action. But I still had my left. Nodding my head forward, pressing my chin hard against the top of his hand, I cocked my left arm at my hip and drove a short jab into his upper arm just above the elbow.

Abruptly, the pressure on my throat went slack. I

grabbed Emikai's half-paralyzed hand, twisted it hard at the wrist, and swiveled on my left foot to bend the arm over, forcing him to bow forward at the waist. "Well, *Logra* Emikai?" I countered.

"Better," Emikai said approvingly. "Much better."

"Thanks," I said, letting go of his hand. "I take it I hit the nerve junction properly that time?"

"Indeed," he confirmed as he straightened up, massaging his right upper arm where I'd hit it and shaking his right hand where my chin had pressed into another sensitive spot. "But you should free your right arm from my left before attempting to turn me over. Otherwise I might pull you over with me."

"Yes, but it might also give you enough time to get your balance back," I pointed out. "Anyway, if this had been a real fight, I'd have followed up with a kick to your torso." I snapped a short kick to the area around his heart, stopping my foot a couple of centimeters short of his body. "Right about there."

"Yes, that would put a normal opponent into the dust," Emikai agreed. "But bear in mind that a professional fighter might have had his heart sac strengthened against such attacks."

I grimaced. He was right, of course. A Filly pro might boast a strengthened heart sac, some extra bone in his fists, and enhanced brow ridges to protect his eyes, and might even have gone to the effort to have his more vulnerable nerve junctions surgically moved to entirely different locations. With the Filiaelian passion for genetic manipulation, a Filly with sufficient money and patience could remake himself into almost anything he or his doctor could imagine.

Which was precisely why we were in this mess to begin with.

I turned to Bayta. "How did it look?" I asked.

"Painful," she said, her eyes smoldering as she looked at Emikai. In her opinion—which she hadn't been at all shy about sharing with me over the past few days—our sparring sessions were way more realistic than they needed to be. Certainly more realistic than she liked.

"Pure illusion," I assured her. Actually, my various bruises and strained muscles were in full agreement with her. But once upon a time I'd been a Western Alliance Intelligence agent, and Emikai and I both knew that the only way to learn hand-to-hand combat techniques was by actually practicing them. "Do we have time for one more?" I asked her.

"I don't think so," she said, a little too quickly.

"How long do we have?" I asked.

Her lip twitched. She really *did* hate these sessions. "Forty-five minutes."

"So plenty of time." I turned back to Emikai. "I want you to try the throat lock you put me in back on the super-express train." I turned my back on him. "I think I've come up with a counter."

His right arm snaked around my neck, his left arm linking with it, his left hand pushing my head forward against the forearm already pressed against my throat. His left foot slapped lightly against the back of my left knee, just hard enough to break my balance and send me to my knees on the floor. He followed me down, maintaining his grip, leaning forward and half over my shoulder.

That was how it had worked the last time he'd pulled this move on me. This time, I had something new to bring to the table. My knees had barely hit the floor when I threw myself forward, pulling Emikai off balance and tumbling over on top of me. As my chest hit the floor I rolled onto my left side, bringing my right elbow up into a shark-fin angle.

And as he belatedly let go of my neck in an effort to break his fall, his torso slammed onto my extended elbow.

In a real fight I would have kept the elbow extended, letting its impact send a shock wave through his heart sac and hopefully ending the fight right there. In this case, since Emikai wasn't an actual enemy and I further-more didn't want to lug his twitching carcass all the way back to third class, I let my arm fold back down again, with the result that instead of bouncing off my elbow in agony he merely landed full length on top of me.

Fortunately, his extended arms took most of his weight, with the result that we both merely oofed in unison in-stead of having the air knocked out of us. "Impressive," he said, rolling off and standing up again. "Aside from the obvious difficulty that if it succeeds you'll be trapped beneath your opponent."

"True," I agreed, getting to my feet and massaging my throat where he'd been gripping it. Maybe Bayta was right about Emikai being a bit on the enthusiastic side. "Given that the alternative is to be comfortable but dead, it seems worthwhile."

"A definite point." He paused, tilting his head thought-fully to the side. "Since we speak of death, what do you intend to tell the director and *santras* of Proteus Station about *Aṣantra* Muzzfor? They will want answers." He eyed me closely. "More complete answers, I hope, than those you have given to me."

"What an odd question," I said, hiding my mild sur-prise. It had been over four weeks since Muzzfor died his violent death aboard the super-express Quadrail travel-ing from the other end of the galaxy, and nearly two weeks since Emikai and I had begun these occasional sparring sessions. Not once in all that time had the Filly asked me for details on exactly how Muzzfor had died.

Now, with our train forty minutes from journey's end, he was suddenly bringing up the subject? "I intend to tell them the truth, of course."

"Good," he said as he retrieved his tunic from where he'd laid it on my bed. "The director and *santras* would not take well to being lied to. By you, or by anyone else they choose to question."

"That *anyone else* being you?"

"I am a former enforcement officer, and was aboard

the train where *Asantra* Muzzfor died," he said. "That makes me a logical person to question."

"Only since you didn't actually witness the event, most of what you can tell them will be hearsay," I reminded him.

"That, plus my trained assessment of the other persons involved."

I inclined my head to him. "Hence, the exercise sessions?"

His cream-colored nose blaze didn't lighten or darken, the usual Filly indicators of sudden emotional change. Emikai already knew or suspected that *I* knew or suspected his reason for suggesting these little playdates. "Yes," he said without apology or embarrassment.

"And what do you intend to tell them?"

For a moment he eyed me in silence. "You have purpose about you, Mr. Compton," he said. "But I do not yet know what that purpose is. You have honor about you, as well, but I do not yet know to which person or ideals that honor attaches." His eyes took on a sudden intensity. "And you have knowledge, but I do not believe you intend to give that knowledge to the director and *santras*."

"An intriguing analysis," I said, trying to keep my voice casual. Damned if he hadn't hit it squarely on the head. "But I *do* intend to tell them the truth."

"I will look forward to hearing it," he said, finishing with his tunic and wrapping his belt and belt bag in place. "I go to prepare the others for departure. Until then, farewell."

"Farewell," I said. He stepped to the door, tapped the release, and disappeared into the corridor.

I crossed to the door and locked it behind him. "You aren't really going to tell them the truth, are you?" Bayta asked.

"Of course not," I said. "Come on, let's finish packing."

Our train pulled into the Ilat Dumar Covrey station exactly on time, which was the way things always worked with the Quadrail system. The Spiders, creatures encased in metal globes carried around on seven spindly legs, kept the trains running perfectly as they facilitated the transfer of passengers, cargo, and information across the galaxy with a calm and understated efficiency.

And as Bayta and I headed across the platform, making our way past Fillies, Shorshians, and assorted other non-Humans, I thought about truth.

It was something everyone wanted, or at least said they did. Emikai wanted it, the director and *santras* aboard Proteus Station wanted it, and most of the people we were passing here in the station probably thought they wanted it, too.

But did they?

Did they really want to know about the Modhri, the group mind that had started out based in exotic Modhran coral and was now also embedded in thousands, perhaps even millions, of unsuspecting beings? Did they want to know that any of their friends might have a Modhran polyp colony inside him or her, linked telepathically to all the other nearby colonies and coral outposts to form a group-mind segment? Did they want to know that that same friend's words or actions might actually be inspired by subtle suggestions whispered to him or her by that mind segment?

Did they want to know that the Modhri was determined to take over the galaxy by turning more and more people into his walkers? Especially the people who were his current walkers' closest friends and associates?

Probably not. Most Humans hated hearing bad news or uncomfortable truths, and I doubted any of the non-Human species of the Twelve Empires were much better at it than we were. They wouldn't really want to know that the Modhri was nothing less than a sentient weapon, created by a group of master-race types called the Shonklaraa, who had finally been defeated and destroyed sixteen hundred years ago by a coalition of their conquered peoples.

That was the truth Bayta and I had been living with for the past couple of years as we, the Spiders, and the Chahwyn, who controlled the Spiders from their hidden world of Viccai, fought a quiet war against the Modhri's plans for galactic conquest. And considering how out-numbered we were, that truth had been bad enough.

Four weeks ago, as Bayta and I traveled aboard the super-express from the Human end of the galaxy, the truth had suddenly gotten a whole lot worse.

Because the Shonkla-raa hadn't been their own indi-vidual species, as the Chahwyn had thought, but merely a genetic variant of the Filiaelians. Someone had appar-ently figured that out, and had also figured out how to re-create that variant.

And that same someone was currently working on his very own master-race breeding program.

The late *Asantra* Muzzfor had been the first of that group that Bayta and I had tangled with, and it had been purely by the grace of God and some unexpected help that we'd survived the encounter. It was from pa-pers Muzzfor had left behind that we'd learned the cen-ter of this new Shonkla-raa operation was somewhere inside Proteus Station, a huge beehive of Filiaelian gene-tic manipulation and a shining example of Filiaelian diplomatic glory and finesse.

The place Bayta and I were currently headed for.

Emikai was waiting near the shuttle bays with the other two members of our party when Bayta and I joined them. "About time," Terese German growled as we came up. "What did you do, stop off for a drink?"

I eyed her, a dozen possible sarcastic rejoinders flash-ing through my mind. Terese was a sixteen- or seventeen-year-old Human girl—I'd never pinned down her actual age—of the type I usually thought of as a mystery wrapped up inside an enigma wrapped up inside of her-self. In this particular case, there was also an outer layer of imported porcupine skin, with the extra-long-quill option. About all I really knew about her was that she'd been assaulted on Earth, that she was pregnant as a result of that attack, and that Muzzfor had pulled some backstage strings to get her aboard the Quadrail and out here to the Filiaelian Assembly.

The *why* of it all, though, still eluded us. I couldn't wait to get hold of the hidden nuggets of truth in *that* one. "Our apologies," I said.

She sniffed. "*Are* we finally ready, then?"

Once again, I resisted the urge to say something sarcastic, and merely gestured toward the shuttle hatchway behind her. She spun on her heel and stalked away, her two small carrybags rolling along behind her. Taking a long step, Emikai settled into place beside her as a good protector should.

"You must forgive her," a soft voice said from my side.

I turned to look at the speaker. Dr. Aronobal was an older Filly, with a graying brown blaze along her long nose and an air of fatigue about her that had grown more pronounced in the two weeks since we'd left the super-express and started wending our way across Shorshian territory into Filiaelian space. "She has been under increasing stress these past few days."

"I'm sorry to hear that," I said, studying the good doctor closely. Tired she might be, but her eyes were clear enough, and I had no doubt that her mind was, too. I didn't know what her role was in this little drama, but I had a feeling it wouldn't be wise to underestimate her. "Any particular reason why?"

"Perhaps merely the additional tension of reaching the journey's end," Aronobal said. "Or perhaps the uncertainty of her future."

"Surely it must be the former," I protested mildly. "Now that we're here, I'm sure your colleagues will take good care of her."

"*My* colleagues?" Aronobal shook her head. "You misunderstand, Mr. Compton. The doctors and genetic surgeons of *Kuzyatru* Station are not my colleagues. *Logra* Emikai and I merely agreed to assist them by looking after Ms. German on her journey here."

"Ah," I said, nodding. And if I believed *that*, I thought cynically, she undoubtedly had some prime Gobi cropland to sell me. "In that case, we'd better make sure she doesn't lose us."

I took Bayta's arm and headed off after the girl, studying the station around us as we walked, my eyes and mind alert for the slow-moving loiterers or casual conversational clumps that might indicate a Modhran mind segment on sentry duty.

If we'd taken this trip a few months ago I might not have bothered. The Chahwyn, who'd been studying the Modhri a lot longer than I had, had assured me that the Filiaelian Assembly was the only one of the Twelve Empires that the Modhri hadn't yet penetrated. The reasoning had seemed solid enough at the time: with the widespread Filly obsession for genetic experimentation, it was hard to see how a group of relatively huge coral polyps could slip through the laser-grid pre-testing required in all genetic restructuring procedures without being spotted. And since the Modhri's best hope for victory was to remain below everyone's radar as long as possible, it followed that he would avoid Fillies, especially the rich upper-class Fillies who would normally be his prime target.

Unfortunately, that comforting logic had gone out the window three months ago on the Human colony world of New Tigris. There, Bayta and I had tangled with no fewer than six *santra*-class Filly walkers whom the Modhri had clearly had no qualms about taking over. Backtracking those Fillies and finding out what the Modhri was up to out here had been the original reason for our trip to Ilat Dumar Covrey, before Muzzfor and *his* unexpected revelation had even come up.

And given that we now knew there were Shonkla-raa at Proteus as well, it followed immediately that they would have someone keeping a close watch on the local Quadrail station.

Only as far as I could tell, they didn't. None of the hurrying passengers gave us more than the quick glance one would normally expect between perfect strangers, none of the people poring over schedules or maps looked up as we passed, and there were no head jerks or widened eyes of recognition as the Modhri spotted his two most notorious enemies.

Maybe he'd simply learned how to better hide his presence and reactions from me. That was one of the group mind's nastiest strengths: as one mind segment got within range of another, the two blended together to form a new, bigger segment, with automatic sharing of experience and memories. That meant that, unless I was able to completely wipe out a given mind segment, anything I did or said would eventually end up as part of the shared memory of every other mind segment in the galaxy. Any trick that worked against him would only work once, and every mind segment knew my face, at least within the limitations of cross-species recognition capabilities.

The other possibility was that the Shonkla-raa and Modhri felt so secure at Proteus that they didn't even care whether or not Bayta and I showed up.

Like every other shuttle hatchway in the Quadrail system, those at Ilat Dumar Covrey were set into the station floor and rimmed with glowing lights indicating whether or not there was a vehicle ready to carry passengers to the transfer station, where torchliners and torchferries waited to transport them elsewhere in the system. Only one of the hatchways in this part of the station was still lit, the one Terese and Emikai were currently heading for. Maybe she'd been right about Bayta and me being a little slow.

Unlike the Tube and stations, which were under Spider control, shuttle design and organization were the province of the species that owned that particular solar system. I'd never been aboard a Filly shuttle before, and I watched with interest as, halfway down the stairway, Terese got her hand and luggage tagged by a laser scanner, which then lit up a holodisplay in English instructing her to put the bags on the conveyor to her left just below the station floor. She did so, and as the luggage disappeared into a wide slot set into the upper part of the shuttle she finished her trip down the stairs. Emikai followed, getting the same tagging and holodisplay, except that this time the instructions were in Fili instead of English.

"Picking up on the passenger's DNA," Bayta murmured from beside me. "Probably marking the luggage with a code based on that."

I nodded. It made sense, considering the Fillies' obsession with genetics. It was certainly more convenient than handing out claim tickets, the way the Spiders did for their secure under-train lockboxes.

Briefly, I wondered if the scanner would spot the fact that Bayta was actually a blend of Human and Chahwyn, then put the thought out of my mind. Surely the Chahwyn Elders who had created her had been smart enough to keep the non-Human elements deep below the surface.

Sure enough, the scanner gave no indication that it had noticed anything unusual. Bayta went through the procedure, followed by Aronobal, followed by me. There was plenty of room in the shuttle, I saw as I reached the deck, and we took three of the four empty seats right in front. Terese and Emikai, I noted, were already seated farther back. We strapped in, and I waited for the hatchway to seal so that we could get under way.

Only it didn't seal. It remained fully open, the muffled sounds of the station drifting down to us. "Hello?" I murmured.

"There's one more passenger still on his way," Bayta murmured back, her eyes distant as she did some of her silent telepathic communication with the Spiders.

And Terese thought Bayta and I had been slow. "What is he, crippled?" I growled.

"Actually, yes," Bayta said, her forehead suddenly wrinkled in concentration.

I looked at the opening. "Trouble?" I asked, lowering my voice.

And then, abruptly, Bayta caught her breath.

"What is it?" I murmured, slipping my hand into my pocket and getting a grip on my *kwi*. Like Bayta herself, the brass-knuckle-shaped weapon was a nearly one-of-a-kind item, this one a relic from the Shonkla-raa war. Once telepathically activated by Bayta or a Spider, it was capable of inflicting three levels of pain or unconsciousness.

Only Bayta wasn't activating it. The *kwi* was just sitting in my grip, showing no sign of its usual start-up tingle. "Come on, girl, look alive," I muttered.

"No, it's all right," she said. But her voice was as tight as her face. "It's not that kind of problem."

I was opening my mouth to ask what kind of problem it was when a shadow fell across the floor and a support chair appeared in the hatchway, descending into the shuttle in the grip of a couple of big drudge Spiders. Seated in the chair was a pale, frail-looking Nemut with an off-center hunch in one of his angled shoulder muscles, slightly watery eyes, and a noticeable distortion in his truncated-cone mouth.

I felt my jaw drop. This wasn't just some random cripple. This was Minnario, one of the first-class passengers on our ill-fated super-express train. "Minnario?" I called.

He didn't respond, but as his chair reached the shuttle deck and he started it swiveling around to face forward I saw a flashing light on the small display fastened to the chair's control box. Minnario was deaf, I remembered now, with the display programmed to transcribe the speech around him. Apparently, it was also keyed to take special note if someone called his name. He continued to turn, bringing his chair around again to face the rest of the passengers, his eyes scanning the crowd for familiar faces. "Here," I said, lifting my hand chest high. "Frank Compton. We met aboard the super-express from Homshil."

He peered at me, then looked down at his display's transcription, and I saw sudden recognition in his face. [Mr. Compton,] he croaked, his Nemuspee marred by a slight lisp. [It's good to see you again. You no longer chase murderers, I trust?]

I felt a tightening in my stomach as the implications of Minnario's presence suddenly flooded in on me. "Not right now," I said carefully. "Tell me, what are you doing here? I thought you were on your way to a clinic for treatment."

[The most extraordinary thing has happened,] he said, his distorted mouth flattening in a distorted Nemuti smile. [I was traveling to Morak Trov Lemanab when I received a message that the genetic surgeons at Vibrant Station had accepted me for treatment.]

"Vibrant—? Oh, right," I said. The place officially known as *Kuzyatru* Station actually had thirty different names, one for each of the Twelve Empires' official languages. *Vibrant* was the Nemuspee version, just as *Proteus* was its name in English. "Congratulations. I understand they're the best in the Assembly. It was very wise of you to apply there."

[Ah! Therein lies the irony,] he said as he swiveled his chair around and maneuvered it into a set of clamps along the wall in front of us. [Knowing how few cases Vibrant Station takes, I *didn't* apply there.]

"Really," I said. "And, what, the director picked your name out of a hat?"

[I don't actually know who decided to offer me treatment,] he said as the clamps locked securely around his chair. [The message carried no name, but merely Vibrant's contract logo.] He swiveled half around, another lopsided smile on his face. [A gift from the heavens, indeed.]

I looked at Bayta, saw the tightness around her mouth. "Indeed," I murmured.

Only I doubted it was the heavens that had supplied the crippled Nemut with this sudden largesse. This gift had come from much lower down, from the general vicinity of hell.

Sometime during our last two weeks of travel, word of *Asantra* Muzzfor's death had made it to Proteus . . . and someone there wasn't buying my story that he'd died in the violent climax of the series of murders that had taken place aboard our super-express. That same person had apparently decided to hedge his bets by bringing in another witness to those events.

Or maybe even more than one. For all I knew, the whole first-class section of that train could be on their way to Proteus right now.

And that could be a problem. A big problem. I knew exactly where Emikai, Aronobal, and Terese had been at the time of Muzzfor's death. Bayta and I had worked it out down to the quarter second and the square meter, confirming that none of them could have seen or heard anything that might contradict my version of those events.

But I had no idea where Minnario had been. It had never even occurred to me to track his movements. And with the Spiders who had served on that train now fifteen thousand light-years behind us there was no way I was going to do it now.

I didn't know if Minnario knew anything. But it looked like someone on Proteus thought he might.

And if he did, the carefully crafted story I'd worked out was suddenly not looking so good.

The hatchway overhead closed, and there was a slight shudder as the clamps holding us to the station floor disengaged. A moment later the shuttle's drive kicked in, angling us away from the Tube and bringing us around toward the transfer station a hundred kilometers away. "Frank?" Bayta asked, just loudly enough for me to hear over the engine noise.

I reached over and patted her hand. "Don't worry," I told her. "I'm on it."

After all, we still had the shuttle ride, the usual customs procedures at the transfer station, and then a three-hour torchferry journey to Proteus itself. Surely in all that time I could come up with a new story that would cover anything Minnario might be able to tell them.

I'd better get started.

Kuzyatru Station, according to all the brochures and encyclopedia entries, was the diplomatic jewel of the Filiaelian Assembly, a high-visibility meeting area for conferences and interstellar meetings as well as a top-rated medical and genetic research facility. It was an odd combination, in my opinion, but it apparently worked well enough for the Fillies. Certainly the photos and holos of the place showed they'd considered it worth dousing with bucketfuls of money.

It wasn't until our torchferry was on its final approach that I realized just how inadequate those holos and descriptions really were.

For starters, the place was huge. It was roughly disk-shaped, with a rounded top and bottom, the whole thing ten kilometers across and ranging in thickness from a kilometer at the edge to three at the center. I was a little vague on my high-school geometry, but I was pretty sure that gave it at least twice the volume of a typical Quadrail station.

That was impressive enough. Even more so was the fact that a Quadrail station was mostly empty space, whereas Proteus's living areas were sliced into three-meter-high decks. That gave the place the carrying capacity of a small nation.

But more even than its size was its sheer grandeur. I

had assumed that the huge historical panoramas decorating the areas around each of the thirty-three main edge-line docking stations were simple hull paintings. In fact, they were intricate mosaics, built of five-centimeter-thick tiles no doubt designed to be resistant to micrometeor damage. The running lights that interstellar law required on every spacegoing vessel or station had here been tweaked into a laser light show that as near as I could tell never repeated itself once during the half hour it was visible from my torchferry window.

And if that hadn't been enough to set it apart from the rest of the galaxy's space habitats, Proteus wasn't just orbiting its sun, but was actually holding itself in constant, stationary position relative to the equally stationary Quadrail station by a massive, brute-force application of Shorshic vectored force thrusters. That meant that, instead of tracing out a long orbital path that might put it anywhere from two hours to four weeks away from the Tube, it was always going to be a convenient three-hour flight for new arrivals to the system.

It was, in short, a huge, self-indulgent, self-aggrandizing stack of metal and plastic and ceramic.

And as I listened to the murmured oohs and aahs of our fellow passengers I felt my heart sink.

Because my plan had been to march into the station, loudly announce the arrival of Terese German, and watch for interested parties from the Shonkla-raa to pop out of the wainscoting. Now I realized that wasn't going to work. Whichever docking station we ended up getting routed to, there was every chance that I would be so far away from the Shonkla-raa that they might not even hear the news that Terese was aboard until long after Reception had thanked me for my service and courteously ushered Bayta and me onto the next outgoing torchferry. Even if I could find some excuse for us to stay aboard, we could wander a facility this size for months without ever finding Muzzfor's fellow conspirators. Especially since those conspirators probably didn't want to be found.

"Frank?" Bayta murmured.

"I know, I know," I murmured back. "I'll figure out something."

"What do you mean?" she asked, frowning. "I was going to ask why we'd changed course."

I frowned in turn. I'd been so caught up with thinking about Proteus and the future of my plans I hadn't even noticed the change in the torchferry's insertion angle.

But Bayta was right. Whereas we'd been heading for one of the docking stations in the upper twenties—probably twenty-seven or twenty-eight—we had now come around and were heading instead into the mid-teens.

Had someone aboard the station belatedly spotted Terese's name on the passenger list and rerouted us accordingly? If so, and if that someone was connected with the Shonkla-raa, Plan A might work after all.

Not surprisingly, the Proteus docking procedure was different from that at every other space habitat I'd ever visited. Instead of simply sidling up beside the station so that our hatchways lined up, we nosed directly into a huge docking bay, complete with clamps and restraints and a collar that looked like it could adjust to anything from our torchferry all the way up to a full-blown torchliner. Personally, I would have simply made a group of docking bays of different sizes, but once again Proteus's designers had decided to go for the more flamboyant approach.

In some solar systems new arrivals had to go through customs twice, once on the transfer station and a second time at their final destinations. Fortunately, the Fillies had dispensed with that nonsense. Outside the wide doors leading out of the docking bay was a long line of desks that served merely as luggage-distribution points. A reader at the door scanned the marks that the passengers had been tagged with at the Quadrail shuttle, and holo-displays then directed each person to the proper pickup desk. Bayta and I were routed to a desk midway down the line, while Emikai, Terese, and Aronobal headed to one a few places farther over.

I maneuvered us through the crowd to our desk and smiled at the female Filly seated there. From the hovering presence of a much older male Filly behind her, I guessed this was probably her first day on the job and he was there to vet her performance. "I greet you," I said, offering my hand to the reader to confirm my identity. "You have a very efficient—"

"Mr. Frank Compton?" the older Filly interrupted as he strode up to the desk.

"Yes," I confirmed. "My bags are those two over—"

"I am *Chinzro* Hchchu, assistant director of *Kuzyatru* Station," he interrupted, raising his hand like the Pope delivering a blessing. In response, three tall Fillies wearing gray and black jumpsuits, who had been loitering behind the row of desks to either side of us, started forward.

"Is there a problem?" I asked carefully, watching the approaching Fillies out of the corner of my eye. In my pocket, I could feel the *kwi* tingling as Bayta activated it.

"A very serious problem," Hchchu said sternly. "You are under arrest." He paused dramatically. "For murder."

TWO :

The entry bay was deathly silent by the time the three jumpsuited Fillies reached us. Two of them took my upper arms in a standard police control hold, while the third got a slightly more polite grip on Bayta's arm. With Hchchu in the lead, we were marched off through the frozen tableau of our fellow torchferry passengers toward a door at the far end.

Which wasn't to say that we went quietly.

"This is absurd," I insisted loudly as we walked, trying to sound bewildered and outraged at the same time. "You obviously have me confused with someone else."

"You are Mr. Frank Compton, New York City, New York, Western Alliance, Earth, Terran Confederation?" Hchchu asked over his shoulder.

"I'm *a* Frank Compton of New York," I acknowledged. "But there must be dozens of us. Besides—"

"Then there is no mistake," he said firmly.

"You have the wrong person," I said, just as firmly. If the Modhri was on to me, none of this protesting would do any good. But it was the way an innocent man would behave and I had to play it through.

Besides, any doubt I could create would only help me. The local Modhran mind segment had only Filly eyes and vision centers to work with, and Fillies in general weren't all that good at distinguishing among Human faces. No matter how suspicious the Modhri might be, he couldn't possibly be as certain as Hchchu sounded. At least, not unless he already had a sample of my DNA aboard.

"What are the specifications of the charge?" a new voice cut in, and I turned to see that Emikai had left Terese and Aronobal and had joined our little procession.

"And you are?" Hchchu challenged.

"*Logra* Emikai," Emikai said. "These Humans are our escort."

Hchchu did a sort of double take, and I caught a brief darkening of his nose blaze as he looked more closely at Emikai. "I welcome you, *Logra* Emikai," he said. "I have words to speak with you, as well. But those words will wait."

"As you wish, *Chinzro* Hchchu," Emikai said. "Again I ask: what are the specifications of the charge against Mr. Compton?"

"Actually, this whole nonsense can wait," I put in. "*Logra* Emikai and I have a task that we've promised to perform, to escort Terese Ger—"

"The charges are plural," Hchchu said, his eyes still on Emikai. "Six counts of murder against citizens of the Assembly."

Emikai looked at me, his blaze paling with surprise. "*Six* murders?" he repeated, sounding sandbagged.

I was feeling a little sandbagged myself. I'd assumed this whole thing was coming from *Asantra* Muzzfor's death aboard our super-express. Where in the world had Hchchu found five more dead Fillies?

[I protest,] a thin voice called distantly from behind us.

I turned my head. It was Minnario, floating through the bay toward us, clearly gunning his support chair for all it was worth. On his distorted face was an expression of full-blown righteous indignation.

But all the determination in the world couldn't make his chair go any faster, and at the rate we were walking he had no hope of catching us before we left the bay. Even if he decided to pursue this further, he wasn't going to get to Hchchu until after Bayta and I had been dealt with and presumably sent elsewhere in Proteus.

And that would be a shame, because I was rather interested in hearing what the crippled Nemut had to say. Bracing myself, I abruptly leaned backward and dug my heels into the floor.

My two attached Fillies came to a jerking halt, stumbling as my unexpected move threw them both off-balance. "What do you do?" Hchchu demanded, spinning around.

"Someone's calling you," I said mildly. "It's rude to ignore him."

Hchchu's eyes shifted to Minnario, still trundling determinedly toward us. "What does he wish to say?" he asked, looking back at me.

"If I knew that, we wouldn't need to wait and hear him, would we?" I said, still leaning back against my handlers' grips.

Hchchu looked at Minnario again, then gestured to my guards. Their pull eased, and I straightened up again.

[You must not do this,] Minnario said as he came up to us, bringing his chair to a gliding halt. [He's an honorable Human, who risked his life to save all of us aboard the galaxy-crosser. He chased down a murderer who would have killed us all—]

"Peace, visitor," Hchchu said. He really needed to work on his habit of interrupting people. "Mr. Compton is not under investigation for activities aboard your galaxy-crosser or any other Quadrail."

[Then what do you do?] Minnario demanded.

"He is charged with the murders of six *santra*-class Filiaelians," Hchchu said. "Specifically, the murders of *Isantra* Snievre, *Isantra* Golovek, *Esantra* Chavine, *Asantra* Morloo, *Asantra* Crova, and *Asantra* Vaermas."

I frowned as he rattled off the names. This was getting more absurd by the minute. I'd never even *heard* of those Fillies.

"*Isantra* Golovek," Bayta murmured suddenly. "New Tigris."

I grimaced. Of course. I *hadn't* known most of those Fillies, at least not by their actual names. But now I did recall *Isantra* Golovek's name going by once or twice. He'd been one of the six Filiaelian walkers who'd tried to keep Bayta and me from sneaking a ten-year-old girl named Rebekah Beach off New Tigris and out of the Modhri's grasp.

Which made the multiple murder charge even more ridiculous. I hadn't killed more than one of those Fillies, and that had been in the middle of a firefight that the Modhri himself had started. In fact, now that I thought about it, I couldn't remember more than four of the six actually dying. The other two had been taken down with snoozers and subsequently hauled off by the local cops to the Imani City lockup.

So I'd been told, anyway. At the time my main concern had been getting Bayta and Rebekah off the planet before the Modhri could regroup for another crack at us.

Minnario couldn't know any of this, of course. But

amazingly enough, that didn't seem to matter. [I don't believe it,] he said firmly. [There must be some other explanation or reason. An honorable person remains honorable in all things.]

"Your comments are noted," Hchchu said, gesturing to his jumpsuited minions as he turned back toward the exit and started walking. One of the Jumpsuits gave me a nudge, and both Fillies started pulling at my arms.

I thought about digging in my heels again. But Minnario had had his say, and as nice as it was to have my own cheerleading section, it didn't make much sense to antagonize Hchchu just for more of the same. Nodding to Minnario, I let them lead me away.

But Minnario wasn't finished yet. [Where did these alleged crimes occur?] he asked, keying his chair forward to try to keep up.

"This is none of your concern, friend Nemut," Hchchu said, clearly starting to get annoyed.

[Justice is everyone's concern,] Minnario countered. [Where did the alleged crimes occur?]

"It was on New Tigris," I told him. "One of the worlds of the Terran Confederation."

[Then it's a cross-empire proceeding,] Minnario said firmly. [Mr. Compton will require a legal defender certified in cross-empire law.]

"*Is* that what you need?" Bayta murmured.

"No idea," I murmured back. My Westali training had included a unit in interstellar law, but only those sections that dealt with jurisdictional disputes. The fact that the New Tigris authorities didn't want me for anything kicked this into an area I knew nothing about.

From the look on Hchchu's face, I gathered this wasn't his area of expertise, either. "I will make inquiries," he said to Minnario. "Perhaps there is someone aboard whom we can consult."

[No need.] Minnario reached into a pouch at the side of his chair and extracted a card. [I am Minnario chu-

DeHak, Attorney of Blue Stature with the Nemuti Far-Reach,] he continued, handing Hchchu the card.

He turned his gaze on me. [If it's acceptable to Mr. Compton, *I* will defend him.]

We ended up in a small room just off the entry bay, our luggage arriving with two more Jumpsuits half a minute behind us. From the room's setup, I gathered that Hchchu's original plan had been to frisk me, frisk my luggage, and then lock me up somewhere out of the way.

But with Minnario on the scene, all such bets were off. Instead, we all stood around waiting while Hchchu sat at the desk making call after call, trying to locate someone on the Proteus staff who knew something about cross-empire law.

Midway through the comm marathon Emikai gave up his part of the vigil and left, promising to check in with me again once he and Aronobal had Terese settled wherever she was supposed to go. I used the occasion to again remind Hchchu that I had my own obligations concerning Terese, but the protest didn't even evoke a reaction, let alone a response.

And while I listened to Hchchu's increasingly irritated conversations, I studied Minnario.

I hadn't seen much of him during our trip aboard the super-express, partly because I'd had more urgent matters on my mind, mostly because Minnario had been a very solitary traveler. Even the Modhran mind segment aboard that train hadn't gleaned more than his name and his reason for traveling to Filly space. I'd spoken to the crippled Nemut only once, just after the train's resident madman had kicked him out of his compartment, and I'd noticed him later among the stream of subdued first-class passengers when they were all finally allowed to return. After that, he'd apparently settled back into his earlier hermit ways.

Yet now here he was, charging to my rescue, volunteering his professional services to a Human he barely knew.

And that worried me, because I knew that the late and unlamented *Asantra* Muzzfor had played his cards very close to his layered tunic. *Logra* Emikai and Dr. Aronobal had both worked for him, though Emikai hadn't known that and Aronobal had given no sign that she had either.

Had Minnario been another of Muzzfor's minions, knowingly or otherwise? More importantly, did he know about my role in Muzzfor's death?

But whatever was going on behind those watery eyes, it wasn't making it to the surface. He scrolled busily through a series of pages on the reader connected to his chair's display, all the while sporting the same poker-faced expression that I'd seen on dozens of other lawyers across the galaxy. My knowledge of written Nemuspee was far too limited for me to follow what he was reading, but from the headings I gathered he was skimming through a compilation of cross-empire laws. Maybe it wasn't really *his* area of expertise, either.

Finally, after nearly twenty minutes, Hchchu closed his comm and put it away. "Our legal representative is on his way with the full specifications of the case against Mr. Compton," he said. "In the meantime, he tells me I have full authority to confiscate any of Mr. Compton's possessions which may pose a threat."

Minnario inclined his head. [You may proceed.]

"Take off your jackets," Hchchu ordered as he lifted our carrybags onto the desk and opened them. "And remove all contents from your pockets."

My Beretta was the first to go, of course, the gun that had served me so well on New Tigris and other occasions. Hchchu turned it over a couple of times in his hands as he examined it, and I could tell he was wondering if this was the very weapon that had slaughtered six of his fellows in cold blood. He also took a close look at the Hardin Industries ID card that our other ally Bruce McMicking had given me, which included a reciprocal galaxy-wide permit to carry the weapon.

Of course, the card was made out in the name of one Frank Abram Donaldson, not Frank Compton. It would have been nice to have gone with the Donaldson identity, but unfortunately Aronobal and Emikai already knew me as Frank Compton. Fortunately, Hchchu was apparently not well enough versed in written English to spot the discrepancy. Without comment, he set both the gun and the ID aside.

My multitool went next, even though not even the Spiders classified it as a weapon. Minnario argued that very point, but Hchchu argued right back that even a two-centimeter blade could kill quite efficiently if the handler knew what he was doing. My watch, lighter, and Bayta's limited selection of jewelry went next, on even flimsier grounds: the necklaces could conceivably strangle, the ear cuffs and watch could be used as throwing weapons, and the lighter obviously would allow me to burn down the station. That was followed by our readers and data chips, with Hchchu not even bothering to float an excuse for those.

Last of all, to my quiet chagrin, went the *kwi*. I'd hoped to hang on to the weapon by claiming it was a bracelet or handwrap, but having already confiscated the rest of our jewelry Hchchu had neatly short-circuited that argument. I couldn't think of anything else to say, and of course Minnario had no way of knowing this strange gadget needed to be argued over.

So in the end the *kwi* wound up sealed inside a lockbox with my Beretta and everything else. "It will be deposited in the security officer's safe," Hchchu said as two of the Jumpsuits took the lockbox and disappeared through a side doorway. "If you're acquitted of the charges against you, it will be returned."

"Can I have a contract to that effect?" I asked.

Hchchu touched a switch and a piece of code-marked

paper slid out through a slot on the desk. "Read," he said, offering it to me.

I grimaced as I took it. My knowledge of written Fili was probably right up there with Hchchu's knowledge of written English. But I had no choice but to try to slog through it.

[May I?] Minnario asked, holding out a thin hand.

"Be my guest," I said. I handed it over and then turned back to Hchchu. "I presume that I'll now be permitted to fulfill my obligations on Ms. German's behalf?"

[I trust you don't intend to lock him away,] Minnario spoke up, his eyes still plowing through the Filiaelian legalese. [You've offered no weight of evidence sufficient for that.]

"Nor does it permit release on his own parole," Hchchu said, a bit huffily. "But there is a third option." He turned toward the doorway through which the lockbox had disappeared. "Bring them," he called.

There was a short pause. Then, one of the Jumpsuits reappeared, leading two of the nastiest-looking animals I'd ever seen.

They were dogs for the most part, or at least that was how my Human eyes and cultural viewpoint reflexively tried to categorize them. They were about the size of adult Dobermans, and there was certainly a lot of canine in their torsos, legs, and snouts.

But with that the resemblance to Fido dozing on the hearth ended. Their ears looked like small seagull wings, their spines bristled with low diamond-shaped spikes, and their backs and the tops of their heads were covered with an organic armor somewhere between armadillo scales and the skin on a pineapple. Their lower torsos and legs were covered with a feathery fur, with an overall color scheme that reminded me of a tabby cat seen through a rose-colored filter. Their eyes, encircled by faint raccoon masks, were deep-set, greenish-white, and decidedly unfriendly. If anyone was planning a remake of the dit-rec mystery *The Hound of the Baskervilles*, I had the perfect casting for the title role. "And what on God's green Earth are *these*?" I asked.

"They are called *msikai-dorosli*," Hchchu said. "They are used as guard animals in many parts of the Filiaelian Assembly."

"I can believe that," I said. The animal closest to me opened its mouth a little, and I spotted a double row of sharp-looking teeth inside a cavernous opening. "So what's the deal?"

"They will accompany you everywhere you go while aboard this station," Hchchu said. It was a little hard to tell, but I was pretty sure there was some malicious amusement in his voice. "They will keep you out of places where you should not go and prevent you from harming anyone."

"What will keep them from harming *us*?" I countered.

Hchchu snorted. "Do you take us for barbarians? They are not merely mindless beasts who rip and tear indiscriminately whenever they are hungry. They have sufficient intelligence to comprehend their duty and understand their orders. Observe." He beckoned the animals forward.

Obediently, they trotted over to him. {Identify,} he said in Fili as he pointed to Bayta and me.

Both animals turned their heads and eyed us balefully. {Identify,} Hchchu repeated, gesturing again.

Reluctantly, I thought, the animals walked over to us. "Offer your hands," Hchchu ordered.

Feeling like a sacrificial goat, I gingerly extended my left hand. Bayta did likewise, and the two animals spent a few seconds sniffing each of us in turn. One of them then turned back to Hchchu and emitted a startlingly dog-like woof. {Limit, and guard against trouble,} Hchchu said.

The lead dog gave another woof and stepped to my right, while his companion settled in on my left. "They are now on duty," Hchchu said.

"I'm so pleased," I said, trying not to sound too sarcastic as I looked down at the pineapple top of my new watchdogs' heads. "Do they have names?"

"Could you pronounce them even if they did?" Hchchu countered.

"Probably not," I said. Most Fillies I'd met had made a point of modifying their own names slightly to make them more pronounceable to the non-Fillies they dealt with. Here in the middle of the Assembly, Hchchu himself apparently felt no need to be so accommodating. "How good are they at learning new ones?"

"They will understand." Hchchu snapped his fingers twice. {The Human will give you new names.} "Proceed," he said in English.

The first watchdog looked up at me, I swear with the same expectant look as a two-year-old Human who's been promised a magic trick. I looked back, trying to think up something appropriate. The watchdogs obviously couldn't talk, so something from the dit-rec comedy silent era? Buster and Charlie? Charlie and Harold?

I focused again on the watchdog's face. Those raccoon masks around their eyes . . . "Doug," I said, pointing to him. I shifted my finger to the other watchdog. "Ty."

Doug snuffed once, then lowered his head again. "What about their care and feeding?" Bayta asked.

"Their food and beds will be delivered to your quarters," Hchchu said. He looked at Minnario. "When you have signed the contract, you may go."

I looked at Minnario. [It seems in order,] he said as he handed me the paper. [You may sign.]

"Thanks." I took the contract and held out my hand to Hchchu. "My pen left with my reader case."

His blaze darkened, but without a word he pulled his contract pen from its tailored pocket in his tunic and slid it across the table to me. I signed on the first line and handed both the paper and the pen back to him. He signed the second line and slid the paper into another slot on the desk. "You may go," he said, putting the pen away.

"We first need to know where Ms. German was taken," I reminded him.

Hchchu tapped a few keys on the desk's computer and peered at the display. {Escort them to Sector 25-F,} he said in Fili. "The *msikai-dorosli* will take you to the proper sector desk," he added in English.

I looked down at Doug's head. "A map would also be handy," I suggested.

"They will take you," Hchchu said. "Good day, Mr. Compton."

Apparently, we were dismissed. "Right," I muttered. "Heel, Doug. Or whatever."

{Go,} Hchchu added.

The two watchdogs turned and trotted toward the door. "You coming?" I asked Minnario.

[I need to wait until the station's legal representative arrives,] he said. [After I've learned the full weight of the case, I'll find you.] He eyed me closely. [At that point, we can discuss the matter further.]

"I'll look forward to it," I said. The watchdogs had reached the door and were standing there expectantly, eyeing me over their shoulders. "My masters call," I murmured, closing our carrybags and setting them on the floor beside us. "Let's go."

According to the material I'd read aboard the Quadrail, Proteus was divided into a number of sectors of different sizes and shapes, each acting like a combination hospital floor and New York City neighborhood. Most of the medical sectors were arranged with the testing and treatment facilities grouped in the center, surrounded by patient and staff quarters, which were in turn surrounded by shops, restaurants, and entertainment facilities. The non-medical sectors, the ones set up for meetings and conventions, had similar layouts, except that the rooms were considerably fancier and the restaurants and entertainment facilities correspondingly pricier.

Living areas for the workers were scattered throughout the disk, most of them consisting of a dozen corridors' worth of apartments grouped around a community-center dome that cut through several decks to give the locals a taste of open space. The brochures were a little vague about how those domes were arranged, and what was in each one, but hinted that the décor was largely up to the inhabitants of the neighborhood.

All of the various living and working sections were in the hundred and fifty decks that ran through the central part of the station's disk, with the domed areas above and below the disk dedicated to storage, recycling, power generation, maintenance, and the vectored force thrusters that kept the station from losing position and starting a long, leisurely fall toward the sun a billion kilometers away.

Sector 25-F was about a quarter of the way around the disk and two kilometers inward from the edge. Fortunately, we didn't have to walk the whole way. The station was equipped with a network of automated bullet trains that ran along their own array of corridors and covered both center-to-rim and circle routes.

Even more fortunately, there was no charge for their use. Just as well, since I wasn't sure where our watchdogs would have carried transit passes.

The Filly at the reception desk by the 25-F bullet train terminus gave us Terese's room number, which turned out to be fifteen floors above us and twenty corridors from the edge of the medical treatment cluster. We took an elevator up and finally arrived at her room.

"I thought you'd been hauled off to jail," she greeted us sourly as she stood in the middle of her doorway.

"Time off for good behavior," I said. "Mind if we come in?"

"I don't know." She nodded to my new pseudo-canine companions. "Are they housebroken?"

I looked down at Doug. "You two housebroken?"

Doug twisted his head to look up at me and gave a little woof. "He says of course," I translated, looking back at Terese.

Reluctantly, the girl stepped aside. "Thanks," I said. I started to walk in, but Doug was faster, slipping in ahead of me. Briefly, I wondered what would happen if I closed the door with him inside and me outside.

But I didn't wonder enough to actually try it. Ty, after all, was still out here with all of those teeth. I waited until Doug was all the way in, then walked in behind him and gave the room a quick once-over.

It was small, not much bigger than a first-class Quad-rail compartment, with a bed, computer desk, couch, half-bath, a wall-mounted entertainment center, a narrow closet that ran the full length of one of the walls, and a compact food-prep and dining area. "Cozy," I commented.

"And only big enough for one," she said pointedly.

That wasn't strictly true, I noticed: while the bed was narrower than a standard Earth queen, king, or emperor, it would be adequate enough for two. "Don't worry, we're not planning to move in," I assured her.

"Then what *are* you planning?" she demanded. "Why are you even here?"

"I told you that back at Venidra Carvo," I reminded her. "*Asantra* Muzzfor asked us to see you safely to Proteus Station."

"With his dying breath, and violins swelling in the background," she said sarcastically. "Fine. I'm here, I'm safe, and I'm happy. So hit the road."

"Unfortunately, it's not that easy," I said. "We still have to meet your doctors, find out what procedures they're planning, double-check the prognosis—basically, make sure you stay as safe and happy as you are right now."

Somewhere in the middle of all that Terese's face had gone rigid. "You're joking," she said. "What if it takes weeks? Or months? What if it takes *years*?"

"Then we'll be here for weeks or months or years," I said calmly. "We made a promise."

"Oh, no, you don't," she growled. "You are *not* going to hang around making a royal pain of yourself. This is my last chance—" She broke off. "Okay, try this. If you don't get lost, I'll call *Logra* Emikai and tell him to throw you out."

"Actually, *Logra* Emikai will probably be on my side," I said. "He was contracted to keep you safe, too, you know."

"Maybe it would help if you told us why you're here," Bayta put in quietly.

"Why?" Terese shot back. "So you can fix it and make me all better?"

I was working on a reply to that when there was a buzz from the door. "You want me to get that?" I asked.

Terese glared her way past me and hit the door release. The panel slid open to reveal Dr. Aronobal, who had changed from her traveling clothes into the crisp tans of a proper on-duty Filiaelian doctor. "Mr. Compton," she said, her blaze darkening briefly as she caught sight of me. Her eyes slipped to the watchdogs, then came back up again. "I didn't know you'd be here."

"We were charged with Ms. German's safety and well-being," I reminded her. "Can you tell me when she'll be seeing the doctors?"

"Right now," Aronobal said. "Come, I'll take you there."

"Great," I said, gesturing Terese through the open door. "After you."

Aronobal stuck her hand out toward my chest. "I'm not certain the doctors will permit you to accompany her," she warned.

"Do I have to go through this again?" I asked patiently. "I made a promise—"

"Yes, yes, I know," Aronobal cut me off. "Very well. I shall ask them."

She turned and headed down the hallway. I gestured again to Terese, and the teen stomped past me and caught up with the Filly. Bayta and I were right behind her, my watchdogs again settling in at my sides.

There were no bullet trains on our level, but two floors down was a major traffic corridor equipped with five-meter-wide fluidic variable-speed glideways at both edges, arranged as usual with the slower sections next to the central, non-moving part of the walkway and the faster ones at the far edges beside the walls. Aronobal got us to the corridor and onto the proper glideway, stepping nimbly across the flow until she'd reached the fast track.

I'd run into this kind of glideway in other places across the galaxy. Their main advantage over a sequence of solid walkways was that there were no abrupt transitions from one speed to another, which made it easier for those with less than perfect balance to get across without falling. Their main drawback was that, since it *was* variable-flow, an unwary rider who stood in a normal forward-facing stance with his feet shoulder-width apart would find the foot nearest the wall slowly but steadily pulling ahead of the other one. More experienced travelers knew to stand with their feet in a straight line, which limited the drift problems to one shoe edge trying to outpace the other and was much easier to compensate for.

I expected Terese to fall into the unwary category, and I was right. She nearly fell twice before Aronobal noticed her trouble and showed her the trick. I couldn't see the girl's face from where I was standing, but from the stiffness of her back I guessed that this wasn't helping her mood.

I'd never seen a quadruped on one of these things, and I watched with interest as Doug and Ty casually kept their two faster feet walking backward to stay in position with the slower pair. Unlike Terese, it was clear they'd done this before.

It was also clear that if I ever decided I wanted to lose the animals, hitting the glideway wouldn't be the way to do it.

We rode the fast track about half a kilometer before Aronobal started us moving back across toward the slow lane. We made our final transition to the stationary part of the corridor, walked up a one-level ramp to the regular corridor system, and arrived at a red-and-gold patterned archway leading into an open space that seemed to be one of the neighborhood domes.

{Ms. Terese German to see Dr. *Usantra* Wandek,} Aronobal announced us to the receptionist.

The receptionist peered at her screen. {You're expected,} she confirmed, waving us all through. {Enter, and proceed to Building Eight.}

I'd expected the dome to be simply a large, gray-walled open space, six or seven decks up and a couple hundred meters across at the base, mostly there just to provide inhabitants and visitors a chance to stretch their eyes. To my surprise, I found myself walking into what appeared to be a EuroUnion Alpine valley, with rugged textured mountains rising up along the dome walls and giving way to an expanse of cloud-flecked blue sky at the top. Scattered across the dome floor were a dozen buildings of various sizes, designed to look like ski chalets. Aside from the corridor we'd entered by, the dome had only one other exit, another corridor directly across from us that led farther inward toward the station's core. "Impressive," I commented as we passed the first of the buildings.

"We are pleased you approve," a voice came from behind me.

I turned to see a heavyset male Filly in physician tans emerge through an open doorway of the chalet we'd just passed. His ears were noticeably wider than the average

Filly's, and his shoulders seemed broader, though that might just have been his general thickness.

More importantly, from my current point of view, there was no sign of the oversized throat that I now knew to be a telltale sign of our new up-and-coming Shonkla-raa. "I do indeed," I told him. "I'm also surprised that you would build an entire Earth-style treatment center on the off-chance that a Human or two might travel to the Assembly for your services."

"You speak nonsense," he said with a snort. "The buildings and dome are of course regularly reconfigured for the comfort and convenience of each patient or group of patients."

"Ah," I said, nodding. Malleable materials were expensive, but hardly unknown across the galaxy. Apparently, the buildings here were cousins to the familiar self-adjusting Quadrail seats, though on a much grander scale. Typical Proteus showmanship.

The Filly's eyes shifted to Bayta, then to Terese. "This is Ms. German, I presume?" he asked.

"It is," Aronobal confirmed.

"Welcome, Ms. German," the Filly said. "I am Dr. *Usantra* Wandek. I pledge on behalf of Proteus Station to do all within our power to relieve you of your trouble."

"Thank you," Terese said. Almost as startling as the Alpine décor, at least to me, was the sudden subdued courtesy in the girl's voice. Apparently, she *was* capable of acting civilized. "I'm ready to begin."

"As always, there will first be some tests to run," Wandek said, gesturing to the building directly ahead of us. "Dr. Aronobal will take you."

Aronobal nodded and gestured in turn to Terese, and the two of them started toward the building. "You must be Mr. Compton," Wandek continued.

"Yes, I am," I said, starting to follow Terese.

I stopped abruptly as Wandek reached out a hand and caught my arm. "I wished you to know," he said, lowering his voice, "how much we appreciate you taking up *Asantra* Muzzfor's duty after his untimely death."

"It was my honor and privilege," I assured him, my mind once again flicking to Minnario and the still unanswered question of what exactly he knew about that episode. "If you'll excuse us—"

"*Asantra* Muzzfor was one of our colleagues," Wandek continued, still gripping my arm. "His services will be sorely missed."

"He was a doctor?" Bayta asked. "He never mentioned that."

"We have many colleagues who are not doctors," Wandek said. "Caregivers, lab techs, gene manipulation specialists, support workers—"

"Which of those was *Asantra* Muzzfor?" Bayta asked.

Wandek's nose blaze did an odd mottling, a type of hue change I'd never seen in a Filly before. Part of his array of genetic alterations, no doubt. "Why do you ask such questions?" he asked. "I thought you knew *Asantra* Muzzfor."

"Not as well as we would have liked," I said, making a concerted effort to pull my arm from his grip.

I could have saved myself the trouble. His fingers were like a machine vise, and from their rigidity I had the impression that the joints had actually locked in place. More genetic fiddling? "Nice grip you've got there, doc," I said. "You get that from all that micro-surgery?"

"I would appreciate a few minutes of your time," he said, ignoring both of my question's possible interpretations. He shifted his weight, pulling me back toward the building he'd first appeared from.

"I may not be allowed in there," I warned, not bothering to resist his pull. He outweighed me by a good fifteen kilos, he still had his iron grip, and I had no real justification to try anything violent. "As you see, I'm under movement restrictions," I added. "Doug and Ty may not allow me to go in there."

I suppose I'd hoped the animals would pick up on the cue. But of course they didn't. Doug and Ty walked docilely at my sides as Wandek pulled me along, without so much as a snort or growl. I threw one final look behind me, just in time to see Aronobal usher Terese into the other building, and then our own door swung open and Bayta and I went inside.

The building seemed deserted as we walked down a light blue corridor. Wandek led us to a double door and pushed it open.

At least now I knew where the building's staff had gone. There were ten Fillies seated around the outer, convex edge of a half-hex table, watching silently as we filed in. "These are some of *Asantra* Muzzfor's other colleagues," Wandek said as he led me to the table's inner edge and planted me in the center of all those silent stares. "While Dr. Aronobal begins Ms. German's tests, we hoped you could spare a few minutes to tell us how it was our friend's life was taken from him."

"Of course," I said, looking around the table. The group was a nice mixture of job specialties, four of the aliens wearing doctor's tans, and two each in similar outfits in brown, blue, and green.

But the variation in wardrobes was the least of my concerns. Along with a host of other, minor genetic variations, all ten Fillies had the same enlarged throats that I'd seen on Muzzfor.

I'd found the Shonkla-raa.

They'd also found me.

THREE :

"First of all, I want to say how deeply I grieve with you at *Asantra* Muzzfor's passing," I said, looking back and forth among the Fillies and memorizing their faces as best I could. "I didn't know him well, but when the crunch came, he came through. Indeed, he saved my life."

The leftmost of the aliens wearing physician's tan stirred in his chair. {Explain,} he ordered.

"Sorry?" I asked, cocking my head slightly toward him. You never know when it could come in handy for people to think you don't understand their language.

"He asked you to explain," Wandek translated.

"Ah," I said. "As you know—well, no, as you probably *don't* know," I amended, "there was a murderer aboard the super-express train from Homshil. He killed four of the passengers before we were able to identify him—"

"This we already know," Wandek interrupted. "How exactly did he save your life?"

"My apologies." So either Aronobal or Emikai had already filled them in on that. "As you may also know, the killer took my assistant Bayta hostage and barricaded himself in one of the first-class compartments. I was able to penetrate the area, but realized I couldn't take him alone. A Filiaelian passenger named *Osantra* Qiddicoj offered to assist me, and persuaded two others, a Tra'ho oathling and a Juri *Krel*, to join us. When *Asantra* Muzzfor learned of our plans he also volunteered for the mission. We penetrated the killer's compartment, and together succeeded in defeating him."

"How did *Asantra* Muzzfor die?" Wandek asked. "We wish details."

"I wish I could give them to you," I said ruefully. "Unfortunately, I can't. I was the first into the compartment, and the killer managed to deliver a blow that knocked me unconscious. When I came to, *Osantra* Qiddicoj, the Tra'ho, the Juri, and the murderer himself were all dead. *Asantra* Muzzfor was still alive, though just barely, but was too far gone for either of the doctors to help him."

{Yet you did not call for them?} one of the green-clad Fillies asked.

"As I said, it was too late," I said after Wandek finished his translation. "I sent word via the Spiders, and would have gone myself, but *Asantra* Muzzfor asked me to stay with him to the end. He told me that he had a contract to deliver Ms. German to Proteus Station, and asked me to fulfill that contract on his behalf."

{Did you see the actual contract?} Tan One asked.

I looked expectantly at Wandek. "He wishes to know if *Asantra* Muzzfor delivered his contract to you," he said.

"No," I said. "He said the killer had destroyed the contract. I don't know for sure, but I had the impression that *Asantra* Muzzfor thought the killer might actually have been targeting Ms. German, with the other victims killed just to muddy the waters."

The Fillies exchanged glances. Aronobal or Emikai would have given the group my explanation of the killer's motives. But for all they knew I could have been wrong, and neither of them had any way of knowing if Muzzfor himself had come up with an alternative theory. "Why would the murderer have destroyed the contract?" Wandek asked.

"I assume he was hoping that *Asantra* Muzzfor would expire before I awoke, thereby leaving Ms. German and Dr. Aronobal stranded at Venidra Carvo with no knowledge of where they were to go next," I said. "And of course, with the contract gone, I myself would have had no way of knowing I even needed to get in touch with them."

{But Dr. Aronobal wasn't summoned?} Green One asked again. {*Asantra* Muzzfor might not yet have been completely dead.}

"According to the LifeGuard, he was," I said. "Anyway, at that point the Spiders intervened, wanting to get all the bodies out of the inhabited parts of the train as quickly as possible. There was some thought that the killer had used an unknown biological agent against his victims, and the Spiders were afraid it might spread."

"But you *did* search for the contract?" Wandek asked.

"I gave the compartment a quick look, but didn't find anything," I said. So that was the real reason for this little interrogation. They wanted to know whether I'd found the evidence of Muzzfor's true affiliation and the Shonkla-raa's existence. "From the smell in the compartment, I'm guessing he burned it."

{What was the smell like?} another of the doctors, whom I dubbed Tan Two, asked.

"Sort of like burnt almonds, with a hint of oregano," I said. That answer I actually knew, because that was what the papers had smelled like when Bayta and I had burned them for real after we'd examined them. "Of course, I'd just been knocked on the head," I amended. "My nose might have been a little off-kilter."

A blue-clad Filly gestured to Bayta. {Has the female anything to add?}

To my mild chagrin, Bayta didn't wait for Wandek's translation. "I was unconscious even before Mr. Compton and the others arrived," she said. "I woke up only after *Asantra* Muzzfor was already dead."

Blue One shifted his eyes back to me, his blaze darkening. {So in other words, we have only Mr. Compton's word for what happened.}

"Were there any other witnesses to these events?" Wandek asked.

"No one who lived through them," I said, letting a little indignation into my voice. It was time I started getting annoyed at being interrogated like this when I'd merely been doing a Filiaelian *santra* a favor. "Look, I'm sorry he's dead, and I honor his memory and all that. But if I'm going to finish the job I've started and get on with my life, I need to get back to Ms. German."

Once again the Fillies exchanged glances. Blue One looked around, and I caught a small twitch of his ear. "You may go," Wandek told me. "We may have other questions to ask later. If you'll follow me, I'll escort you to Ms. German."

"Thanks, but we'll find her ourselves," I said, taking Bayta's arm and backing toward the door. The watchdogs, who'd been standing patiently at my sides, came along with us.

Wandek's hand lanced out and again caught my arm. "Forgive us if we sound harsh," he said. "It was a terrible blow to lose such a close colleague. Naturally, we wish to know all we can about his death."

"I understand that," I said, dialing back on my annoyance. "You'll forgive me in turn if I'm not in the best mood. It's highly unpleasant to have come all this way only to be immediately put under arrest for crimes I didn't commit."

"Yes, we heard about that," Wandek said, letting go of my arm. "If there's any way we can assist in your defense, please don't hesitate to call on us."

"Thank you," I said, letting my eyes drift around the group.

It was like looking at a group of sharks. These Fillies were my enemies, every one of them. They knew who I was, or were ninety percent sure of it. They knew about my war against their ally the Modhri, they knew I was lying about what had happened to Muzzfor, and they wanted to kill me.

The only thing keeping them from doing exactly that was the small sliver of doubt that I was not, in fact, lying about Muzzfor's death and how it related to the murders aboard the super-express. If there was another player in this game, someone who had in fact tried to get Terese German away from them, they needed to find out the who and the what and the why. Right now, I was the best source of information that they had.

But I was only valuable as long as they thought such information might actually exist. The minute they were convinced otherwise, Bayta and I would be in serious trouble.

We had to make sure we were finished with our own investigation and far from Proteus before that happened.

Predictably, I suppose, Wandek followed us out of the building. "As a small gesture of gratitude for your time," he said as we headed toward the building Terese and Aronobal had disappeared into a few minutes ago, "allow me to escort you to Ms. German."

"That really isn't necessary," I told him. "We saw where she went. We can find our own way."

"Of course you can," Wandek said. "But this way you will not need to deal with questions or forms at the reception desk."

We had made it halfway there when Doug suddenly stopped, turned his head, and gave a sharp yip. I was starting to look down to see what the trouble was when there was an answering yip from the distance.

I turned to look. Near the edge of the dome another watchdog was striding along at the side of a Filly, this one not in simple doctor's garb but dressed in the usual upper-class set of ancient-Mongolian-style layered tunics. The watchdog was peering across toward us, the Filly himself ignoring us completely.

I was trying to figure out what another criminal would be doing here, especially such a well-dressed one, when Ty gave a yip of his own. Once again, the other watchdog answered.

And with that, all three animals went back about their original business. "What was that all about?" I asked Wandek.

"You mean the greetings?" he asked, gesturing down at the watchdogs.

"Yes, if that's what those were."

"The sounds function as a greeting and identification between *msikai-dorosli*," he explained. "Each burst contains a wide range of ultrasonics unique to that particular animal."

"Some kind of jailer-to-jailer code?"

"That Filiaelian you saw was not a prisoner," Wandek said, a little stiffly. "Many citizens, even aboard *Kuzyatru* Station, keep *msikai-dorosli* as companions."

I looked dubiously down at Doug's non-furry and decidedly non-pettable back. "They're considered *pets*?"

"They're considered *companions*," Wandek repeated, leaning on the word a little. "They can be trained to assist their owner with various tasks."

"Like what?" I asked. "Making tea? Calling up the morning mail?"

"They can perform simple tasks such as fetching objects, particularly for those with post-operative weakness," Wandek said. "They can also be fitted with harnesses for carrying medium-weight items."

I looked down at Doug. I hadn't considered the possibilities of him as a pack animal. "How much weight can they carry?"

"Why all the questions?" Wandek asked, frowning. "They're really very simple animals."

"I have a very simple curiosity," I said. "How much weight?"

"I don't know," Wandek said, a little impatiently. Clearly, he had more important things on his mind right now. "If you really wish to know, you can look them up on the computer in your quarters. Everything there is to know about *msikai-dorosli* can be found there."

We reached the building and went inside. Unlike the Shonkla-raa nest, this one was bustling with activity, with doctors in tan striding purposefully along or holding conversations in corners. Other Fillies in the full range of colored outfits manned desks or pushed carts or joined the doctors in their consultations. I spotted a couple more of the enlarged throats that I'd seen back in the other building with our Gang of Ten, but everyone else seemed normal. Or at least, what passed for normal in this genetics-crazy society.

A receptionist at one of the desks looked up as we approached. {We're visiting Terese German,} Wandek said.

{Room 22, *Usantra* Wandek,} the Filly said, and gestured us down a side corridor. Midway along it was an open door with half-audible English mutterings emanating from inside. We reached it and went in.

In the middle of the room was a diagnostic bed similar to the Fibibib models common elsewhere in the galaxy but with some distinctly Filiaelian modifications to its design. Terese was lying on the bed, dressed now in a loose hospital gown, her eyes locked rigidly on the ceiling above her. Three doctors were standing around her, busily hooking up sample-taking equipment, while a blue-clad Filly was seated at an electronic console in one corner. Aronobal was off in a different corner, watching the procedure closely.

Trying to keep out of everyone's way, Bayta and I slipped around to Aronobal's corner. "How's it going?" I asked.

"They have begun the preliminary tests," Aronobal murmured, her eyes never leaving Terese.

"And then the treatment starts?"

"Once the tests have been evaluated, yes."

I looked at Terese. She was still gazing at the ceiling, her face stony with nervous determination. "What sorts of tests are you running?" I asked.

"Tests that are none of your freaking business," Terese bit out before Aronobal could answer. "Can someone throw them out? Please?"

"Hold still," one of the other doctors said brusquely.

I frowned, taking another look at the activity around Terese. There was a hard edge to it all that I hadn't noticed before.

I took a step closer to Aronobal. "What's wrong?" I asked quietly.

She looked sideways at me, then nodded silently toward the door. I nudged Bayta, and together the three of us sidled along the edge of the room and escaped out into the corridor, followed by the watchdogs and Wandek. "Well?" I asked as Aronobal led us a few meters farther away.

Aronobal looked at Wandek, as if seeking permission

to speak, then turned back to me. "The problem is not with Ms. German," she said, keeping her voice low. "What I mean is that, although she has many physical problems of her own, our immediate concern is with her child. There appears to be some kind of unexpected stress in his heartbeat and brainwave pattern."

I looked at Bayta. Her face looked a little pinched. "How bad is it?" I asked. "Better question: what are they doing about it?"

"They will begin by taking samples of the fetal tissue and of the fluid in the birth sac," Aronobal said. "Unfortunately, until this is settled we cannot begin work on Ms. German's own problems."

"Which are what exactly?" I asked. "I've never gotten a straight answer on that."

Aronobal sighed, a soft whinnying thing. "She has at least four genetic disorders," she said. "Possibly more—we have not yet done a complete mapping. Any one of the flaws could prove fatal to her over the next thirty years. Together, they are a virtual promise that her life will be cut tragically short."

"Can you fix her?"

"We believe so," she said. "But our knowledge of Humans and Human genetic structure is still woefully incomplete. That is indeed one reason she was invited to Proteus Station: to see whether we could map her genetic flaws and correct them."

"But that's now on hold?"

"It is the only safe way," Aronobal said. "The work on Ms. German is extensive and deep, with the potential to put additional stress on the child. Were he healthy it would be a simple matter of screening out the treatment chemicals and monitoring his condition. But until we know what is causing these other anomalies we cannot risk any action that might precipitate his death."

"And Ms. German cares about that?" I asked. "As I understand it, this child is the product of a vicious attack on her. Yet she still wants it to live?"

"*We* want it to live," Wandek put in firmly. "Despite what some Human cultures believe, all sentient life is sacred and must be protected and nurtured to the fullest extent of our abilities."

"Very noble," I said, watching him closely. "Yet the baby is Ms. German's, not yours. Doesn't she have a say in the matter? Especially since the baby is now getting in the way of her own treatment?"

Wandek drew himself up, his blaze mottling again. "The baby *will* be protected," he said curtly. "We have not—" He broke off. "All sentient life is sacred," he repeated.

"Of course," I said, ducking my head humbly. I'd gotten what I'd been looking for. Time to backpedal. "Naturally, I agree. It's just that there are many regions on Earth, with laws that vary widely from place to place."

"This is the Filiaelian Assembly, not Earth," Wandek said frostily, the mottling of his blaze slowly fading back to normal. "Only Filiaelian law has any bearing."

"Of course," I said again as I turned back to Aronobal. "Any idea how long the tests on Ms. German's baby will take?"

"No," Aronobal said. "If you like, I can put your name and comm number on the list of those to be informed of progress."

"I'd appreciate that." I gave her my number and Bayta's and watched as she keyed them into her comm. "Can you tell me who we talk to about getting accommodations somewhere in this sector?" I asked when she'd finished.

"That has already been arranged," Wandek said. "Speak with the receptionist at the door where we entered."

"Thanks." I started to turn away. "Oh. Does she happen to speak English?"

"You Humans," Wandek said, his tone more resigned than angry. "So many of you seem to believe the galaxy must necessarily accommodate your needs and desires."

"Yes, we're funny that way," I agreed. "Does she speak English, or doesn't she?"

Wandek made an impatient-sounding rumble deep in his throat. "I will send an English-speaker to meet you at her desk," he said, pulling out his comm. "I must return now to my work."

"And I to observe the work on Ms. German's child," Aronobal added.

"Of course," I said. "Thank you. Both of you."

Whatever else one might say about Wandek, he definitely got fast results. By the time we reached the receptionist's desk there was a young Filly in a pale green outfit already waiting for us. "You are the Human Compton?" he asked.

"Yes," I acknowledged.

"Come with me," he said, walking toward one of the corridors and motioning for us to follow. "Your quarters have been assigned."

"Are they near Ms. German's?" I asked, making no move to follow. "They have to be near Ms. German's."

"Your quarters have been assigned," he repeated. "Come with me."

He headed down the corridor, not checking to see if we were following or not. Taking Bayta's arm, I headed us off after him.

We retraced our steps out of the dome, down the ramp to the traffic corridor, along the glideway, and back to Terese's room. The door our guide led us to was two doors farther down. "Here," he said, gesturing toward a plate beside the door. "It is already keyed to your nucleics."

"Thank you," I said. I touched my hand to the plate, and with a soft click the door slid open. With my watchdogs crowding at my sides, I went inside.

And stopped. The room was a photocopy of Terese's, right down to the color scheme on the blankets on the bed.

The single, barely double-size bed.

One.

I felt the movement of air as Bayta came in and stopped beside Doug. "Cozy," I commented.

She didn't say anything. But I suspected that she wasn't looking at me just as hard as I wasn't looking at her.

I should have expected this, of course. I hadn't, but I should have. One of the Modhri's best and most insidious methods of infiltration was through something called thought viruses: subtle suggestions—sometimes not so subtle—that were passed telepathically from a Modhran walker to an uninfected person. Usually the suggestion was geared to get the victim to touch a piece of Modhran coral, which would get a polyp hook into his bloodstream and eventually grow him an internal Modhran colony of his own.

The most horrific part of the technique was the fact that thought viruses transmitted best between those who already had emotional attachments. That meant friends, allies, confidants, and coworkers.

And lovers.

I stared at the single bed, feeling a cold and angry sweat breaking out on the back of my neck. Did the Modhri think Bayta and I were lovers? We weren't, and weren't likely to go that route any time soon, either—we both knew how thought viruses worked, and neither of us was stupid enough to increase our risks that way. We'd shared only a single kiss, and even that had been driven more by lingering fear and pain and exhaustion than anything else.

Even now, I still wasn't sure how much of that kiss had been affection on Bayta's part and how much had simply been that same shared fear and exhaustion coming through. In many ways, the deepest core of Bayta's mind was still a mystery to me.

But she and I had been living and fighting side by side for a long time now, and the Modhri certainly knew enough about human biology to know we were ripe for that kind of attachment if we weren't there already. Apparently, he was hoping a little nudge might be enough to push us the rest of the way.

Well, he could just keep hoping.

I turned to the Filly, waiting expectantly in the corridor like a dit-rec comedy bellhop expecting a tip. "Unacceptable," I told him. "This room is designed for one. We are two."

It was clearly not the response he'd been expecting. He drew back a little, his eyes darting uncertainly from me to the room to me again. "Call your superiors," I said. "Tell them we need a larger room or a second room in this same area."

"Yes, of course," he said, finally unfreezing enough to pull out his comm. {The Human wants a larger room,} he reported to whoever picked up at the other end. He listened a moment— {No, he also wishes it to be near the Human Ms. German.} There was another pause, and I watched his blaze for signs of emotional distress. But the blaze remained unchanged. {I'll tell him,} he said, and shut down the comm. "There is a second room available," he told us. "But it is on the other side of the medical dome, the inward side."

I looked at Bayta. The far side of the medical dome would put whichever of us took that room over half a kilometer away from Terese. More importantly, it would put us that same half kilometer away from each other. "I'm afraid—"

"Would you show it to us, please?" Bayta asked.

"Certainly," the Filly said. "Follow me."

He led the way to the glideway, and we wended our way back to the dome. The receptionist looked up as we passed, but neither she nor our guide said anything to each other. The Filly led us into the dome, past the building where they were presumably still working on Terese and her unborn baby, and out into the corridor on the far side. Two corridors later, he stopped at another door. "This is the one," he said, gesturing to it.

I nodded. "Open it."

"It is not yet keyed to your nucleics."

"I realize that," I said patiently. "That's why I asked you to use your passkey."

For a moment he hesitated, perhaps wondering if he was supposed to admit he even had a passkey. Then, silently, he pulled a card from inside his tunic and waved it past the touch plate. The door slid open, and he gestured us through.

The room, as I'd expected, was exactly like the other two we'd already seen. "This is good," Bayta said briskly, turning to block the Filly as he started to come in behind us. "We'll take both rooms. How long will it take to key the lock to our nucleics?"

"I will call a room server immediately," the Filly said, clearly relieved that the awkward situation had been resolved. "It will be ready within the hour."

"Thank you," Bayta said, putting a hand on his shoulder and easing him gently but inexorably all the way out into the corridor. "We'll wait here until that's been done."

The Filly started to say something else, seemed to change his mind, and merely nodded. He was pulling out his comm when the door slid shut in his face.

I looked at Bayta. "You're kidding," I said.

"Why not?" she countered, starting along the edge of the room, her eyes darting everywhere. "I stay near Terese where I can watch over her. You stay here, where you can slip into the medical building when no one's looking and figure out what they're up to."

"And what happens if they *do* come after Terese, with me a good fifteen minutes away?" I asked. Bayta was heading toward the bed, so I went in the opposite direction, circling the room toward the computer desk.

"They aren't going to hurt her," Bayta said. She reached the bed and knelt down to peer at its underside. "They'd hardly bring her across the galaxy for that."

"Unless she isn't the one they actually care about," I said, running my fingers beneath the computer desk.

Bayta paused long enough in her examination of the bed to throw a frown at me. "What do you mean?"

"In a minute," I said, studying the edge where the desk met the wall. If the Fillies hadn't had time to code the lock to our DNA, they probably hadn't had time to install any listening devices, either, or at least nothing so subtle that we couldn't spot it.

Of course, the fact that I wasn't all that familiar with Filly bugging devices theoretically meant that one of their normal, non-stealthy versions might still be able to slip past us. But listening devices shared certain characteristics, and I figured I had a fair chance of finding anything they might have put in here.

Bayta was clearly on that same wavelength. One of the hazards of having hung around with me all this time, I supposed. We completed our respective sweeps, meeting halfway around the room. Then, again by unspoken but clearly mutual agreement, we both continued on, each of us now checking the areas the other had already searched.

We finished without finding anything. I had no doubt that the other room, the one they'd planned for us, was bugged to the ceiling. But this one seemed safe enough, at least for the moment. "Of course, it's only an assumption that they didn't already have the lock coded for us," I reminded Bayta as she sat down on the edge of the bed and I settled into the computer desk chair facing her. "Our helpful native guide might have used that passkey just to throw us off."

"I don't think so," Bayta said. "I touched the pad on my way in, and there was no click."

"Maybe that was because the door was already open."

She shook her head. "The first room door was also already open when I touched the pad there, but it still clicked. Why don't you think they care about Terese?"

I hesitated. Bayta had already shown she had a soft spot for the young and helpless, first with Rebekah

Beach back on New Tigris and then for Terese herself aboard the super-express. I wasn't at all sure how she was going to react to my current suspicion. "Here's the score as I see it at the moment," I said. "You remember, back on the super-express, we speculated the attack on Terese might have been staged as an excuse to get her to Proteus Station?"

Bayta's lip twitched. "Yes."

"I've been thinking about how to prove that," I said. "So a while ago, when Aronobal brought up the fact that the baby was in trouble, I tossed out the possibility that Terese might want to abort him. Did you notice Wandek's reaction?"

Bayta nodded. "He was very upset."

"He was more than just upset," I said. "The way his nose blaze was going, it was clear the whole idea made him furious." I paused. "As furious as if the baby was his own."

Bayta stared at me. "Are you saying," she said slowly, "that the baby isn't *Human*?"

"No, of course—" I broke off. I most certainly *hadn't* been saying that. All I'd been saying, actually, was that Wandek was treating the baby like it was certified Filiaelian property.

But now that I thought about it, why not? With the Filly obsession with genetic manipulation, why the hell not? "We need to talk to Terese," I said grimly. "Find out exactly what happened to her."

"She won't talk to you," Bayta said. The color had come back into her cheeks, and a quietly simmering anger into her eyes. "When do you want me to do it?"

I started to glance at my wrist, then remembered that Hchchu had taken my watch. "No time like the present," I said, standing up. "Let's go see how much longer they're going to keep her. Maybe you can take her out to dinner."

I wasn't sure my watchdogs would let me into Terese's examination building a second time, particularly now that we didn't have an official or even an implied invitation. But they apparently decided that since we'd been inside once, we now had legal run of the place. That could be very useful down the line.

Unfortunately, that was all we got for our trouble. Aronobal intercepted us outside Terese's room and told us that the girl's tests were going to run at least two more hours, and that once they were over she would probably be spending the night in the building under observation instead of going back to her room. She did promise, though, to pass on Bayta's offer of a dinner invitation for future consideration.

"Now what?" Bayta asked as we emerged again into the crisp pseudo-Alpine air.

"We wait for them to be done with her," I said, running my fingers across the building's wall and looking up at the caves. I'd seen other varieties of malleable materials, but this one took the cake for looking and feeling solid. "Just because Aronobal says we can't talk to her doesn't mean we actually can't. You want to grab some dinner while they're working?"

"Let's not go too far away," she said. "Just because Dr. Aronobal says it'll take two hours doesn't mean it actually will."

I eyed her. Bayta was on fire, all right. A slow, simmering fire, maybe, but Bayta on fire was not to be trifled with. It almost made me pity whoever had done whatever the hell they'd done to Terese. Almost. "You want to camp out here at the door, or shall we be a little more subtle?"

Bayta looked around the dome. "Let's see if we can get into one of the other buildings," she suggested. "Maybe we can sit by a window and watch for them to bring her out."

I looked down at Doug, remembering all those sharp teeth. "As long as you're willing to take *no* for an answer," I said.

"Of course." Bayta pointed to a building near the edge

of the dome. "That one doesn't look very busy. Let's try it." Without waiting for an answer she headed off. Ty, apparently figuring that Doug already had me adequately covered, trotted off alongside her.

"Fine," I murmured as I trailed after her. Bayta on fire was Bayta on fire, but a little healthy caution wouldn't be out of line, either. Maybe she hadn't had a good look into the watchdogs' mouths and didn't know about all the teeth. Or maybe the prospect of being ripped limb from limb simply didn't bother her. I made a mental note to see if the entertainment center in her quarters carried any of the versions of *The Hound of the Baskervilles*.

We were nearly to the building when I heard someone call my name.

I turned around. It was Emikai, striding toward us with a determined expression on his face. Fanned out in a moving wedge behind him were four more Fillies wearing the same gray-and-black jumpsuits as the ones who'd hauled me out of the entry bay four hours ago. "Uh-oh," Bayta muttered.

"Steady," I cautioned her. I stood still, keeping my arms at my sides, as they came up to us. "I greet you, *Logra* Emikai," I said, nodding to him. "I'm rather surprised to see you still here. I'd have thought that having delivered Ms. German safely to Proteus you'd be on your way elsewhere."

"My way is now here," he said. "My contract has been bought by *Chinzro* Hchchu. I will remain until he dismisses me."

I cocked an eyebrow. "And you don't like that?"

"I was an enforcement officer," he reminded me. "My personal preferences are of no account." He gestured to the Jumpsuits still grouped behind him. "But that is of no account. I have come to tell you that you are summoned. The preliminary hearing on your trial is about to begin."

I frowned. "That was quick."

"The law as practiced aboard *Kuzyatru* Station requires justice to be meted out in a timely fashion," he explained.

Something with cold feet took a walk up my back. "Not so timely that the defense won't have a chance to prepare its own case, I hope?"

"Have no fear," he assured me. "This is merely a preliminary hearing." One of the Jumpsuits muttered something under his breath. "And we must leave at once," Emikai added. "The hour is rapidly approaching, and we have some distance to travel."

"How much distance?"

"The hearing will take place in Sector 16-J," he said. "That is the core administrative area nearest where we entered the station."

I suppressed a grimace. Which would put us a quarter of the way around the station just when Terese was due to be released. How very convenient for someone.

But there was obviously nothing I could do about it. Emikai might be cajoled or otherwise bargained with, but I very much doubted Hchchu could. "Fine," I said with a sigh as I took Bayta's arm. "I presume my attorney's been notified?"

"Your pardon," Emikai said, holding a hand up in front of Bayta. "She will not be permitted to attend."

The cold-footed thing on my back broke into a gallop. "That's absurd," I insisted. "She's my assistant."

"You have a right to an attorney," Emikai said. "But I do not think your assistant has any such rights."

"You don't *think*?" I asked. "You're an ex-cop. Don't you *know*?"

"*Kuzyatru* Station currently operates on different rules of law from those I am familiar with," Emikai said, sounding a bit defensive. "Director *Usantra* Nstroo and Assistant Director *Chinzro* Hchchu have chosen to reinstitute the ancient protocols of Slisst." He cocked his head. "That is why *Chinzro* Hchchu will be prosecuting you himself. Under the Slisst Protocols, that role falls to a friend or acquaintance of the injured party."

"And he was a friend of the Filiaelians I'm supposed to have murdered?" I asked.

"Not a friend, precisely, but I am told he was acquainted with all of them," Emikai said.

"I see," I said, wondering uneasily if Minnario had even heard of this Slisst Protocol stuff, let alone knew his way around it. "All very interesting, but I'm still a non-Filiaelian accused of a crime in non-Filiaelian territory. My situation still comes under the jurisdiction of cross-empire law."

"I believe *Chinzro* Hchchu is still studying that question," Emikai said, looking a little uncomfortable. "A final ruling is expected soon. Until then, you must still appear at the hearing."

"*With* my assistant," I said firmly.

One of the Jumpsuits stirred. {Why do we waste time?} he demanded. {We're many. He's one. Bring him and be done with it.}

{I hear and obey,} Emikai said reluctantly. "Mr. Compton—"

"Tell you what," I put in quickly. "If the big legal minds are still wrestling with this, it's certainly nothing the two of us are going to solve on our own. Why don't you call Minnario, clue him in on what's happening, and get him to the hearing? Then he and *Chinzro* Hchchu can hash out together whether or not Bayta can watch the proceedings."

"That seems reasonable," Emikai said, a note of relief in his voice as he pulled out his comm. Clearly, the rapid pace of Hchchu's brand of justice wasn't sitting well with him, either.

{The Protocols don't require this,} Jumpsuit insisted.

{Neither do they forbid it,} Emikai countered. He punched in a number and lifted the comm to his ear.

{This is *Logra* Emikai,} he said. {I wish to speak with Attorney Minnario chu-DeHak.}

{This is wasted time,} Jumpsuit muttered.

I watched him out of the corner of my eye, hoping I wouldn't have to use any of the combat techniques Emikai had taught me during our sparring sessions. At five-to-one odds, I wasn't likely to last very long.

But I sure as hell wasn't going to let them take me away and drop me into some dark hole somewhere where Bayta wouldn't even know where to start looking for me. Not without a fight.

{Understood,} Emikai said.

I looked back at him. The grimness in his voice was mirrored in his face. "What's the matter?" I asked.

"*Chinzro* Hchchu has been attempting to contact Attorney Minnario for nearly half an hour," Emikai said. "There is no answer on his comm. Nor have any patrollers or operational personnel seen him during that time.

"Your attorney, Mr. Compton, has vanished."

FOUR :

The nearest security nexus was ten floors directly above the medical dome. We arrived to find a full-scale search operation already in progress.

{There continues to be no response from his comm,} a jumpsuited patroller standing by the door reported as Emikai escorted Bayta and me into the room and over to a bank of monitors that stretched all the way up one wall and angled onto part of the ceiling.

{Keep trying,} Emikai ordered. "He is still not answering his comm," he translated for my benefit.

I nodded, looking over the monitors. About half the screens were cycling through visual images of important offices or key intersections, but most of the displays seemed to be readouts of environmental, power, or equipment usage. I spotted two different views of our Alpine medical dome go by in the rotation, one apparently from just above each of the two corridors leading into it. "Do you keep records of any of these images?" I asked.

"For one hour only," Emikai said. "Under the Slisst Protocols, anything more is considered a violation of privacy."

"That's unfortunate," I murmured. But probably very convenient for the Shonkla-raa as they scurried around on whatever nefarious schemes they were up to aboard the station. An excellent reason all by itself for Proteus's directors to have adopted the Protocols. "I guess we'll just have to do it the old-fashioned way, then," I continued. "We know Minnario was in the security station with me when our torchferry docked. We start by talking to everyone who was also there at that time, from *Chinzro* Hchchu on down, and try to track his movements."

"That is already being done," Emikai said, pointing to a display filled with Fili characters. "That is a list of those who have been spoken to, plus summaries of their testimonies to the patrollers. But it has already been over four hours since our arrival, and the trail has started to go dry. Many of the relevant personnel have dispersed to evening meals and quarters."

"Unless the Human expert wishes to offer a better method?" a sarcastic voice suggested from behind me.

I turned. It was *Usantra* Wandek, working his way toward us through the crowd of Jumpsuits. His blaze was showing the same odd mottling I'd seen during our earlier conversation down in the medical dome. "Greetings, *Usantra* Wandek," I said, nodding to him. "Did someone call for medical assistance?"

"The Nemut has a long list of medical problems," he said grimly. "His disappearance strongly implies one or more of those problems may have intensified." He cocked his head. "But my question was serious. Have you any better options to suggest?"

"Oh, please," I scoffed. "If you're going to set a trap, at least make it an interesting one. I was an Intelligence agent—of course I know about the locator transponders in most comms. I also know where they're located, how they function, and how to disable them." And, I didn't add, routinely did so, dropping my comm and Bayta's out of the system whenever we looked to be going into danger. "And since Minnario apparently hasn't been located that way, I presume his locator was in fact disabled. *Logra* Emikai?"

"You are correct," Emikai acknowledged.

"The more interesting question," I went on, watching Wandek closely, "is whether *Usantra* Wandek is suggesting I might have done away with my own lawyer. What reason could I possibly have for doing such a thing?"

"Who knows how Humans think?" Wandek countered, the mottling of his blaze intensifying a bit. The effect was oddly hypnotic. "More importantly, there can be only a handful of individuals on the station who have the knowledge and skill to disable the transponder."

"Really?" I looked at Emikai. "How many of the patrollers aboard Proteus have that skill?"

"I would guess between one and ten percent," Emikai said. "I believe many communications techs would also possess the necessary knowledge."

"There you go," I said to Wandek. "Ten percent of the patrollers on a station this size means we're talking hundreds or thousands of people. And that's just the Filiaelians."

"Do you accuse one of us?" Wandek demanded stiffly.

"I accuse everyone, and I accuse no one," I said. "It's no different than a doctor who suspects all illnesses until he's narrowed down the list of possibilities."

"Perhaps," Wandek said reluctantly. "Just be certain that your list of possibilities include *all* aboard *Kuzyatru* Station, and not merely the Filiaelians." He turned to Emikai. "I assume you are in charge of this investigation. How do you intend to proceed?"

I looked at Emikai in mild surprise. "*You're* in charge here?"

"*Chinzro* Hchchu has assigned me to supervise all matters concerning you and your pending case," Emikai explained. "Since Attorney Minnario is with you, his disappearance falls within my authority."

"So what *do* we do?" I asked. "Because *Usantra* Wandek is correct: if Minnario's lying injured off in some corner, his physical problems could make his situation critical."

Emikai gave a whinnying sigh. "Unfortunately, the tools at our disposal are severely limited," he said. "None of the monitors shows his location, we have no recordings of his movements, and so far no one interviewed remembers seeing him after his departure from the security office over two hours ago."

"What about DNA sniffers?" I suggested. "Surely you still have the records from when he entered Proteus Station."

"That has already been tried," one of the Jumpsuits said in badly accented English. "There is insufficient remaining nucleic in the security station."

"The air in *Kuzyatru* Station is cleaned as it is recirculated," Emikai explained. "That limits the usefulness of nucleic sniffers."

Another nice bonus for the Shonkla-raa. "Then we need to focus the search in the most likely places for him to have gone," I said. "In order, I would guess those to be places where he could get food or rest, look up the details of the Slisst Protocols, or get medical attention."

"What would he wish with the Protocols?" Wandek asked.

"He needs to know how the Proteus legal structure will affect our defense," I said.

"Your analysis makes sense," Emikai said, gesturing to the Jumpsuit at the monitor bank. {Institute a search of Mr. Compton's suggested target areas.}

{I obey.} The Jumpsuit swiveled back to his board and began speaking rapid Fili into a microphone.

"Have you any other thoughts?" Emikai asked.

I hesitated. This one, I knew, was *not* going to go over well. "We also need to consider motive," I said. "Specifically, who would benefit from Minnario's disappearance."

To my mild surprise, Emikai was already ahead of me. "You thus name *Chinzro* Hchchu," he said calmly.

I heard the faint whisper of a dozen necks against jumpsuit collars as every nearby Filly turned toward us. "According to the Slisst Protocols, he's the one who'll be prosecuting me," I pointed out for their benefit. "There are any number of reasons why he might want to delay the proceedings."

"What about *your* reasons?" Wandek put in.

"Such as?" I asked.

"I am told you were reluctant to attend this evening's preliminary hearing," Wandek said. "That hearing has now been unavoidably postponed."

"Pretty weak motive, if you ask me," I said. "Especially since the reason for my reluctance was that my assistant Bayta wouldn't be permitted to attend with me." I gestured toward Emikai. "And given that I've been under direct observation since I first learned about the hearing, it would have been well-nigh impossible for me to have done anything to him."

"Perhaps Attorney Minnario informed you ahead of the official notification," Wandek suggested darkly. "Perhaps you called for a meeting to discuss the matter, and you"—he threw a look at Bayta—"*and* your assistant then disposed of him."

"No," Emikai said flatly.

Wandek's blaze went all mottled again. "*No?*" he echoed. "You dare—?"

"They have not been alone aboard *Kuzyatru* Station." Emikai pointed at Doug and Ty. "Ever."

Wandek looked at the watchdogs, his expression and

posture reminiscent of a schooner that's just had all the wind knocked out of its sails. "Oh," he said in a suddenly subdued voice. "No, of course not."

"The *msikai-dorosli* would not permit them to harm another being," Emikai went on, in case Wandek hadn't fully grasped the point. "*Chinzro* Hchchu would have ordered them—"

{Yes, yes, I understand,} Wandek snapped. {Don't belabor the point.}

{My apologies, *Usantra* Wandek,} Emikai said.

Apparently, the words weren't enough. Wandek's hand twitched imperiously, and Emikai bowed his head toward the other. {My apologies,} he repeated.

"If you two can stop babbling a minute, can we get on with this?" I put in. Watching Emikai grovel in front of Wandek was nearly as irritating as Wandek making him do it. "My attorney's missing. I'd kind of like someone to find him."

They were still at it an hour later when my growling stomach finally forced me to go with Bayta in search of food. Fortunately, the security nexus included a station with a selection of quick foods available for the duty personnel. I decided Bayta and I qualified, and we had a quick meal there before returning to the monitor room.

Three hours later, when I finally gave up, they still hadn't found Minnario.

The door to Bayta's room was still keyed to both our DNA signatures. I opened the door, turned on the lights, and gave the room a quick scan as we walked in. Bayta's luggage had been delivered and was set neatly at the foot of the bed, but aside from that everything was just the way we'd left it. "What do you think happened to him?" Bayta asked quietly as I closed the door and locked it.

"Nothing good," I said, crossing to the half-bath and peeking inside. It, too, appeared untouched. "I just wish

I knew how they could have gotten to him without *someone* seeing it and coming forward."

"Maybe whoever saw his abduction or disappearance didn't realize the significance at the time," she suggested as she walked over to the bed and stood beside it.

"Maybe," I said. There was considerably more I wanted to say, facts and speculation both, and from the look on Bayta's face I could tell she was equally eager to have that same discussion. But this was the room that had been prepared for us, in all senses of that word, and neither of us was interested in having that conversation where little pitchers with big ears would undoubtedly be listening in. "We can hope so, anyway. Well. Good night, I guess."

"Good night, Frank," Bayta said.

For a long moment we just gazed across the room at each other. We'd said these same good-nights a thousand times before, and for most of those nights it had been a routine and largely meaningless ritual.

But not tonight. Tonight a Nemut was missing from Proteus Station, with every evidence of foul play. Tonight we were a long ways away from the Tube, with its multitude of Spiders and its weapon-free environment.

And tonight we weren't going to be sharing a double Quadrail compartment with nothing but a collapsible divider separating us. We were going to be half a kilometer apart, with neither of us able to quickly come to the other's aid if any of that foul play headed in our direction.

I wanted to say the hell with this, to just lock the door and settle down here for the night where I could protect Bayta while she in turn watched my back. But I didn't dare. We were already too emotionally close for comfort, and the Modhri was just waiting for his chance to ensnare us.

And if he got me, I would rather die than be the conduit through which he also got Bayta.

So I nodded a last farewell and stepped out into the hallway, Doug padding out beside me. I waited there until I heard the snick of the inner lock, then headed through the quiet corridors toward my own distant quarters.

Most of the space stations I'd visited over my career with Westali had run on a more or less round-the-clock schedule, with a noticeable drop in traffic and activity after midnight but nothing even approaching a complete halt. Proteus Station was different. The corridors were largely deserted as I walked along them, with only the jumpsuited patrollers still out and about. The lights were noticeably dimmer than they'd been when Bayta and I had left the security nexus, but they'd faded gradually enough that I hadn't really noticed until Doug and I were on the glideway and I realized that I couldn't make out the same details at the far end that I had when traveling this route earlier that afternoon. I assumed the station's schedule was set to mimic that of the Fillies' homeworld, but that was only a guess and with my reader locked up a quarter of the station away there was no way to look that up until I got back to my room and fired up the computer there.

I spent most of the trip trying to think up a fresh approach to finding Minnario. But it had been a long, full day, and I couldn't marshal enough brain cells to make even a dent in the problem. Maybe in the morning I would be able to think again.

Maybe in the morning Minnario would already be dead.

The receptionist station at the entrance to the medical dome was deserted. A few of the chalets were still showing lights, probably marking the presence of doctors or techs or maybe Shonkla-raa burning the midnight oil. The building where they'd been treating Terese was dark, and I briefly considered seeing if I could sneak inside.

But a closed building at night would almost certainly be on Doug's forbidden list, and there were all those sharp teeth to consider. Besides, even if Doug didn't have a problem with it, the two small cameras set on the dome's inner walls just inside the corridors would hold the images of me breaking and entering for the next hour. With the search for Minnario presumably still going on, the chance that someone would notice me was probably higher than I wanted to risk.

And so I continued on through the dome without stopping. I did, however, make a few mental notes as to which windows in which buildings still showed lights.

I half expected my door to still be sealed, with the techs having forgotten to code the lock to my DNA. But if the renowned Filly efficiency couldn't locate a lost Nemut, it was at least able to handle routine maintenance. The door opened at my touch on the plate, and I wearily stepped inside.

I was reaching for the light switch when I heard a soft grunt.

I took a long step to the side, out of the potentially lethal backlighting of the low glow from the corridor. Dropping into a combat stance, I tried to pierce the gloom in front of me.

And then, as the door slid closed, I caught a glimpse of something crouching motionlessly beside my bed.

I mouthed a curse, a flood of adrenaline kicking my brain back into gear. The light control was still within reach to my right—a flick of the switch and I would have all the light I needed to see who or what was waiting for me.

But for that first couple of seconds my dilated pupils would be momentarily blinded. If the intruder was ready for that, with optical filters or whatever, those couple of seconds could mean the difference between life and a very quick death. Doug was standing beside me, but his breathing was calm and rhythmic, with no sign of distress or extra alertness. No help for me there.

Or was there? If I picked him up and lobbed him across the room at the crouching figure, it might put the intruder out of action long enough for me to get my eyes adjusted and either jump him or get the hell out of the room. Silently, I squatted down and slid my arms around Doug's torso—

[Hello?] a Nemuti voice called groggily from the direction of the squatting figure. [Hello? Is someone there?]

For a long moment I just crouched there, my mind spinning on its rails. Then, letting go of Doug, I straightened up again and flicked on the light.

Minnario was half sitting up in bed, one hand shading his squinting eyes against the sudden glare. The figure I'd thought I'd seen lurking beside the bed was nothing more sinister than his support chair. [Mr. Compton,] he said, and there was no mistaking the surprise in his voice. [What in the FarReach are *you* doing here?]

I took a deep breath and reached for my comm. "Someone's been sleeping in my bed," I murmured. "And he's still here."

[I'm so terribly sorry to have caused such distress,] Minnario apologized, his voice low and embarrassed as he looked around at me, Emikai, and the half-dozen Jumpsuits who had intruded upon his privacy. [I had no idea that I was even considered missing, let alone that foul play was suspected.]

"How did you get in here, anyway?" I asked. "I was told this was my room."

[As was I,] Minnario said. [Which is what I then told the technician who was keying the lock when I arrived.]

"And it didn't concern you that he was coding it to my nucleics?"

[I assumed you'd instructed him to do that so you would be able to enter for consultations without my having to come to the door to let you in.] He frowned. [Though now that I think about it, the tech did say something about *me* coming to visit *you*. I confess that I was so tired that the comment didn't register at the time. I'm so very sorry to have caused such trouble.]

"It is not your fault," Emikai assured him. He'd come charging into the room in response to my call looking both relieved and annoyed. Now, he just looked tired. "It will be straightened out in the morning." He turned to one of the Jumpsuits. {Where can we assign Mr. Compton for the night?}

{There's nothing available in this sector,} the other Filly said, punching keys on a reader. {I can try to find him something in one of the adjoining sectors.}

"There are no other empty rooms nearby," Emikai translated for me. "Could you perhaps stay with Bayta? It would only be for the one night."

"No problem," I said. "In fact, forget about looking for something else. She and I will just share the room as originally planned."

Emikai's blaze paled a bit with obvious surprise. "I was told you wished your own quarters."

I shrugged. "I've changed my mind."

And to my own surprise, I realized that I had. That long, lonely walk from Bayta's room to this one had finally solidified my misgivings about our forced separation, and I realized that the risk of deepening our emotional involvement was far less than the danger of splitting our forces in the middle of hostile territory. When the Shonkla-raa and Modhri decided to make their move, Bayta and I needed to be standing together as we faced it.

"Very well," Emikai said, eyeing me another moment before turning to the Jumpsuit with the reader. {Log the fact that Mr. Compton now shares quarters with his assistant,} he ordered.

[A moment,] Minnario put in, reaching down and sweeping the blankets away from his useless legs. [At this point, I believe it would be easier for Mr. Compton and Bayta to move in here and for me to take the other room.]

"How exactly would that be easier?" I asked.

[Because this room is already set for your *msikai-dorosli*,] he said, pointing toward the closet. [It would be more trouble to collect and move it than for me to move myself and my few belongings.]

Frowning, I walked over to the closet and looked in. He was right: jammed into the narrow space were two long dog beds, plus bowls of water and food, plus a hefty bag of the latter over in the far corner.

It was only then that my preoccupied brain suddenly registered the fact that Doug was the only watchdog here with me. Ty, for some reason, had stayed behind with Bayta.

Ty, and all those sharp teeth . . .

I whipped out my comm and punched in Bayta's number, my pulse hammering in my throat. "Yes?" Bayta answered.

"Are you all right?" I demanded, my voice harsher than I'd planned.

"I'm fine," she assured me, her own voice going suddenly tight in reaction. "What's the matter?"

I took a careful breath. "Nothing," I said. "I just wanted to tell you we found Minnario. In my room. Rather, in *our* room—he's decided to swap with you."

There was a brief pause. "All right," Bayta said, clearly having trouble following the half-story she was getting. "Do you want me to pack right now?"

"If you would," I said. "Uh . . . how is Ty?"

"Ty?" she echoed, sounding confused.

"Yes," I said. "Any problems with him?"

"No, nothing. Should there have been?"

"No, of course not," I assured her. Only why the hell had he ended up staying with her instead of coming with Doug and me? "I'll be over shortly to get you."

"All right," she said. "Good-bye."

"Bye."

I hung up and gestured to the watchdog supplies. "Was all this delivered after you arrived?" I asked Minnario.

[Actually, it was already here,] he said. He had eased himself into the chair while I'd been talking to Bayta, and now twisted the control that sent it rising smoothly to waist height on its thrusters. [I wondered about it, but again was too weary to make inquiries before turning off my comm and going to bed.]

"Speaking of your comm," I said, "there's supposed to be a tracker in it for police to use in case of emergency."

[Yes—the location transponder,] Minnario said, nodding. [My comm did indeed come with such a device. But it unfortunately interfered with the control systems of my chair and I had to have it removed. Are you ready?]

I looked at Emikai, who gave a little shrug. "However you wish to arrange your sleeping quarters is of no matter to me or to *Kuzyatru* Station," the Filly said. "But you should know that the preliminary hearing postponed from this evening has now been rescheduled for tomorrow at ten o'clock."

I nodded. "Bayta and I will be there."

Emikai seemed to brace himself. "*Chinzro* Hchchu has also ruled that your assistant is not permitted to attend."

[Of course she may attend,] Minnario spoke up. [Not as Mr. Compton's assistant, but as my chief witness of the events surrounding the charges against him. As such, she may attend all proceedings.]

I felt my cheeks warming. The most blatantly obvious logic possible, and I'd missed it completely.

So, apparently, had Emikai. "Ah," he said, sounding as bemused as I felt. "Are you certain that is part of the Slisst Protocols?"

[Very certain,] Minnario said firmly. [As it happens, I happened to be studying that very section of the Protocols just before I settled down to sleep.]

"I see," Emikai said. "I will be certain to bring that to *Chinzro* Hchchu's attention." He turned back to me. "A patroller will meet you here at nine o'clock to escort you to the hearing room."

"I'd prefer that you come yourself," I told him.

He seemed to measure me with his eyes. "As you wish," he said. "I will meet you here then." He looked at Minnario. "I presume you will be content with an ordinary patroller as your escort?"

[Quite content, thank you,] Minnario assured him. [But for now, I'm still very tired. If you'll be good enough, Mr. Compton, to show me to my new quarters?]

Minnario's chair couldn't safely use the glideways, which meant we had to walk the normal corridor the entire way, which meant that it was another long and tiring hour before Bayta and I and my watchdogs—both of them this time—were finally in our new quarters.

Doug and Ty, at least, seemed pleased with the new arrangement. They made a joint beeline for the closet and food dishes, and a minute later the room was filled with the sound of chomping and slurping.

"Any idea why Ty decided to stay with you?" I asked Bayta as we watched them eat.

"No," she said. "I suppose it's possible that *Chinzro* Hchchu actually intended one of them to stay with each of us."

"That wasn't what it sounded like when he gave the orders," I reminded her.

"Maybe there are nuances in his Fili that neither of us caught."

"Maybe." I looked at the bed, then headed for the couch. "I'll be over here if you need me," I said over my shoulder. "You can have first crack at the bathroom."

"Are you sure?" she asked, her voice oddly strained.

"Of course." I tried to look her in the eye, but for some reason I was unable to do so. "Unless you had some different arrangement in mind."

"No." She paused. "But someone else apparently does. Either the Shonkla-raa or the Modhri."

I felt my throat tighten. "Luckily, we don't care what

they want," I said. "I'll need to steal one of your pillows
and a blanket, though."

"Of course." She paused again. "Do you think the
room is safe?"

I shrugged. "If Minnario's timeline is right, he got
here pretty much right after we left, right while the tech
was coding our DNA—well, mine, anyway—into the
lock. That doesn't leave much time for someone to nip
in here and plant a bunch of bugs."

"I suppose," Bayta said. But her eyes were troubled.
She opened her mouth—

"Meanwhile, it's been a long day, and tomorrow's
looking to be just as bad," I said before she could speak.
"Go get your bedtime prep done so that I can do mine,
and let's get some sleep."

"All right," she said, gazing at me with the kind of
wary intensity that told me she was on the same wavelength that I was.

Minnario's timeline did indicate that no one would
have had time to bug our quarters. But there was no
way to know whether Minnario's timeline was accurate.

Bayta headed into the half-bath, and then it was my
turn. By the time I emerged she was already snuggled
down in bed, the blankets pulled up to her chin.

So, to my surprise, was Ty. He had taken up a cross-
ways position at the very head of the bed, his pineapple
back pressed against the headboard as if he'd been sta-
pled there. I didn't know whether or not Bayta had made
an effort to get rid of him, but fortunately the bed was
long enough that she had enough room despite his presence. She'd also managed to snag the remaining pillow
before he got to it.

Doug, for his part, had also skipped out on his doggie
bed and was curled up in front of the door. If I'd been
thinking about going for a solitary walk during the
quiet of the Proteus night, I would have had to seriously
revise my plans.

I padded over to the bed and, with only a little hesitation, lay down on top of the blankets beside Bayta. "You okay?" I whispered in her ear, feeling the warmth of her body through the bedding as I pressed myself close to her.

"Yes," she said. But I could hear the tension in her voice.

Small wonder. We'd done this pretend-snuggling thing once before, also as a way of talking without our conversation being picked up by the bugs that had been planted in that room.

But things had been different then. I'd hardly known Bayta, hadn't trusted her farther than I could throw a drudge Spider, and hadn't found her all that attractive.

Now all of that had changed. *All* of it.

I didn't know what Bayta was thinking or feeling. Most of me really didn't want to know.

"Do you think he was lying?" she whispered.

"I don't know," I admitted, rolling my eyes toward the feathery underbelly a few centimeters from the top of my head, an underbelly that had started a low rumbling. Either Ty had a snoring problem, or the damn things actually purred. "On the other hand, I'm almost positive the other room was bugged, so there was zero chance there of a private conversation," I went on. "Here, at least we've got a shot at it. Besides, what reason would Minnario have to lie?"

"The answer to that might depend on why Attorney Minnario is on Proteus in the first place."

I grimaced in the darkness. "Theoretically, for medical treatment."

"And we both know that's not the whole story."

"Right, but what is?" I asked. "My first assumption was that he was brought in to be a witness against me in Muzzfor's death. But Hchchu hasn't even mentioned Muzzfor. It's also counterproductive for your hoped-for star witness to suddenly decide to represent the other team."

"So why did he do *that*?" Bayta persisted. "Why would he decide on the spur of the moment to donate his time to a Human he barely knows? Especially a Human who's facing serious charges that could very well be true?"

"There are still a few crazy idealistic crusading attorneys out there," I said. "Maybe he's a fan of old dit-rec courtroom dramas. Or maybe he really believes that anyone who could take down a multiple murderer is deserving of a good legal defense."

"Or *Chinzro* Hchchu or the Shonkla-raa brought him in to defend you so that they could get close to us," Bayta countered.

"Could be," I agreed. "The problem with that is, why bother? There have to be dozens of lawyers right here on Proteus they could recruit without having to haul Minnario in, especially with what we all agree is a pathetically weak excuse. Without an attorney of our own on hand, we would have to take whoever Hchchu offered."

"Except that we might suspect an appointed attorney of being in league with them."

"Not a Filly lawyer," I said firmly. "Genetic engineering, remember? I don't think they're capable of being in cahoots with anyone except their current client. Anyway, if Minnario was working with Hchchu, why on Earth did he so inconveniently disappear this evening, thereby screwing up Hchchu's hearing schedule? For that matter, why did he volunteer to move to a room that now has a whole bunch of useless bugs in it?"

"Useless because we're not there?"

"Useless because there are Shorshic vectored force thrusters operating in there," I said. "Bugs by definition are tiny microphones and transmitters, and thruster harmonics screw up most radio frequencies something fierce. That's probably why Minnario's phone transponder messes up his controls—there are only a few frequencies that the thrusters don't blanket, and phones and local control systems have to share them. No, whoever's listening in on Minnario's room is going to get nothing but unreadable and unfilterable static."

"I didn't know that," Bayta said thoughtfully. "Maybe we should start carrying a thruster around with us."

"High-level diplomats often do, actually," I said. "One final point: if Hchchu and Minnario were trying to separate us, why would Minnario remind everyone that you qualify as a witness? *I* sure hadn't thought of that dodge."

"Could we have two different sides working at cross-purposes?" Bayta suggested slowly. "Perhaps *Chinzro* Hchchu wants to convict you of those six murders and doesn't want me around for the trial, while the Shonkla-raa *does* want me at the trial so that we'll both be away from Terese."

I pursed my lips. Another angle I hadn't thought of. I was definitely slipping. "Could be," I agreed. "Certainly the whole idea of saddling us with these watchdogs theoretically gives them the power to control all our movements . . ."

I trailed off as something suddenly struck me. "What is it?" Bayta asked tensely.

"I was just wondering about the way Ty stuck with you tonight," I said. "Clearly, the Fillies—presumably including Hchchu—expected both of them to come here with me, even though they knew we were supposedly going to be staying in different quarters. That implies there wasn't any subtle nuance in Hchchu's instructions to the watchdogs."

"Maybe they misunderstood their orders," Bayta suggested.

"Or maybe you're right about two groups working at cross-purposes."

"Perhaps." Bayta was silent a moment. "Do you suppose one or the other of those groups may have planted trackers in them?"

"Unlikely," I assured her. "Without a collar or other similar add-on, the only place for anyone to put something like that is inside the animal itself. That requires a fair amount of prep work, more than anyone got after Minnario charged up on his white horse and disrupted everyone's plans. No, I'm pretty sure they're clean."

"That makes sense, I suppose," she said. "It's not like someone couldn't put us under nearly constant observation anyway, assuming they had access to the security camera system."

"Exactly," I agreed. "Which I'm guessing they won't do, since it would involve awkward questions from the patrollers. Much easier to simply have us followed." I frowned down at Doug. "Which still leaves us with our watchdog tag-team puzzle. I wonder who aboard Proteus is authorized to give these things orders."

"Maybe Attorney Minnario can find out."

"Or maybe I can do it myself," I said. "I think I'll take a few minutes and see what files the computer will let me get into."

"Do you want any help?"

"No, you'd better get to sleep," I said. "Remember that Emikai will be here bright and early."

"Do you trust him?"

I shrugged. "I've got no particular reason not to. He was a cop, which means he's got his own set of genetic engineering and behavioral restraints."

"Only his loyalties aren't to us," Bayta reminded me. "They're to the Filiaelian *santras*."

"There's that," I conceded. "And when I say there's no reason not to trust him, I also mean there's no reason *to* trust him, either. We'll have to watch him—and Minnario—and see how this all plays out."

"While also watching Terese and Dr. Aronobal?"

"Like I say, tomorrow's going to be a full and rich day," I said. "Get some sleep." I patted her shoulder through the blankets and started to roll off the bed.

"Why *Ty*?" she asked suddenly.

"What?" I asked, frowning, as I rolled back to her again.

"*Doug* I understand," she said. "They look a little like Earth dogs. But why do you call the other one Ty?"

"Actually, *Doug* has nothing to do with the word *dog*," I said. "It's the mask sort of things they have around their eyes. They remind me of an old character from Earth literature named Zorro. *Doug* and *Ty* come from Douglas Fairbanks and Tyrone Power, the actors who played the character in the first two dit-rec adventure adaptations of the stories."

"Oh," Bayta said. "I don't think you've ever showed me those."

"I'll put them on the list," I promised. "Right after *The Hound of the Baskervilles.*"

"The what?"

"Never mind," I told her, climbing off the bed. "Get some sleep. I'll see you in the morning."

FIVE :

The couch was too short for me to stretch out comfortably, but I was able to take off the cushions and lay them out on the floor instead. That, along with the extension provided by the pillow I'd taken from the bed, made my pallet long enough to serve as a tolerable sleeping platform.

It was colder on the floor than I'd expected, and even wrapping myself up in my blanket like a burrito left me on the cool side of comfortable. Fortunately, a few minutes after I got settled Doug seemed to realize I was in for the night and padded over to lie down beside me. He wasn't exactly cuddly, certainly not in the way a real dog would be, but the radiated heat was welcome. Besides, I could hardly feel his hard pineapple hide through the blanket.

Emikai and a pair of Jumpsuits arrived precisely at

nine o'clock the next morning. Bayta and I were ready, and together we headed off through the station's labyrinth of corridors, glideways, elevators, and bullet trains. I tried to keep track of the twists and turns, but within the first ten minutes I was thoroughly lost. If for some reason Emikai refused to guide us back home, we would likely be sleeping in somebody's doorway tonight.

I'd seen dozens of courtrooms over the years, and the Proteus version was right up there with the best of them. Tall double doors led into a chamber that was large and imposing, with a high and long judge's bench at the far end and only marginally less grand places for the prosecution and defense. Unlike the usual high-class wood-paneled Human courtroom, though, this one was done completely in dressed stone, from floor to ceiling, extending even to the seats and tables. Fortunately, the seats had been furnished with cushions and back rests.

Hchchu was waiting, seated at the prosecutor's table with no fewer than four readers spread out on the table in front of him. Either he was planning to refer to four separate versions of Filly law or else he didn't trust bookmarks for retrieving the relevant pages. Minnario was also there, peering at his reader as he hovered in his chair at one end of the defense table.

More interestingly, at least to me, the judges also were already seated, a marked departure from the Human custom in these matters. There were four of them, each dressed in an identical outfit of layered gray and dark blue with elaborate shoulder points and collar and sleeve tucks, the whole ensemble topped by a floppy hat. I'd never seen such garb on Fillies before, not even in pictures, and as Emikai ushered Bayta and me to the defense table I wondered if the clothing was something out of the Slisst Protocols. Something I might want to ask about later.

"You will sit with your attorney," Emikai murmured to me as I started forward. "But your assistant must wait back here with us."

I looked at Bayta. "I'll be all right," she assured me. "Go on."

I nodded to her and crossed the expanse of stone toward my seat. Way too much empty space, I knew, for the kind of economy of scale demanded by anything built in space. The open area probably served as a visitors' gallery during high-profile cases.

[You're late,] Minnario chided quietly as I sat down on the stone bench beside him. There was a scuffling noise, and I looked down as Doug and Ty settled themselves comfortably on the floor beside my seat. Apparently, whatever order or mistaken assumption had briefly kept Ty with Bayta last night was all over now.

"I make it three minutes till," I told Minnario.

[The guardlaws and your opponent are already here,] Minnario countered. [By arriving last you've given up any challenge to the high ground.]

I was opening my mouth to ask what the hell that was supposed to mean when the Filly at the far end of the judges' bench gave a startlingly bird-like trilling whinny. {The groundstage is begun,} he announced in a loud voice. A loud *and* familiar voice.

I took a second, closer look. I was right. The judge was none other than *Usantra* Wandek.

Minnario nudged me and pointed to the table in front of me. I looked away from Wandek, to see that a section of the table had lit up with an English translation of the Fili. It made a nice counterpoint to the Nemuspee translation running on Minnario's chair display. {You of the adversaries are met to seek truth, divide honor, and find justice,} Wandek continued. {We of the guardlaws are met to hone the sword and guide the spear.}

I grimaced. Not exactly the conversational direction a defendant liked to hear from his judges. "Is this standard courtroom procedure?" I murmured to Minnario.

The Nemut twitched his fingers in a shushing motion. {If any here has words of confession or remorse, let him speak now,} Wandek continued. His eyes were steady on me, but that might have been because he'd spotted me talking over his speech. I held his gaze, and after another couple of seconds he shifted his attention to Minnario. {You speak for this adversary?}

[I do,] Minnario replied. Now that the proceedings had begun, I noted that the table was also running a translation of his Nemuspee.

{And you have studied the rules and precedents of the Slisst Protocols?}

[I have.]

{Then you should already be aware that adversaries' companions are not permitted on this ground,} Wandek said, giving a sharp nod toward Bayta.

[She is not merely a companion, but a witness,] Minnario pointed out.

{This is the groundstage,} Wandek said, his tone the annoyance of a teacher trying to deal with a slightly dim student who keeps making the same mistake over and over. {Witnesses are not yet to be examined.}

[I understand,] Minnario said calmly. [But Mr. Compton is on trial for a crime that can carry the death penalty. In such a case, Protocol Fifty-seven states his life partner may be present for all proceedings.]

I sat up a little straighter on the stone bench. My *life partner*? That was stretching reality a bit far.

Wandek wasn't buying it, either. {I see no ring, mark, or sash,} he said pointedly.

[No such indicators are necessary,] Minnario said. [They are Humans, and Human custom provides for what is called common-law life partnership. All that is required is a period of cohabitation and a commitment to one another.]

Wandek looked at me, and I worked hard to keep my face expressionless. Minnario was definitely playing fast and loose with this one, especially the cohabiting bit.

But sifting through Human legal terms was tricky enough for Humans, let alone Fillies. And if it kept Bayta and me together through this mess, I was willing to play along.

{Very well,} Wandek said at last. I could tell he still wasn't buying it, but at the moment he didn't have anything solid to hang his suspicions on. {Until the court has had an opportunity to assess the validity of your claim, she may remain.}

He looked down the table at his fellow judges. But none of them seemed inclined to go any further out on this particular limb, and after a moment he straightened up and nodded to Hchchu. {Proceed,} he ordered.

Hchchu nodded back. {Proper form states that a list of charges be the first item under consideration,} he said. {But in this case, we must first establish who, in fact, my opponent truly is.}

He lifted one of the readers and tapped a button. Beside the running translation on our table, a repeater display lit up with an image of my diamond-edged first-class Quadrail pass. {His Quadrail pass identifies him as Frank Compton of New York City, Western Alliance, Earth, Terran Confederation,} he continued. {Yet this document—}

{Which sector?} the judge beside Wandek interrupted.

{The Terran Confederation has only one sector,} Wandek told him.

The judge gave me an odd look, probably wondering how Humans dared even show their faces around the galaxy with such a pathetically small tract of real estate to call our own. {Proceed,} he said.

{*This* document, in contrast—} Hchchu tapped the button again, and my Quadrail pass was replaced by my fake Hardin Industries ID card {—names him as Frank Abram Donaldson. This speaks of duplicity and fraud.}

Wandek turned to our table. {Does *Chinzro* Hchchu's opponent have a parry?} he asked.

[We do,] Minnario said. [At heart is our opponent's

contention that having two names is an intent to deceive this court.]

{Do you take us for fools?} the judge in the fourth position demanded. {Humans are not Cimmaheem, who randomly take different names at different lifepoints.}

[I did not imply that they were,] Minnario assured him. [To repeat: Mr. Compton's intent was not to deceive *this court*. As a security agent of the cross-galaxy corporation Hardin Industries, it is necessary at times for him to conceal his true identity from his opponents.]

{No Human corporation can be considered truly cross-galaxy,} the third judge said disdainfully. But he nevertheless nodded and made a note on his reader.

{Parry accepted,} Wandek said. {Riposte?}

[Yes,] Minnario said, turning toward Hchchu. [I claim that from the evidence thus presented, *Chinzro* Hchchu had no reason to suspect my client of the crimes for which he is accused. As a second riposte, I claim that the evidence he presents is improper and flawed.]

{Explain,} Wandek ordered.

[*Chinzro* Hchchu states that his evidence comes from a Filiaelian scholar who traveled to the Human world of New Tigris to retrieve the bodies of the six *santras* and investigate the circumstances surrounding their deaths,] Minnario said. [But the information she collected pertained to a Human named Mr. Frank Abram Donaldson.]

{Which is one of Mr. Compton's assumed names,} Wandek reminded him.

[But from the evidence presented, *Chinzro* Hchchu could not have known that at the time Mr. Compton entered *Kuzyatru* Station,] Minnario said. [Mr. Compton entered under his own proper name, with proper identification.] He looked at Hchchu. [So I ask: for what reason of expectation did *Chinzro* Hchchu search Mr. Compton for other identity papers?]

It was, I decided, a damn good question. From the suddenly wooden texture of Hchchu's face I gathered he thought so, too. {A valid question,} Wandek agreed. {Parry, *Chinzro* Hchchu?}

{I have another source of information concerning Mr. Compton's identity and crimes,} Hchchu said reluctantly. {It was this source who informed me that the Frank Abram Donaldson of the scholar's report was the same as the Frank Compton soon to arrive aboard *Kuzyatru* Station.}

[The name of this source?] Minnario asked.

{At this time, I'm not at liberty to disclose it,} Hchchu said.

Clearly, Minnario had been expecting that reply. [The Slisst Protocols specify that a defender must have a clear view of all weapons in the opponent's array,] he said. [Unless the identity of this source is revealed in a timely manner so that I can assess its strength and temper, I must request that the attack against my client cease without risk of blood, honor, or spirit.]

{I ask time to consult my source,} Hchchu said before any of the judges could respond.

Wandek murmured something down the line of judges, and received other murmurs in reply. {You have one day to lay this weapon on the table,} Wandek told Hchchu. {We will reconvene on this field at this same time tomorrow. The groundstage has ended. The opponents may leave the field.}

Silently, Hchchu stood up and began putting his collection of readers into the pouches of a belt bag fastened around his waist. I started to stand up, stopped as Minnario laid a hand on my arm. [Wait,] he murmured. [You were last to arrive. We must similarly be last to depart.]

Hchchu finished his packing and strode down the center of the room, not looking at either of us, and disappeared through the double doors. As they closed behind him, the judges gathered their own paraphernalia and filed off their bench, Wandek bringing up the rear as they too marched toward the doors. Like Hchchu, the first three judges ignored us, but Wandek paused as he passed. "Come by quickly," he murmured. "Ms. German's condition worsens."

I started to speak, again stopped at the touch of Minnario's hand, and watched as Wandek followed the others out through the double doors. "Now?" I asked, standing up.

[Yes, we may depart,] Minnario confirmed, making no move to maneuver his chair away from the stone table. [But there are matters we need to discuss. This is as good a place as any to do so.]

I looked at the double doors, thinking about what Wandek had said about Terese. But Minnario was right, on both counts. With our quarters possibly bugged, and me with no faith whatsoever that an attorney/client conference room would be any cleaner, the courtroom itself was probably our best bet. Especially a courtroom made entirely from stone, which would make hardwired microphones extremely hard to install.

And to be doubly sure . . .

I stood up and turned back to the doors. "Thank you for your assistance, *Logra* Emikai," I called, beckoning Bayta toward me. "I need to speak with my attorney for a few minutes."

Emikai hesitated, then nodded. "Very well," he called back. "But I've been informed that there are new developments in Ms. German's case."

"Yes, I know," I said. "If you'd like, go on ahead and assess the situation. We'll find our way back from here."

"Very well." Emikai pushed open one of the doors and ushered the two Jumpsuits ahead of him out into the corridor beyond.

"We *can* find our way back from here, right?" I asked Minnario.

[Of course,] Minnario said. [There are directories at each major intersection. Touch the green emblem, speak your destination, and follow the directions you're given.]

"Oh," I said, feeling more than vaguely foolish as Bayta came up to us. "I must have skipped that page in the guidebook."

[Now we may speak?]

"Sure." I pointed toward the judges' bench. "Up there."

Minnario looked at me in astonishment. [In the *guard-laws'* positions?]

"I won't tell if you don't," I said. "If there's any place in a courtroom guaranteed not to be bugged, it's the place where the judges discuss their side of the case."

[You may be right,] Minnario said reluctantly. [All right, but we must be quick about it.]

We crossed to the stone table, Doug and Ty padding along behind us, and I climbed up into the place where Wandek had been sitting. "Plenty of room," I pointed out.

"That's all right," Bayta said, standing beside me as Minnario stopped his chair at her side. "What exactly do we need to discuss, Attorney Minnario?"

[To begin with, *Chinzro* Hchchu's mysterious information source,] Minnario said. [Have you any idea who it might be?]

"Emikai and Dr. Aronobal are the most likely suspects," I said. "They were both on our super-express Quadrail, which gave them opportunities to see me in action, and both were on Earth when the reports of the New Tigris incident filtered in. Either of them could have put those two pieces of data together and come to at least a suspicion, if not a conclusion."

"Could they have obtained a private police report?" Bayta asked.

"Assuming they have a top-level contact in the Filiaelian embassy, sure," I said. "I'm more interested in who exactly this Filly scholar is that Hchchu mentioned, and how she was conveniently on hand in that part of the galaxy to go around collecting bodies and evidence."

[I have her name,] Minnario said, scrolling through his reader. [But I've done a search, and she seems to have no connection to *Chinzro* Hchchu or anyone else aboard *Kuzyatru* Station. It appears she was simply on Homshil when the report of the *santras'* deaths reached the Assembly, and as the nearest Filiaelian with governmental connections she was ordered to delay her return and travel to New Tigris.]

"So she has no actual expertise in police procedure?" I asked.

[None,] Minnario said. [And to tell you the truth, it shows. Her report's full of oddities, curiosities, and the occasional contradiction.] He smiled lopsidedly. [Those are technical legal terms, of course.]

"Like the laying out of weapons that *Usantra* Wandek mentioned?" I asked.

[The Slisst Protocols are filled with such expressions,] Minnario said. [They came from the ancient Filiaelian mode of honor-satisfaction via combat, and retain much of the same form and language. That's why the overseers are called guardlaws instead of judges. They don't so much rule on the case as watch what *Chinzro* Hchchu and I do and award the verdict on the basis of the strength and validity of our arguments.]

"Like martial-arts referees awarding points," I said, nodding. "Not so different from the way a lot of Earth courts work, actually. Can I assume the Protocols won't degenerate at some point into actual armed combat?"

Minnario laughed, a sort of pleasant rippling-brook babble that I'd heard before only in recordings. It sounded even more cheerful in person. [Be of confidence,] he assured me. [Filiaelian society is far beyond such primitive behavior.]

"Glad to hear it," I said. "So tell me more about the scholar's report. Starting with how I managed to get saddled with six murders."

[You didn't commit all the murders?] Minnario asked. [I'm your attorney, you know—you can tell me the truth without fear of bias or betrayal.]

"The truth is that I didn't commit *any* murders," I told him firmly. "I may—*may*—have killed one of the Fillies in a firefight, but I'm not even sure about that."

"Which *they* started in the pursuit of criminal activities," Bayta added.

Minnario made a sort of hissing sound. [Incredible,] he said. [*Santra*-class Filiaelians.]

"Evil comes in all shapes and sizes these days," I said. "And as I say, even that one killing is questionable. I was in the middle of a bunch of cops at the time and all of us were trying very hard to get to the *santras* before they got us. You'd have to do ballistic and residue tests on all our weapons to figure out who shot whom, and I'm not sure the New Tigris cops even bothered."

[I see,] Minnario said thoughtfully. [Well, as I said, the scholar's report is full of problems. It shouldn't be a problem to pick at it until it falls apart.]

"I'll hold you to that," I said. "Was there anything else?"

[I have no other questions, no,] Minnario said, easing his chair backward. [Now that I have possible names for *Chinzro* Hchchu's information source, I can begin backtracking and hopefully have some material on hand when he officially reveals the name.]

"So as to have your sword in the en garde position?" I suggested.

Minnario laughed again. [Indeed,] he said. [I should have known that a Human would have little trouble adapting to the legal flavor of the Slisst Protocols. Your recent history's still so bloody.]

"Thanks," I said dryly. "I think."

His smile faded. [Speaking of blood, did I hear *Usantra* Wandek say that your companion's medical condition has worsened?]

"Yes, and Bayta and I need to get back there," I said.

[Do you wish me to escort you?] Minnario offered. [But no—you can surely travel to her side faster by yourselves.]

"Probably," I said. "But if you'd feel better traveling together . . . ?"

[No, no, I'll be fine.] He looked ruefully down at his chair. [Someday, Mr. Compton, I'll be free of this chair.]

"Absolutely," I assured him. Though if he figuratively bloodied Proteus's assistant director by beating him in this ridiculous trial by verbal combat, it might be a long time before anyone aboard the station found the time to treat him.

Firmly, I shook the thought away. Surely Hchchu wouldn't be that petty. Even if he was, I could only deal with one crisis at a time. "Then we'll see you later," I said, sliding off the stone bench and taking Bayta's arm. "Oh, and this time will you do me a favor and leave your comm on?"

[I will,] he promised. [My regards to your friend.]

The green directories worked exactly the way Minnario had described. I used them four times on the trip back to Terese's medical dome, the last three times just to double-check my memory, and I felt a flush of warmth in my cheeks each time I did so. I really *should* have picked up on that on my own.

We arrived at the door to Terese's building to find Emikai waiting for us. "How is she?" I asked.

"I am not certain," he said, beckoning. "Come and see."

Dr. Aronobal was waiting in Terese's room. So, to my mild surprise, was *Usantra* Wandek, dressed now in his doctor's tans instead of his guardlaw outfit. "Mr. Compton," he greeted me gravely. "It's good of you to come."

"Nice to see you again, too," I said, shifting my attention to the bed. At first glance Terese didn't seem to have changed much since our last meeting, though she was hooked up to more wires and monitors than she had been before.

But on my second look I noticed her sunken cheeks, the dark circles around her eyes, and her slightly sallow skin. "Hello, Terese," I said. "How are you feeling?"

"Crowded," she said, a little of the old fire coming back into her eyes and voice as she looked pointedly around at all of us.

"I don't doubt it," I said. "Shall I ask *Logra* Emikai to throw all of us out?"

She snorted. "I can ask him myself if I want to."

"Yes, I'm sure you can," I said, catching Bayta's eye and nodding fractionally toward Terese. "Actually, I have a few questions for Dr. Aronobal, so I can at least get two of us out of your way. And I think *Logra* Emikai and *Usantra* Wandek have a matter or two of their own to discuss." I looked at Emikai. "For one thing, I'm concerned about the security arrangements at my trial."

For once, someone actually picked up on one of my cues. "As am I," Emikai said. "If I may have a moment of your time, *Usantra* Wandek?"

"What security arrangements are these?" Wandek asked, his blaze mottling a bit with obvious confusion.

"Oh, come now," I said reproachfully. "I'm a Human aboard a Filiaelian space station accused of murdering six other Filiaelians. Of course I'm going to need security." I gestured down to Doug and Ty. "Preferably something with a bit more of my own welfare in mind than *Chinzro* Hchchu's watchdogs."

Wandek was still looking unconvinced, but he nevertheless nodded. {There's a small conference room down the hallway,} he told Emikai. {We can go there.}

The two of them left the room. "Dr. Aronobal?" I invited, gesturing toward the doorway. "Perhaps outside would be best—I could use the fresh air."

Aronobal hesitated, then looked at Terese. "I will return shortly," she said. "Call for an attendant if you need anything."

The dome was, as usual, reasonably deserted when Aronobal and I emerged from Terese's building. There were a handful of Fillies moving around, most of them walking from one building to another, but that was about it. As far as the mainstream of Proteus' traffic flow was concerned, this dome definitely wasn't in it. "Please make this quick," Aronobal said. "I have a patient to treat."

"I appreciate your devotion," I said. "I wanted to ask about the status of Terese's unborn baby."

"Ms. German is aware of our concern for him," Aronobal said, a little reproachfully. "We could have spoken of this in her presence."

"Maybe yes, maybe no," I said, feeling a frown creasing my forehead as I took another look around the dome. I'd brought Aronobal out here purely to give Bayta a little privacy in which to quiz Terese about the attack she'd suffered back on Earth. But now that we were here, something was tingling at the back of my neck.

The dome was wrong. Something about this place was simply *wrong*.

"What do you mean, maybe yes, maybe no?" Aronobal asked.

That was a good question. With my mind preoccupied with the vague new riddle that was suddenly nagging at me, I grabbed at the first thought that came to mind. "I mean you might not want her around," I said, "when you tell me the baby's going to die."

I expected that to spark some kind of reaction. I didn't expect Aronobal to grab my upper arms and pull me toward her until my face was bare centimeters from her nose blaze. "Who told you he was going to die?" she demanded.

"No one," I protested, leaning as far away from her as I could. Beside me Doug gave a low warning growl, no doubt assuming that I was the aggressor.

"He must live," Aronobal insisted. Abruptly, she seemed to realize what she was doing and hastily released her grip. "My apologies," she said stiffly as she took a step back. "Do you have new information on the child's welfare?"

"No, that's why I asked *you* about him," I said. "But I apologize in turn for my comment. It's what Humans call hyperbole, the deliberate stretching of a situation to its worst possible conclusion in order to make a point. Let me rephrase: there may be things about the child's condition you wouldn't want to say in Ms. German's presence."

"If that was what you meant, that was what you should have said," Aronobal said severely. "And my answer is that there has been no such worsening of the child's condition."

"And Ms. German herself?"

Aronobal hesitated. "We do not understand what is happening to her," she admitted. "But her health index is definitely deteriorating."

"Could whatever you're doing to the baby be affecting her?"

"We are *doing* nothing to the baby," Aronobal said. "We are simply taking fluid and tissue samples and studying his brainwave and metabolic patterns. No genetic work is being performed."

"Maybe not, but tests themselves can sometimes adversely affect people," I pointed out. "And you can't have much experience with treating Humans here."

The words were barely out of my mouth when I suddenly realized what it was that had been nagging at me.

I looked around the dome again, at the charming EuroUnion Alpine village the Fillies had created. Only this time, I looked at it all with new eyes.

And with new understanding.

Damn them, anyway.

"You forget our consultation work with Pellorian Medical Systems," Aronobal reminded me. "We have had enough experience with Humans to know what cannot and must not be done."

"I hope so," I said, my voice sounding distant in my ears. "I wonder if I could get a full update on Ms. German's condition, her treatment, and any prognosis you might have."

Aronobal snorted gently. "Could you read such a document?"

"The computer in my quarters can translate it for me," I said. "I swore an oath to *Asantra* Muzzfor—"

"Yes, yes, I remember," Aronobal interrupted. Apparently, she was as tired of hearing Muzzfor's name as I was of invoking it. "I will have the appropriate documents sent to you."

"And similar documents concerning the treatment of Ms. German's unborn child, too, if you would," I said. "But I've taken up enough of your time. When you get back to Ms. German's room, will you ask Bayta to join me out here?"

Aronobal gave me an odd look, and I had the feeling that she was surprised by the brevity of the conversation. Apparently, she'd been expecting something longer and more drawn-out. But she merely nodded. "I will," she said, and went back inside.

I stepped around the corner of the building and sat down with my back to the wall, massaging my calves as if the morning's travel had left me with tired muscles. As I did so, I once again looked casually around the dome, watching the meager flow of Fillies back and forth. This time, I paid special attention to which buildings seemed to be the centers of attention.

"Frank?" Bayta's voice came from somewhere near the door.

"Over here," I called.

Bayta appeared around the corner. Once again, Ty seemed to have inexplicably stayed with her instead of coming outside with Doug and me. "You get anything?" I asked her.

"You didn't give me much time," she countered, a little crossly. "Was Dr. Aronobal that anxious to get back?"

"I was that anxious to get rid of her," I said. "First

things first. Come sit down and tell me what you found out from Terese about her attack."

Bayta frowned, but obediently walked over and sat down beside me. "It happened outside her apartment building as she was coming home from a late party," she said. "She never saw—"

"Do you have a nail file with you?" I interrupted. "Or anything you can cut or poke with?"

She gave me an odd look. "I have a set of tweezers."

"No good," I said. "I need something that can dig into wood or plastic."

"*Chinzro* Hchchu already took everything I had like that." She pointed at Doug, who had settled down a couple of meters away. "If what you want isn't too complicated, maybe Doug or Ty would let you use their claws."

I frowned at Doug's feet. They looked to me like clawless dog feet. "What makes you think they have claws?"

"Because I saw them," Bayta said. "I woke up last night while Ty was shuddering against the headboard—probably having a dream—and saw them sliding in and out of his paws."

"Lovely," I said, wincing at the thought of something with sharp teeth *and* claws having nightmares that close to Bayta. "Any idea how I would go about asking?"

"I don't even know what it is you want," Bayta said. "But I would recommend saying *please*."

"Thanks." I lifted up a hand and beckoned. "Here, Doug. Come here, boy."

For a moment he just looked at me, displaying all the semi-sentience of a Chesapeake Bay mollusk. Then, he heaved himself to his feet and trotted over. "Right here," I went on, patting the ground beside me. "Come stand over here."

Again, he took a moment to think it over before obeying. "I just need to borrow this paw a minute," I said soothingly, getting a light grip on his front paw. "I'm not going to hurt you."

To my surprise, he not only didn't fight me, but read-ily shifted his weight onto his other three legs and raised the paw I was holding. Maybe his last owner had taught him how to shake hands. "They just slide out, you said?"

"Like cat's claws, yes," Bayta said. "Try squeezing the foot just behind the toes."

"And maybe get my face clawed off," I muttered. Shifting my hand to the spot Bayta had suggested, I gen-tly squeezed Doug's foot.

The watchdogs had claws, all right. Big, long, sharp, nasty things. Scary, but exactly what I needed. "Easy, now," I soothed as I pressed the lifted foot against the wall beside me and began carefully scratching with the extended claws. "Okay, so Terese was heading home from a party and never saw anything?"

"She never saw her attacker," Bayta said, picking back up on the story. "He hit her from behind and dragged her down off the street into a stairwell. There he must have hit her again, maybe more than once—her memories are pretty foggy. When she came to she was alone, half dressed—" She grimaced. "And, as she found out later, pregnant."

"Mm," I murmured, half my attention on Bayta, half on the gouges I was making in the wall with Doug's claws. "Anything else?"

"Isn't that enough?" Bayta asked. "I'm surprised she was willing to give me that much."

"She's sick, she's a long way from home, and as much as she probably hates it you and I are the most familiar faces around," I pointed out. "On top of that, I get the impression she's never been exactly flush with close friends. This thing's probably been bottled up inside her for a long time."

"And I'm a fellow woman?"

"With this sort of thing, that's usually the way it works," I said. "So she never saw her attacker. Interest-ing."

"Why is it interesting?"

"Not sure yet." I nodded across the dome. "New subject. Remember what Wandek said when I asked him why all these buildings were Human design?"

"He said they were reconfigured for the comfort of the patients."

"Right," I said. "So why, if Terese is the only Human patient around, did they bother putting together a whole dome's worth of buildings? Especially since the things *aren't* made of malleable material like he said they were?"

"They're not?"

"Take a look," I invited, lowering Doug's foot back to the ground and pointing to the gouges I'd made in the wall with his claws. "Every malleable material I've ever seen automatically heals small tears like this. But not this stuff. This stuff is simple, ordinary wood." I raised my eyebrows. "Which leads directly to the question of what the hell is going on in here."

"The Filiaelian who showed us to our first quarters," Bayta said slowly. "He needed to confirm who you were." She looked at me. "But he shouldn't have, should he?"

"Not if I was the only male Human in this part of Proteus." I nodded across the dome. "I've been watching the Fillies going in and out of those buildings. The same buildings, maybe not coincidentally, that were still showing lights after I dropped you off at your first room last night."

Bayta let out a sort of soft hiss. "There are other Humans in there."

"That's where the logic is heading." I levered myself to my feet and offered a hand to her. "What do you say we go and find out?"

We headed across the dome toward the particular chalet I'd tagged as number one on my list of potentially interesting tourist attractions. We were within ten meters of it when the door opened and a Filly dressed in doctor's tans stepped out.

Only this wasn't just an ordinary Filly doctor. This was the alien I'd dubbed Tan One, one of the Shonkla-raa at Wandek's informal interrogation yesterday afternoon.

Tan One hadn't seemed all that friendly during that meeting. Today, he was even less so. {Where are you going?} he asked sternly.

"Good afternoon," I greeted him cheerfully, not breaking stride.

{This building is off-limits to visitors,} he growled, planting himself directly in our path three meters in front of the building.

"Sorry, I don't understand," I said, still not slowing. I would maintain my course, I decided, until I was about half a pace away from him, at which point I would feint left with my shoulder and try to slip around him to the right.

"He said you were not permitted to enter that building," Wandek's voice came from behind me.

I swallowed a curse as I came to a halt and turned around. No chance now of pretending I simply didn't understand what Tan One was blathering about. "Hello, *Usantra* Wandek," I greeted him. "Did you and *Logra* Emikai sort out the security arrangements?"

"They are being dealt with," Wandek said, eyeing me closely as he came up to us. "What are you doing here?"

"I was hungry," I said. "I saw all the people going in and out of this building, and thought there might be a food service here like the one in the security nexus upstairs."

"There are no public dining places in this area," Wandek said. "The computer in your quarters can provide a list of nearby facilities."

"Yes, I know," I said. "I was just hoping we could grab something quick and get back to Ms. German."

"She is resting now after her treatments," Wandek said, taking my arm in one of his iron grips and pulling me gently but determinedly back the way Bayta and I had just come. "In an hour, perhaps two, she will be able to receive visitors. This would be a good opportunity for you to seek refreshment elsewhere."

"And maybe get a little rest ourselves," I conceded, pulling experimentally against his grip. Now that I was moving in the right direction, Wandek took the hint and let go. "Good day."

I turned back to face Tan One. "And good day to you, too, Doctor," I added, giving him a short bow of my head. Under cover of the movement I took a good, hard look at the door behind him.

Turning back again, I took Bayta's arm, nodded a farewell to Wandek, and headed toward the corridor leading back to our quarters.

We were nearly there before Bayta spoke again. "We're not really giving up, are we?" she murmured.

"Of course not," I said. "But I *am* hungry. Let's go find something to eat."

SIX :

We didn't bother going into our room, but simply consulted the green-emblem directory in the main corridor leading out of the dome. With usual Filiaelian efficiency, it pointed us to what turned out to be a very nice row of restaurants of various types three corridors from our quarters. Bayta had no preference, so I chose a small Jurian café that was wafting the familiar scent of braised *flirdring* out into the corridor.

I found it interesting, considering my suspicions about what was going on in the rest of the chalet village, that there weren't any Human restaurants among them. We ate, then returned to our room.

There, for the next two hours, I sifted through every bit of data I could find on the medical dome, the corridors and service ducts surrounding it, and the various types of locks used aboard Proteus Station.

Not that everything I needed was just sitting there waiting for the general population to access it. But part of my Westali training had been in the art of taking what was shown and filling in what wasn't.

And after those two hours were over, mindful of the bugs that I still assumed were planted in our room, I took Bayta out on a nice, long walk.

"The cameras are the big problem," I told her as we walked. "The locks, the building itself—no sweat. But unless we can disable the cameras, it's not going to work."

"They're not that high off the floor," Bayta pointed out. "Three meters at the most, at least the two are that are just inside the dome. Could you hit them or push them or something?"

"Theoretically, sure," I said. "The way they're set up on those gimbals, a good hard shove upward with a push broom ought to point them toward the top of the dome and away from the buildings. But it would have to be a really good shove, because from the images I saw in the security nexus last night it looks like they're modified wide-angles, and a small nudge would still leave them with a view of the building we want to get into. And of course, since they're within each other's view, they'd both have to be taken out at the same time."

"So dead end?" Bayta asked.

"Not necessarily," I said. "There appear to be a whole bunch of service crawlways and ventilation ducts in the area around the dome. I may be able to find one that'll get me to the cameras from behind, or at least to their power and signal cables. And even if I have to take out the camera itself, the access port ought to be small enough that I won't be visible."

"So you can take out one camera without being seen on the other," Bayta said, nodding. "Then you could circle the dome and take out the other one."

"Right," I said. "Of course, that assumes that whatever self-checks the security system has for spotting broken equipment don't instantly send a tech to the trouble spot. If company arrives on the scene too quickly, the whole thing will be a waste of effort."

"Even worse if they catch you."

"There's that," I conceded. "But I think it's worth a try."

Bayta was silent for another few steps. "When?" she asked at last.

"Tonight," I said. "I'll wait a couple of hours after the lights finish their dimming. That ought to have the corridors as empty as they're going to get."

"What will you want me to do?"

"Basically, stay in the room," I said. "If they get someone on the case faster than I can move, I might end up having to play a little hide-and-seek before I can shake them. You'll need to cover for me when they call to make sure I'm innocently tucked away in bed." I glanced furtively at her. "I meant, tucked away on my floor cushions."

"I know what you meant," she said evenly. "So that's tonight. What about right now?"

"Let's see if Terese is up and receiving," I suggested. "That'll give us an excuse to go back into the dome and maybe scope out that building some more. If we catch Wandek napping we might even find a way to sneak in right now. That would save us a lot of effort and sleep tonight."

I sensed her shiver. "You really think the others won't be watching for us to try that?"

I shrugged. "You never know. They might assume we won't be dumb enough to try the straightforward approach twice in a row. Sometimes people outsmart themselves."

Terese was indeed up when we arrived at her room. Not that she was receiving, or at least she wasn't receiving us. Standing outside in the corridor, I could distinctly hear her tell Aronobal in no uncertain terms that she did *not* want any company, especially if that company consisted of Bayta and me.

Fortunately, I never let things like that bother me. She was still in the middle of her quiet tirade when I took Bayta's arm and walked in.

The nap had definitely done Terese some good. Her cheeks had more color in them, and the fire in her eyes as she glared at me was several degrees hotter than the pale glow she'd been able to generate earlier. "Damn it all, Compton," she bit out. "What do I have to do to get rid of you?"

"It's tricky, I'll grant you that," I conceded. "But enough chitchat. We came by to see how you were feeling."

"I'll feel better when you're gone."

"Terese," Aronobal murmured, a hint of disapproval in her voice.

Terese grimaced. "I'm doing a little better," she said in a marginally more civil tone. "But I'm still pretty tired."

I looked at Aronobal. "Does she need a longer nap time?" I suggested. "Or is this a reaction to the drugs you're giving her?"

"We are using no drugs," Aronobal said. "All we have done so far is take samples for study."

"Then what's causing all the trouble?" I persisted. "Her trouble *and* her baby's?"

"Do you mind not discussing me like I was a side of beef?" Terese put in crossly. "Look, I know you're trying to help." Her eyes flicked to Bayta. "Both of you," she added, almost grudgingly. "But you're not a doctor. You're a—I don't even know *what* you are."

"Troubleshooter?" I suggested. "Fixer?" I cocked my head slightly. "Friend?"

"Yeah, whatever," Terese said. "My point is that Dr. Aronobal could give you the full names and pedigrees of everything they're doing, and you still wouldn't have a clue whether it was helping or hurting me. Tell me I'm wrong."

I pursed my lips. "No, probably not."

"So stop trying to pretend you understand and let them get on with it," she said. "Okay?"

"If that's what you want." I turned to Aronobal. "I wonder if I might have a moment alone with Ms. German."

Aronobal hesitated, then bowed her head. "A few moments only," she said. Nodding to Terese, she backed out of the room. I caught Bayta's eye and twitched my head toward the door, and she slipped out, too.

"What?" Terese demanded warily.

"I just wanted to ask you a couple of questions," I soothed. "First of all, what are they giving you to eat? Is it Human-style food, or something Filly?"

"It's Human," she said. "Bland stuff, mostly—soup, whole-grain bread, and crackers. Oh, and dinner last night was a fillet of something that tasted like chicken."

"Any odd tastes to any of it?" I asked. "Especially bitter tastes?"

She shrugged. "Not really. Like I said, it's all pretty bland. The chicken had a sort of glaze on it, but it was more sweet and sour than bitter."

"What about liquids?" I asked. "They're mostly giving you water, I assume, but are there any odd tastes in that?"

"No," she said, an edge of exaggerated patience creeping into her voice. "What, you think they're trying to poison me or something?" She gestured at the rolling stand beside her bed, with its impressive array of hypos and drawers full of medicine vials. "With my *food*?"

"I guess it really doesn't make much sense," I conceded. "But I'd appreciate it if you'd pay close attention to what you eat. Especially anything about the food that smells or tastes odd."

"Yeah, I'll do that," Terese growled.

"Thanks," I said. "One more thing. If Dr. Aronobal or anyone else asks what we just talked about, tell them I wanted to know where I could find Human-style food aboard Proteus, and that you told me you didn't know."

Terese stared at me, a sudden uncertainty in her eyes. "You're serious, aren't you?" she murmured. "You really think I'm being poisoned?"

"Actually, I can't see any logical reason why anyone would do that," I assured her. "I just believe in covering all the bases." I gave her my best the-policeman-is-your-friend smile. "But don't worry. We're watching out for you, Bayta and I." Beside me, Doug picked that moment to make a snuffling noise. "And Doug and Ty, too, of course," I added.

Terese looked down at the watchdog. "Right," she said dryly.

"I'll be back later," I said. "Try to get some rest." With another smile, I left.

Bayta was waiting just outside the room. Again, I noticed, Ty had elected to go with her instead of stay with me. "Anything?" she asked quietly.

"Later," I said. "Where's Dr. Aronobal?"

She nodded toward one of the doors halfway to the reception desk. "Checking on some tests."

"Good." I took Bayta's arm and turned in the opposite direction. "Let's see if we can get out this way."

No such luck. We'd gotten maybe five steps when Aronobal's voice boomed out from behind us. "Mr. Compton! A moment, if you please."

With a sigh, I stopped. I'd hoped to avoid any questions about what exactly Terese and I had talked about, preferring to let Terese's version be the only one she got to hear. No getting around it now. "Yes, Dr. Aronobal?" I said politely as she caught up with us.

But to my surprise, the doctor didn't launch into an inquisition. Instead, she glanced furtively behind her and then gestured quickly to an open door nearby. Frowning, I stepped in, nearly tripping over Doug as he scampered in ahead of me. Bayta followed, followed by

Ty, followed by Aronobal. "My apologies," the doctor said quietly as she closed the door behind us. "I understand this is not your concern. Nor perhaps is it mine. But I am troubled, and I have no one else to turn to."

"I'll of course do whatever I can to help," I said, putting on my earnest face. This was some kind of trick, of course, but I didn't mind playing it straight and dumb until I spotted the hook. "What seems to be the problem?"

Aronobal hesitated. "Building Twelve," she said. "The one you tried to enter earlier."

"Before *Usantra* Wandek stopped me?"

"Yes, that one," she confirmed. "Something is being done in there, Mr. Compton. Something terrible."

"What sort of something?" I asked. "And to whom?"

"I have neither answer," Aronobal said. "But I heard *Usantra* Wandek when he returned. He was very upset, and made it clear to all that you were not to enter any building in the dome but this one."

"Really," I said, adding some interest to my earnestness and carefully filtering out the bemused disappointment. Did they really think I was this easy to manipulate? "Have you spoken to *Chinzro* Hchchu about it?"

Aronobal gave a sort of two-toned snort. "How can I?" she countered. "I am a mere doctor. He is *chinzro*."

"That might make sense if I knew what it meant," I said. "What kind of title is *chinzro*, anyway?"

"It is an ancient and noble title," Aronobal said. She'd been speaking softly already, but now she lowered her voice even more, as if she fully expected Hchchu to hear her all the way over in Sector 16-J. "It means guardian, leader, and lord highest."

"Impressive," I said. "An old title from the Slisst Protocols, I assume?"

Aronobal drew back sharply, her blaze paling. "You have heard of the Protocols?"

"It's what Proteus is running on at the moment," I said. "I assumed you knew that."

Aronobal shook her head. "I deal with illness, not philosophies."

"Yeah, I have that in my business, too," I said. "So I gather that you, a mere doctor, can't talk to someone as lofty as the *chinzro* of this whole place?"

"Not when my suspicions involve one of *usantra* rank," she said. "Not without evidence of wrongdoing."

And there it was: the hook. Cue the earnest but gullible Human. "Well, maybe that's something I can help with," I said.

"Thank you," Aronobal said quietly. "I knew that one who stands faithfully by his duty to protect the Human Terese German would be trustworthy."

"Just call me *Logra* Compton," I said dryly. "That means—what does it mean again?"

"I believe the title translates to the Human word *bulwark*," Aronobal said.

"Right," I said, nodding. "A defender of the people, or some such, I think was how *Logra* Emikai defined it for me once." I reached up and gave Aronobal a conspiratorial pat on her shoulder. "You just concentrate on taking care of Ms. German. I'll poke around and see what I can come up with."

We had left the dome and were walking along the corridor toward our quarters before Bayta spoke again. "You're not serious," she said.

"Oh, come now," I said reproachfully. "I get a perfectly good, wonderfully polite invitation into a trap, and you want me to just ignore it?"

"You shouldn't joke about things like that," Bayta said, her tone suddenly tight.

I looked sideways at her. Her face was grim, her eyes shiny with suppressed tears. "Hey," I said softly. "You okay?"

"Of course I'm not okay," she bit out. "They're *here*, Frank. The people who once enslaved half the galaxy, slaughtered billions—"

"Hey, hey," I interrupted, catching her hands and

pulling her to a stop facing me. "Calm down. I may not have had the same history course you did, but we really are on the same page here."

"Are we?" she shot back, glaring at me with a simmering passion that looked to be equal parts anger, frustration, and fear.

This time I didn't say anything, but just held her hands in silence and watched as she pulled herself back together. "Here's the deal," I said when her emotions were safely back in the dark trunk where she usually stored them. "Someone who was on Earth when the New Tigris reports came in brought a heavily edited version of those reports to Proteus. The most likely candidates for that role are Emikai and Aronobal."

"I know that."

"Right," I acknowledged, glancing both ways down the corridor. This particular hallway didn't seem all that well-traveled, and there was currently no one else in sight. But sooner or later that would change. "In the same way, Aronobal's pitch just now has two possibilities. It could be an innocent concern over something she's seen in Building Twelve, or it could be deliberate bait. We don't know which, so we play along. If it *is* a trap, it'll eventually get sprung, at which point we can probably safely assume that Aronobal was the one who fingered me. Does that make sense?"

"Everything except the part about the trap springing," she said. "What if you get caught inside it?"

"That's the tricky part," I admitted. "The usual technique is to do something they don't expect and hopefully haven't prepared for."

"Like going in through the service crawlways?"

"Exactly." A motion caught the corner of my eye, and I turned to see a pair of Fillies strolling toward us down the corridor. "So for now we head back to our room," I continued, shifting to a one-handed grip on Bayta's arm and starting us moving again toward our quarters. "Actually, it might be smart to start by messaging Minnario that I have someone who would like an audience—or whatever the Protocols call it—with His Royal Highness *Chinzro* Hchchu."

"You want to bring Minnario into this?" Bayta asked, puzzled.

"Sure, why not?" I said. "It's not like defending me hasn't put him into the crosshairs alongside us anyway. Besides, making an effort to go through proper channels is the sort of thing a helpful but naive bystander might do."

"Thereby adding a little extra confusion to *Usantra* Wandek's assessment of who and what you are?"

I shrugged. "Every little bit helps."

Minnario, when I finally got through to him, wasn't very encouraging about my chances of getting a meeting with Hchchu, particularly since I wouldn't give him the name of the party requesting the audience. But he promised to do what he could. He reminded me that we were due in court at ten o'clock the next morning, and bade me a pleasant evening and a restful night's sleep.

Bayta and I spent the rest of the afternoon and early evening poring over the various station schematics I'd been able to access, looking for any possibilities I might have missed. The level immediately above the dome floor would be my best shot, and I considered taking a stroll around the dome area to see if I could spot the access hatchways. But Bayta didn't like the idea of me roaming around looking devious before the bulk of the Proteus populace retired to their quarters, and I wasn't sure how much it would gain me, either, so we dropped that part.

We'd had a large and late lunch, so instead of going back to restaurant row we found a small grocery store and bought the makings for sandwiches and fruit salad. Doug and Ty had shown themselves to be connoisseurs of Jurian cuisine at lunch, and now demonstrated an equal fondness for roast *quipple* on toasted *poro* bread. Between their eagerness and my generosity, they ended up polishing off an entire sandwich each.

Bayta pointed out that getting them used to expecting table scraps would probably not be appreciated once we returned them to the Proteus security force. As far as I was concerned, that was just one more reason to encourage them.

I'd already decided to start my foray two hours after the end of the lights-down ritual, which the computer's day schedule informed me would begin at ten o'clock and be completed forty-five minutes later. I set the computer's clock for a twelve-thirty wake-up call and lay down on my floor cushions to get some rest. Well before I drifted off to sleep Ty and Doug also settled into their preferred spots, the former at the head of Bayta's bed, the latter curled in front of the door.

Bayta stayed up a while longer, working silently at the computer. I thought about asking what she was doing, but the set expression on her face wasn't one that encouraged conversation. Besides, I was likely to be up half the night, and this might be my only chance to get some sleep for a while. Closing my eyes against the soft glow of reflected light from the computer display, I drifted off to sleep.

And awoke with a jolt.

Through my closed eyelids I could tell the room was dark and quiet. For a few seconds I lay still and listened, locating the three soft sounds of breathing coming from where Bayta and the two watchdogs should be. There were no stealthy footsteps, no extra sounds of breathing, no buzz of a sonic weapon or the scent of a gaseous one. Everything seemed fine.

Only it wasn't. Somehow, I knew it wasn't.

I eased my eyes open. Only then did I spot it: a subtle hint of red light flashing slowly across the walls and door. I studied as much of the room as I could without moving, then carefully rolled over.

It was the computer. Something on the display, which Bayta had left turned toward the wall, was flashing red.

I looked around the room one last time, using the light from the slow flashes to confirm that Bayta and Ty were indeed curled up on their parts of the bed and Doug was by the door. Rolling off my cushions, I went over to the computer desk.

There, in the lower corner of the display, were the flashing red words MESSAGE WAITING.

I sat down in the chair, mouthing a curse. The computer's clock read 12:02, which meant the stupid message indicator had robbed me of half an hour of sleep. Mentally flipping a coin between a reminder from Minnario of our morning court date and a worried pestering from Aronobal about the mysterious Building Twelve, I keyed for the message.

The way is clear. Go now, before the evil ones close the path. The way is clear. Go now.

There was no signature.

I stared at the display, reading the message twice more, my brain skidding on its tracks. The way is *clear*? What the hell was *that* supposed to mean?

And then, abruptly, I got it.

I looked over at the door. My movements had awakened Doug, who was looking at me with the expectant air of a dog whose master has just picked up the leash. "Sure, why not?" I murmured. A midnight stroll through the quiet Proteus night was hardly a crime, and if my walk happened to take me through the medical dome, that wasn't a crime, either.

And if the way to Building Twelve was indeed clear . . .

The corridors were as empty of pedestrians as they'd been the previous night. Actually, they were noticeably more deserted, since with Minnario no longer AWOL the extra groups of Jumpsuits who'd been prowling around were no longer in evidence.

The medical dome was similarly deserted, though once again there were a scattering of lights in several of the buildings, including Building Twelve. I stayed on my path, heading straight across the dome as if aiming for the exit corridor on the far side.

I was halfway across the dome when I noticed that the security camera I was walking toward looked odd. I continued toward it, trying to pierce the twilight darkness and see what it was that had caught my attention.

Two steps later, I got it. Talking earlier with Bayta, I had commented that someone with a push broom could shove the camera up on its gimbals and aim it out of line with the dome floor.

Apparently, someone had done just that.

"That's interesting," I murmured aloud. Turning, I looked toward the other camera, the one I'd just walked beneath, wondering if the fellow with the broom had had a similarly equipped friend.

He'd had a friend, all right. Only the friend seemed to have had a pocket chain saw instead of a broom. The other camera was completely missing.

I felt a shiver run up my back. *The way is clear,* my mysterious correspondent had said. The only question now was whether the way was clear for me to investigate Building Twelve, or clear for me to incriminate myself by breaking and entering.

Or clear for me to casually walk to my death.

I took a deep breath. *So we play along,* I'd told Bayta. Unfortunately, that was still the best strategy I had. "Heel, boy," I murmured to Doug, and started across the dome.

With the soft glow from the handful of lit windows throwing the front of Building Twelve into compara-

tively deeper shadow, I was nearly there before I spotted
the body lying crumpled in front of the door.

I should have simply stopped in my tracks and
punched the emergency button on my comm. But I'm
never that smart. Besides, if the victim wasn't quite
dead, a few minutes' delay could mean all the difference
in the world.

And so instead of stopping I broke into a run, closed
the last five meters, and dropped to my knees beside the
body. It was a male Filly, I noted automatically, dressed
in either a green or blue medical tech's outfit, I couldn't
tell which in the dim light. His body was limp, he was
still warm, and he was lying in a pool of blood.

He was also very dead.

I was reaching for my comm when the door in front
of me abruptly opened, flooding the crime scene with a
blaze of light coming at me from around the silhouette
of a second Filly.

I sprang sideways, squeezing my eyes shut against the
blinding glare, trying desperately to get out of the line of
fire. If I could get around the side of the building before
my assailant got his weapon lined up, I might still have
a chance.

I hadn't gotten two steps when I caught Doug's side
with my leg and went sprawling face-first over him onto
the ground. I got my hands under my chest to try to
push myself back up—

{Help!} a female Filly voice screeched from the direction of the doorway, the harmonics from her terrified
shout rising well into the ultrasonic range. {Assault!
Death! Murder! Help!}

And even as I shakily made it back to my feet, more
lights in the buildings around me began to come to life.

With a sigh, I pulled out my comm and punched for
Bayta. "It's me," I said when she answered. "Get dressed
and get up to the security nexus. I'm about to head that
direction myself."

I looked back at Building Twelve. Three husky Filly males had now appeared, two of them dropping down beside the dead body, the third striding purposefully toward me. "And you'd better give Minnario a call," I added. "I think I'm going to need my lawyer."

SEVEN :

I'd already discovered that the security nexus upstairs had an employee snack area. Now, I learned they also had a processing room complete with a pair of holding cells.

The cells weren't much in the way of prisoner restraint, actually, certainly not compared to some of the high-tech prisons I'd seen across the galaxy. They were composed of plain high-impact plastic bars, with simple DNA-key locks, and extremely spare accommodations, each boasting a cot and sink/toilet combo. A single monitor camera covered the doors of both cells, and probably not much else. My guess was that the whole setup had been designed more as a drunk tank than with any expectations that they would someday play host to an actual accused felon.

But whatever the cells lacked in physical security was more than made up for by the half-dozen Jumpsuits milling around the processing room, every one of them keeping a sharp eye on me. They were clearly shaken, some of them stunned at the killing, others enraged by it.

And for the first time since I'd arrived at Proteus, they were carrying sidearms. From where I was sitting I couldn't tell what kind of weapons they were, whether they were lethal or something more humane. I wasn't especially anxious to find out, either.

Bayta was the first visitor to arrive, but she wasn't allowed in to see me. I could see her out in the main nexus room, Ty at her heels, gesturing as she talked inaudibly to one of the Jumpsuits. Working solely from their body language, I tentatively concluded that she was demanding to see me while the Filly was insisting she couldn't.

The next new arrival was *Usantra* Wandek. Him, naturally, they let right in.

"Good evening, *Usantra* Wandek," I greeted him politely, standing up as he strode across the room toward my cell, the Jumpsuits melting out of his path like butter in front of a laser scalpel. "I don't suppose it would help for me to tell you this is all a huge mistake."

He didn't answer. He didn't speak at all, in fact, until he had stopped just outside the bars. "Why?" he demanded.

"Why what?" I asked. "Why was I out for a walk? Or why did I try to help someone I thought might be hurt?"

"Why did you kill him?" he snarled. His blaze was mottling like crazy, the changes coming fast and furious. Clearly, he was as shaken as any of the Jumpsuits around him.

"I didn't kill him," I said. "And I'd like to request a replacement guardlaw for my trial."

He twitched oddly. Apparently, that one had caught him completely by surprise. "What?"

"You heard me," I said. "A guardlaw who instantly jumps to conclusions regarding my guilt in one situation can't be trusted to be impartial in his judgments in a different situation."

For a moment he just stared at me, as if not believing an accused murderer on the wrong side of a cell door would dare lecture him on the responsibilities of his rank and position. He drew himself up—

[Say nothing more, Mr. Compton,] Minnario called from the doorway. [You're under my guidance now. Please let me through. Let me through, please.]

Most of the Jumpsuits moved more or less promptly out of his way. A couple of them, those who seemed angriest about the murder, did just the opposite, placing themselves between Minnario's chair and the cells.

Useless spite, of course—even something as archaic as the Slisst Protocols undoubtedly allowed a prisoner free access to his attorney. Or to his second, as the Protocols probably phrased it. I waited, memorizing the uncooperative Jumpsuits' faces for future reference, as Minnario made his way through the crowd. I also noted that Wandek made no attempt to intervene on Minnario's behalf.

But Minnario was just as stubborn as the Fillies, and eventually he got through the obstacle course and glided to a halt beside Wandek. [What's this about?] he asked tersely. [Bayta messaged that you were in custody. Now I hear from the patrollers that you're accused of *murder*?]

"Yes, I am, and no, I didn't do it," I said. "But you have to admit, there's a certain charm in this kind of consistency."

Minnario finished reading the transcription on his display and then looked at Wandek. [I'll speak to my client alone, if you please,] he said firmly.

"He has not yet made an official statement of his activities this night," Wandek countered, just as firmly. "He might as well speak it to both of us together."

[The requirements of the law—]

"That's all right," I interrupted. "I have nothing to say that *Usantra* Wandek can't hear. Besides, it's a long story, and I'd hate to have to tell it twice."

Minnario's conical mouth puckered, but he nodded. [Proceed,] he said.

"And in that same vein," I added, "we might as well have Bayta in here, too."

This time it was Wandek's turn for a puckered mouth. Clearly, I wasn't making anyone happy tonight. "She is not necessary to this conversation."

I folded my arms across my chest and remained silent. His blaze did its mottling thing, and then he half turned toward the door. {Bring the Human,} he called.

For a moment nothing happened. Then, one of the Jumpsuits appeared in the doorway, with Bayta and Ty following close behind. The Filly led her to Minnario's side, took one look at Wandek's thunderous expression, and beat a hasty retreat.

"Are you all right?" Bayta asked anxiously.

"I'm fine," I assured her. "Okay, here's how it went down. I was awakened about twelve o'clock by the message light on my computer. The message said only that the way was clear and that I needed to go."

"What does that mean, the way is clear?" Wandek asked.

"Good question," I agreed. "Unfortunately, I really don't know. Even more unfortunately, since the message was unsigned, I didn't have any way to write or call back and see what it was all about."

"You should have called the patrollers," Wandek said severely.

"What, to report a confusing message?" I scoffed. "Because at the time I thought that was all it was. Since it was in English, and since I gather not a whole lot of people aboard Proteus are fluent in the language, I just assumed the sender had garbled the translation."

"The computers aboard *Kuzyatru* Station do not make translation errors," Wandek said stiffly.

"I'm sure they don't," I said. "But the station's computers weren't involved. Computer translations are always tagged, and I know what the Proteus mark looks like—I saw it when I was looking up restaurant listings. No, whoever sent the message typed it in just the way I got it."

[So if the message was mistranslated, what did you think it was supposed to say?] Minnario asked.

"I didn't know then, and I really don't know now," I told him. "But since the reason I came to Proteus was to watch over Ms. German, I assumed it had something to do with her. So I got dressed and headed for the medical dome to see if something was going on that I should know about."

[Did you speak to her doctors?] Minnario asked. [What did they say?]

"Nothing, because I never got to any of them," I said. "The building was completely dark, so I figured everyone was down for the night. I was heading toward one of the other buildings, one of the ones that *was* showing lights, to see if someone there might have sent me the message, when I saw the body."

"Why did you not use your comm to signal an emergency?" Wandek asked.

"Because my trained response to such things is to first check them out myself," I said. "Who was he, anyway?"

"One of the techs from Building Eight." Wandek cocked his head. "The building in which Terese German is being treated."

I felt a shiver run up my back. So this hadn't been just some random killing of some random person. Whoever had set me up had done a good job of paying attention to the details. "Was he on the night shift?" I asked.

"His position and rank are irrelevant," Wandek said. "So you then approached the body—"

"Excuse me, but the victim's life and particulars are very much *not* irrelevant," I put in. "If he was night shift, he must have gone to Building Twelve for some reason. What reason? If, on the other hand, he was day shift, what was he doing in the dome at night? Was he lured there the same way I was?"

For once, Wandek seemed at a loss for words. He looked at Minnario, then at Bayta, and finally back at me. "Yes," he said, his voice subdued. "Yes, I see what you mean. Perhaps . . ." He trailed off, and did another glance around at Minnario and Bayta. "Please continue."

"That's basically it," I said. "I went over to see what had happened, but before I could do more than confirm he was dead and start to call for help, the door opened and someone started screaming. Ninety seconds later the place was crawling with Jumpsuits, half of them trampling the crime scene while the other half hauled me up here."

"They did not *trample the crime scene*," Wandek growled, the momentary introspective mood having apparently passed. "They were attempting to resuscitate the victim."

"Well, whatever they were doing, the scene looked to be pretty well demolished," I said. "So that's how I spent my evening. Where do we go from here?"

Wandek seemed to brace himself. "You were found at the scene of a killing," he said. "You must be processed and formally charged with that crime."

For a moment I considered asking how he thought I could have pulled off a cold-blooded murder with my station-issue conscience Doug at my side. But given that both Doug *and* Ty were presumably supposed to be sticking close to me, and given the fact that only one of them was actually there with me in my cell, I decided it might not be the wisest thing to bring that up. I still didn't know what this tag-team game was that the watchdogs were playing, but I didn't want to draw any attention to it until I had a few answers of my own. "Understood," I said instead. "What about the rest?"

Wandek frowned. "The rest of what?"

"The rest of the suspects," I said. "I figure the list includes everyone who works in Buildings Twelve and Eight, plus the night crews in the other buildings—oh, hell, let's just make it everyone in the medical dome and be done with it. Plus all the victim's friends and enemies, of course."

"Do not mock me," Wandek warned darkly. "You are the one who was found with the body."

"Which either makes me the dumbest murderer in this half of the galaxy or else makes my story true," I countered. "But suit yourself. If I were you, though, I'd get that autopsy up and running as soon as possible. There's this thing we Humans call the 24/24 rule: the most important part of a murder investigation are the twenty-four hours immediately before the crime, and the twenty-four hours immediately afterward."

"I will keep that in mind," Wandek said with an edge of sarcasm. "In the meantime, you will stay here." He turned a glare onto Minnario and Bayta. "The discussion is over. Return to your quarters."

I looked at Bayta, noting the fresh tightness in her expression. "Bayta will be staying here," I said quickly.

"What did you say?" Wandek demanded.

"I want her here with me," I told him. "Which part of that didn't you get?"

Wandek turned to Bayta, his blaze going into full mottle mode again. "That is ridiculous," he insisted. "She is charged with no crime."

"No, but since you haven't yet charged the real suspects with the crime, it's got a sort of weird yin/yang to it," I said. "She can bunk down in the other cell."

"No," Wandek said firmly. "Keeping her here could be construed as an unstated charge, permitting the possibility of counteraction against *Kuzyatru* Station. I cannot permit it."

[There would be no such liabilities if the cell door was left open,] Minnario spoke up. [If her actions aren't hindered, there would be no construing that she was under charges.]

"She could even sign a contract waiving her right to counteraction if those parameters are met," I added.

Wandek bit out a phrase that had somehow been missed in the Westali language classes. But contracts were king, queen, and the whole royal flush in the Filiaelian Assembly, and now that I'd invoked that magic word he would have a hard time turning down my request. "I will prepare the contract," he said reluctantly. He turned a baleful eye on Bayta and raised his voice. {Lieutenant of the Guard? Come at once and open this cell.}

One of the Jumpsuits hurried forward. He reached for my cell door—{The other one, fool,} Wandek gritted.

The Jumpsuit frowned in obvious confusion. But an *usantra* had spoken. Dutifully, he touched the pad of the unoccupied cell. The door gave a snick, and he pulled it open. {Is the Human female also to be charged with murder?} he asked.

{She merely wishes lodging for the night,} Wandek growled. {She may come and go as she pleases. See that she and the prisoner are fed in the morning.}

{I obey, *Usantra* Wandek,} the Jumpsuit said.

Without another word, Wandek spun around and strode from the room. Once again, the loitering Jumpsuits made sure to get out of his way.

[I take my leave, as well,] Minnario said. He looked around and leaned in close to me. [Whatever speech you wish to share, remember there's a camera pointed at you,] he added quietly. Getting a grip on his chair's controls, he swiveled around and headed out in Wandek's wake. This time, none of the Jumpsuits bothered to interfere.

"What did you want to talk to me about?" Bayta asked softly.

I looked behind me. The two cells were set up as mirror images of each other, with the cots pressed end to end against the dividing set of bars. "Later," I said, giving an elaborate yawn that required no acting whatsoever. "Let's get to bed, shall we?"

Bayta's eyes flicked past me to the cot arrangement. "Good idea," she said.

She stepped through the door of her new quarters and walked to her bed, lying down with her head to the bars. Ty, for once, didn't try to hog the headboard position, but merely curled up on the floor beside her. I lay down, too, my head toward Bayta's, then gave the three remaining Jumpsuits in the room a baleful look. "Do you mind?" I asked. "A little privacy, if you please. You can also turn off the lights while you're at it."

Taking their own sweet time about it, the three Fillies strolled from the room. The lights, naturally, stayed on.

"Are you all right," Bayta whispered. "I mean, *really* all right?"

"As all right as someone can be who's being framed for yet another murder," I told her sourly. "They're doing an especially terrific job on this one, too. Did I mention that the two cameras in the dome had already been taken out when I got there?"

"No, you didn't," she said. "How was it done?"

"One of them was twisted up on its gimbals where it couldn't see anything but the top of the dome," I said. "The other isn't even there anymore. No idea when it was done, but certainly sometime before the murderer got busy."

"So that no one would see the killing," Bayta murmured.

"*And* so that I couldn't prove when in the timeline I arrived on the scene," I said. "Fortunately, I have an ace in the hole that so far no one seems to have noticed."

"The *msikai-dorosli*?"

"Exactly," I said. "I didn't see much of the victim before I was hauled away, but I saw enough to know that he'd been stabbed at least twice. They looked a lot like the wounds Muzzfor inflicted on our allies aboard the super-express."

"Allies." Even in a whisper, I could sense the odd flatness to the word. "I'm sorry, but it still sounds wrong to talk about the Modhri that way."

"Don't worry, you won't have to get used to it," I assured her. "That was a specific mind segment, in a specific situation, and the truce we had died when he did. So just forget it."

"I'm trying," Bayta said. "So you're saying one of the Shonkla-raa was the killer?"

"I'll know better if and when I get a look at the autopsy," I said. "Those fancy self-locking stabbing fingers Muzzfor had aren't likely to be mistaken for a knife or any other kind of weapon. It's probably too much to hope that we'll be able to match the wounds to any specific fingers, but we should at least be able to prove they *were* fingers."

"Though a specific match may not be impossible," Bayta said thoughtfully. "The Proteus computer system is quite extensive."

"So I've noticed," I said. "Speaking of which, what exactly were you doing on the computer when I went to bed?"

There was just the briefest hesitation. "I was mostly just looking around," she said.

"Mostly?"

"Yes," she said, her tone warning me to drop it. "We've talked about how those enhanced Shonkla-raa throats look like the ones Filiaelian opera singers sometimes get to extend their range and volume."

Whereas the Shonkla-raa used their additional vocal capacity to send out an ultrasonic tone that could paralyze Spiders and take control of Modhran walkers. All things considered, I'd rather have opera. "So what were you were looking for, the headquarters of the Proteus Operatic Society?"

"Actually, yes, I was," she said, sounding a little miffed at my tone. "And every other musical and singing group aboard."

I grimaced. "Sorry," I apologized. "Actually, that's a very good idea."

"Not really," she said with a sigh. "It turns out that there are dozens of groups devoted to songs and singing, scattered all across the station. Not to mention at least five operatic associations. Dead end."

"Not necessarily," I said. "Maybe we can figure out a way to refine the search. Were any of the operatic societies in this sector?"

"No, the nearest was in Sector 25-C."

Three sectors away from us in the direction of the station's rim. On a station this size, that was a long walk and a hell of a lot of Fillies away. "It's still a good idea," I said. "Let's think about it some more and see what we come up with." I yawned again. "Or rather, let's sleep on it. I don't know about you, but I'm about half dead."

"You think we're safe here?" Bayta asked quietly.

So she'd figured out why I'd insisted on her staying with me tonight. "What, surrounded by Proteus patrollers?" I countered, trying for a cheerfulness that I didn't really feel.

"Most of whom think you're a murderer."

"Most of whom have had one murder on their watch and want to make damned sure they don't have a second one," I pointed out. "I was a cop, Bayta. I know how cops think and feel. Besides, Filly cops are designed with very specific behavioral boundaries. I doubt they could get up a good lynch mob even if they wanted to."

She didn't answer, and it wasn't hard for me to guess what she was thinking. That was all well and good for your run-of-the-mill Filly cops, but these cops were on Proteus Station, under the authority of the ancient Slisst Protocols. Neither of us had a clue what the Protocols had to say about lynch mobs.

"It'll be all right," I said into the silence. "I'll see you in the morning, okay?"

"All right." Bayta paused. "It's almost like being in the middle of a dit-rec drama, isn't it?"

"That does seem to be the way our lives have been going these days," I agreed. "Any one in particular springing to mind?"

"I was just thinking tonight about the one you showed me last week," she said. "The Hitchcock dit-rec where the man was framed for murder and found himself caught up in a huge conspiracy."

"Right—*The 39 Steps*," I said, making a face. "That one's definitely hitting a little too close to home tonight. I don't think Proteus's bullet trains go anywhere near Scotland, though."

"Too bad," she said. "The landscape looked very pleasant."

"I'll take you there someday," I promised. "Your choice as to with or without the handcuffs."

She exhaled, just loudly enough for me to hear. "If we

ever make it there, I think we'll have had enough of handcuffs."

"I suppose," I conceded. "Joking aside, try not to let any of this worry you. We've gotten out of much worse situations. We'll get out of this one, too."

"I know," she said. "Good night, Frank."

"Good night, Bayta."

There were some soft creakings as she resettled herself on her cot, and with a grimace I did the same. Maybe she was right. Maybe we *would* be murdered in our beds. If we were, I'd never forgive myself.

There was a little woof from across my cell. I opened my eyes to see that Doug had once again settled himself in front of my door, once again keeping me from sneaking out alone. The fact that the lock on this particular door was on the other side had apparently escaped him.

Still, even a Jumpsuit lynch mob wouldn't be stupid enough to kill me in their own security nexus. And if Doug was keeping me from getting out, he was also keeping anyone else from getting in. It was, I decided, a fair enough trade.

Closing my eyes again, I rolled over to face the wall, where the glaring light was the least intrusive, and drifted off to sleep.

I slept straight through the night, without any of the disturbances or interruptions that might have been caused by on-duty Jumpsuits "accidentally" dropping tools or equipment where the clatter might startle a prisoner awake. There were no such incidents, I wasn't murdered in my bed, and when I did wake up it was to the delectable aroma of a hot breakfast on a tray just inside my cell.

The Jumpsuits might think I was a murderer, but that clearly wasn't interfering with their professionalism. Genetic engineering, I thought as I ate, could be a wonderful thing.

I had finished my breakfast, and Bayta was just starting to stir in her cell, when we had a visitor.

"Good morning," *Logra* Emikai said gravely, glancing around the processing room as he walked across to our cells. "I trust your treatment has been proper?"

"I couldn't have asked for better," I assured him, waving around the room. "What do you think? Professionally, I mean."

"Very nice," he said. "More compact than other processing areas I have seen, but well and properly equipped." He gave my cell a quick once-over. "Though the holding facilities are not as secure as I would prefer."

"I doubt they usually have to deal with anything more dangerous than the occasional rowdy," I pointed out. "I hope you didn't come here to escort me to my morning court appearance. It looks like I'm going to be tied up for a while."

"Indeed," Emikai agreed. "But not in the way you think." He half turned. {Lieutenant of the Guard?} he called.

A Jumpsuit appeared in the doorway, striding toward me with a darkened blaze and a decidedly unhappy expression on his face. He reached the cell and touched the pad, and the door popped open. Turning on his heel, he strode from the room.

Emikai beckoned to me. "Come."

"Come where?" I asked, not moving. "*Chinzro* Hchchu's court?"

"That proceeding has been put on indefinite suspension," Emikai said. "You have been assigned to investigate last night's murder."

I felt my jaw drop. "I've been *what*?"

"An unexpected turn of events, to be sure," Emikai agreed. "But as you yourself already stated, the experience of the *Kuzyatru* Station patrollers is largely limited to overenthusiastic revelers and threats to property. As it happens, there are only two trained investigators aboard." He barked a small laugh. "You, and I."

"And they're desperate enough to actually put me in the game?" I asked, still not believing it. "The chief suspect in the case?"

"You are no longer a suspect," Emikai said. "*Chinzro* Hchchu has so ruled."

I glanced at Bayta, who was now sitting up on her cot listening to us. "You're kidding," I said. "A prosecutor declaring his very own defendant innocent? That's one for the books."

"Only for this particular crime," Emikai clarified. "The events surrounding the other six murders must still be examined, because at that time you did not have *msikai-dorosli* observing your actions." He looked down at Doug, then across to where Ty was still dozing beside Bayta. "*Chinzro* Hchchu realizes you could not possibly have committed such a crime in their presence."

"Glad someone agrees with me, for whatever reason," I said, turning to Bayta. "You ready to play detective?"

"Of course," she said, looking over at her breakfast tray. "Do I have time to eat first?"

"She can remain here and join us after her meal," Emikai offered. "Or she could simply stay here. She is not a trained investigator, is she?"

"No, but she's terrific at holding the flashlight," I said. "Just take the tray along, Bayta—you can eat on the way down." I cocked an eyebrow at Emikai as something suddenly occurred to me. "And I'll also need my reader, data chips, and the rest of the gear the patrollers took away from me."

Emikai's blaze darkened a bit. He'd seen that reader in action, back on the super-express train, and he knew all about the sensor/analyzer hidden inside its innocent-looking exterior. "I do not know if *Chinzro* Hchchu will agree to that," he warned.

"Then *Chinzro* Hchchu had better find himself another investigator," I said bluntly. "I need my data files, investigative templates, pattern dissectors—all the stuff a modern detective relies on."

"I shall make that point," Emikai said. He hesitated. "Do you also demand your weapon be returned?"

"That would be awfully nice, what with a murderer running around Proteus and all," I said. "But I doubt even under these circumstances that *Chinzro* Hchchu would be willing to go that far. If you can get me everything else, we'll call it even."

"I shall do what I can," he promised. "Are you ready?"

I looked at Bayta. She was crouching on the floor beside her breakfast tray, feeding one of the fried *giggra* strips to Ty. I winced—I'd completely forgotten about Doug when I'd eaten my own meal. "Yes, we're ready," I said. "Let's stop by the duty station on our way out and see if there's something more convenient for Bayta to carry her breakfast in than that tray."

I looked down at Doug. He was looking back at me, his mouth open just far enough for me to see the sharp points of his front teeth. "And," I added, "we should also probably pick up a few more of those *giggra* strips."

EIGHT :

As was traditional in these things, the first stop on our tour was the crime scene.

I'd suggested last night, admittedly in a rather snide way, that the Jumpsuits swarming around the victim had probably trampled any useful clues into oblivion. Unfortunately, as it turned out, I'd been right.

"So they didn't find anything?" I asked, gazing down at the dried blood still staining the ground.

"Not once they finally began searching," Emikai said, an edge of contempt in his tone. "If I had been informed in time, perhaps something could have been salvaged. But they did not call me until several hours had passed."

"Really?" I said, frowning. "Interesting."

"How so?"

"Because you're supposed to be the person riding herd on me," I said. "Two minutes after I was picked up, someone should have been yelling in your ear about your pet Human having committed a murder and why the hell weren't you already on top of it. Do we know who's been in charge of the investigation up to now?"

"Captain of the Guard Lyarrom," Emikai said. "I have spoken to him by comm, but not yet in person."

"We should make a point of doing that," I said. "What do we know about the victim?"

"His name was Tech Yleli, and he worked the evening shift in Building Eight," Emikai said. "That is the shift from the hours of four until twelve."

"So he should have already left for home by the time I found him," I said. "Unless he'd been killed earlier?"

Emikai shook his head. "His death was between twelve and twelve-fifteen."

I cocked an eyebrow. "You can be that accurate?"

"Filiaelian blood coagulation follows a well-known curve," Emikai explained. "When all the genetic parameters are known, a time of death can be defined to within a single minute."

"That's handy," I said, frowning. "So why do we have a fifteen-minute window on Yleli?"

"Because he was undergoing genetic restructuring at the time of his death and his coagulation curve is no longer valid," Emikai explained. "But his progress charts have been requested and should be filed soon. At that point, we will be able to considerably narrow down the time of death."

I looked across the dome toward Terese's building. "Was his treatment by any chance taking place in Building Eight?"

"No, it was being done in a facility designed specifically for Filiaelian use near his home in Sector 25-C."

I felt an eyebrow twitch. That was the same sector Bayta's research had tagged as the location of one of Proteus's operatic societies. "We'll want to go take a look at the place later," I said. "In the meantime, what exactly was his job here? Specifically, did he deal directly with Ms. German?"

"He dealt with her case, but I do not yet know whether he personally interacted with her," Emikai said. "His job was to analyze tissue and fluid samples to create baselines and search for anomalies."

Out of the corner of my eye I saw Bayta pull out her comm and hold it up to her ear. "Let's try a different approach," I suggested. "Do we know exactly how many patients there are in Building Eight besides Ms. German?"

"I am not certain," Emikai said, pulling out his reader. "Up to now, I have only been given limited data. If that particular number is not here, we can ask the receptionist."

"Frank, I have to leave," Bayta announced, putting away her comm. "Dr. Aronobal says that something's happening with Terese."

"What kind of something?" I asked. "Never mind—we'll go ask in person. *Logra* Emikai has some questions for the receptionist, anyway."

We headed back across the dome and into Building Eight. As Bayta and I dropped Emikai off at the receptionist's desk I looked around, trying to get a sense of activity and tension levels. But everything seemed about the same as it had been on our previous visits.

Everything, that is, except in Terese's room. Aronobal was there, along with two other Fillies in doctor's tans and two techs in blue. Aronobal was standing beside Terese, her hand on the girl's shoulder as she murmured softly to her, while the other two doctors huddled over one of the girl's attached monitors and talked quietly between themselves. One of the techs was across the room by a narrow table, laying out a series of sampling hypos, while the other tech was carefully taking a blood sample from Terese's arm. "We seem busy this morning," I said briskly as we walked in. "Good morning, Terese. How are you feeling?"

"Not so good," she said, her normal animosity toward me nowhere to be seen. Her face was pale and drawn, even more so than usual. "Dr. Aronobal tells me my baby is dying."

"*May* be dying," Aronobal corrected firmly. "We still have more tests to run."

Terese nodded, a short, choppy jerk of her head, and closed her eyes. Aronobal caught my eye and nodded to the side, toward the table where the tech had set down his freshly drawn blood sample and was headed back to Terese with another hypo. Bayta and I drifted over in that direction, arriving at the same time as Aronobal. "Well?" I asked softly.

"I do not know," Aronobal said, her voice anxious and frustrated. "Her physiology is like that of no Human I have ever dealt with. Nor is there anything like it in the literature."

"In the *Filiaelian* literature, maybe," I said. "Earth's medical community has had a lot more experience with Human genetic disorders than you have."

"Obviously," Aronobal said tartly. "But there has yet been no reply to our queries."

"What can we do to help?" Bayta asked.

"She is frightened," Aronobal said. "Though she would not admit it, you are the closest people she has to family or friends in this part of the galaxy." She hesitated. "Perhaps even in her own part of the galaxy. I do not believe she has many people even on Earth she is close to, or who care for her. Certainly not the way you do."

"That's very touching," I said. It was also laid on way too thick, but I decided not to mention that part. "Unfortunately, we're a bit busy with an important investigation at the moment."

Aronobal shivered. "Yes—Tech Yleli's horrible and senseless murder."

"Horrible, yes," I agreed. "Senseless, no. We just have to figure out where the sense lies."

"Perhaps," Aronobal said. "But surely an hour spent

comforting a frightened child could not harm your investigation."

I gazed at her, an unpleasant feeling tingling the back of my neck. The time constraints of the 24/24 rule were already getting pretty short. And now Dr. Aronobal was proposing that I run that clock down even more in order to sit here and hold Terese's hand.

Bayta was obviously thinking along the same lines. "Can you give us a minute?" she asked Aronobal.

"Certainly," Aronobal said. She looked over her shoulder as Terese gave a little grunt, then turned and hurried back to the girl's side.

"What do you think?" Bayta asked quietly. "I could stay here with Terese while you and *Logra* Emikai continue the investigation."

"I don't like the idea of leaving you here alone," I told her, frowning at the line of hypos. Up close, I could see now that the table had lines marked on them, with three of the hypos in each of five hourly boxes, their needles capped by plastic sterilizer sheaths. Apparently, Aronobal was serious about getting up-to-the-minute information on what was going on with Terese's biochemistry.

Or maybe not. The three hypos in the box labeled for the previous hour were still there, two of them containing bright red blood, the other holding a pale amber liquid I didn't recognize. Apparently, whoever was supposed to have taken the fluids away for analysis had fallen down on the job.

Maybe that job was supposed to have been Tech Yleli's.

Whatever the reason for the foul-up, though, the current hour's draws were now already under way. One of the hypos in the current time box was already filled, with the tech at Terese's side working on the second.

"I'll hardly be alone," Bayta pointed out. "The building is full of Filiaelians, and that's not likely to change." She hesitated. "Actually, I'm more concerned about you being alone with *Logra* Emikai. We still don't know whether it was he or Dr. Aronobal who told *Chinzro* Hchchu about your part in the New Tigris events."

"True," I agreed, running a finger gently over the sterilizer cap on one of the empty hypos. Something about this wasn't adding up, somehow. "And the main reason we don't know that is because Tech Yleli's untimely death has canceled today's hearing, where Hchchu was supposed to give us the name. Coincidence?"

Bayta's eyes widened. "Are you saying that's why Tech Yleli was murdered?"

"It *does* seem rather ludicrous, given all the simpler stalling tactics in a lawyer's repertoire," I conceded, my eyes still on the damn hypos. "But crazier things have happened. And we know our friends don't seem to have a problem with multiple murders when it suits them . . ."

I trailed off, my vague uneasiness suddenly snapping into focus. *Multiple.*

Why the hell were there two different hypos with blood in them? Why not just draw twice the amount in a single, larger hypo?

One from Terese and one from her baby? But Aronobal had said they were concentrating on the baby right now. And even if they were sampling from Terese, too, why only one hypo with the other fluid instead of two of them?

I looked over my shoulder at the tech. He was just finishing the draw, this one from an access port taped to Terese's abdomen. "Move over here," I murmured to Bayta.

Obediently, she stepped close beside me. With her body blocking the Filly's view, I reached over and took one of the blood hypos from the previous hour's box, flipping it around and sliding it deftly up my sleeve. I glanced back again as the tech arrived and courteously moved out of his way. He set down his full hypo, picked up the last remaining empty one, and hurried away again.

"Better take all three," Bayta advised quietly, once again moving to block everyone's view of the hypos.

I smiled tightly. She was definitely getting good at this skulking stuff. One missing hypo would raise eyebrows, but three missing hypos would naturally imply that someone had collected them for processing. Scooping up the other two hypos of the group, I slipped them up my other sleeve.

"So am I staying with Terese?" Bayta asked.

I'd almost forgotten the reason we'd been alone over here in the first place. "If you think it would be helpful," I said reluctantly. "I suppose it might give you a chance to prod her for more information about the aftermath of her attack."

"Yes, I can do that," Bayta agreed. "What do you want to know?"

I turned around again, watching Aronobal trying to soothe the girl. "For starters, where and when exactly Aronobal and Emikai came into her story," I said. "I want to know how fast they were on the scene, where they come from, how quickly they offered the Assembly's aid—that sort of thing."

"Should I also find out if she ever met Tech Yleli?"

"Absolutely," I agreed. "And if she did, how much interaction did they have, and how much interaction did she see between him and Aronobal or him and Wandek." There was a motion at the door, and I looked over to see that Emikai had returned from his conference with the receptionist and was waiting unobtrusively out in the corridor. "Looks like Emikai's ready," I continued. "I should be back in a couple of hours. If it looks like it's going to take longer, I'll call you."

I fixed her with a stern look. "And if anything happens here—*anything*—you call me. Immediately."

"I understand," Bayta said. Her voice was solid enough, but I could see the worry in her eyes. Not for herself, but for me. "Be careful."

"Trust me," I said dryly. Reaching down, I took her hand. "And don't forget what I said. You get so much as a strange shiver, you get on the comm."

"You, too," she said, making no attempt to withdraw her hand. "Don't worry about me, Frank. They want the baby alive, remember? *Usantra* Wandek's reaction earlier proved that much. They wouldn't do anything to me when there was a chance that Terese or the child would be put at risk."

"I suppose," I said. "Stay alert anyway." Giving her hand a final squeeze, I let go and slipped out of the room.

Emikai caught my eye with a questioning look. I gestured silently toward the exit, and he nodded and strode off. I followed, Doug as always padding along at my side. Halfway down the corridor, I slipped the purloined hypos from my sleeves into more permanent carrying places in my side jacket pockets. "Well?" I murmured.

"Ms. German is the only patient in this building," he murmured back. "I was told she is a special case."

I grunted. "I'm sure she is."

We were nearly to the receptionist's station when the outside door opened, and to my surprise Minnario floated into the building on his support chair. He started to turn to the receptionist, caught sight of me, and changed course to head instead in our direction. [Mr. Compton,] he greeted me. [The very Human I wanted to see.]

"Good morning, Minnario," I greeted him back. "What can I do for you?"

He warbled a brief, growling laugh. [You may do for me what you may do for everyone else aboard *Kuzyatru* Station,] he said grimly. [Find and imprison this murderer who's arisen among us.]

"Have you any thoughts as to who it might be?" Emikai asked.

Minnario seemed taken aback by the question. [I hardly even know my way around the station, let alone any of its people or politics. I couldn't even begin to guess why anyone would want the late Tech Yleli dead.]

"Of course," I said. Though the murder *had* occurred only two days after Minnario had come aboard. Timing like that was always a little suspicious.

But of course, that same logic could also be applied to Bayta and me. Probably better not to bring it up. "So what brings you here this morning?" I asked. "You come by to offer moral support?"

[I actually had something more practical in mind,] he said. [I'm told your murder trial is on hiatus for the moment. But of course, that moment will last only until you have captured the murderer. I know you're busy, but I thought that if you could spare Ms. Bayta for a while, I'd like to hear her version of the events on New Tigris.]

I suppressed a grimace. So now Bayta would not only be closeted with Aronobal, whom I didn't especially trust, but also with Minnario, whom I also didn't especially trust. Terrific. "Well, actually—" I began.

"He did not commit the murder," Emikai murmured.

I frowned at him. "And you know this how?"

The Filly nodded at Minnario's chair. "His vectored thrusters would have left a ripple pattern in Tech Yleli's spilled blood."

I felt my face warm with embarrassment. Of course they would have. I should have spotted that one myself. "Right," I said. "My apologies, Minnario."

[No offense taken,] Minnario assured me. His face seemed to darken. [And no need to apologize for your concern for Bayta, either. The first test of every person, whether Nemut or Human, is how he guards and protects his friends and companions. I honor you for taking that duty so seriously.]

They were fine words, and laid on almost as thickly as Aronobal had delivered her speech a few minutes ago. Unlike hers, though, Minnario's I actually believed, though I wasn't exactly sure why. "She's down the hall in Terese German's room," I told him. "Feel free to stay as long as you'd like."

[Thank you,] he said, leaning over the side of his chair and patting Doug on the head. [Good hunting to you.]

Emikai and I had made it out of the building and half-way to the outbound corridor when my comm vibrated: Bayta calling to check whether I'd indeed sent Minnario to talk to her. I confirmed that I had, told her to cooperate with him as best she could while still comforting Terese, and signed off.

"An excellent assistant," Emikai commented as we reached the end of the dome. "The ability to take on several tasks at once is rare indeed."

"She's definitely good at that," I agreed. "Wait a second—I want to check out the camera."

"An effective bit of sabotage, was it not?" Emikai asked, pointing up at the monitor camera still angled toward the top of the dome. "I have only had a moment to study it, and insufficient time for a full examination."

"We'll want to find a ladder and do that sometime," I said, craning my neck. "Any idea what was used to push it?"

"I do not see any obvious marks that would indicate the method," Emikai said. "But from the stress lines on the metal gimbals, I believe it was done in a single, solid thrust instead of via several smaller ones."

"That would make sense," I said. "Standing here nudging the thing would be a little obvious." I turned around to look at the far side of the dome and the corridor that led toward my quarters. "What about the other one?"

"It was removed completely," Emikai said.

"That much I know," I said. "I meant, why it was removed instead of simply pushed up like this one?"

Emikai shook his head. "That I cannot say. Though it surely would have been more difficult to remove than simply push out of line."

"Unless the plan was to remove both of them, only some of their equipment failed," I said. "And no one up in the security nexus monitor room noticed any of this?"

"As you must have noticed last night, the images on

the displays rotate among many cameras and status boards," Emikai said. "The patroller on duty would have first had to notice that the dome camera was misaligned."

"Which he obviously didn't."

"Or he noticed and was unable to fix it," Emikai went on. "It is likely the twisted gimbals would not permit a remote adjustment. In that case, a repair order would automatically be logged."

"As I assume would also be the case with the camera that was suddenly missing," I said, eyeing the remaining camera closely. "How soon after the orders were logged would there have been someone on the scene?"

"Normally within thirty minutes," Emikai said. "In this case, of course, the murder of Tech Yleli intervened."

I looked across the dome at Building Eight. "And now that the whole place has become a crime scene, I assume they'll be left just the way they are. Conveniently leaving the whole dome unwatched."

"Hardly that," Emikai said. "I am told there have been extra patrollers assigned to the area."

"Really?" I made a show of looking around. "Where?"

"I presume they are stationed inside the buildings," Emikai said. But he was looking around, too, and he didn't sound so sure anymore.

"I didn't see any hanging around Building Eight," I pointed out.

"Nor did I," he conceded. "Perhaps I should call the security nexus and inquire."

"That'll only help if it's an honest oversight," I said. "Otherwise, all you'll get will be more empty promises."

"Let us see which," he said, pulling out his comm.

I listened with half an ear while Emikai spoke to the controller, studying the twisted camera mount as I did so. A single, solid punch, Emikai and I had both concluded. But as Emikai had said, there was no sign of denting in any part of the mounting hardware. Whatever the tool was that our mystery man had used, he'd made sure its business end was well padded.

I looked back as Emikai put his comm away. "The controller agrees that the assigned patrollers have not taken their posts," he said. "Other security matters took priority."

"What other security matters?" I asked.

"He did not list them," Emikai said. "But he has promised they will be here as quickly as possible."

"Of course they will," I growled.

Emikai eyed me closely. "We could examine the cameras and mounts now," he suggested. "By the time we finish, the patrollers might be ready to return to their posts. Regardless, we could then allow the maintainers to replace the cameras and thus restore monitor service to the area.

"And Tech Yleli's acquaintances?" I asked.

"We would speak with them after that."

I chewed at my lip. I would definitely feel safer with Bayta in the middle of a milling group of genetically engineered Filly cops. But we also had a murder to investigate, and the sand was rapidly running out of our 24/24 hourglass. "No," I said, coming abruptly to a decision. "Our first priority is to nail down the victim's movements as quickly as we can, before anyone's memory starts to fog up. Let's go."

Besides, I reminded myself firmly as we left the dome and headed down the corridor, the Shonkla-raa wanted Terese's baby alive and unharmed. They wouldn't try anything against Bayta here.

Surely they wouldn't.

The foot traffic in the area around our quarters and Terese's medical dome had always been rather on the sparse side. Not so elsewhere in the station. As Emikai and I took the elevator to the bullet train deck and headed outward, we found ourselves traveling amid Manhattan-level crowds of Fillies. Most of them gave us a quick glance as we passed, apparently impressed by the novelty of having a Human aboard Proteus, while other no doubt more cosmopolitan residents ignored us completely. In contrast, there was one couple aboard the bullet train who stared at me the entire time, whispering back and forth to each other. I felt more than a little relieved when we left the train and they went off in one direction while Emikai and I headed off the other.

Twenty decks down, we finally reached the late Tech Yleli's neighborhood.

Up to now all my time on Proteus had been spent in the official and medical sections of the station, which also turned out to be the areas that had been photographed for the professionally prepared pamphlets and brochures I'd seen. Nowhere in any of those publications had I seen pictures of what the staff and worker residence areas looked like.

As we walked into Yleli's community-center dome, I finally understood why.

It wasn't that the center was squalid, or unkempt, or even unphotogenic. It was that it was so utterly *alien*.

For a long moment I just stood there at the archway leading into the dome, my mind spinning as I tried to take it all in. The curved dome surface caught my eye first: patterned with odd splotches of subtle color and an asymmetric pattern of clinging vines that climbed nearly to the top. Birds of some sort perched on the vines, and small creatures, half caterpillar and half slug, crawled slowly along both the vine network and the dome surface itself. Where Terese's medical dome featured a calmness of blue sky and white clouds, the top of this dome was done in brilliant reds, yellows, and oranges, an image of flaming death that could have been either a representation of a volcanic explosion about to rain down on the landscape below or else a Filly interpretation of Dante's hell.

The stores and parkland lying beneath the frozen waves of fire were no better. Buildings were buildings, I'd always assumed, with form following function and all that. But even given that purely practical basis, there was still something about the shops, community buildings, and meeting clusters that took me a long moment to wrap my mind around. The angles, textures, and perspective seemed to be at war with one another, leaving the sort of feeling I always got looking at an optical illusion and watching it go from a pair of faces to a vase and back again. Above the buildings were probably thirty helium-filled balloons of various sizes, shapes, and colors, arranged in three separate vertical levels as they circled the dome slowly in the air currents. Arranged on the ground outside their three-level circle was a ring of blazing torches, whose updrafts were apparently designed to keep the balloons contained within their proper flight area.

And then, as my brain finally got all the rest of it more or less sorted out, I focused for the first time on the Fillies themselves.

I'd seen Fillies hundreds of times before, in person, in holos, or in recordings. And yet, suddenly I felt as if I was seeing them for the very first time. There were at least two hundred of them in the dome, dressed in brightly colored clothing, walking stolidly among the dome's structures. At first glance it looked like just random pedestrian milling, but as I studied it I saw that the crowd was divided into linear groups, rather like hands-free conga lines. Each line was making its own version of a solemn procession across the dome floor, curving and weaving like a Chinese New Year dragon, each group moving in a different direction and with a different flow pattern. As two lines met they might combine, or pass through one another, or simultaneously veer off in brand-new directions. It was like a huge field-show marching squad pageant, mixed with a dit-rec costume drama of an eighteenth-century royal ball, with a bit of Japanese kabuki tossed in. Another couple of hundred Fillies were standing around the dome's perimeter watching the performance, most of them in pairs or small clumps set in between the six corridors leading into the dome.

And the whole group of them were doing everything in perfect silence. "Tech Yleli's funeral service?" I murmured.

"His remembrance processional, yes," Emikai answered. "I believe the movements are designed to represent various aspects of his journey, as well as the people whose lives he touched. This particular cultural form is one I am not very familiar with." He paused, and I could feel his eyes on me. "You probably find it quaint."

With a supreme effort, I forced back the chilling alienness of the scene. "Not at all," I assured him. "I've just never seen anything like this before. From Filiaelians or anyone else."

"Our private cultural lives are not to be set out for strangers to witness," Emikai said grimly. "My error. I should have called before we came."

"If it helps any, I promise not to tell anyone about it," I offered. "Actually, I doubt I could do it proper justice even if I wanted to."

"Thank you," he said. "That would be appreciated."

I nodded, a tightness forming in the pit of my stomach. Cops were supposed to try to put aside any emotions they might feel for the victims in their investigations. But nevertheless I could feel anger-tinged sadness as I gazed at the spectacle before me. From the number of people who'd showed up to act out his life, it was clear that he'd been a well-liked member of his community.

And yet, someone had killed him. Possibly because of Terese, and whatever the hell the Shonkla-raa wanted with her and her baby.

Or maybe he'd been murdered because of me.

"They have noticed us," Emikai murmured.

I snapped out of my gloomy thoughts. Sure enough, a handful of the spectators, mostly the ones nearest us, had turned in our direction and were staring at us, still in eerie silence. "We should go," Emikai continued, taking a tentative step backward. "We can come back later and ask the necessary questions."

I was opening my mouth to agree when one of the Fillies who had spotted us turned and sidled casually to the next corridor clockwise from us around the dome's perimeter. As he reached it, he threw one last look at us and disappeared around the corner.

And though I couldn't be positive at that distance, it had sure looked like he had an enlarged throat. The kind favored by professional singers and Shonkla-raa.

"Better idea," I murmured to Emikai, taking a couple of backward steps of my own. "I'll go. You can stay until the end of the performance and then talk to them about Tech Yleli."

He frowned at me. "Are you certain?"

"Absolutely," I assured him, backing up a couple more steps and then turning around and heading at a fast walk down the corridor. "I'll talk to you later," I added over my shoulder.

The corridors in this particular part of Proteus had a slight bend to them, and by the time I was halfway to the next major intersection the dome itself was no longer visible around the curve. Now that I was out of view, I picked up my pace. The whole area seemed to be deserted, with everyone in the neighborhood apparently in the dome at Yleli's funeral performance.

The silent part of the proceedings had apparently ended. Wafting down the corridor from behind me was the sound of someone giving a speech or eulogy or something of the sort, his voice rising and falling in an odd singsong pattern. I wondered if it was their particular cultural form, or something out of the Slisst Protocols, or neither.

The next major intersection was two more corridors away. I reached it and tapped the green emblem on the wall. "Neighborhood map," I ordered.

The wall lit up with a map, complete with a helpful mark showing my current location. Unlike the more prosaic rectangular pattern around Terese's dome, this part of Proteus was arranged like a wheel, with the six curved corridors I'd already noted radiating outward from the community center and all the cross-corridors arranged in concentric circles centered on the dome. The corridor the Filly had taken had also already passed two other intersections, but assuming he was still on that path, the cross-corridor I was currently standing beside ought to give me a fair chance of cutting him off. Taking one final look at the map, making quick note of the various public places the Filly might have ducked into if he *wasn't* still in his original corridor, I headed out.

The cross-corridor was just as deserted as the previous one had been, and I took advantage of the lack of obstacles to break into a fast jog. Fortunately, Doug didn't jump to the wrong conclusion, like that I might be trying to ditch him, but merely trotted along beside me, with no indication that he thought a nice afternoon run was anything out of the ordinary. Probably he was enjoying the exercise. I reached the end of the curved corridor and turned into the main radial one.

I'd been wrong earlier about everyone in the neighborhood being at the funeral. There were three of them waiting twenty meters down the radial corridor from my intersection: big, strong males, all of them dressed in the same style as those I'd seen in the dome. Apparently, they'd been at the funeral and had decided to duck out of the proceedings early. They were clustered together in the middle of the corridor, glowering at me as I came skidding around the corner. Directly behind them was an apartment door decorated with an archway made of pieces of colored paper, in the same color gradation from bottom to top that I'd noticed with the floating balloons in the dome.

{You desecrate Yleli's former place of life,} the Filly in the center of the group said, his thin nose blaze darkening with anger, his voice just loud enough to be audible above the eulogy still going on down in the dome. {You will leave here at once.}

"Hello there," I said cheerfully, slowing to a casual walk and continuing toward them. Out of the corner of my eye I saw Doug suddenly turn his head to look behind us. "Any of you speak English?"

The three Fillies exchanged quick and slightly confused glances. Apparently, my presumed lack of understanding of their challenge was something they hadn't expected. {You desecrate Yleli's former place of life,} Thin Blaze tried again, his voice still angry but now with a tinge of uncertainty. {You must leave at once.}

"Did you see one of your fellows come this way?" I asked, picking up my pace a little. Walking up to three angry Fillies, all of whom were bigger than I was, was not my first choice on how best to spend a quiet morning. But Doug's over-the-shoulder look a moment ago strongly implied there was a fourth member of the group back there, and stopping or slowing would just give him time to catch up and jump me from behind. Better to play the ignorant tourist as long as I could and hope for a decent opening before I reached the point of no return.

I made it three more steps, and was just starting to wonder if this had been such a good idea after all, when I got my break. Stepping away from his fellows, Thin Blaze started toward me. {You will leave at once!} he snarled, bunching his hands into fists.

I smiled grimly to myself. Now, instead of facing three-to-one odds, I would have a one-to-one followed by a two-to-one. It wasn't perfect, but it was the best I was going to get.

I was two steps from combat range with Thin Blaze when I suddenly remembered Doug.

They will keep you from traveling where you should not go, Hchchu had said about the watchdogs' job, *and prevent you from harming anyone.*

And suddenly, I realized this might not be a simple

single and duo after all. It might instead end up as a single and a duo plus a pineapple-backed dog under strict orders and with the teeth to back them up. I had no idea how far Doug would go to prevent me from taking out the Fillies, but even if he just hung on to my ankle he was going to severely cramp my style, possibly badly enough to get me killed.

Unless I got creative.

Thin Blaze was almost to me now. I extended my right arm toward him, as if offering to shake hands. Back on the super-express Quadrail I'd successfully nailed Emikai with this one. Time to see if the average non-cop Filly would fall for it, too.

He did. He reached for my extended arm, and as he did so I smoothly withdrew it, forcing him to lean forward as he tried to chase it down.

His full attention was still on the annoyingly elusive arm when I reached across with my left hand, grabbed his right hand, and twisted it up and back. Simultaneously, I grabbed and locked his elbow with my right hand and swiveled around on my left foot, twisting the trapped arm upward and forcing the Filly to bend forward at the waist.

During my sparring sessions with Emikai aboard the Quadrail, I'd always stopped at that point. Here, with three-plus assailants whose ultimate intentions were still unknown, I couldn't afford to be so charitable. Turning the helpless Filly another ninety degrees, I gave his arm a hard shove and sent him flying straight into his two startled friends.

Their shrieks of surprise, protest, and anger were drowned out as Doug let out a howl of his own, possibly a shot-across-the-bow warning that I'd just crossed the line. The howl turned suddenly into a startled yip as I reached down, scooped him up by his midsection, and hurled him as hard as I could behind me.

My aim and timing were perfect. The two Fillies who were hurrying in from that direction had just enough time to goggle in disbelief before Doug slammed across both their torsos. The impact sent all three of them sprawling in a confused tangle of arms and legs and claw-tipped paws.

There was a farcical aspect to it, but I didn't have time to properly appreciate the show. Spinning around again, I charged into the first group of Fillies, still off-balance after having had their spokesman slammed into them. Thin Blaze still had his back to me, so I took him first, hammering a blow into one of his upper-leg nerve centers and dropping him hard onto the deck. One of the others, attempting to do a tiger leap at me, instead caught a foot on his friend's shoulder and took himself down even more efficiently than I could have done. The third managed to actually get off a punch, which I dodged with relative ease before taking him down with a pair of jabs of my own. Leaping over the twitching bodies, putting them between me and my final two opponents, I turned around and prepared for round two—

Only to discover that the fight was over. The two who'd been trying to sneak up on me were still extricating themselves from their entanglement with a dazed-looking Doug, but already they were backing as quickly as they could toward the cross-corridor behind them. By the time they disappeared around the corner the three at my feet were heading in the same direction, crawling then hobbling and finally limping as feeling and function began returning to the relevant parts of their bodies. I watched them go, ignoring their looks of impotent rage, until the last of them had vanished around the corner.

{Incompetent fools,} a voice growled from behind me.

I turned around, simultaneously taking a long step away from the voice toward the middle of the corridor. The door to Yleli's apartment had slid open, and standing beneath the arch of multicolored paper was the Filly whose furtive exit from the funeral ceremony had caught my attention and sparked this whole thing in the first place.

And now, up close, I saw that I'd been right. Sticking prominently through the V-neck of his tunic was the oversized throat the Filly genetic engineers had given him. The mark of professional singers and Shonkla-raa.

{So be it,} he said, taking a step out of the apartment toward me and letting the door slide closed behind him. {I'll simply have to do this myself.}

NINE :

The mourners in the dome had gone silent again, giving the air the quiet stillness of a midcontinental Western Alliance afternoon just before a thunderstorm. The Filly's eyes were dark and malevolent, his hands large and ready, the whole package topped off with an unholy glitter of anticipation.

Which didn't mean I should assume he knew everything. "Sorry—what did you say?" I asked, reprising my ignorant tourist role and wondering how far I could push the game this time.

As it turned out, not very. "Don't play the fool, Compton," the Filly said contemptuously, switching to excellent English. "We know all about you, and about your war against my servant the Modhri. A Human of your talents and experience most certainly is capable of understanding Fili."

"Which you expect to be the language of the future?" I suggested, giving him a quick but careful study. Filly faces were tricky for Humans to tell apart, but I was almost positive that this was the Filly I'd dubbed Blue One, one of the group of Shonkla-raa that *Usantra* Wandek had dragged Bayta and me in to see when we first arrived at Terese's medical facility.

"Of course," he said. "As it was also the language of the past."

"I'll have to take your word for that one," I said. He

hadn't bought my game of pretending not to understand Fili, but maybe I could still convince him I didn't know the Shonkla-raa were on the rise again. "As to that comment about incompetent fools, what did you expect from local talent? What did you do, grab the nearest bunch of yokels and tell them I was going to trash Yleli's place?"

"Something like that," the Filly said, taking another step toward me. "But I didn't expect anything more from them than to soften you up."

"You might be surprised at how little softening has actually taken place," I warned, taking a couple of hasty steps back.

"Oh, don't look so concerned," the Filly chided, coming to a halt. "At the moment, you're worth more to us alive than dead."

"That's comforting," I said, a hard knot forming in my stomach. Of course I was worth keeping alive. Why kill me when a touch of Modhran coral would turn me directly into one of their slaves? "How about you? Are *you* worth more alive, too?"

He smiled, a thin, evil thing. "If you wish for more combat, I can certainly oblige you."

"I'm sure you can," I murmured, trying desperately to think. He could almost certainly take me —that much we both knew. Yet for all that brimming confidence, he didn't seem in any hurry to get things started. Was he waiting for backup to arrive? More locals, or another Shonkla-raa or two? In either case, giving them time to get into position was a guarantee that I would get my head handed to me.

But what were my other choices? Turning tail and trying to run for it wouldn't work—from my fight with *Asantra* Muzzfor aboard the super-express Quadrail I knew that Shonkla-raa were pretty fast on their feet. Besides that, I didn't much care for the image of being run to ground like an antelope on the Serengeti.

But facing him straight-up and unarmed this way

wasn't going to work, either. What I needed was to find a weapon.

Or maybe I already had one.

There was a slightly dazed-sounding rumble from somewhere to my left. "Doug?" I called, wanting to look and see how he was doing but not daring to take my eyes off Blue One. "Hey, boy. You okay?"

The watchdog rumbled again. Maybe he'd hit the deck harder than I'd realized. "Yeah, sorry about that," I apologized.

"A most clever maneuver, by the way," the Filly commented. "Although I expect *Chinzro* Hchchu will be annoyed if you permanently damage one of his *msikai-dorosli*." He smiled thinly. "If you wish to try throwing him at me as well, feel free to do so."

"Sorry, I never do a trick twice for the same audience," I told him. "Speaking of tricks, why did you kill Tech Yleli? If it's not a professional secret, of course."

"If anyone bears the blame for his death, it's you," he said darkly. "You were the one who disabled the monitors in the dome. That was what allowed him to die unseen."

I felt my forehead crease. *I* was the one who'd disabled the monitors? "An act of petty vandalism hardly rises to the level of murder," I pointed out. "I also notice you're ducking the question. What did he do? Or did he see something he shouldn't?"

The Filly snorted again. "You Humans have such a narrow way of viewing the universe," he said. "You insist on dealing with reality purely in terms of cause and effect."

"And how *should* we deal with it?"

"By seeing through to the ultimate goal," he said. "The path itself is meaningless. You must look to the goal, and to reach it no matter what obstacles lie in your way."

"Ah, yes—the old end justifying the means," I said, nodding. "We tossed that one into the ethical ash heap centuries ago."

"Of course you did," he said calmly. "You're an inferior being, among a race of inferior beings. *Your* goals certainly don't justify your path."

"That's only for superior beings like you, I gather," I said. "My mistake. So which of your higher goals did Tech Yleli's death serve?"

The Filly lifted his finger, his head half turned in the direction of the community center. "Wait," he said. "Do you hear?"

I frowned. Then, drifting down the corridor toward us, came the first strains of music.

It began as a single voice lifted in quiet song. A few bars later a second voice joined in, then a third, then a fourth, and then an entire chorus in full Filiaelian five-part harmony.

"The time of meditation is over," the Filly said, a grim satisfaction in his voice. "And with the raised voices to mask your screams of agony, we may finally proceed." Settling his hands into the lock-jointed knives I'd faced aboard the super-express Quadrail, he started toward me. "Or would you prefer to come quietly?" he added.

"Careful," I warned, backing up at his advance. "You and your friends want me alive, remember?"

"*Alive* can also mean not quite dead," he pointed out. "It makes little difference to me."

"I suppose not," I said, still backing up. I passed Doug, who was standing more or less where I'd tossed him earlier. He turned to face me as I continued by, his eyes tracking me balefully, his mouth half open to show his teeth. I'd caught him by surprise the last time, but he wasn't going to fall for my quick-grab tactics again. The Filly picked up his pace, closing the gap.

And I took a long step to my left, putting Doug squarely between the two of us.

The Filly stopped, his blaze paling a little with clear surprise at my maneuver. "You're not serious," he said, looking at Doug and then back at me.

"I'm not?" I asked. The Filly took a step to his right,

and I responded with a step to mine, keeping Doug between us.

"Please," the Filly said condescendingly. He did a little two-step, clearly enjoying the novelty and, probably, the ultimate uselessness of my stalling technique.

I did a mirror-image two-step and jammed my hand into my side pocket. "Okay, that's far enough," I said in as stern a voice as I could manage. "Back off, right now, or you'll regret it."

"You disappoint me," the Filly said, a tone of regret in his voice as he feinted left and then took another step to the right. "Do you Humans truly believe your skill at bluffing is so potent a weapon? *Chinzro* Hchchu is barely intelligent enough to qualify as a sentient being, but even he knows how to properly disarm a potential threat to his precious station."

I grimaced. "Someday you're going to be wrong," I said, reluctantly withdrawing my hand from the pocket. "I just hope I'm there—"

Right in the middle of my sentence he leaped toward me, his tucked feet clearing Doug's head and back by a good half meter as he arced over the oblivious watchdog. I caught a motion-blurred image of his right hand extending toward my throat and his left cocked ready at his waist just in case he needed to kill me after all.

And flipping around the uncapped hypo I'd palmed, I twisted my head and torso out of the Filly's path and stabbed the needle as hard as I could into his left thigh.

He shrieked, a resonating combination of pain and rage and disbelief that included a set of upper harmonics that nearly took off the top of my head. His left hand knifed reflexively toward me, as he perhaps momentarily forgot he wanted me alive, but the sudden jolt of agony had thrown off his timing and aim and the hand slashed harmlessly past my shoulder. He hit the ground, his newly paralyzed left leg collapsing beneath him and sending him tumbling toward the floor. I took a step toward him, my second hypo ready in my hand.

And dodged back barely in time as he twisted around at the waist and slashed his right hand viciously toward my torso. The blow missed, and he slammed shoulder-first against the deck. His hand slashed out again, this time aiming for my knee, and as I again dodged the blow I reached over and down and buried my second needle in his upper arm.

He was making another attempt to kill me with screeched sound waves as I pushed his long nose to the side with my foot and slammed my fist into the nerve center beneath his right ear. His screech abruptly cut off, and he collapsed limply onto the deck.

For a moment I stood there, one foot on his good wrist, the other on the side of his nose, breathing heavily and trembling as my adrenaline level slowly subsided. "To see it," I finished my interrupted sentence.

I crouched down beside the Filly and looked over at Doug. "You okay, boy?" I asked. "He attacked first, you know."

Doug gave a snuffle, and plodded a little unsteadily over to me. I tensed, but he merely pressed his snout against my sleeve as if reminding himself who I was. He had a sort of lopsided, dit-rec-cartoon look in his eyes, and I winced a little as I wondered briefly if my toss had done him any serious damage.

But he merely gave my sleeve another sniff and then sat back on his haunches. "Right," I agreed. "Back to work."

The singing from the dome was still going strong, making for an odd but pleasant counterpoint as I went through the unconscious Filly's clothes. Lady Luck was definitely on my side today: the first two pockets I tried yielded a handful of plastic quick-lock restraints and one of the passkey cards that our Filly escort had used to let Bayta and me into our room two days ago.

I got the restraints securely onto his wrists and ankles, then took a moment to look around. Yleli's apartment, where Blue One had lain in wait for me, was the one place within reach where I was pretty much guaranteed we wouldn't be disturbed. On the other hand, it was also the first place his buddies would come looking for him when he failed to bring me in on schedule.

But I didn't have much choice. The singing down the hall had all the earmarks of a finale, and I absolutely couldn't be found out here in the open with a turkey-trussed Filly when the funeral broke up and people started returning to their homes. At this point, Yleli's place was my best bet.

I stood up and got a grip on Blue One's sleeve. "Feel free to help," I offered, looking again at Doug.

He just looked back at me with his masked eyes. "Right," I said, and started pulling.

Yleli's apartment was at least three times the size of the one Bayta and I had been given, which made sense given that we were transients and techs like Yleli actually lived here. Leaving Blue One in the living room, I gave myself a quick tour, noting the nice but unpretentious furnishings, and making sure the place was, in fact, unoccupied.

I returned to the living room, and for a minute gazed down at my unconscious prisoner, the itching feeling of having just climbed on top of a tiger creeping through me. I'd beaten off this first overt attack by the Shonkla-raa, but what was I supposed to do now? Leave him here, knowing that someone would eventually come looking for him? The mood he would be in when he woke up wasn't something I really wanted to face, certainly not with my Beretta locked away in Hchchu's security office.

On the other hand, trying to move a Filly's worth of deadweight across Proteus Station by myself presented its own set of challenges.

Doug padded over and nuzzled the sleeping Filly's face. "No, no, we don't want him awake yet," I admonished, frowning at the watchdog. I'd always known he was the size of an adult Doberman, and I knew now that he was about as heavy as one, too. Wandek had told us they could carry light burdens, but I'd never gotten around to checking just how much weight they could handle.

Maybe it was time I did.

I glanced around the room, looking for Yleli's computer. But even as I spotted it I realized that accessing Proteus's network from a deceased person's apartment would probably kick up red flags from here to Hchchu's office and back again.

Fortunately, there was another way. Pulling out my comm, I punched in Bayta's number.

She answered on the first ring. "What's wrong?" she asked tautly.

"Nothing," I assured her. "How about you?"

"I'm fine," she said, her voice still tense. "I'm sorry, Frank, but I've had a bad feeling ever since you left."

"Well, you can give your intuition full marks," I said. "Our friends had a go at me, but so far I'm winning. Listen, I need you to look up something for me. Is there a computer you can get to without anyone noticing?"

"Yes, I think so," she said. "What do you need?"

"I need to know how much weight these watchdogs can carry," I said. "I've got a package I need to lug, and I don't want to risk breaking Doug's spine. I've already abused him enough for one day."

"Just a minute."

The comm went silent. I pulled a chair up beside Blue One and sat down, watching his slow breathing and wondering how long before that punch I'd given him wore off. Not long, probably, which meant I was going to have to come up with something a little more long term.

There was a click from the comm. "I think I can get you something even better," Bayta said. "Where are you?"

"Why?" I asked warily.

"Why do you think?" she retorted. "I'm coming to give you a hand."

"That may not be safe," I warned. "Our friends could be back on the warpath at any time."

"Then we need to get you and your package out of there as quickly as possible, don't we?" she countered. "Where are you?"

I grimaced. "In Tech Yleli's former residence," I said, and gave her the number. "Maybe I should meet you halfway, though. Better yet, I'll meet you at the bullet-train station at—"

"We'll be fine," she cut me off. "Wait there and watch your package."

Once again, the comm went dead. Cursing under my breath, I put it away. Should I call her back and insist on meeting her along the way? Or should I just show up at the bullet-train stop and walk her the rest of the way, whether she liked it or not?

But whenever the Shonkla-raa realized their plan had gone awry and came out in force from under their rocks, it would be me they would be looking for. Much as I hated to admit it, for the moment Bayta might actually be safer without me.

I was still trying to come up with a good reason why she *wouldn't* be safer out there alone when there was a chime from the door.

Silently, I got to my feet and headed across the room, grabbing the two hypos I'd stabbed Blue One with from the end table where I'd left them. By the time I reached the door, I had the hypos arranged in a V-shape in my right fist, the plungers set firmly against my palm, the needles angled outward on either side of my middle finger. If the Shonkla-raa were here for a rematch, the first one in line, at least, was going to hurt a lot. I pressed my ear to the door . . .

"Compton?" Emikai's voice came softly through the panel. "Compton, are you in there?"

Sighing, I stepped back and keyed the release. Emikai caught sight of me as the door slid open, glanced both ways down the corridor, and stepped hurriedly inside. "I thought you might have found a way into—" he began.

And broke off as he caught sight of my prisoner. "What happened?" he asked in a subtly altered tone.

"He sent a few locals to try to beat me up," I said. "When that didn't work, he took on the job himself. You have any idea how to keep him quiet for the next hour or two? Apart from punching him behind the ear every ten minutes, I mean?"

"Possibly," Emikai said, still staring in a sort of fascinated repugnance at the unconscious Filly. Probably wondering why I hadn't called the Jumpsuits, and whether he should do it himself. "Have you looked in the medicine cabinet?"

"No, I just had the quick tour," I said. "You think Tech Yleli might have left us some sleeping tablets?"

"It is likely," Emikai said, finally tearing his eyes away from Blue One and heading toward the rear of the apartment. "He might have needed them himself, or kept some to sell to others."

"To *sell*?" I echoed. "You mean he was dealing?"

"Not at all," Emikai said huffily. "Filiaelian medical techs are often tasked with providing minor health care to neighborhood residents. It relieves some of the strain on doctors and other care providers."

"Ah," I said, wondering if I should take that explanation at face value or press the issue further. Still, I knew Filly warriors and cops had been genetically engineered for loyalty and professional ethics. Why not medical techs, too?

If Yleli had been a dealer, he was either very good at it or very bad. The medicine cabinet was nearly empty, with no more than a dozen vials and bottles of various sorts lined up on the shelves. "Not looking good," I commented.

"On the contrary," Emikai said as he lifted out one of the bottles. "Though primarily designed for relieving the symptoms of a vision disorder, this medication also carries powerful soporific qualities."

"And you'd know that how?" I asked, taking the bottle from him and peering at the label. A complete waste of time—I could read the Filly characters, all right, but the words they spelled out were technical terms my Westali courses had never covered.

"Even enforcement officers must occasionally improvise," Emikai said with a hint of dry humor.

"Ah." I wasn't entirely sure what he meant by that, and I was pretty sure I didn't want to.

"But this form is a liquid that must be injected," he continued. "Are the hypodermics you met me with at the door still functional?"

"Yes, but the needles have been bent a little," I said, digging into my pocket. "Fortunately, I happen to have a spare."

I pulled out my third hypo, the one with the pale amber liquid in it, feeling a twinge of regret as I got my fingers around the rests and my thumb on the plunger. So much for doing my own analysis of Terese's condition. But it couldn't be helped. Aiming the needle into the sink, I pressed the plunger.

Nothing happened.

I frowned, pressing the plunger a little harder. But it didn't move. The fluid level stubbornly remained right where it was, without so much as a drop seeping out the end of the needle.

"Is there trouble?" Emikai asked.

"Yes, but I don't know what," I said, peering closely at the hypo. I couldn't see anything wrong with it. "I can't get the fluid to expel."

"Let me see."

I handed it over, and for a few seconds he carefully turned it over in his hands as he studied it. "Well?" I asked.

"I do not see any problem," he said. "But it seems bulkier, somehow, than the hypos I have used in the past."

"Interesting," I said. "With Human equipment of this sort, the goal is usually to make things lighter and simpler rather than bulkier."

"That is generally the same with us, as well," Emikai said. "Can you tell me what fluid this is?"

I shook my head. "I can identify Human blood and a couple of other fluids by sight. But I don't know this one."

"But you *did* see it being withdrawn from Ms. German?"

"I—" I broke off, a strange thought tugging suddenly at the base of my skull. "I saw a tech stick the needle into one of the access tubes they've got plugged into her," I said slowly. "I also saw him pull on the plunger. But that's not what you asked, is it?"

"No, it is not," Emikai said, and from the tone of his voice I could tell he was thinking the same thing I was. "Shall we perform an experiment?"

I gestured. "Go for it."

He shifted the hypo to a two-handed grip, shot me a final look, and carefully pulled on the plunger.

The level of the amber fluid didn't change, as it should have if there were a little of the stuff still inside the needle itself. Nor did bubbles appear in the fluid, as there should have if the needle was instead empty and Emikai was merely sucking air.

And then, as we watched, something *did* happen. A small droplet of a clear liquid oozed from the end of the needle.

I eyed the droplet a moment, then shifted my gaze back to Emikai. "Well, well," I said. "Isn't *that* interesting?"

"A reverse-valved hypo," Emikai rumbled, still staring at the droplet. "But this makes no sense. She is in a hospital facility, where injections and medications are both expected and commonplace. Why use deception of this sort?"

"Precisely because she *is* in a hospital facility," I said darkly. "Everything she's officially given has to be identified, double-checked, and recorded. But with these, they can pump her full of stuff that's completely off the radar, all under the guise of taking samples."

I nodded toward the living room. "That also explains why there were two blood-sample hypos instead of just one. The first was a regular hypo, with a genuine blood sample, while the other was one of these tricked-out jobs."

"Two reverse-valved hypos," Emikai murmured thoughtfully. "One injection going to her and the other to her unborn child?"

"Or one intramuscular and one intravenous," I said. "Or one into the bloodstream and the other into the intestines or liver. Take your pick."

Emikai turned his gaze in the direction of the living room. "The *santra* you have taken prisoner. Is he one of those involved?"

"I think so," I said. "If not directly, then at least peripherally. Who is he?"

Emikai shook his head. "I do not yet know."

"You just said he's a *santra*," I said, frowning. "If you don't know who he is, how do you know that?"

"It is obvious he has had a great deal of genetic work done," Emikai said, gesturing toward his own throat. "From that it follows that he is a *santra*."

"I thought *santra* was a social or political title," I said. "It means *exalted one*, doesn't it?"

"A more accurate translation would be *distinguished one*, and as such can also be applied to those with extensive genetic alterations," Emikai said. "In actual practice, of course, those two populations largely coincide."

"I suppose that makes sense," I said, though the idea of getting your DNA remodeled just because you had the money and status to do it sounded slightly ridiculous. Still, it wasn't any crazier than getting elaborate tattoos or jewelry implants, each of which had been fashionable for a time in various upper-class Human societies. "So what exactly does his status mean to all this?"

Emikai cocked his head. "I do not understand."

"Back on the super-express you said that as an ex-cop you were still required to obey orders given to you by Filiaelian *santras*," I reminded him. "Does that mean you have to take orders from him once he wakes up?"

I'd been hoping for a quick answer, a firm and automatic assurance that even *santras* weren't above the law. The lengthening silence wasn't a good sign. "Well?" I prompted.

"I can certainly restrain any Filiaelian who has clearly broken the law, *santra* or otherwise," he said. "I also would have no difficulty in turning over a suspected lawbreaker to currently active enforcement officers." He hesitated. "But I have as yet seen no evidence that this *santra* has committed any crime. I also infer that you do not wish to turn him over to the *Kuzyatru* Station patrollers at this time."

"He *did* assault me," I pointed out.

"A crime for which I have no proof other than your statement," Emikai countered. "Proper protocol would call for an interrogation of both parties in an attempt to determine the truth."

I grimaced. This was starting to get awkward. "If we turn him over to the patrollers, his friends will know he's been taken," I said. "They'll also find out what happened between him and me, which they'll then try to twist against me."

"We could arrange to keep him incommunicado."

"Trust me, they'd get around that," I said grimly. "Once they've figured out what we know—which isn't much, but they don't know that it isn't much—they would have two options. Either they would step up whatever they're doing to Ms. German, or else they would shut down completely and go to ground. At this point, we aren't ready for either option."

"But there are legal requirements at play," Emikai said. "You have no proof that this person has committed a crime."

"We have that hypo," I pointed out. "That proves some kind of crime is under way." I snapped my fingers. "He also has a passkey that lets him into other people's apartments. That can't be legal for him to have, can it?"

For a long moment Emikai gazed down at the gimmicked hypo in his hand. "What do you wish from me?" he asked at last.

"Let me find a place where I can stash him for a few days," I said. "Bayta's on her way to help with the move, so you don't have to be involved with that if it makes you uncomfortable. A couple of days will hopefully buy us enough time to figure out what they're up to."

"If he is allied with others, his disappearance will not go unnoticed," Emikai pointed out.

"True, but a complete disappearance is a lot more enigmatic and disconcerting than having him pop up in the local nexus lockup," I said. "Any uncertainty and hesitation on their part is to our advantage."

"And if they counter by attacking Ms. German?" he asked, his voice dark and ominous. "My contract requires me to protect her."

"It's a calculated risk," I admitted. "But right now, it's our best option." I hesitated. "If it helps any, I think they're more likely to come after me than they are to go after Ms. German. After all, I was apparently the one on today's menu."

"Perhaps." Carefully, Emikai laid the hypo down on the sink. "You ask for several days. I will give you one. If at the end of that time you have no further leads or proof of criminal actions, I must turn him over to the patrollers."

"It's a deal," I said. One day wasn't much, but it was better than I'd hoped for. "We should have one blood-filled hypo out there in the living room that's actually real. Let's go get it and see about sending our friend off to dreamland."

TEN :

It took us a few minutes to figure out which hypo was the useful one, get the needle straightened enough to be functional, dump Terese's blood, and load the drug from Yleli's medicine cabinet into it. By then, Blue One was starting to show the first signs of returning consciousness.

Fortunately, the sleeping potion was a potent one, and the twitchings and random grunts faded quickly away as the drug did its magic.

Our next task was a quick search of the apartment. From the way Blue One had been talking before our fight, I was beginning to wonder if there had been an actual purpose to Yleli's murder. But I wasn't ready yet to give up on my inferior Human way of seeing the universe in terms of cause and effect, and so Emikai and I went through the papers in his file cabinet and sifted through drawers and closets in the hope of finding something that would explain why a lowly Proteus Station medical tech had been worth killing.

We had finished our first search, and Emikai had started on a more detailed one, when Bayta and Ty arrived.

To my annoyed surprise, they weren't alone.

"What is this, a party?" I demanded, glaring at Minnario as he floated through the doorway into the apartment. "Bayta, what in hell's name—?"

"He wanted to help," Bayta said, her tone just barely on the civil side of snappish. "I asked him to look up on his encyclopedia if *msikai-dorosli* could be used to carry things, and he said he could do better than that."

I took a deep breath, willing myself to calm down. Bayta's edgy defiance was a sure sign that she'd done what she'd thought to be right, knowing full well that I would probably be furious about it when I found out. The tension in her face also showed she'd continued to worry about my reaction the entire way here. "I appreciate his willingness to help," I said in as controlled a voice as I could manage. "The problem is that even though he's my attorney, he's also an officer of the Filiaelian court. That means he can't just sit back and watch a crime being committed. He has to report it."

"What crime?" Bayta shot back.

"Kidnapping, for starters," I said. A small voice at the back of my mind warned me that making a handy checklist for Minnario to refer to was probably not a good idea. But as was usually the case with those small voices, I ignored it. "Also criminal restraint, trespassing, medicating without proper credentials—"

[Please,] Minnario interrupted, one hand waving for attention, his eyes on the transcript on his display as it tried to keep up with our argument. [Mr. Compton, in general your analysis is correct. But in this case, fortunately, it's not.]

"What's the part that's wrong?" I growled.

[The part that defines me as an officer of the court,] he said. [As you know, *Kuzyatru* Station is running on the Slisst Protocols. Those state that an attorney isn't simply a defendant's advocate, but also his partner and second in this form of combat. Though I'm required to turn over any evidence involved with the specific case at issue, I'm *not* required to impugn my client's character or actions by bringing up anything outside of the case that he might have done.]

He gave me one of his lopsided smiles. [Including anything that he might still be doing, or that might be construed as criminal.]

I looked at Emikai. "Is he right?" I asked.

"I do not know," Emikai said thoughtfully. "I have not studied the Protocols extensively." He gestured to Minnario. "But he clearly has. Unless offered proof to the contrary, I would trust his interpretation."

[Actually, I'm more concerned about *Logra* Emikai,] Minnario continued, eyeing Emikai warily. [As a former

Filiaelian enforcement officer, his duties and responsibilities are far more rigid than my own.]

"Fortunately, they're also a bit vague," I said. "Moreover, since he agrees there are indications of wrongdoing on the part of our sleeping friend here, he's agreed to give me a little slack. Specifically, I have one day to dig up something concrete before he brings this to the patrollers." I cocked an eyebrow at Emikai. "Correct?"

"Correct," Emikai said. He still didn't look happy with the situation, but there was nothing in his expression or tone that might indicate he was thinking of reneging on his promise.

"Meanwhile, that clock is ticking merrily along," I continued, turning back to Minnario. "You told Bayta you could help. How?"

[With my chair, of course,] he said, as if it was obvious. [Its lifting capability is provided by a set of eight Shorshic thrusters. As a highly redundant system, though, it will function quite well with only three of them.]

Leaving us five to use in getting Blue One out of here. "How hard are they to remove?"

In answer, Minnario touched a couple of controls, then reached over the side of his chair and got a grip on the nearest of the cylinders poking out from beneath his chair. He gave the cylinder a half turn, and to my astonishment the tube popped right out. [Not very,] he said, holding it up for my inspection.

"I'll be damned," I said, frowning as I took it from him. The whole chair was obviously designed to be operated from the main control board, yet this individual thruster also had its own on/off switch and level and focus controls. "It has its own power supply, too?"

[Yes, it's fully self-contained,] Minnario said.

I shook my head in amazement as I handed the thruster back to him. "I don't think I've ever heard of a chair design like this before."

[As far as I know, it's the only one,] Minnario said, a

note of pride in his voice. [I travel a great deal, and had it custom-designed and built this way so I could swap out defective thrusters without having to take apart the entire chair.]

"Very efficient," I said, bending over and peering at the underside of the chair. The thrusters were arranged down there in a three-by-three array. "You said there were eight of them?"

[Yes,] he said. [The central position of the array is a stabilizer, not a thruster. Oh, and even though each of the thrusters has individual controls, I can also control them directly from my chair while they're detached, provided I'm close enough.]

I looked at Bayta. Her overt defiance was gone, but there was still a tightness in her throat and cheeks. "Do you want an apology now?" I asked. "Or would you rather save it until later when you can enjoy it more?"

She gave me a tentative smile, and as she did so the last of the stiffness faded away. "Later will be fine," she said. "Right now, we have work to do."

Having the means to carry our prisoner across Proteus was only the first half of the problem. We also had to somehow disguise the fact that we were carrying an unconscious Filly through busy hallways without someone becoming suspicious enough to call the Jumpsuits down on us.

Fortunately, Emikai had already laid the groundwork in his brief post-funeral questioning of some of Tech Yleli's neighbors. One of the standard questions in a murder investigation always centers around the deceased's employment history, which for Fillies would mean a list of his contracts. Yleli must have had a lot of such history, because each of the three drawers in his file cabinet was over half full. Naturally, the team investigating his murder couldn't be expected to set up camp in his apartment, which meant the cabinet needed to be taken somewhere else.

The fronts of the file drawers were attached to the drawers themselves with simple screws, which Emikai's multitool made quick work of. The cabinet was considerably shorter than Blue One, but it was deep enough that we were able to put him inside in a sort of half-sitting, half-crouching position that would probably have been pretty uncomfortable if he hadn't already been asleep. After that it was simply a matter of putting the drawer faces back on and wedging them into place, turning the cabinet on its back onto four of Minnario's thrusters, and we were ready to go.

Or so we thought. We had maneuvered the cabinet nearly to the door when it suddenly gave a hard twitch to the side and settled to the floor. "What happened?" I asked, reflexively grabbing for the side of the cabinet. "Minnario?"

[Yes, I set it down,] he said, frowning at his chair controls. [But I didn't make it twitch. There's something not right here.]

"What sort of something?" I asked. "Are the thrusters losing power?"

He shook his head. [No. Something seems to be interfering with the control signal.]

I looked down at the cabinet, the back of my neck tingling. Our first night here, when the Jumpsuits had gone crazy trying to find a non-missing Minnario, he'd mentioned that the locator in his comm interfered with his chair's controls. "Emikai, you did relieve our friend of his comm, right?" I asked.

"Of course," Emikai said. "It is over there on the side table."

"Yeah." I held out a hand toward him. "Multitool, please?"

We found the extra tracker pinned to the inside of Blue One's inner tunic lapel. "Very cute," I said, taking the device across the room and setting it beside the comm. "Minnario, how's it running now?"

[It seems all right,] Minnario said, sending the cabinet on a few tango-like maneuvers around the living room. [Yes, that was the problem.]

"Good," I said. There was a wafting of air as Bayta came up beside me. "Emikai, would you mind putting the drawer faces back on?"

He nodded and set to work. "So we were supposed to walk into a trap?" Bayta murmured.

"Or else they were just being careful," I said. "Do you recognize our friend, by the way?"

She nodded. "He was one of the Filiaelians at the interrogation *Usantra* Wandek took us to. Do you think he was the one who killed Tech Yleli?"

"Could be," I said. "I was trying to steer the conversation that direction when the noise from the funeral started up again and he tried to take me out."

Bayta shivered. "If there isn't a trap waiting out there now, there will be soon," she said quietly. "They'll be furious when they discover what we've done."

I shrugged. "Just gives us more incentive to figure out how they fit into the murder, and then find a way to nail them for it."

"*Logra* Emikai's only giving us one day."

"It'll be enough," I assured her. "If not to nail the Shonkla-raa, at least to persuade Emikai to give us more time."

Emikai finished wedging the last drawer face in place and straightened up. "Are we ready?" he asked.

"We're ready," I confirmed, taking Bayta's arm and rejoining the others. "Let's get this show on the road."

"Where exactly are we going?" Bayta asked.

I looked at Minnario, busily maneuvering the file cabinet into line with the door. "Don't worry," I said. "We'll find something."

The bullet trains would have been the fastest way to get back across the station. But they would also harbor more prying eyes and idly inquisitive minds than I wanted to have staring at our party and our cargo. So instead we took the back route, traveling the regular corridors and hallways and avoiding even the major traffic lanes and glideways.

We did what we could to disguise the oddness of our party by letting Emikai walk alone beside the floating file cabinet, with Minnario hanging back at the very limit of his control range, while Bayta and I and the watchdogs hung back even farther.

The marching order was helpful, but it was also open to exploitation by any Shonkla-raa who might have tumbled to what had happened and managed to track us down. I kept a close watch, but while we got plenty of curious looks from the other pedestrians no one started any trouble.

And finally, we arrived at the hiding place I'd had in mind ever since Bayta and Minnario had first showed up at Yleli's apartment.

Minnario's room.

"I do not like it," Emikai said flatly as I started pulling the drawer covers off the cabinet. "It is well known that you are Attorney Minnario's client. This is the first place his allies will look for him."

"The second place, actually," I corrected, taking hold of one of Blue One's arms. "The first place they'll look will be my room. Give me a hand, will you?"

Together, he and I got the sleeping Filly out of his makeshift coffin and up onto the couch. He didn't fit on this one any better than I had on the one in my room, but I wasn't particularly worried about how comfortable he would be with his feet hanging off the end. "Good," I said, reaching behind him to confirm that his wrist restraints were still secure. "Phase one, complete. On to phase two."

"Which is?" Emikai asked.

[To prepare for trial,] Minnario spoke up. While Emikai and I had been getting Blue One out of the cabinet, he had settled in at the computer and was peering at the display. [I'm informed your next hearing will be tomorrow morning at ten o'clock.]

"I thought *Chinzro* Hchchu wanted me to investigate Tech Yleli's murder," I protested. "How am I supposed to do that while I'm sitting around listening to lawyers?"

[Obviously, he thinks you can,] Minnario said, gesturing toward the display. [The message is very clear. Ten o'clock tomorrow.]

So much for Emikai's grace period. Depending on how much legalese *Chinzro* Hchchu decided to pull out of his sleeve, Minnario and I could be stuck there the whole day. "In that case, I've got the rest of today to figure out who Blue One is and find a connection with Tech Yleli. Do either of you have a camera I can use to take his picture?"

[I do,] Minnario said, pulling a small, flat disk from his chair pouch. [You call him Blue One?]

"Only until I get his real name," I said, taking the camera and getting a few shots of Blue One's face from different angles. "When we first met, he was wearing a blue tech's outfit."

"You did not say that you and he had previously met," Emikai said, eyeing me oddly.

"It just hadn't come up yet," I assured him. "I wasn't hiding it, if that's what you're getting at."

"What were the circumstances of this meeting?" Emikai persisted.

"*Usantra* Wandek wanted to ask me about *Asantra* Muzzfor's last hours aboard the super-express," I said. "Blue One was part of the audience. End of story." I turned back to Minnario. "Did you and Bayta—?"

"That is *not* the end of the story," Emikai interrupted. "You have not even told *me* all of what happened to *Asantra* Muzzfor. What did you tell them?"

"I told them the truth, the same as I told you," I said. "Besides, all of that is irrelevant. You heard Minnario—we're dealing with the New Tigris incident, and no one has any business looking at anything else."

Emikai's blaze darkened. "I am not a member of the court," he rumbled. "*I* choose what is relevant to me."

"Fine," I said. "You come up with some questions, and I'll be happy to answer them. But later. Right now, I have to get back to my room and my computer and see what I can dig up on this guy."

For a moment Emikai glared at me. Then, reluctantly, he nodded. "Very well," he said. "But this conversation is not yet over."

"I'll look forward to finishing it," I assured him as I turned back to Minnario. "As I was starting to ask, were you and Bayta finished with your witness prep work?"

[Yes,] the Nemut said, looking back and forth uncertainly between Emikai and me. [Before you leave, though, do you have more medication for my guest?]

"Yes, of course—sorry," I said, digging the bottle and hypo out of my pocket and handing them to him. "Give him—what was it, about two of the little hypo marks?" I asked, looking at Emikai.

"Yes," he confirmed. "Two *vikka* every six hours."

[I understand,] Minnario said. [What about food and water?]

I gazed over at our sleeping Shonkla-raa. If Emikai's six-hour time estimate was accurate, he should be coming to in about three and a half hours. "Tell you what," I said. "Forget any fresh injections for now—I'll come by about the time he's due to wake up and handle it. I think by then I'll want to talk to him anyway."

[Are you sure that'll be all right?] Minnario asked, looking apprehensively at our prisoner. [What if you're late? He's considerably bigger than I am.]

"He's a lot meaner, too," I said. "But don't worry, he's not going to break out of those restraints any time soon."

"But if we're not here by the time he starts to wake up, call one of us at once," Bayta added.

"Right," I agreed. "We'll see you in a couple of hours." I raised my eyebrows at Emikai. "You coming?"

"In a moment," Emikai said. "I would like a word first with Attorney Minnario."

I frowned, looking back at Minnario. [It's all right,] he assured me. [Actually, I'd like a word with *Logra* Emikai, as well. Until later.]

"Until later," I said. With a final look at Blue One, I took Bayta's arm and left the room.

The corridors were crowded as we made our way back toward the medical dome. But that was okay. I didn't really want to talk right now, and I could sense Bayta was in a deep study of her own. The only ones of our group who said anything for most of the way, in fact, were Doug and Ty, each of whom sent out a yip greeting to another watchdog and his master as they went in the opposite direction on the glideway.

The traffic had mostly cleared out, and I could see the archway into the medical dome ahead, when Bayta finally spoke. "If you don't mind, I'd like to check on Terese before we go to our room," she said. "Make sure she's all right."

"No problem," I assured her. "Were you able to find out anything new about the attack?"

"Not really," Bayta said. "She didn't seem to want to talk in front of Minnario."

I grimaced. "Yeah, I was afraid that would cramp your style a little. Did anyone notice the missing hypos?"

"I think Dr. Aronobal might have," she said. "I saw her looking at the area where they were all laid out, and then she went out in the corridor and had a short conversation with one of the techs. I couldn't hear what they were saying, but he left in something of a hurry."

"Well, I wouldn't worry too much about it," I said. "They can't prove anything. At least, not until they talk to Blue One."

Bayta exhaled loudly. "There's something wrong here, Frank," she said pensively. "Everything that's happened here is just *wrong*, somehow."

"For example?" I asked. I already had my own list, but I wanted to hear hers.

"The attack on you, for one thing," she said. "Why did they send only one person? Were they really that overconfident? Or did they want you to win so that you would do exactly what you did?"

"You mean wrap Blue One in cotton and drop him in a hole?"

"Or they may have hoped for something worse," she said, a brief shiver running through her. "They might have thought they would lose on the New Tigris killings, and were hoping to get something else to accuse you of. If we hadn't found that spare tracker, it would have led them right to him. Whether he was alive or . . . not."

"True," I agreed. "Okay, so we've got the attack. Anything else bugging you?"

"Yes, several things," she said. "Why lure you to the scene of Tech Yleli's murder? Just so they could jump out at the right time and frame you? But that didn't work. More importantly, they should have *known* it wouldn't work." She gestured down at Doug and Ty. "As *Logra* Emikai and *Chinzro* Hchchu quickly realized."

I looked down at the watchdogs, thinking about Doug's lack of action when the locals accosted me at Yleli's funeral. "Actually, that alibi may actually not be as tight as they all think," I said. "Doug didn't exactly leap to the defense of all those fine, upstanding citizens who jumped me. I wouldn't mention that to anyone else, of course."

"But why try it at all?" Bayta persisted. "In fact, it's worse than that. Not only did the frame-up not work, but in a way it actually backfired on them."

"How so?"

"It brought you and your Westali training back to *Chinzro* Hchchu's attention," she said. "I assume that's why he asked you to investigate the murder."

"Which led me to Sector 25-C, where no one knew me, and into an ambush," I reminded her. "Maybe it didn't backfire as badly as you think."

"Oh," she said. "Right."

"But let's not be hasty," I continued. "They may have gotten me hired so as to set me up for the ambush. But on the other hand, it could also be that the ambush was their response to me getting hired. In which case, we could argue that there's something about Yleli or his murder that they don't want us to find. Or else they want us to *think* there's something about the murder they don't want us to find."

"I hadn't thought about that," Bayta said slowly. "I don't know, Frank. This whole thing's starting to sound like a bizarre game."

"Not if *Asantra* Muzzfor was a representative member of the group," I said grimly. "He could get as convoluted as the best of us, but there was always a solid core of intent and motive beneath all the foam. If this is a game, there's some deadly reason for them to be playing it."

Bayta snorted. "All it's doing . . ." She trailed off.

"All it's doing is what?" I prompted.

"I was going to say all it's doing is wasting time," she said slowly. "But then I realized it's mostly wasting *our* time. *And* keeping us away from Terese."

That was a thought that had been hovering around the edges of my mind ever since Emikai and I discovered the tricked-out hypos. "Well, if that was their plan, it's about to come to a screeching halt."

"What are you going to do?" Bayta asked. "Tell someone about the extra drugs they've been giving her?"

"Not *someone*," I said with a tight smile. "*Everyone*."

She frowned at me. "What?"

"You heard me," I said. "I'm going to write up the

whole thing and put it on the station's main computer network. An hour from now, every pea-picking horse-faced Filly on Proteus is going to know about it."

"That should certainly stir things up," Bayta murmured.

"I hope so," I said. "At this point, stirring is exactly what we want."

We passed the receptionist at the archway and headed across the dome. Foot traffic seemed a bit lighter than usual, and I wondered briefly if this might be a good time to drop in on Building Twelve and see what the hell was going on in there.

But there were two figures loitering outside that particular building's main entrance, and I doubted they were just sampling the air. Making a mental note to check on the place again when I headed back to interrogate Blue One, I continued on to Building Eight, courteously opening the door for Bayta and the two watchdogs. I nodded a greeting to the receptionist as we passed, pressed myself against the wall halfway down the corridor to get out of the way of a tech with a loaded equipment cart, and turned into Terese's room.

To find an empty, neatly made-up bed.

I walked to the side of the bed, my eyes and brain taking a quick inventory. The narrow cabinet that had held a change of clothing was empty. So was the under-bed shelf where she'd kept her reader and music headphones.

I turned around to find Bayta standing just inside the doorway, her eyes wide. "Frank—"

"Come on," I said, taking her hand and heading back into the hallway. I nearly ran down the same Filly tech along the way and brought us to a halt in front of the receptionist. "Where is she?" I asked shortly.

The Filly gave me a quizzical look. {Who?}

"The Human girl, Terese German," I said, striving to keep my voice civil. Maybe there was a reasonable explanation. "She's gone. Where did they take her?"

The receptionist dropped her gaze to her computer display and punched a few keys on her board. {Terese German was checked out an hour and twenty minutes ago,} she reported. {Her condition had worsened, and her doctors decided to move her to an intensive-care facility.}

I clenched my teeth. An hour twenty would put it right after Bayta and Minnario had left. Also right after Aronobal had discovered that two of the gimmicked hypos were missing. "Which one?" I asked. "One of the other buildings here in the dome?"

{No,} the receptionist said, her blaze paling a little in confusion as she peered at the screen. {She's not here.}

"Then where?"

{I don't know,} she admitted, still studying her screen. {The location should be listed. But the reference point is blank.}

I looked at Bayta's ashen face. She'd been right. The Shonkla-raa had indeed wanted to keep us away from Terese.

And now they'd succeeded.

ELEVEN :

"You must try to calm down, Mr. Compton," Captain of the Guard Lyarrom said in probably the closest he could get to a soothing voice. "We are doing our best to locate your friend."

I looked at Bayta, who was sitting in a corner of the security nexus, her face rigid with her efforts to hide her emotions. I looked at Emikai, whom I'd summoned back from Minnario's room and who was now standing stiffly beside her. "I appreciate your words of concern, Guard Captain Lyarrom," I said. "You'll forgive my impertinence if I say that's not good enough."

"One's best is all that one can do," he said in a sage, grandfatherly way.

"Then maybe it's time to bring in more people and add *their* best to the mix," I countered. "For starters, you could start a trace on Dr. Aronobal's comm—chances are she's still with Ms. German. You could bring in patrollers from other parts of Proteus and get them started on a room-by-room search, starting with her quarters—"

"Ms. German's quarters have already been searched," he put in. "There is nothing of any help to us there."

"—and finally, if you can't or won't get through the bureaucratic inertia," I concluded, "I suggest you bring in *Chinzro* Hchchu to streamline things."

Lyarrom's face had grown stiffer, and his blaze darker, with each suggestion. "Mr. Compton, you are seriously overreacting," he said stiffly. "There is no evidence of criminal wrongdoing in this matter. Nor is there any evidence that Dr. Aronobal is in danger, impaired, or engaged in criminal behavior, which are the legal requirements for activating her comm's tracker. Finally—"

"So get *Chinzro* Hchchu in here to override those requirements."

"Finally, your verbal contract regarding Ms. German's safety ended when she came aboard *Kuzyatru* Station," Lyarrom said, raising his volume. "As to your final suggestion, I am *not* going to call in *Kuzyatru* Station's assistant director to deal with a bookkeeping error."

I took a careful breath, fighting back the urge to punch the complacent idiot in his snout. "Fine," I said between clenched teeth. "You just stay inside your nice, comfortable guidelines and limitations. When dead bodies start showing up, don't blame me."

Without waiting for a reply I stalked over to Bayta and Emikai. "You okay?" I asked Bayta quietly.

"I shouldn't have left her," Bayta murmured, her voice

on the edge of tears. "I should have just sent Minnario when you called and stayed with her."

I grimaced. Minnario. If the Nemut hadn't pulled his own vanishing act that first night, it might have been easier to convince Lyarrom that Terese's disappearance was something more serious than a bureaucratic glitch. But then, that had hardly been Minnario's fault.

Nor was Terese's disappearance Bayta's. "You had no way of knowing," I reminded her.

"Didn't I?" Bayta countered darkly. "I knew Dr. Aronobal knew about the missing hypos. I should have guessed she and the others wouldn't just leave things the way they were."

"And what exactly would you have done to stop them?" I shot back, more harshly than I'd intended. I should have anticipated this, too. Even more than Bayta should have. "In fact, I'd go so far to say that, under the circumstances, I'm just as glad you *weren't* in their way when they decided to move her. Who knows what they would have done to you?"

"I'm not as helpless as everyone thinks," she said stiffly. She sighed and lowered her eyes. "But you're probably right."

Which wasn't to say that I *was* right, or that she believed I was right, or that any of my soothing logic was making her feel better. "Regardless, what's past is past," I said. "We need to focus on finding her and getting her back."

"Right." Bayta took a deep breath. "What do you want me to do?"

"Go back to our room and start figuring out who Blue One is," I told her. "If and when you finish with that, start making a list of all medical facilities in this part of Proteus—yes, I know there are a lot of them, but we have to start somewhere. *Logra* Emikai, would you escort her back to the room?"

"Of course," Emikai said, his voice dark and grim. His contract to keep Terese safe had ended, too, but that clearly wasn't making any more difference to him than it was to me. "What will you do?"

I looked over at the Jumpsuits poring over their controls in front of their fancy monitor banks. Fat lot of good any of it, or any of them, had done us. "I'm going to have a word with my attorney," I said. "Watch yourselves. Both of you."

Minnario was understandably surprised to see me. [I thought you would be at least another hour,] he said, wiping his mouth with a cloth as he backed his chair out of the doorway to let me in. [Forgive me—I'd just brought in my dinner.]

"No problem," I assured him, looking over at the couch. Blue One didn't seem to have moved. "You left him alone?"

[The restaurants don't deliver,] he reminded me. [But I checked his restraints before I left, and I was gone less than fifteen minutes. May I offer you something?]

"No, thank you," I said, walking over to the couch and reaching around behind the Filly. The quick-locks were still securely in place. "Please go ahead with your meal," I added as I pulled over the computer desk chair and sat down facing the prisoner. "Just pretend I'm not here."

Among the Human diplomats I'd escorted during my early days in Westali, Nemuti were considered fairly low on the list of desirable dinner companions. The species in general tended to chomp their food, and their truncated-cone-shaped mouths added an odd echo effect to the sound of their mastication. The additional distortion of Minnario's mouth, I quickly discovered, greatly enhanced the overall effect.

Back on the super-express, the Modhran mind segment I'd dealt with had mentioned that, as far as he knew, Minnario always took his meals alone. Now I knew why.

He'd finished his main meal and was starting on his dessert cheese when Bayta finally called.

"I can't get a match on Blue One's face with anyone aboard the station," she said tightly. "Staff, visitors, clients—no one. As far as the main computer is concerned, he simply doesn't exist."

"Terrific," I growled. "Is Emikai there with you?"

"No, he left as soon as we reached the room," she said. "He said there were some things he had to do."

"You've double-locked the door, though, right?" I asked. "Blue One had a passkey, remember. Some of the others might have them, too."

"Double-locked, one of the dining chairs is pressed against it to make it harder to slide, and Ty's lying down beside it," she assured me.

Clearly, my native paranoia had started rubbing off on her. Aboard Proteus, that was increasingly looking like a good thing. "And you've been through all the records?"

"Everything I can find," she said. "Do you want me to keep digging?"

"Probably no point," I said. "But there are bound to be areas of the computer you haven't been able to access. Maybe we'll call Emikai in later and see if his cop training included system hacking."

"You think it might?"

"Mine did," I reminded her. "Besides, he did say earlier that even enforcement officers sometimes have to improvise. Go ahead and get started on that listing of nearby medical areas."

"All right," she said. "Is he awake yet?"

I looked at Blue One. His eyes were still closed, his face still slack. From all outward appearances he seemed to still be in the depths of dreamland.

All appearances but one. His breathing, while still slow, was definitely faster and stronger than it had been when I'd first begun my vigil. "Actually, he just woke up," I said. "I'll talk to you later."

I keyed off the comm and reached out a foot to nudge Blue One in his side. "Come on, look alive," I said. "I haven't got all night."

For a moment he didn't move. I was picking out a spot for my next kick, a harder one this time, when he opened his eyes. "Interesting, that last conversation," he said. "Have you misplaced someone?"

"Only temporarily," I said. "You want to tell me what you know about it? Or do I have to beat it out of you?"

He favored me with another of his thin, evil smiles. "Address me by name," he said.

"Sure," I said. "What name would you like me to use?"

"By my name," he repeated. "Or this conversation is ended."

"I don't know your name."

"A pity," he said, and closed his eyes again.

I felt my lip twitch. In other words, he wanted to know how much I actually knew. "How about *Shonkla-raa*?" I asked. "That close enough?"

He opened his eyes again, his blaze darkening. "So we were right," he said quietly. "You did indeed examine *Asantra* Muzzfor's papers aboard the Quadrail." He cocked his head. "And if he didn't destroy them, it follows that everything else you told us concerning his death was a lie."

"Most of it," I agreed. "The truth is that he attacked me after the murder investigation was over. Without warning or provocation, of course."

"And?"

I looked him squarely in the eye. "And during the fight I killed him."

His blaze darkened even farther. "Impossible," he said flatly.

"I'm sure you'd like to think so," I said. "But it might just be that you don't know as much about me as you think you do." I leaned back deliberately in my chair. "You ever hear of the mystery of Quadrail 219117?"

"The outbound train from Homshil to the Bellidosh

Estates-General," he said. "The one that . . ." He trailed off, an odd expression suddenly on his face.

"The one that disappeared a couple of years back," I finished for him. "Vanished from the tracks into thin air with everyone aboard and was never heard from again. You want to know what really happened to it?"

His eyes were locked on me. "Tell me."

"One of the mind segments of your friend the Modhri had decided I had information he didn't want me to have," I said. "He'd also brought some coral aboard the train, which he used to infect the rest of the passengers. He figured a trainful of walkers ought to be more than enough to take me down."

I paused. "And?" Blue One asked.

"It wasn't," I said. "I killed him."

He smiled again. But this time it was forced and uncertain. "*All* of him," he said.

"Every last bit of him," I confirmed. It hadn't been nearly that easy, of course, any more than it had been easy to take down *Asantra* Muzzfor. And I'd had a lot of help in both situations.

But Blue One didn't know that. And he wasn't going to. "There's a reason the Spiders hired me, Shonkla-raa," I continued. "I'm good at what I do. And if I don't get some answers about Terese German, I'll probably have to kill a lot more people. Starting with you."

For a dozen heartbeats he remained silent. Across the room in the dining area, Minnario had stopped chomping, and even Doug at my feet seemed to be listening in anticipation. "I'm not afraid of you," Blue One said at last. "But I also have no desire to see blood flow in the corridors of *Kuzyatru* Station."

"A wise decision," I said, "especially since you're probably trying as hard to operate under the radar as I am. Where is she?"

"I don't know," Blue One said. "Moving her wasn't part of the plan. I can only assume it was done in response to this." He twitched his shackled arms. "If you'd care to release me, I could go ask them."

"Maybe later," I said. "Fine—let's assume you really don't know where she is. Where *might* she be?"

He snorted. "What, aboard *Kuzyatru* Station?"

"I'm not talking about the whole station," I said. "I'm talking about the limited number of ratholes you and your limited number of fellow Shonkla-raa have set aside for yourselves."

He smiled again. "You delude yourself, Compton. There are far more of us than you can possibly imagine."

"And they'll be jackbooting their way down the corridors to Director *Usantra* Nstroo's office any time now," I said. "Heard it before. I want a list of those boltholes."

He shook his head. "A waste of time. She's a medical patient in poor condition, which means they'll have taken her to another medical facility."

"That makes sense," I said, watching him closely. "Except that she wouldn't be in poor condition if you hadn't been dosing her with sickness juice. Did I mention we'd found your gimmicked hypos?"

His face changed, just enough to show I'd hit a nerve with that one. "Did you think we weren't expecting you to?"

"Actually, yes, I do think that," I said. "Seems like a lot of wasted effort, though. Why not just have Dr. Aronobal spike Ms. German's normal meds? Aronobal *is* on your team, isn't she?"

He hesitated, then shrugged. "I suppose there's no point in denying it. Yes, she was our agent looking for likely prospects on Earth. She heard about Ms. German's condition and arranged for her transport here."

"And the rest of the Humans, the ones in Building Twelve?" I asked. "Did Aronobal bring them in, too?"

Again, his expression shifted subtly. "You're well informed, Compton," he said. "I was told you hadn't been closer to Building Twelve than the spot where I left Tech Yleli's body."

A cold feeling settled around my heart. I'd tentatively tagged Blue One as Yleli's killer, but I'd never had any actual proof of that. Now I had a confession. "You're right, I didn't," I said, managing to keep my voice as casual as his. "Just observation plus simple logic. Once I knew *Usantra* Wandek was lying about the buildings being malleable, it followed that no one would put up a whole dome's worth of Human buildings unless he also had a whole dome's worth of Human patients to put there. I gather from the décor that most of them were taken from the EuroUnion?"

"Many were, yes," Blue One agreed calmly. "A few were from other places on your worlds."

My coldness at Blue One's confession of murder dissolved into the warmth of anger. I'd already deduced that the Shonkla-raa had been taking Humans like Terese out of the Terran Confederation. But to have it so casually confirmed, as if Earth was nothing more than their own private butterfly preserve, was just plain galling. "Why?" I demanded.

"Do you really want me to tell you here?" he countered. His eyes flicked over my shoulder to Minnario. "When we win this field of battle, everyone who knows will have to die."

I grimaced. That threat probably wasn't a bluff, either. My neck was already in the Shonkla-raa's noose; there was no point in putting Minnario's in there with it. "Minnario, turn off your transcriber for a minute," I said. "Our Filly friend here and I have something we need to discuss in private."

[Are you sure that's wise?] Minnario asked, a bit uncertainly.

"No, but I'm sure it's necessary," I said. "I'll let you know when you can turn it back on."

I heard the faint click of a switch. [It's off,] he said.

Blue One eyed him another moment, then shifted his

gaze back to me. "How much do you know about the original Shonkla-raa?"

"Enough," I said. "They ruled the galaxy for a thousand years before being defeated and slaughtered by their slaves. There's a moral in there somewhere."

"Fables and morals are for inferiors," the other said contemptuously. "Did it ever occur to you to wonder why Earth wasn't included in their empire?"

I frowned. Actually, somehow, it hadn't. It was a damn good question, too. "I'm sure you have an answer," I said.

"That's just it: we don't know," he said, his blaze darkening. "There are many theories: diseases that frightened the Shonkla-raa away, oppressive climatic or cultural factors, your uselessness as slaves, or simply that there was nothing in your system they couldn't get more efficiently elsewhere. But it's something we need to find out before we set out on our road to conquest." He smiled suddenly. "I'm sorry: on our *final* road to conquest."

"No need to apologize," I assured him. "We've had plenty of would-be conquerors of our own who talked about how long their reigns would last. It's a typical delusion with megalomaniacs."

"You think we will fail?" he asked, his voice rich with arrogance and challenge.

"Pretty sure," I said. "Bunny trails over; back to Terese German. Do I get that list of bolt-holes, or do I have to show off my expertise in the fine art of stimulating Filly nerve junctions?"

He sighed. "No need," he said. "But it will do you no—"

And with a soft snap of plastic he yanked his formerly secured arms from behind his back and shoved off the couch, his hands reaching for my throat.

They'd made it halfway to their target when I snapped my right foot up and slammed my heel hard into his chest.

With a strangled *whoof* the air went out of him, the impact of the blow killing his momentum and sending him tumbling to the floor, his eyes wide with pain and fury. I kicked him again, just to be sure, then stood up and stepped over to the computer desk and the neat stack of quick-locks I'd left there.

[What is it?] Minnario gasped, and I felt the movement of air as he hurriedly brought his chair up behind me. [What happened?]

"Our clever friend gnawed through his ropes," I said, selecting three of the quick-locks and returning warily to Blue One's side. The caution was unnecessary—his whole upper torso must have felt wrapped in cotton right now, his arms pretty well useless. And of course his legs were still securely tied together. He wasn't going to be starting any more fights for a while, and he certainly wasn't going to be winning any. "More precisely, he used his nails to dig through parts of his quick-lock," I continued. "I felt the notches when I checked it after I came in."

[And you didn't immediately fix it?] Minnario said, his tone somewhere between incredulous and livid. [You risked both our lives?]

"It wasn't that much of a risk," I assured him as I got Blue One's wrists behind his back again and tightened a fresh quick-lock around them. "With his legs still useless he would have had to take me down in that first attack, and I was pretty sure he couldn't."

[But for what end?] Minnario persisted. [What did it gain you?]

"Information," I said. Pushing the backs of Blue One's hands together, I looped another quick-lock around his palms, and then another around his upper fingers, immobilizing all his nails where they couldn't reach any of the restraints. "People get careless when they think they're in control. They also talk too much." I raised my eyebrows. "Like, for instance, confessing to Tech Yleli's murder."

"It will never be believed," Blue One spat. "The word of two aliens in collusion, against that of a *santra* of the Filiaelian Assembly? No court would accept that without physical evidence."

"That's okay—physical evidence is the next thing on our scavenger-hunt list," I said. "See, Minnario? We know now that he's a *santra*, too. Okay, he's ready to be put back to bed. Can you give me a hand?"

Minnario moved his chair close to Blue One's other side, and between us we got the Filly back up onto the couch. "All nice and comfy again?" I asked as I looked down at him.

"I will kill you, Compton," he said quietly, gazing up at me with a coldness that even the Modhran walkers I'd faced over the years hadn't matched. "When the time comes I will personally end your life."

"Interestingly enough, the Modhran mind segment on Quadrail 219117 said the same thing," I told him. "Minnario, where'd you put the hypo and sleep juice?"

[Here,] Minnario said, pulling the hypo gingerly from his chair pouch and handing it to me. [It's already loaded.]

"Thanks," I said. I confirmed it was the amount Emikai had specified and slipped the needle into Blue One's arm. "Anything else you'd like to say?" I invited.

"I'll also kill your friend Bayta," he said. "You will be there to watch it happen."

"Got it," I said, and pressed my thumb on the plunger. "Pleasant dreams."

Once again, the stuff worked its magic with gratifying speed. Within a minute, Blue One's breathing had slowed back down again. "Okay," I said, handing the hypo back to Minnario. "It looks like he's got a slightly better metabolism than the average Filly, so you'd better not count on him getting a full six hours per dose."

[I understand,] he said. [I'll give him another dose in five hours.]

"Thanks," I said. "Unless you want me to come back and do it."

[I can manage.] He smiled self-consciously. [For all of a lawyer's high-sounding talk of searching out the truth while protecting those in need, I have to say that I've never before felt so much like I was actually doing that. It's frightening, but curiously refreshing.]

"I'm glad you're having fun," I said, deciding not to ruin his evening by mentioning how quickly that glow of satisfaction faded once you'd actually been in the field for a while. "Call me right away if he looks to be waking up. Or if anything else odd happens."

[Such as someone attempting to break down my door?] he inquired with a bland smile.

I grimaced. "Something like that."

The smile faded. [A foolish jest,] he apologized. [My apologies.]

"That's all right," I said. "If it helps any, at the end of the day they're probably not going to bother with you."

[I know,] he said soberly. [You and Bayta are their real targets. That's why I apologized.]

"Don't count us out yet," I said. "We've been in tight scrapes before. By the way, you mind telling me what you and Emikai discussed after we left earlier?"

Minnario shrugged. [Not very much, as it turned out,] he said. [*Logra* Emikai wished to know what I knew about you and Bayta.] He gave me a half smile tinged with embarrassment. [Which was also what I wished to know from him. As it happened, neither of us knew much more than the other.]

"I've always said we have no secrets from our friends," I said dryly. Which wasn't even close to being true, of course. "Anyway, get some rest. And be sure to double-lock the door behind me."

TWELVE :

The corridors were quiet as Doug and I headed back toward the medical dome. Not just quiet, in fact, but completely deserted. I wondered about that until a check of my watch reminded me that it was the Proteus dinner hour, which probably explained why no one was out and about. It also explained why my stomach was growling.

Which was fine with me. The quiet was conducive to thought, and between Yleli's murder, Terese's disappearance, and Blue One's defiant stubbornness I had a lot to think about.

I had reached the traffic corridor and was working my way leftward across the glideway's variable-speed fluid toward the fast track when Doug, who had decided to walk in front of me for once, suddenly turned his head and looked behind us.

An unpleasant tingle ran up my back. The last time Doug had reacted like that, it had been because a pair of Fillies were doing their best to sneak up on me. It seemed reasonable to assume that the same watchdog behavior might portend the same type of attack.

I'd been expecting some kind of Shonkla-raa reaction to Blue One's disappearance. This could be it.

Mirrored walls would have been handy, but Proteus's interior decorator had unfortunately missed out on that one. I continued toward the fast track as if nothing was happening, keeping my eyes forward, feeling my back muscles tightening in anticipation of a hand, a fist, or a knife. Blue One had said that I was worth more alive than dead, but I hadn't believed him then and I certainly wasn't going to count on it now.

We were one step away from the fast edge when I made my move. Before Doug could shift over onto the fast track I stepped onto it myself, ran three quick steps forward to pass him, and finally stopped and allowed him to move over behind me.

And with my watchdog now between me and whatever was back there, I finally turned around.

He was striding silently toward me along the fast track, his oversized throat bulging through the neck of his tunic, his hands stiffened into Shonkla-raa knives, an unholy glitter of anticipation in his eye. A flicker of something crossed his face as I turned to face him—surprise or disappointment, I couldn't tell which—but he didn't even break stride.

"Hello, there," I called pleasantly to him. "I'm new in town. Can you recommend a good restaurant?"

He didn't answer, but merely continued walking toward me. I watched his face, and as he approached Doug I saw his dilemma suddenly dawn on him.

He couldn't simply step around Doug to come at me, because moving to his right would put him in a slower section of the glideway, requiring him to break into a jog just to stay even or an actual run if he wanted to catch up with me. I had no doubt he could do either, but having to run to catch up to an opponent who was standing still put an attacker at a definite disadvantage. He could look as eager as he wanted to about the upcoming fight, but he had to be thinking at least a little about the fact that Blue One had also been sent to take me down and hadn't been heard from since.

Which really left him only two options. He could pick up Doug and physically move him out of his way, which would leave him even more vulnerable during the brief period when his hands were occupied, or he could do what Blue One had done outside Yleli's apartment and simply jump over the animal.

It took him maybe half a second to run through the analysis and come to a decision, and as he stepped up to Doug's tail he bent his knees and leaped.

Unfortunately for him, I'd already done the analysis

myself and had planned my response. Even as he arced over Doug's back, I threw myself to the side onto the mid-speed section of the glideway.

I hit the fluid with a thud and a brief skid as the glideway damped out the extra inertia I'd brought with me from the fast track. My shoulder had barely slowed to that speed when the faster track at my feet grabbed my legs and spun me ninety degrees around, leaving me lined up along the section that my shoulder had landed on, feet forward with my head to the rear. Rolling onto my back, I shoved awkwardly against the different-speed tracks on either side of me and pushed myself back to vertical.

In an ideal world, my maneuver would have taken the Shonkla-raa completely by surprise, and he would still be standing on the fast track where his leap had put him, gazing stupidly back at me as he and Doug faded off into the sunset. But it wasn't an ideal world, and the Shonkla-raa was anything but stupid. By the time I was back on my feet he had already picked his way across the glideway to the slower track just to my right and was waiting there patiently for me to catch up to him again.

And suddenly I was in a dilemma of my own. Staying where I was would bring me within range of those hands in probably twenty seconds or less. I could try going to my right, passing his track and getting onto an even slower section of the glideway. But he could easily match that maneuver, which meant all I would accomplish would be to delay the inevitable.

Which left me just one other choice. Stepping to my left, I headed back toward the fast track, moving as quickly as I could without losing my balance. If I could get to the higher speed faster than he could, I might be able to bypass him while he was still out of striking distance.

But again he'd already duplicated my analysis and

conclusion. Even as I made my move he was matching it, step for step, making sure he stayed just to my slow side where the glideway would bring me straight to him. I tried reversing direction, hoping to buy myself a little time. But again, he was right on top of it, easily matching my every move.

Behind him, I caught sight of Doug working his four-footed way across the glideway onto the slower tracks, for once sensing trouble before it actually happened. If I didn't do something fast I would probably end up fighting both him and the Shonkla-raa at the same time.

I waited until I was almost within the Shonkla-raa's reach. Then, shoving off the glideway, I again threw myself onto my side to my right, trying to get as far into the glideway's slow section as I could. The Filly was right on top of it, making an easy leap the same distance and landing directly in front of the spot where my shoulder landed.

Only I had thrown myself onto my side, whereas he'd chosen to remain vertical, which meant that his feet were suddenly going a slower speed than the rest of his body. He staggered violently as Newton's Laws kicked in, and he was forced to throw one foot behind him to keep himself from falling flat onto his back. He won the battle with momentum and straightened up again—

Just as my legs, again caught by the glideway's speed gradient, swung around in a ninety-degree arc and kicked his feet completely out from under him.

He went down with a bellow, slamming onto the glideway and scrambling for purchase even as the same forces that had spun my legs into him now also turned him around. I didn't wait to see how he handled his predicament, but began rolling sideways as quickly as I could toward the slow edge. If I could get to the unmoving part of the corridor, cross it, and make it onto the glideway going the other direction, I might be able to put enough distance between us to escape.

I reached the edge of the glideway and rolled onto solid ground. Giving myself one final half-roll onto my stomach, I started to push myself back to my feet.

Only to slam flat onto the deck again as Doug leaped onto my back, growling straight into my ear.

I don't know much more of a reprimand for my uncivil behavior the watchdog had planned to deliver once he had me down. But whatever it was, it was instantly preempted as his growl turned into a startled yip and he toppled sideways off me, a trio of bright red balls tied together by red cords suddenly appearing across his side, belly, and back.

I leaped to my feet, catching sight of a second Filly as he shot past on the fast edge of the glideway, and ducked as a second spinning flash of red shot just over my head. It was some kind of bola weapon, I saw now, with the added bonus of an adhesive to make sure that once the target was down he stayed that way. The newcomer was already heading away toward the slow edge of the glideway, gazing balefully back at me as he readied a third bola. Farther ahead down the corridor, I could see that my first opponent was back on his feet and also moving toward the slow edge.

So now it was two against one. And with Doug tangled up in his bola, he wasn't going to be available for me to use as a shield or throwing weapon unless I picked him up and carried him with me.

And then I caught sight of a figure approaching on the other glideway. He was too far away for me to tell whether he had a Shonkla-raa throat, but from his stiff posture and air of alertness I suspected he wasn't just some random citizen returning from dinner.

Suddenly, it wasn't two against one, but three.

And now I was well and truly trapped. If I did nothing, the third Filly would shoot past me, step onto the unmoving part of the corridor, and I would be bracketed. If I ran, no matter which glideway I chose, there would be an opponent on my tail within seconds.

Better to make a bad choice, I decided, than to lose by default. Clenching my teeth, I stepped back onto my original glideway and headed as quickly as I could toward the fast edge. So far only one of the Shonkla-raa had demonstrated he was carrying any weapons, and I would rather be facing him when he threw his next bola than have my back to him.

But once again, the Shonkla-raa had thought things through. The one with the bolas had already stopped moving toward the corridor; but instead of attempting to close the distance to me he was merely standing there on his section of glideway, waiting for me to pass him by on my faster section.

At which point, I realized, I would be only about half a glideway's width away from him. Even with the speed differential, I would be pretty damn impossible to miss.

But there was nothing I could do, nowhere I could go. I crouched down, making myself as small a target as I could, angling my arms into defensive combat positions in front of me. If I could catch the bola on my arms and torso and keep it away from my legs I would at least still have the theoretical option of running. I swept to and past him, and he raised the bola to throw.

And abruptly jolted forward as something slammed hard into his back. Even as he tried to regain his balance, a second object slammed into him, jarring the bola loose from his hand and sending him flailing forward to crash face-first onto the glideway.

I looked across at the other glideway. While my full attention had been on the Shonkla-raa with the bola, the Filly approaching from the other direction had closed the distance between us and stepped off onto the corridor floor.

Only it wasn't a third Shonkla-raa, as I'd thought.

It was Emikai.

Even as my brain registered that fact, he swiveled

around, brought the gun in his hand to bear on the remaining Shonkla-raa, and fired.

But his target was already in motion, diving toward the glideway's fast end and taking Emikai's pancake-sized projectile in a glancing blow off his shoulder instead of getting it full-force against his torso. The pancake ricocheted off the wall, did another bounce off the ceiling, and went wobbling off somewhere behind me. The Shonkla-raa himself hit the glideway chest-first, lay there just long enough for the speed gradient to spin him around and align him along the glideway the way it had already done twice to me, then rolled his way quickly over to the fast track. The other Filly, the one Emikai had first shot, had also managed to get himself to the same part of the glideway and was following his comrade as fast as it could take him.

"Compton!" Emikai called. "Let them go."

I didn't need any persuasion. I crossed the glideway, watching as the two prone Fillies disappeared off into the distance, and stepped off.

Emikai hurried up beside me. "Are you all right?" he asked.

"I'm fine," I assured him. "Thanks for the assist." I looked down at the weapon in his hand, short-barreled but with a long grip and an extended magazine. "Nice toy. What does it fire?"

"They are called expanders," he said. "Expanding impact disks, non-lethal but with a high degree of stopping power."

"A beanbag gun," I said, nodding. "We use them sometimes in the Confederation. I usually prefer snoozers—you can get a higher magazine count with them. But of course they don't have any stopping power to speak of. I don't suppose there's any chance I can persuade Captain Lyarrom to issue me one?"

"I doubt it," Emikai said. "I only have one myself because I have been temporarily reinstated as an enforcement officer aboard *Kuzyatru* Station."

I felt my eyebrows creeping up my forehead. "Congratulations," I said. "Someone recognized your skill and merit?"

"Someone recognized the anomalies in the evacuation drill coverage," Emikai corrected, his voice going grim. "This has them seriously concerned."

"No doubt," I agreed, wondering what the hell he was talking about. "Am I supposed to know what that means?"

"Exactly my point." Emikai looked over his shoulder. "But come—I believe your *msikai-dorosli* is going to need our assistance."

I'd almost forgotten about Doug. I turned to see him limping toward us on three legs, his fourth partially tied to his belly by the balls and cords still glued to him. "So he is," I agreed, starting toward him. "Tell me about this evacuation drill."

"They are safety drills that are scheduled at irregular intervals, each usually involving a single sector or subsector," Emikai explained as he fell into step beside me. "They are supposed to be announced in every public area within the drill region, with a duplicate message sent to each comm within the area."

"Which area was involved?"

"Subsector 25-F-4, extending from the medical dome outward to the edge of the sector and for five corridors to either side of this one." He looked at me. "The area we are currently in."

I stared at him, a creepy feeling running through me. "My comm never went off," I said. "Neither did Minnario's."

"Nor was it announced in this corridor," Emikai said, his voice and blaze going dark. "Or in the side corridor leading to Attorney Minnario's quarters. That was the discovery that led me to request a weapon and come looking for you."

"I'm very glad you did, too," I said. "How many

comms besides Minnario's and mine were left out of the general announcement?"

Emikai sighed. "As best as could be established, none."

No wonder I'd had the whole place to myself. "Cute. Seems a little like overkill, but still cute. Any idea how they pulled it off?"

"We know some of it," Emikai said. "The order for such drills comes from the office of the sector overseer. This one seemed to follow the proper protocol, which is why it was passed and activated."

"So they know how it's supposed to be done," I concluded. "That tells us they're either highly placed locals, or else have a connection to highly placed locals. What gave away the show?"

"As it happened, I was working a deep-level analysis at the time and my search picked up an anomaly," Emikai said. "I investigated, and discovered that instead of originating in the overseer's office, the message had merely been echoed from that site." He looked sideways at me. "It had originated from the computer in the late Tech Yleli's apartment."

"So they have a computer whiz on their team," I said thoughtfully. "Bayta told me earlier that the station computer hadn't been able to identify our friend Blue One. Now we know why. Either somebody slipped him into the station without the computer noticing, or else scrubbed him out once he was in."

"An unpleasant and ominous ability, indeed," Emikai mused.

"Yeah," I grunted. "Tell me about it."

We reached Doug and crouched down beside him. "What are these things, anyway?" I asked as I gave one of the red balls an experimental tug. It seemed to be glued solidly to both his feathery belly fur and his pineapple back. "I'd think something like this wouldn't be welcome here."

"The *kristic* is a weapon for hunting small game," Emikai said. "Upon sharp impact the balls secrete a strong adhesive through micropores. And they are most definitely *not* welcome aboard. They are forbidden, in fact."

"So whoever it is who sneaks people aboard Proteus also likes playing with cargo manifests," I said. "Is there any way to get the things off him?"

"The security nexus will have a solvent," Emikai said, pulling out his multitool and popping out a knife blade. "Cutting the cords should enable him to walk properly."

"Good idea," I said. "I'd rather not have to carry him."

"Yes." Emikai set to work cutting through the cords. "I have a question. One which you may not like."

"I get those all the time," I assured him. "Go ahead."

"How well do you truly know your assistant Bayta?"

"Extremely well," I said, frowning. "Why?"

"I told you I was working on a deep-level analysis when the drill order came through," he said. "I was attempting to backtrack the message you told me appeared on your computer, the one that instructed you to go to the dome just prior to Tech Yleli's murder."

"What did you find?"

"That there is no record of you having received any such message," he said. "Not through the *Kuzyatru* Station system, or from any computer aboard."

"Which just means our friends are better at this stuff than I thought."

"That is one possibility." Emikai cut through one of the cords and started working on the next one. "There is another."

"That I'm lying?"

"That the message did not travel through the system because it originated on your computer."

I snorted. "Right," I said. "Doug sent it. Or maybe Ty—he's the more literary of the two."

"Or Bayta did."

I shook my head. "Not a chance."

"Are you sure?"

I opened my mouth to tell him that of course I was.

Only I wasn't. There was no way I could be. Not with all the battles and other contact we'd had with the Modhri since this whole thing began. Certainly not with him lurking somewhere aboard Proteus. There was always the possibility, however small, that he'd gotten to her.

Or that he'd gotten to me.

And if there was a Modhran colony inside me, then it was all over. Any thought I had, any conclusion I came to, any plan I hatched—I would never know whether any of it was truly real, or pure illusion. I would be nothing but a puppet dancing on the Modhri's strings, carefully and cleverly rationalizing every order he gave me, no better than any of his thousands or millions of other walkers.

No better, and a whole lot worse. Because unlike all those other walkers, I was in a position of authority and power unlike anything the Modhri had ever had before. I was in contact with Bayta, agent of the Chahwyn, and through her with the Spiders and the Chahwyn themselves. My words and actions could fatally affect the Chahwyn efforts against not only the Modhri but also his Shonkla-raa masters. Like it or not, I was a pivot point around which the fate of the galaxy teetered.

And then, the dry ice that had formed in my veins turned to liquid nitrogen. Because there was another, even more horrifying possibility.

What if the Modhri wasn't involved in this at all? What if it was Bayta's other half, the Chahwyn symbiotically encased within her? What if the defender Spiders aboard the super-express had reported back on my flagrant breaking of Quadrail rules, and the Chahwyn had decided I'd become a loose cannon that needed to be dealt with? What if they'd decided it was time that they took over the operation personally?

What if they'd decided to start with Bayta?

I looked sideways at Emikai's profile. The Modhri, I knew, could take direct control over his walkers' bodies without their permission or knowledge. Could the Chahwyn inside Bayta do the same?

Or was such a thing even possible? The way Bayta described it, her Human and Chahwyn halves were in close, permanent, conscious contact. But now that I thought about it, I realized that my understanding of their relationship was built mostly on my own assumptions.

I shook my head, a short, violent, brain-clearing movement. No. Bayta was my ally, and my friend. She wouldn't betray me that way. Not unless she herself had also been betrayed.

Meanwhile, Emikai was still waiting for an answer. "No," I said as firmly as I could. "She'd never do something like that."

Emikai tilted his head slightly. "I know you would prefer to think not."

"It's not a preference, it's simple logic," I insisted. "What reason could she possibly have had to do that? To give me a reason to go over to the dome in the middle of the night? Ridiculous. I'm not a prisoner—I don't need an excuse or reason to leave my quarters."

"I make no suggestion as to reasons or motivations." Emikai nodded at Doug. "But do you not also find it curious that one of the two *msikai-dorosli* assigned to you by *Chinzro* Hchchu has chosen to remain instead with Bayta?"

I grimaced. So Emikai had picked up on that, too. And if he had, had Hchchu or the Shonkla-raa? If so, what had they made of it? "What makes you think Hchchu *didn't* assign us one each?" I countered.

"Did he?"

"I'm actually not sure," I said. "I was concentrating on other things at the time and wasn't paying attention to the nuances of his words. Even though I'm the one under indictment, maybe he figured we both needed watching."

"Perhaps," Emikai said. "But surely you noticed that both *msikai-dorosli* stayed close to your side during the preliminary hearing, when *Chinzro* Hchchu was present. Clearly, *they* understood that they were both supposed to watch you."

"Yes, I noticed that," I conceded. "I assumed it was just the grandeur of the setting and circumstances that had them both sticking with me at the time."

"Perhaps," Emikai said. "But turn that thought around. Perhaps it is at other times, not in *Chinzro* Hchchu's presence, that they sense your companion needs to be watched."

"Even if they were ordered to do something else?"

He shrugged. "It is known that the lower animals sometimes have senses and instincts beyond those of us who are fully sentient. Those senses can allow them to perceive and understand things we ourselves cannot."

Like when Bayta stopped being Bayta and became a Modhri? Or a Chahwyn? "I'll think about it," I said. "You about done there?"

The last cord snapped. "Yes," Emikai said, putting away the multitool. "Do we go to the nexus?"

"Yes," I said, straightening up and looking around the deserted corridor. Round two was over. I wondered what the Shonkla-raa had in mind for round three. "Let's get the hell out of here."

I called Bayta on our way, confirmed she was still safely in our room, gave her a thumbnail of what had happened, and told her to stay put.

The Jumpsuits in the security nexus seemed decidedly annoyed that someone had smuggled a *kristic* aboard, and made all the usual police-type noises about looking into it, bringing the perpetrators of my assault to justice, etc. I'd made plenty of the same noises during my time with Westali, and I knew not to expect much to come out of it. Especially since they also had to admit they'd still made no progress in locating Terese.

I also wasn't surprised that they turned down my request for a gun.

Still, they were efficient enough about getting the *kristic* glue balls off Doug. An hour after arriving at the nexus we finally headed out, with Emikai insisting on escorting me back to my quarters. We stopped by one of the restaurants on our way to pick up some dinner, and at long last I was finally home.

"Do not forget the court proceedings at ten tomorrow," Emikai reminded me as Bayta undid the inner lock and opened the door. "I will be here an hour before that time to escort you."

"Better make it an hour and a half," I said. "Minnario said we lost points last time by being the tail end of the parade."

"An hour and a half it will be." Emikai eyed me. "Until then, I suggest you remain here."

"With the door double-locked," I agreed. "Don't worry, I've had more than enough excitement for one day. Farewell, and thank you again."

"Farewell." Nodding to each of us, he turned and strode down the hallway, his gun bouncing at his hip.

I stepped inside, waited for Doug to pad his way in behind me, then closed the door and double-locked it. "I hope you're hungry for Shorshian beef and rice squares with imported Human chili sauce," I said as I crossed the room toward the dining area. Ty, I noted, was already sacked out on the bed in his usual spot by the headboard, apparently completely unaware of the ordeal his buddy had been through this evening. Briefly, I wondered if the animals were intelligent enough to share that kind of information, and whether Doug would bother, and whether Ty would care.

"Never mind the food," Bayta said, taking my arm in a firm and very worried grip. "How are *you*?"

"They never laid a hand on me," I said. "That's actually true, by the way. Which isn't to say they didn't try."

For a long moment Bayta gazed into my eyes, her face drawn and pale and tense. Then, reluctantly, she let go of my arm and sank down into one of the dining table chairs. "What are we going to do, Frank?" she asked. "I've never felt—how do I explain it? Pulled in so many directions at the same time."

"Our Shonkla-raa friends have definitely been busy little bees," I agreed, sitting down across from her. "And you're right, one way or the other we're being chased all over the countryside." I opened up the bag. "Maybe it's time we cut through some of the ground clutter."

"What do you mean?"

"I think I know how I can end this stupid trial once and for all," I told her. "Or at least get it postponed to the point where we can effectively cross it off our list of things to do. Once that's done, we can concentrate on turning Proteus upside down until we find Terese."

Bayta shivered. "If she's still even aboard the station. Or if she's still . . ."

"She's alive, and she's aboard," I said firmly. "They want her baby, remember?"

"They want *him* alive," Bayta murmured. "They may not care about her."

"At this point, the simplest and safest life-support system for Terese's baby is Terese," I said. "Anyway, there's no point in thinking or worrying about any other possibilities, so we won't. Understand?"

Bayta took a deep breath. "You're right," she said, some of the frustration fading from her voice as the calm, cool part of her took over again. "And we *will* find her."

"That's the spirit," I said approvingly as I laid out the bowls and utensils and the packages the restaurant had packed. "But right now, it's time to eat. Can't rescue a maiden in distress on an empty stomach, you know. Especially one who isn't very keen on being rescued."

"She appreciates us more than she lets on," Bayta said quietly. "I think Dr. Aronobal is right. She's been alone for a long time."

Several snide comments flashed across my mind, most of them revolving around how a lot of that might well be Terese's own personality. But I left them unsaid. Bayta wasn't in the mood.

Besides, she could be right. She'd spent more time with Terese than I had, after all. "Well, she's not going to be alone much longer," I said instead. "Motherhood has a way of doing that. Eat up, and then I for one am turning in. It's been a long, rich day."

"Especially for you." Bayta started spooning rice squares into one of the bowls. "What about Blue One?"

"What about him?"

"I was wondering about tomorrow morning," she said. "If we're all going to be in court—you, me, *Logra* Emikai, and Minnario—there'll be no one available to watch him."

"True," I said. "Unfortunately, there's not much we can do about that. We'll just have to double-dose him in the morning and hope for the best."

"What if the Shonkla-raa search all of our quarters while we're out?" she persisted. "There isn't anywhere in any of these rooms where you could hide an unconscious body for very long."

"Sure there is," I said, watching her closely out of the corner of my eye as I spooned some of the rice squares into my bowl. "We'll just stuff him back in the file cabinet. No reason why the Shonkla-raa would suspect that it was full of Filly instead of files."

Only I knew that they'd already been in Yleli's apartment, when they'd sent that fake evacuation drill message. I knew they'd seen the file drawers we'd left behind and wouldn't be fooled for a minute by a supposedly full file cabinet in Minnario's room. If Bayta had been infected by the Modhri and knew about the Shonkla-raa's computer scam, and if I was very lucky, she might show some reaction to my nonsensical argument.

But she didn't, at least not in any way that I could detect. "I suppose that'll work," she said, a bit doubtfully as she picked up her fork. "Can Minnario lift him all by himself?"

"Shouldn't be a problem," I said. "It's only his legs that don't work. His upper body's strong enough. And he can always use a couple of his chair's thrusters if he needs help."

"I suppose." Bayta hesitated. "Do you think Blue One knows where Terese is?"

I shrugged. "He says he doesn't, but I'm not ready to believe him. Tomorrow, right after the hearing, we'll see about finding out for sure."

Bayta shivered. "That sounds . . . not very pleasant."

"It won't be," I agreed grimly. "You don't have to watch if you don't want to."

"Yes, I do," she said. Her expression was still disturbed, but her voice was firm enough. "I'll be there."

We ate our dinner mostly in silence. Afterward, as promised, I got ready for bed. Bayta stayed up a while longer, working on the computer, but after an hour or so she gave up and went to bed herself, maneuvering carefully so as not to disturb Ty. Doug, as usual, had taken up his self-appointed guard post at the door.

I waited for two hours after Bayta settled in under the blankets, dozing a little but mostly staying awake, watching and listening. Finally, when her breathing had settled down into the slow rhythm of deep sleep, I got up, dressed, and crossed to the door.

I had wondered how I was going to get Doug out of my way without waking him, but it turned out to be a moot point. Once again, my quiet activity had aroused him, and he was standing to the side of the door, clearly wondering where we were going on this newest exciting outing. Crossing my fingers against the possibility that there would be a Shonkla-raa waiting for me, I opened the door and slipped out.

The corridor was deserted. I headed quickly toward the traffic corridor and the glideway, the low nighttime lighting giving the station an eerie, graveyard feeling. The perfect time, as generations of thieves, muggers, and murderers had discovered, for creating chaos and death.

But for once, the Shonkla-raa had missed a bet. Either that, or they'd also had enough for one day. No one was loitering in the hallways or lurking around corners. In fact, the only figures I saw were a handful of Jumpsuits roaming the corridors on patrol.

Ten uneventful minutes later, I arrived at my destination.

Minnario's eyes were half-closed with sleep as he opened the door at my buzz. They came all the way open in obvious surprise as he saw who it was. [Mr. Compton!] he gasped. [What are you—? Never mind. First things first—come in.]

"Thank you," I said, giving a quick glance in both directions before walking inside. "Sorry to bother you at this time of night, but something's come up that can't wait until morning."

[Not a problem,] he said as he closed and locked the door behind me. [What can I do for you? It's still an hour yet until I'm supposed to give Blue One his injection.]

"Actually, I'll go ahead and do that, as long as I'm here anyway," I said. "But before that, I need to move him."

[To hide him in case of a search later this morning by his friends,] Minnario said, nodding. [Yes, I've been wondering that as well. I presume you intend to take him back to Tech Yleli's apartment?]

"That was my original plan, yes," I said. "But as of a couple of hours ago, that's no longer an option."

I gave him a quick summary of my fun and games

earlier on the glideway, and how Blue One's buddies had cleared the arena so that they wouldn't be disturbed. "The point is that we know they have access to Yleli's apartment," I concluded. "Not only do we not want his friends to find him, but the patrollers may also be in and out of the place for the next couple of days, and we don't want them falling over him, either."

[Agreed,] Minnario said slowly, his face puckered with thought. [But you can't put him in your quarters, either. *Logra* Emikai's?]

I shook my head. "Even if he gave me permission, I wouldn't trust Blue One there. No, I had something hopefully a little less obvious and a lot closer in mind. Ms. German's quarters."

Minnario's eyes widened. [The Human girl? But—oh. Yes, of course. She's been spirited away, hasn't she?]

"And according to Guard Captain Lyarrom, the patrollers have already searched her room," I said. "It's not perfect, but it's as close to guaranteed privacy as we're likely to get."

[Agreed,] Minnario said, turning his chair around and heading toward the couch. [I presume we'll want him back in the file cabinet, in case his friends decide to drop by?]

I hadn't actually been planning to go quite that far. But now that I thought about it, he had a good point. If the Shonkla-raa had followed the same reasoning I had, they might conclude that a place the Jumpsuits had already searched would be a perfect spot to stash Terese. Having them walk in on Blue One dozing on the couch would be just slightly counterproductive. "Good idea," I said. "In that same vein, we should also change the labels on the drawers so that it won't be obvious that the cabinet came from Yleli's apartment."

It took a few minutes for me to attach four of Minnario's thrusters to the file cabinet and get Blue One inside. By the time I was finished Minnario had written out and attached new labels to all the drawer faces. I gave Blue One his next sedative shot, a double one this time that would hopefully last through not only the rest of the night but also through the morning's hearing. Closing up the cabinet, I made sure the hallway was still deserted and nudged my burden outside.

Terese's quarters were only two doors down, which was the reason Bayta and I had been assigned that particular room in the first place. Blue One's contraband passkey card got us inside, and I maneuvered the cabinet into the closet, where it would be inconspicuous, though not so inconspicuous that it would look like someone was trying to be inconspicuous. I positioned it so that we would be able to haul him out with relative ease once we were back from the hearing, then removed the borrowed thrusters. Again checking the hallway, I stepped out, closed the door behind me, and returned to Minnario's quarters.

The Nemut was waiting, and had the door open again practically before I hit the buzzer. [Everything all right?] he asked as I came inside.

"As all right as I can make it," I said, handing him the passkey and the thrusters. "Here's the key in case you want to check on him before the hearing tomorrow. If you don't have time, or the hallway seems too crowded, don't bother. He should have enough juice in him to last until early afternoon."

[When we will again interrogate him as to Ms. German's whereabouts?] Minnario asked, a dark anticipation in his voice.

"Exactly," I said. "Anyway, I'm off, and this time I promise I won't be back. Sleep well."

[You, too,] he said as he opened the door again. [Don't be late.]

Once again, the Shonkla-raa and whatever local skulkers Proteus Station had aboard had all apparently cashed it in for the night. Fifteen minutes later, I was safely back inside our room.

Bayta was still asleep. I got undressed again and sank

gratefully back onto my couch cushions. I still didn't know if Bayta had gone rogue, under either Modhran or Chahwyn influence, but I'd now done everything I could to prevent either faction from getting to Blue One before I was finished with him.

Of course, if I was the one carrying a Modhran colony under my brain, all my effort would count for less than nothing. But then, if the Modhri had gotten to me, we were all dead anyway.

There was a quiet, questioning snuffle at my ear. "Yes, we're done for the night," I assured Doug softly, reaching over and scratching his belly. "You can go back to sleep now."

He snuffled again and left, and I heard him padding his way back to the door.

I was asleep before he actually got there.

THIRTEEN :

Emikai was right on time the next morning, this time with an escort of six Jumpsuits instead of just two. Bayta and I were ready, and the whole crowd of us trooped off together.

Along the way I tried to engage Emikai in conversation, but he was strangely taciturn this morning. About all I could get out of him was that the patrollers still hadn't located Terese, Dr. Aronobal was still missing, and there'd been no further progress on last night's phony evacuation drill, Tech Yleli's murder, or the various assaults on me.

Our escort was even quieter, responding to my greetings or conversational openers with no more than three or four syllables each. Bayta wasn't much better, and we weren't very far along our way before I gave up the effort entirely. You'd have thought they were the ones functioning on four hours of sleep, not me.

My strategy of leaving a half hour earlier than the last time was only partially successful. Again, *Chinzro* Hch-chu was already seated at the prosecutor's table when we arrived, as was Minnario at our table. Three of the four guardlaws were also there, with *Usantra* Wandek the only one missing. Eyeing his empty seat as I crossed the stone floor toward Minnario, I wondered briefly if he, too, had been up late. Maybe consulting with his Shonkla-raa buddies about Blue One's disappearance.

As had happened the last time I'd been in this room, both Doug and Ty stayed at my side instead of dividing themselves up between me and Bayta.

[Good morning,] Minnario greeted me as I sat down. [I trust you had no further adventures on your way home last night?]

"It was actually rather boring," I assured him. "Anything new on our guest?"

[Unfortunately, yes,] he said, lowering his voice as he glanced casually around. [The passkey wouldn't open the door this morning. I'm guessing that it's designed to only be good for a single day, or even just a few hours.]

"Damn," I muttered. Stupid, stupid, stupid, and I should have seen it coming. "Fine. We'll just have to get hold of someone else's passkey."

[How?]

"Working on it," I assured him. "I also have a statement I want to make to the court as soon as possible. Will the Slisst Protocols have a problem with that?"

[No, I don't think so,] Minnario said, peering oddly at me. [What sort of statement?]

"If we're lucky, one that should get this whole thing closed down," I told him. "If not in a flat-out acquittal, at least in complete and utter confusion."

[That sounds like quite a statement,] Minnario said, his odd expression going a little odder. [Perhaps you should share it with me before we present it to the court.]

Across the room, the door opened and Wandek entered

the room. "Too late," I murmured. "Trust me, though. You're going to love it."

The opening ceremonies were pretty much the same as last time around. After they were finished, Hchchu informed the guardlaws that it was indeed Dr. Aronobal who had informed him of my dual identity as Frank Compton and Frank Abram Donaldson. Unfortunately, since Aronobal had now disappeared, he continued, it would be impossible for the guardlaws to ask her any questions as to how or where she'd obtained that information.

And then it was my turn.

"I have a point of order to raise," I said, rising to my feet. "I confess my relative ignorance of the Slisst Protocols on this matter, and I beg the guardlaws' indulgence and clarification."

{Continue,} Wandek said, his voice wary.

"Thank you," I said. "My question is in regard to this court's right to jurisdiction in this matter."

That one got them. Two of the guardlaws shifted in their seats, while the third sent a sharp look over at Hchchu. Wandek, in contrast, kept his eyes unblinkingly on mine. {This is an old argument, Mr. Compton,} he said, {and one which numerous courts have ruled on over the last three centuries. All those rulings have been against you.}

"But you haven't even heard my question," I protested politely.

{I don't need to,} he said. {You seek to claim that since the six victims of your crime were *santras*, with the genetic variations that often accompany that title, they cannot be considered true Filiaelians.}

{Even at the time of the Slisst Protocols it was accepted that *Filialian* was a wide-spanning title,} one of the other guardlaws put in. {If a person has Filiaelian blood and Filiaelian appearance, he is indeed a Filiaelian.}

"So it's the appearance that matters?" I asked.

{Not at all,} Wandek said, shooting a brief glare at the other guardlaw. Hardly surprising, really—allowing me to get away with framing the argument in terms of appearance was a quick road to a possible legal minefield.

Unfortunately for him, that wasn't actually the direction I was headed. And though he didn't know it, he and the whole Slisst Protocols were already in the middle of that minefield. "So what *is* it that makes a person a Filiaelian?" I asked.

{His heart,} Wandek said. {Not the physical heart, of course—that can be altered in any way desired. I speak of the way he views life.}

{A Filiaelian's identity is in his heart, his mind, and his soul,} the other guardlaw added. {No matter what genetics were worked on you, Mr. Compton, you would never and could never be a Filiaelian.}

"I see," I said slowly, as if trying to work it through. "So it's basically a person's mind that makes him truly Filiaelian?"

{Yes,} Wandek said.

"Good," I said. "Then if the court will indulge me, I'd like to tell you about a strange being who is even now attempting to conquer the galaxy.

"A creature who calls himself *Modhri*."

I laid it out for them. All of it: the Modhri's history, his nature, his essence, and the fact that all six of the Fillies on New Tigris had been Modhran walkers.

I left out the details of the war itself, of course, including how long Bayta and I had been involved with it. I also didn't talk about the true nature of the Spiders, and I absolutely didn't even hint at the existence and importance of the Chahwyn. The details of our various cases, as well as why the Modhri had been interested in New Tigris in the first place, I also kept to myself.

Still, even without all of that, the recital was clearly riveting. The guardlaws listened in silence, the darkening and paling of their blazes betraying their swirl of emotions. Most of my attention was on the guardlaws, but out of the corner of my eye I could see Hchchu sitting just as unmoving at the prosecutor's table. Beside me, Minnario listened with fascination, and even Doug and Ty seemed entranced by the firm, resonant sound of my voice.

Finally, I ran out of things to tell them. "The bottom line is this," I said. "Since the beings I fought on New Tigris were, at the time of the combat, Modhran walkers and not Filiaelians, I claim that no regular court of the Assembly has jurisdiction over the case. I therefore request that I be released without prejudice until such time as a proper court can be established to deal with what is surely an extraordinary and unprecedented situation. Thank you." Nodding to each of the guardlaws in turn, I sat back down.

Beside me, Minnario stirred. [A most interesting argument,] he murmured.

"Thank you," I said, inclining my head to him.

[I didn't say it was *good*,] he warned. [Merely interesting.]

Wandek looked down the table at his fellow guardlaws, and for a couple of minutes they all murmured back and forth. Then Wandek straightened up and looked back at me. {No,} he said flatly.

Even Minnario seemed taken aback. [I beg your pardon?] he said.

{The six murdered Filiaelians came from *Kuzyatru* Station,} Wandek said. {That's already been established. Even if this Modhri truly exists—and without actual proof, we cannot grant that as fact—even if it exists, it has no presence here. We therefore have no choice but to conclude that the murdered Filiaelians were not so infected.}

I cleared my throat. "Perhaps I wasn't entirely clear on how the Modhri operates," I suggested. "His polyp colonies are *designed* to hide within a walker's body where they can't be detected."

{Perhaps not by Humans or Shorshians or Juriani,} Wandek retorted with an edge of offended pride. {But they cannot hide from Filiaelians.}

{*Usantra* Wandek is correct,} Hchchu spoke up. {As assistant director of *Kuzyatru* Station, I can confirm there is no such alien presence aboard.}

"But that's the point: you *can't* confirm that," I persisted. "The polyps simply lie in place, unmoving and undetectable—"

{But they still live,} Hchchu interrupted. {Which means they must absorb nutrients and secrete waste products. Both processes leave subtle but detectable indicators that a full biochemical scan would be able to find.}

"And how often would something that complete be done?" I scoffed.

{Four times a year,} Hchchu said. {On everyone.}

I stared at him. Of all the answers he might have given, that was probably the last one I'd expected. "What do you mean, everyone?" I asked.

{Everyone aboard the station,} he said. {Every resident, every patient, every visiting lecturer, doctor, or researcher. Everyone.}

"Four times a year," I said, stalling for time while I tried furiously to get my brain in gear. If that was true, then maybe he was right. Maybe the Modhri *hadn't* penetrated Proteus Station.

But the Shonkla-raa were here. Surely they wouldn't have set up shop without having the Modhri here along with them. Would they? "Is that a Proteus Station year, or a Sificarea Standard?" I asked.

{The latter, of course,} Hchchu said. {A *Kuzyatru* Station year is over eleven Sificarea Standards. Once every three Sificarea Standards would hardly be a useful monitoring schedule.}

"No, of course not," I murmured. "May I ask the reason for such extensive bio testing?"

{The widespread genetic manipulation practiced

aboard *Kuzyatru* Station can by its very nature create instabilities and anomalies,} Wandek said, his tone shifting subtly into what was probably his lecturing doctor mode. {It can also lead to drastic changes in infectious disease organisms. Testing everyone aboard allows such problems to be detected and dealt with before they can escalate into general risks.}

{In addition, the vast majority of Filiaelians aboard take advantage of our facilities to have genetic work done,} Hchchu added. {There is absolutely no doubt that a preoperative scan would detect something as large and obvious as alien polyps.}

I grimaced. He was right on that one, too. Even Human medical scans were that good. "And the testing is universal, and not random?" I asked, just to be sure.

{Yes,} Wandek confirmed.

"I see," I murmured. Maybe the Chahwyn's threat assessment had been right, after all. If the whole Assembly was as careful about watching out for biochemical anomalies as Proteus Station, I could see how even the Modhri might find it impossible to make any headway here.

{Have you anything else to add?} Wandek asked.

Grimacing, I stood up again. "Despite your precautions, the six Filiaelians *were* Modhran walkers," I said. "If they were clean when they left Proteus, they must have become infected somewhere on their way to New Tigris."

{Where was it done?} Wandek countered. {*How* was it done? Such a statement requires proof, and that burden rests upon you.}

"I know," I said. Minnario had been right: an interesting defense, but obviously not a very good one. "That's why I'm formally requesting full records of the Filiaelians' itineraries, from the time they left Proteus Station until their arrival on New Tigris. I'd also request a one-week recess to give me time to analyze the data."

{Impossible,} Wandek said. {Such an itinerary doesn't exist, except perhaps in the records of the Spiders and the Quadrail.}

"Then let me query the Spiders," I offered. "I could laser a message to the Tube—"

{Request denied,} Wandek cut me off. {This is a clear and outrageous attempt to delay these proceedings. Such tactics will not be tolerated.}

{A moment, *Usantra* Wandek,} Hchchu spoke up. {I, for one, am curious about Mr. Compton's claims.}

{When the combat has been decided, you'll be free to indulge that curiosity,} Wandek said acidly. {Until then, the proceedings will continue on their proper schedule.}

Hchchu looked at me. {In that case, *I* hereby request a one-week recess.}

Even from my distance I could see the sudden mottling of Wandek's blaze. {*You* request a delay?} he demanded.

{Yes,} Hchchu said. {I wish to send a request to the Spiders for the itinerary Mr. Compton has requested.}

{On his behalf?} Wandek said, sounding both astonished and outraged.

{On *my* behalf,} Hchchu corrected. {I'm the prosecutor in this trial. I have the right to sheathe one weapon while I examine the possible use of another.}

Again, Wandek looked down the table at his fellow guardlaws. But if he was looking for support on this one, he wasn't getting it. {Very well,} he said stiffly. {But I remind you that all four of us have other duties aboard this station. If during your delay we're called to other activities and cannot resume our duties here, the Slisst Protocols require the trial to be ended and the Human given his freedom.}

{I'm aware of the law,} Hchchu assured him. {I'm willing to take that risk.}

For another moment Wandek locked eyes with him. Then, with a snort, he turned to me. {The combat is ended for one week, or until such time as *Chinzro* Hchchu is prepared to resume,} he announced formally. {The defendant is free to return to other activities.} He paused. {Or rather, to return to the investigation of Tech Yleli's murder as you have been ordered by Assistant Director *Chinzro* Hchchu,} he added, with a last glare toward Hchchu.

Stuffing his reader back into its pouch, he left his seat and strode past me out the door. His three fellow guard-laws were right behind him.

I looked across at Hchchu. He was again looking at me, a twitch of his hand indicating that I was to stay put. I gave him a small nod in reply, then turned half around in my seat and gestured in turn to Bayta.

She was already headed across the room toward me, Emikai at her side, her face taut with a whole mix of emotions. "What are you doing, Frank?" she demanded. "Why did you tell them about the Modhri?"

"Why shouldn't the Fillies get in on the fun?" I countered. "They're under the same threat as the rest of us, and all the fancy testing in the galaxy won't change that." I gestured around us. "Besides, the more paranoid eyes there are watching everyone's every move, the harder it'll be for the Shonkla-raa to take another crack at us. So. Next thing on the agenda—"

I broke off as Bayta's eyes shifted warningly to something past my shoulder, and I turned again as Hchchu walked up to us. "If you would, Mr. Compton," he said, "I would like to see you for a few moments in my office."

"Isn't that slightly improper?" I asked. "You being the prosecutor and me being the defendant and all?"

"It won't be a problem," Hchchu assured me. "If you come with me, I believe I can provide you with the itinerary you asked for."

I felt my eyes narrow. "That was fast," I said. "You have an instant pipeline to the Spiders I don't know about?"

Hchchu's eyes flicked to Bayta and Emikai. "I would prefer to discuss it in private," he said.

I was about to tell him his preferences weren't a high priority for me when I took a good look into his eyes.

He was frightened. More than frightened, in fact. He was terrified.

And anything that terrified the assistant director of the Fillies' showcase space center was something I'd damn well better look into. "Bayta, why don't you and *Logra* Emikai head back," I said casually. "I'll get the itinerary from *Chinzro* Hchchu and rejoin you."

"What about our other friend?" Bayta asked. "He's going to want to see us."

"There'll be plenty of time for that later," I said. I could hardly tell her I'd moved our prisoner to Terese's room, not with Hchchu standing right there. "Go ahead—I'll be there as soon as I can."

[I'd like to go with you, if I may,] Minnario spoke up.

"I would prefer to speak with Mr. Compton in private," Hchchu repeated, his voice making it clear that that was an order.

[I'm his attorney and advocate,] Minnario said, his voice making it clear that he didn't care. [Besides, as Mr. Compton has already pointed out, you and he are on opposite sides of the arena. The presence of a third person will be as much for your protection as for his.]

Hchchu sighed. "Very well," he said reluctantly. "Follow me."

He turned and strode off toward a door on the side of the courtroom. I gave Bayta an encouraging smile and followed.

The door led into a corridor that was similar to all the others I'd traveled through on Proteus, yet at the same time was subtly different. The unobtrusive color scheme was more vibrant, and the patterns of grooves and sculpted florets that decorated the upper walls and ceiling were more elaborate than I'd seen elsewhere. Officers' country, I decided, the place where Proteus's senior staff worked and played.

We'd made two turns into an even more elaborate

hallway when I suddenly realized that, once again, Ty had deserted me, leaving Doug trotting alone at my side.

Did that mean Bayta going off the rails again? Or was it just a precaution?

Either way, I needed to do something quick before Hchchu noticed I was a watchdog shy of my quota and sent some patroller to bring Ty back. "You definitely have a nice part of the station here," I commented, picking up my pace a bit.

"This is the main administrative center for *Kuzyatru* Station," Hchchu explained, picking up his own pace to keep up with me.

Which was exactly what I'd hoped he would do. Now, with Doug and Minnario both trailing behind us out of Hchchu's view, he hopefully wouldn't notice Ty's absence until it was too late to be worth the effort of getting him back. "How many administrators and staff are there?" I asked.

"Too many administrators; not nearly enough staff," he said, with the first touch of humor I could remember ever hearing from him. "My office is down here."

He turned into a short hallway guarded by yet another of the ubiquitous receptionists and receptionist desks that Proteus Station never seemed to run out of. At the far end of the corridor he pushed open the door—a real, hinged, hardwood door, not one of the sterile sliding types—and gestured me inside.

I got three steps before the sheer grandeur of the place brought me to an abrupt halt.

It wasn't the office per se. The place was nice enough, and certainly roomy enough, but the large central desk and display cases and curved plant stands along the walls and scattered around the floor were of only simple design.

It was the view through the floor-to-ceiling window across from the door that had grabbed my full attention. Against a brilliant blue sky I could see the tops of a cluster of slender, impossibly green trees, surrounded by a ring of pillars that reminded me of stylized Filly hands reaching for the sky, the whole view embedded in a soft, drifting mist. To the right of the trees, the blue sky faded into the star-scattered blackness of deep space.

"You like my view?" Hchchu asked dryly.

"Very much," I said. Ungluing my feet, I headed across the room for a closer look.

"It is merely one of the many domes scattered around *Kuzyatru* Station," Hchchu said as he angled away from me toward the desk. "Though perhaps more elaborately furnished than most."

It was indeed a standard Proteus dome, I saw as I reached the window, of apparently the same size as Terese's medical dome and the neighborhood center where Yleli's funeral services had been held. But unlike both of those, this particular dome was arranged as a park. The trees were part of a central pocket-forest area, surrounded by the sculpted reaching hands I'd seen and, lower down, a series of narrow fountains, the source of the floating mist. Arranged around the fountains were some smaller trees, flower beds, and clusters of bushes, all woven together with meandering pathways lined with chairs and benches. On the far side of the central area, I could see a bit of what looked like a small children's play area. Other windows lined the rest of the dome at my same level, all of them privacy-shielded to allow the occupants to look at the park without anyone from the park being able to see in.

"Here," Hchchu said from behind me.

I turned. Hchchu was now seated in the desk chair and was holding a data chip toward me. "What is it?" I asked as I gave the view one last look and walked over to him.

"The itinerary I promised," Hchchu said.

I glanced at Minnario, who had pulled his chair up to one corner of the desk. He was gazing at the data chip, an intense expression on his face. "You really need to work on your sense of drama," I told Hchchu as I plucked the chip from between his fingers. "Here you have the perfect chance to sit at your desk, gazing steely-eyed at your computer display as you sift through vast quantities of data—"

"Why should I do that?" Hchchu interrupted. "The itinerary was already prepared because I was the one who sent them."

I felt my mouth drop open, a sudden chill running through me. If Hchchu had been the one in charge of their mission . . . "*You* sent them to New Tigris?" I asked carefully.

"No, nor to any other world in Human space," he said. "Please; sit down."

I glanced again at Minnario, resisted the urge to also glance at the closed door behind me, and sat down in one of the guest chairs across from Hchchu. "Maybe we should start at the beginning," I suggested.

"The beginning is with you and your tale of the Modhri," Hchchu said, opening one of the desk's drawers and pulling out a reader. "Here—you will need this."

Only it wasn't just any reader, I saw with mild surprise as I took it, but my very own reader, the fancy, gimmicked gadget that Hchchu and the Jumpsuits had taken away from me the minute I'd stepped aboard Proteus. "Thanks," I said, turning it on and plugging in the chip. "I was telling the truth, you know."

"Indeed I do," Hchchu said grimly. "Rumors and stories of this Modhri have circulated for many years throughout the highest levels of the Filiaelian Assembly. Yet we have seen no evidence of penetration into our species, not even in travelers or diplomats who have spent extensive time outside our borders."

"Actually, that makes perfect sense," I agreed, pulling up the file.

"How so?" Hchchu asked. "If the Modhri's goal is to control the galaxy, why leave us untouched?"

"Because he's ambitious, but he's not stupid," I said, skimming the itinerary. The six Fillies had taken a

Quadrail from Proteus to Venidra Carvo, boarded a super-express train for Homshil, and from there had visited three more places in the Jurian Collective. There was no mention of New Tigris, just as Hchchu had said, or of any other world, for that matter. "He knows all about the genetic work and biochemical testing you do," I continued. "Right now, stealth and secrecy are his greatest weapons, and he's not going to risk certain exposure by infecting a Filiaelian diplomat who's probably going to be tested the minute he gets back home."

"Yet if you are right, these six Filiaelians *were* infected," Hchchu pointed out. "Why? And where?"

"I don't know the *where*," I said. "It could have been anywhere along the way, basically any time after they left Filiaelian space." I gestured toward my reader. "Or possibly after this listing ends. I notice that the last stop is over two months before they showed up on New Tigris."

"Yes, their reports stopped at that point," Hchchu said heavily. "Their mission, if you hadn't already guessed, was to search for evidence of this Modhri in Halkan and Jurian space. They had sent back several reports that seemed to indicate they had discovered the rumors were true, and were near to capturing a sample to bring back for study. But then the reports suddenly stopped, and all my subsequent messages to them were left unclaimed."

"Sounds like they found him, all right," I said. "And as to the *why*, they were infected because they were needed. There's something in Filiaelian physiology that apparently links uniquely with the Modhran hive mind, giving him an ability he apparently can't get from anyone else."

"What ability is this?"

"Sorry, but I can't tell you that," I said. "Even if I could, I don't understand it myself well enough to explain it."

For a moment Hchchu sat in silence. Then, he gave a soft, whinnying sigh. "Stealth and secrecy, you say," he murmured. "Yet they were infected, Filiaelians who would soon have returned to the Assembly. Does that mean that a new phase is about to begin? Is the Modhri finally ready to launch a full assault on the Filiaelian people?"

Briefly, I thought about telling him that there was a group of Filiaelian people who would not only welcome the Modhri's incursion but was actively working to facilitate it. But he didn't need that extra news dumped on him. Not yet. "I don't know what his current plan is," I said instead. "But aside from his existence, you know now two other important facts. One: the reason he hasn't yet penetrated the Assembly isn't because there's something about Filiaelians he can't connect with. We know now that you're as easy a target for him as anyone else in the Twelve Empires. You may be able to spot him, but only after the fact."

"And the second thing?"

"That you're not only vulnerable, but also uniquely useful. But that also means he's not going to try a full assault on the Assembly until he's damn sure he's ready."

"Yes," Hchchu murmured. "Something else strikes my thoughts. If the Modhri is wary of allowing himself to come under Filiaelian scrutiny, it follows that, no matter what happened on New Tigris, the six *santras* would not have been permitted to return to Proteus alive."

I winced. That one hadn't yet occurred to me. "Which probably explains what happened to the two that I know were taken alive," I said. "They were undoubtedly killed in custody by their polyp colonies to make sure you never got a chance to properly examine them."

"Indeed." Hchchu peered suddenly at me. "How exactly do *you* fit into all this, Mr. Compton?"

"I'm just a simple Human who got caught up in the whole thing and is trying to make a difference," I said, more or less truthfully. "Along the way I've run into a few others who recognize the Modhran threat and are working to stop him."

"No." Hchchu shook his head. "I have been studying you, Mr. Frank Compton, learning all I can about you." He pointed at my reader. "That device, for instance, is more than it appears. No, you are not simply a lone, isolated soldier in this war. You also are more than you appear."

I felt my stomach tighten. I knew how special I was, the Modhri and Shonkla-raa knew, and now Hchchu had figured it out as well. I might as well take out a full-page ad and paint a bull's-eye on my back. "I'm flattered that you think that," I said. "But in reality—"

{*There* you are,} a familiar voice growled from behind me.

I turned around, to see Wandek standing in the open doorway glowering at Hchchu. {I've been looking all over for you,} he continued, pushing the door closed behind him and striding across the room toward us.

{Is there a problem?} Hchchu asked, sounding confused.

{Indeed there is,} Wandek said. He strode past Minnario and continued around the end of the desk.

And without warning, he swept his right hand outward, catching Minnario with a backhanded blow across the Nemut's conical mouth. The force of the impact spun him and his chair a quarter turn around and sent him flying out onto the floor.

I was still goggling at the sheer unexpectedness of it when Wandek took another two steps to Hchchu's side and drove his stiffened hand into the assistant director's torso.

"Don't," Wandek warned, turning to face me as Hchchu collapsed without a sound onto his desk.

I was already scrambling to my feet, kicking my chair backward out of my way. A quick leap up onto the desktop, a kick to Wandek's head or torso before he could move away—

"No, no—let him try," another voice came from the door.

I froze, my knees still bent for my leap, and turned my head. Stalking across the room toward me were a pair of Shonkla-raa. The one in the lead, the one who had spoken, was Blue One. "Please," he said softly, his eyes burning with hatred as he stared at me, "let him try."

FOURTEEN :

I didn't try. At three against one, trying would be suicide, and I wasn't yet ready to die. Slowly, I straightened up again and stood perfectly still, raising my arms slightly away from my body just to prove I knew the proper drill. The second Shonkla-raa, thinner than the others and with an unattractive, jagged-edged nose blaze, strode up to me, gave me a quick pat-down, and took away my comm and my newly reacquired reader. Stuffing them into his belt bag, he headed over to Minnario, who was sprawled unmoving on the floor, his eyes closed, blood seeping through his skin beside his snout where Wandek had hit him. Jagged Nose patted him down as he had me, then crossed to the Nemut's chair and started unfastening the storage pouches.

"Three of you this time, huh?" I said, looking at each in turn. "Is that your typical pattern, then? First you send one of you after me, then you send two, and now three. I suppose next time it'll be four?"

"There will be no next time," Wandek said. He waved toward my overturned chair, a few drops of Hchchu's blood spattering from his hand onto the desk as he did so. "Please sit down, Mr. Compton. You have nothing to fear from us. As I'm sure *Isantra* Kordiss told you, we'd prefer to keep you alive for the moment."

He looked over at Blue One. "Though he himself may not be feeling so generous at the moment. He didn't appreciate the way you treated him, locking him in that file cabinet."

"I'm sorry he feels that way," I said, looking at Kordiss. His expression was still begging me to start trouble. "But if he's not ready to run with the big dogs, he needs to stay on the porch."

Kordiss took a step toward me, his blaze darkening almost to black. "What does that mean?" he demanded.

"Please," I said, putting a little condescension in my voice. It was risky, I knew, goading him like this. But Wandek had already said they wanted me alive, and getting an opponent angry was still one of the best ways to get him to make a mistake. Right now, I desperately needed one of them to make a mistake.

But if Kordiss was poised on the brink of stupidity, Wandek wasn't. "An excellent try, Mr. Compton," he said approvingly. "But there's no need. You can't possibly win a fight, certainly not against three of us. And we really *aren't* going to kill you. Not unless you absolutely insist on it."

I eyed Kordiss. But Wandek's interruption had given him time to think, and already I could see the blind fury fading from his face. I flicked a glance to the side, where Doug was watching the situation with the oblivious interest of a dumb animal who hasn't realized that the situation requires him to act outside of his official orders. Still, if I could get to him and throw him at one of the Shonkla-raa . . .

"And I wouldn't count on your *msikai-dorosli* to intervene on your behalf either," Wandek added. "I'm fairly certain *Chinzro* Hchchu ordered him to prevent you from attacking others aboard *Kuzyatru* Station, not vice versa. Is that the correct use of the term, by the way? Vice versa?"

"Close enough," I said. Reaching down, I picked up my chair from where I'd kicked it and set it upright again. "Tech Yleli showed you weren't shy about murder," I said as I sat down. "I wouldn't have guessed you'd go as far as killing the assistant director of the whole station, though."

"Great rewards are worth great risks," Wandek said.

{*Usantra* Wandek?} Jagged Nose spoke up. He was peering into one of Minnario's bags, his fingers sifting through the contents. {His comm is missing.}

{You've checked his clothing?} Wandek asked.

{Thoroughly,} Jagged Nose confirmed. {It's not here.}

Wandek eyed me, probably wondering if he should have the other Shonkla-raa search me again, just in case I had somehow teleported the comm out of Minnario's pocket and into mine. But he merely shrugged. {He must have left it in his quarters,} he said. {Get to your main task.}

{As ordered.} Closing up the bags, Jagged Nose tied them to his own belt like saddlebags, then crossed to the desk. Casually shoving Hchchu's body out of the chair onto the floor, he sat down and started typing on the desk computer. "But then, you already know the magnitude of the rewards we seek," Wandek continued, coming around the end of the desk and settling himself on the corner facing me.

"You've got ambition to burn, I'll give you that," I said. "But if you'll pardon the observation, your methods stink like three-day-old fish. What exactly do you think *Chinzro* Hchchu's murder is going to gain you? Control of the station?"

Wandek gave what was probably supposed to be a chuckle. "We've badly overestimated your intelligence, Mr. Compton," he said sadly. "Even now, with all you've learned, you still have no idea what we're actually doing."

"You're probably right," I agreed, listening to my heartbeats count off the seconds. Even as we sat here talking, Hchchu's blood would be coagulating along the well-defined curve Emikai had told me about yesterday. If I could keep the conversation going, the patrollers and techs who investigated the murder should be able to narrow down the time of death to the exact period when Wandek and his buddies were here in the room. I didn't know how much that would help, but it certainly couldn't hurt. "But I imagine you're dying to tell me."

"As it happens, I am," Wandek agreed. "And since we have a few minutes to spare, I'll indulge your curiosity. Do you have any idea why the Shonkla-raa left Earth alone two thousand years ago when they were busy conquering the rest of the galaxy?"

"No, and neither do you," I said. "That's why you're experimenting with all those Humans in Building Twelve."

"In point of fact, we *do* know why," Wandek corrected. "We also know how to correct that deficiency. That's why we brought the Human females here, so that we could turn their babies into our future servants."

I stared at him. "Are you saying Building Twelve is full of pregnant women?"

"Building Twelve, and two of the others," Wandek said. "You understand now why, after your confederates disabled the cameras and we realized you would soon be arriving, I ordered *Isantra* Kordiss to kill the first likely person he could find and leave him in your path. If you'd seen the other pregnant Humans, even you couldn't have failed to realize what it was we wanted with Ms. German."

He waved again, a more expansive gesture this time. "You see, Mr. Compton, we of the Shonkla-raa don't rule the way Humans or even most Filiaelians do, by way of spoken orders and written contracts. We are telepathic. Not very strongly, admittedly, but strongly enough to impress our thoughts and commands on other beings." He lifted a bloody finger like a college professor trying to underline an important point for a dull pupil. "But only if those other beings have some telepathic ability of their own. Reception *and* transmission."

"Like the Modhri," I murmured.

Wandek's face brightened. The dull pupil had gotten one. "Exactly like the Modhri," he agreed. "Except that the Modhri is much more telepathic than most species— designed that way, of course—which gives him a higher resistance to us than other species. That's where this"—he tapped his throat—"or rather those," he corrected, pointing at Kordiss's and Jagged Nose's oversized throats, "come in."

"Let me guess," I said. I knew perfectly well what the throats were for, having seen Muzzfor in action aboard the super-express. But I wasn't ready yet to show him that particular card. "You sing grand opera to calm him down?"

"We sing a set of very specific notes, a tonic plus several of its harmonics," he said. "All telepathic species can theoretically be reached with the proper tones, though so far we have only discovered the frequency necessary for bringing the Modhri and Modhran walkers under our control. Though it may be that the Modhran tone will also affect a Spider, at least enough to confuse it," he added thoughtfully. "We still need to experiment with that. It's possible we'll need to engineer specific Shonkla-raa with different throat specifications to deal with them."

"Is that why you haven't had one of your own installed?" I asked, nodding toward his own normal-sized throat. "You're waiting to get a Spider throat?"

"I was actually waiting for a Human one," he said, his eyes glowing. "My plan was always to become the prince of your world once we were again the rulers of the galaxy."

"Really," I said. "Out of thousands of possible worlds, you chose our modest little split-level? We're flattered."

"You speak sarcastically," he said. "But you really have no idea. Earth and its solar system have resources beyond anything you can imagine, simply because you in your ignorance haven't known to look for them." He smiled. "One of those resources being your people themselves. If all Humans are as effective at combat as you, I will soon have a force that even the other Shonkla-raa will look upon with respect."

He gestured in the direction of the medical dome, a

quarter of the way around the station. "And those un-born Humans in Building Twelve will be yet another step toward achieving that goal."

"Thanks, I'd already figured that one out," I growled. "You're trying to graft some telepathic ability into them, aren't you?"

"Not *trying*," he corrected mildly. "*Succeeding*. Another few weeks and we'll be sending all of them back to Earth, their mothers secure in the belief that their babies' alleged medical problems have now been corrected."

"Genetic engineering at its finest," I said sourly. "No wonder you went ballistic when we suggested Terese might abort her baby."

"What, you mean this?" he asked, pointing to his nose. Suddenly his blaze began to go mottled, seething with the indications of emotions that clearly weren't there. "A toy I had the engineers install when they turned my hands into weapons," he said offhandedly as the blaze faded back to its normal shade. "It adds an additional level of supposed emotional depth to my performances, wouldn't you say?"

"I would indeed," I agreed. "Good thinking, that. I'm not so impressed by your army of toddlers, though."

Wandek shrugged. "We have time," he assured me. "As to Ms. German, yes, we had originally brought her here to create another slave from her offspring. But shortly after your arrival, we realized we had a far bigger prize waiting for us."

I raised my eyebrows politely. "Me?"

"Of course not," Wandek said. "Bayta."

My stomach tightened into a hard knot. "You must be joking," I said as contemptuously as I could manage through the pulse pounding in my throat. "She's barely competent to be my assistant, let alone one of your junior world-conquerors."

"Please," Wandek chided calmly. "Did you really think Dr. Aronobal hadn't noticed on your journey that Bayta could communicate with the Spiders? And since we know Humans aren't telepathic, it immediately follows that Bayta is something different. A hybrid of Human and Spider, perhaps, since her nucleics are indeed Human. Or perhaps she's a member of a species we haven't yet discovered, which has encased itself in a Human shell to avoid detection." He eyed me closely. "Or possibly she's one of the beings we've always suspected are quietly controlling the Spiders and the Quadrail."

"Or else Aronobal is just imagining things," I offered.

"I don't think so," Wandek said. "Regardless, I'm sure Bayta will be a most interesting test subject." His blaze mottled a bit. "Who knows? If it turns out she *is* one of the beings controlling the Spiders, I may decide to leave Earth in someone else's control and—what is the term? Trade something?"

"Trade up," I supplied. "But in all honesty, I really think Bayta's going to be a big disappointment for you."

"We shall see." Wandek snorted. "Now that we'll actually have a chance to find out."

"Oh?" I asked. Behind Wandek, Jagged Nose was still fiddling with Hchchu's computer, and I wondered uneasily what exactly he was doing. "What's been stopping you?"

"Not you, certainly," Wandek said. "The fact is that pure happenstance has thwarted our every move. First, we arranged to put the two of you in separate quarters, so that she would eventually be forced to travel the hallways of *Kuzyatru* Station alone. But then *he*"—he jabbed a finger contemptuously at the unconscious Minnario— "somehow was assigned one of those same rooms. Our next thought was that you would attend the preliminary hearings alone, which would again leave her vulnerable. But again, the Nemut brought her in as a witness."

"Lawyers are often pests on our worlds, too," I said. Suddenly, a lot of the strange things that had been happening aboard Proteus were starting to make sense. "And the reason you killed Tech Yleli instead of just trying to clobber me was so I'd be arrested for the murder and locked up, which would again leave Bayta alone. Only she spent the night with me in the security nexus, where you couldn't get at her without going through a whole wall of patrollers first."

"Indeed," Wandek said, scowling at the memories. "Still, we knew you wouldn't be under suspicion for long, not with that *msikai-dorosli* tagging along wherever you went. So we maneuvered *Chinzro* Hchchu into assigning you to investigate Tech Yleli's murder, knowing it would take you far across the station."

I grimaced. "That one nearly worked, too."

"Yes," Wandek agreed. "We even chose to risk our investment in Ms. German and her child by making her ill, hoping Bayta would stay by her side, out in the open where we could get to her, while you carried out your investigation." He snarled an evil-sounding Fili phrase. "Only yet again this stupid Nemut spoiled it, coming in to prepare her to testify at your trial."

"And then *Isantra* Kordiss tried to take me out and failed, and you chased everyone out of the subsector with a fake evacuation drill and sent two more of your goons after me, who also failed," I offered helpfully. "And Ms. German's disappearance was presumably again designed to split us up, with me handling the investigation while Bayta went off hunting for her."

"Correct," Wandek confirmed sourly. "Only this time it was *Chinzro* Hchchu who intervened by restarting the trial."

"Which again kept Bayta and me together," I said. "You're really not batting very well on this one, are you?"

"Perhaps," Wandek said. "But as with all games, it's only necessary for us to win once. And now we have." He half turned. "*Asantra* Prllolim?" he invited.

"It is done," Jagged Nose announced, tapping one final key on the computer and standing up.

"Excellent." Wandek turned back to me. "Let me explain to you what is about to happen. In two minutes' time my companions and I will depart, leaving the door locked. You have no comm, we have all the Nemut's equipment, and *Chinzro* Hchchu's computer and intercom are both frozen. Approximately ten minutes after that, the receptionist will return from the errand I sent her on and resume her position as guardian of *Chinzro* Hchchu's office. I should mention that the office door is completely soundproof, so you won't be able to call out to attract her attention. But you're welcome to try."

"Let me guess," I said. "Eventually, she starts wondering why she hasn't been called in to water the plants, and comes in to find Minnario and me all alone with Hchchu's body."

"Not at all," Wandek said calmly. "Approximately ten minutes after she returns, the computer will send out an emergency signal, which will be received by both her and the nearby patroller office. One minute after that, to allow for their response time, the door will unlock. *Then* they will all enter to find you and the Nemut and the body."

"Nice," I complimented him. "There might be a couple of problems, though."

"How so?" Wandek asked politely.

"First of all, the coagulation curve on *Chinzro* Hchchu's blood will prove he was dead long before he supposedly sent out his distress call," I said. A small part of me was screaming that warning him about potentially fatal errors wasn't a particularly smart thing to do. But Wandek had such obvious contempt for Humans that I needed to let him know that, in my field of expertise at least, I was smarter than he was. "And second, it'll be obvious to anyone with half a brain that my hands couldn't possibly have made the wound that killed him."

"How foolish of us to have forgotten such things," Kordiss said sardonically.

"How foolish, indeed," Wandek agreed. "*Asantra* Prl-lolim?"

"The coagulation curve in *Chinzro* Hchchu's records has been reset," Prllolim said. "It will now show his death to have occurred less than a minute after the emergency call is made."

"And as to your second point, the capabilities of Human hands are not nearly as obvious to untrained Filiaelians as you might think," Wandek continued. "Director *Usantra* Nstroo and the patrollers will have to turn to an expert in Human physiology to determine that."

I felt my brief flicker of professional pride fade away. "You?"

"Who else?" Wandek said. "And I will naturally need several days of study before I can come to a conclusion. I will certainly want *Logra* Emikai to be standing by during that time in case you try to escape."

"Of course," I said, feeling my heart sink even lower. And with Minnario injured and probably needing medical attention himself, Bayta would be completely alone. Every direction I tried, every turn I made, the Shonklaraa had already closed it off.

Maybe Wandek could see the growing despair in my face, or else he simply knew Human psychology as well as he knew our anatomy. "Please don't assume that I'm telling you all this in order to gloat in your presence," he said. "As I'm sure you long ago deduced, the Modhran strategy for slipping through mental defenses is to insert suggestions along lines of respect, familiarity, and trust. For us, the preferred strategy is to break down resistance through the creation of fear and hopelessness."

He stood up and leaned over me. "Do you feel fear and hopelessness, Mr. Compton?"

"Fear is a biochemical response that can be controlled or ignored," I said as firmly as I could. "And hopelessness is a lie and an illusion. There's always hope." I locked eyes with him. "Always."

Wandek shook his head. "You Humans are remarkable beings indeed," he said as he straightened up. "I shall look forward to having all of you under my authority. Until later, Mr. Compton."

He started toward the door, then paused and turned around again. "One other thing," he said. "Up to now, our plan has included only the modification of unborn Humans. But since you'll be our guest anyway, I think it will be worth examining whether or not the same techniques will work on a fully developed Human brain."

"Sure, why not?" I said, fighting down a surge of horror at the thought of Wandek and the other Shonkla-raa poking around inside my skull. "You might as well be efficient about this."

"Exactly," Wandek said. "Of course, the technique may also kill you. But if it succeeds, you too will be able to look forward to a lifetime in my service."

He took a step back toward me. "So tell me now, arrogant Human," he said softly, "whether hopelessness is only an illusion."

He turned again and started across the room. Prllolim and Kordiss joined him, Kordiss walking backward so that he could keep an eye on me the whole way. Even a last-second act of desperation was going to be denied me.

They were halfway to the door when an unexpected question hammered through my growing swirl of despair.

Why the hell were they bothering to alter Human brains?

There was no reason to go to all that time and effort. *Asantra* Muzzfor had already demonstrated that the Shonkla-raa could take control of the Modhri, and the Modhri had just as conclusively proved he could take control of Humans. Instead of spending all this time and energy fiddling with baby brains, why not simply scratch the babies—*and* their mothers—with some Modhran coral and be done with it?

The answer seemed obvious. As Hchchu and Wandek had both stated, there wasn't any Modhran presence aboard Proteus. No Modhri, no coral, no Modhran walkers.

And yet . . .

I lowered my gaze to Doug. He was sitting on his haunches, his body motionless, his masked eyes gazing intently back at me. Doug, my faithful watchdog, who had accidentally alerted me to at least two attacks since our arrival here. Doug, whose partner Ty had inexplicably deserted me in order to stay close to Bayta, whom the Shonkla-raa had been furiously trying to get alone. Doug, who had never once greeted Ty with the same yip that both watchdogs invariably exchanged with other watchdogs they happened to meet.

Doug, who by Dr. Aronobal's own statement belonged to a species that the Fillies knew so well they had no reason to study further.

Deliberately, I turned my eyes from Doug to Minnario. The Nemut was still lying motionless, his breathing still the slow rhythm of unconsciousness.

And then, as I peered into his face, I saw his conical mouth shift in a small, knowing, hard-edged smile.

The three Shonkla-raa had reached the door now. "*Usantra* Wandek?" I called.

He turned around. "Yes?"

"The next time you come after me," I said softly, "you'd better bring *all* of you."

He snorted and turned away. A moment later, the door closed and sealed behind them.

I turned back to Minnario. "Hello, Modhri," I said.

"Hello, Compton," Minnario murmured, his eyes still closed, his distorted mouth speaking English for the first time since we'd met. "It's a long way indeed since the super-express." He hesitated. "Are we still allies?"

"Yes," I said firmly.

"Good," he said. "Then we must hurry."

Doug stood up and trotted to me. Lowering his head, he opened his mouth wide.

And out onto the floor slid Minnario's missing comm.

"Bayta is in terrible danger," Minnario continued, his voice urgent as I reached down and picked up the comm. "We must move swiftly if we're to save her."

FIFTEEN :

Bayta answered on the second ring. "Where are you?" I asked without preamble.

"On the bullet train heading back to our quarters," she said, her voice suddenly taut. "What's wrong?"

"Pretty much everything," I said grimly, walking over to the door and trying the release. It was locked, all right. "There's been another murder, the Shonkla-raa are trying to frame me for it, and you're in danger," I continued, turning and heading for the desk. "You need to get off that train at the next stop and find a place to hide. Is Emikai with you?"

"Yes, he's right here," she said. "Do you want to talk to him?"

Minnario's hand twitched. "There's a place nearby that will serve," he said.

"No, that's all right," I told Bayta, nodding to Minnario in acknowledgment. "I don't think the Shonkla-raa particularly want him, so he should be safe enough for now. But tell him he has to make a choice—"

"This is Emikai," Emikai's voice came abruptly. "What has happened?"

"The people who killed Tech Yleli have killed again," I told him, walking around the side of the desk and trying to activate the computer. It was as solidly locked down as the door.

"Who was murdered?"

"Why?" I asked suspiciously. "You going to call it in if I tell you?"

"Of course," he said. "I have no choice."

"In that case, I can't tell you," I said. "The killers are trying to frame me for the murder. I have to get away from the crime scene before the whole Proteus security system piles on top of me."

"Leaving the scene will not help you," he warned. "You will have left samples of your nucleics behind."

"In this case, that won't matter," I said. "Put Bayta back on, will you?"

"Wait." There was a brief pause. "What do you want me to do?" he asked.

"I don't know," I said. "What *can* you do?"

The pause this time was longer. "Assuming you escape the scene, how much evidence will there be against you?"

"If I get out fast enough, none," I assured him, looking at the locked door and then at Hchchu's desk. "In fact, depending on how much noise I make, and how fast the patrollers get here after me, they're going to be left with one hell of a puzzle. Don't ask me to explain— it's way too complicated."

"No explanation is necessary," he said, and I could hear the relief in his voice. "If you are innocent, and if the evidence will show that, there is no requirement for me to hinder your movements."

"That's good to hear," I said, going over to where Minnario's empty chair was quietly hovering. Taking one of its arms, I pulled it over beside the desk. "I'd like you to accompany Bayta to a place of safety. She'll show you where."

"Understood," he said. "We will await your arrival."

"Thanks," I said. "Now put Bayta on."

There was a pause— "Frank?"

"Okay, we're all set," I told her, searching the chair's control board for the off control. "Emikai will go along and help keep you safe until I can catch up."

"Where do you want me to go?"

"I don't know yet," I said, looking at Minnario. "Minnario?"

The Nemut's fingers twitched again. "Ty can guide her."

I grimaced. Of course Ty could guide her. Sometimes I forgot just how useful a group mind could be. "Ty will show you where," I told Bayta. "Just follow him."

"*Ty* will show me?"

"Yes," I said. I found the control and twisted it, and the chair settled smoothly to the floor. "It turns out our super-express ally had an extra card up his sleeve."

Even over the comm I could hear the hiss as she inhaled sharply. *"Minnario?"*

"Bingo," I said. "Fortunately, the truce appears to still be on. Doug and Ty are also members of the club—go ahead and follow him."

"Are you sure?" she asked, her voice strained. "I mean—"

"I know, I know," I cut her off. "But go back and think about everything that's happened here. He's been running interference for us against the Shonkla-raa ever since we set foot on the station. Including having Ty stay with you for protection, despite the fact the animal had been ordered to stay with me."

"Yes, but—"

"More to the immediate point, up until thirty seconds ago Wandek and his buddies had me in an airtight frame-up," I went on. "There's no game the Shonkla-raa and Modhri could possibly be playing that would put us in a worse predicament than they already had us in. So just go—I'll join you as soon as I can."

"All right," she said, still reluctant but with a firmness in her voice that meant she was ready to go along with the new plan.

"And watch yourself," I added. "See you soon."

I keyed off the comm and slipped it into my pocket. "How is he?" I asked as I tipped the chair over on its side and started removing the thrusters. The central stabilizer Minnario had mentioned the first time we'd taken the chair apart was visible from this angle: a plain cylinder the size of the other thrusters, but with six vertical lines of hash vents instead of the thrusters' three.

"He's very much unconscious," the Modhri said grimly. "At the very least he has a mild concussion. It may be more severe than that."

"Can you do anything to help?" I asked. Freeing two of the thrusters, I slid them up under two of the desk's corners, giving them just enough juice to lift that side of the desk half a meter off the floor.

"Do you think I function as a medical implant?" the Modhri retorted.

"So that's a no," I said as I pulled two more of the thrusters from the chair. "That means we'll have to find someplace where we can get him proper medical attention."

"If you think that's wise," the Modhri said doubtfully. "It's certainly not necessary—I can function well enough without him."

"That's the kind of talk that makes people not like you," I admonished as I set the thrusters beneath the desk's other two corners.

"Yes, of course," he said. "I understand. Forgive me."

I paused, frowning around the corner of the desk at Minnario's unmoving form. Had the Modhri actually *apologized* to me? "It's okay," I said as I keyed in the thrusters and cranked up the other side of the desk. "Besides, unless Doug's a lot better at charades than he looks, we definitely still need Minnario, or at least his mouth. Speaking of which, how are you hearing me right now? Or isn't Minnario really deaf?"

"Yes, he is," the Modhri said. "I'm hearing you through Doug's ears."

"Ah," I said, detaching two more of the chair's thrusters and looking for some way to attach them to the rear of the hovering desk. "So how come you didn't join the party when Muzzfor called up everyone else back on the super-express? You could hear his siren song through the other walkers' ears, couldn't you?"

"I don't know the answer to that," he said. "But I suspect that the sound works on an Eye's polyp colony directly through his auditory system. Hearing it through the group mind isn't the same as having the physical effect of the physical sound coming through the Eye's own ears. But whatever the reason, I wasn't affected that way."

Minnario's body gave a sudden shiver. "You don't know what it was like, Compton. You can't possibly know. I could feel the tug of his orders, could feel the helplessness and horror of it filling my mind. For the first time in any part of my experience this particular part of the mind was cut off from all the rest. It was terrifying."

"It's called being alone," I said, pulling out the two middle desk drawers and probing with my hand at the panels at the back ends. The wood seemed thick enough to handle the pressure the thrusters would be exerting. "Very popular among all the rest of us."

"So I understand," the Modhri said, some of the horror fading away. "But it's not something I'm accustomed to. What's your plan?"

"To get us the hell out of here before the receptionist gets back," I said, sliding one of the thrusters into each of the empty drawers. "Any idea how we're doing on time?"

"If *Usantra* Wandek's numbers were right, we have another five minutes."

And Wandek's estimate could easily be off by a minute or two. "Okay, here's the rundown," I said as I stood up and turned Minnario's chair upright again. "The door's locked, and it may be soundproof, but it isn't particularly thick or strong."

"So you're going to ram the desk into it?"

"Right," I said, looking at the controls. Earlier, when

we'd been moving the unconscious Kordiss inside Yleli's file cabinet, I'd watched how Minnario had operated the detached thrusters. I wouldn't have nearly his finesse, but I was pretty sure I could duplicate his technique as far as I needed.

Only with four of the thrusters now taking the desk's weight and two more positioned to push it across the room, there were only two thrusters left to power the chair. The chair that Minnario had said required three to function.

"Is there a problem?" the Modhri asked.

"Minnario's chair is one thruster short," I told him as I lugged the chair over to Minnario's sprawled body and got a grip under his arms. My brief Westali medical training had mentioned the risks of moving someone with a head injury, but it would be a hell of a lot more dangerous to leave him here. "If we've got time to retrieve at least one of the thrusters after we crash the desk, we'll be okay," I went on as I carefully lifted Minnario and eased him into his chair. It was harder and a lot more awkward than it looks in dit-rec dramas.

"Why won't there be time?" the Modhri asked.

"Because if Wandek has any brains at all he'll have someone loitering out there to make sure things go as planned," I said. "In which case, we'll have a very limited number of seconds in which to barrel our way over, around, or through him."

"And thus may not have time to retrieve the thrusters," the Modhri said. "Yes, I understand. Have you a plan?"

"We'll find out in a second." I adjusted Minnario so that he was more or less upright, and keyed the switch. The chair rose a few centimeters on the remaining thrusters and stopped, hovering a bit uncertainly. Functional, but barely, and only if there weren't any obstacles along the way taller than someone's foot.

Which meant we were going to have to get creative.

"Doug?" I called, beckoning to the watchdog. "Front and center."

For a second the animal hesitated, and I could swear I could see an inquisitive frown on his face. Then the look cleared away. He trotted over, nudged his muzzle under the edge of the chair, and slid the whole thing up onto his back.

"Even with the thrusters taking some of the weight, he won't be able to carry it very far," the Modhri warned.

"He shouldn't have to," I said. "I just need you to be able to make a run for it if I end up tangling with one of Wandek's buddies."

"You mean you would fight him alone?" the Modhri asked, his voice suddenly tense. "No, you mustn't. I've fought against Shonkla-raa. You can't possibly survive such a battle."

"I fought him too," I reminded him, "and I'm very open to suggestions. You think Doug could take one of them?"

"By himself, no," he said. "But he could delay a single enemy long enough for us to escape."

"You mean before the Shonkla-raa killed him?"

"Well . . . yes," the Modhri conceded.

I grimaced. It made sense, I knew, certainly if it came down to a question of Doug or Minnario and me. But the idea of deliberately sending even an animal to die in my place didn't feel very good. "Let's see how it plays out," I said. Switching to the proper section of the chair's control panel, I ran a little more power to the four supporting thrusters.

The desk rose to waist height. I lowered it back down to knee height and got a grip on the power controls for the remaining two thrusters.

And paused as an odd thought suddenly struck me. Before he was murdered, Hchchu had said he had been studying me. He'd also had my reader right there in his top desk drawer.

And if he'd wanted to take a closer look at my reader . . .

"Only three minutes left," the Modhri said urgently. "Is there a problem?"

"Hang on," I said. Mentally crossing my fingers, I stepped to the desk and pulled open the drawer.

And found my lips tightening in my first genuine smile in a long, long time. Collected neatly together in the drawer were all the items Hchchu had taken from Bayta and me our first hour aboard the station: my multitool, watch, lighter, and data chips; Bayta's jewelry, her reader and data chips, and the *kwi*.

And, most wonderful of all, my Beretta.

"No problem at all," I told the Modhri as I grabbed everything and stuffed it all into my pockets. I checked the Beretta's magazine, then flicked the selector to the snoozer side and chambered a round. "Brace yourself," I warned as I stuck the gun into my belt and resumed my grip on the chair's thruster controls. "This is probably going to be loud."

I keyed the driving thrusters, and the desk took off like a carved wooden bat out of hell. It shot across the room and with a thunderous crash slammed into the door, bending and then shattering the panel as it was itself bent and shattered. Thumbing off the Beretta's safety, I charged.

The Modhri was faster. Doug leaped out in front of me, loping along the floor like a greyhound who's spotted a rabbit. He reached the crumpled remains of the desk, still hovering on its thrusters, and leaped up and over it.

Minnario wobbled violently as the animal negotiated the wreckage now wedged into the doorway, but remained in his seat. Landing on the far side, Doug paused just long enough for the chair to mostly come back to balance, then took off down the hallway. I did a sort of half jump, half climb over the desk that wasn't nearly as graceful as the watchdog's and followed.

I had just registered the fact that the receptionist's desk was still unoccupied when Jagged Nose suddenly charged into view from around the corner.

Whatever he'd expected to see in the aftermath of all that noise, the sight of Doug and Minnario bearing down on him like an undersized elephant carrying a howdah on his back was definitely not it. Even at this distance I could see the Shonkla-raa's eyes widen and his blaze pale as he took a reflexive step backward.

But almost before he'd finished that step he was back on mental balance. He set one foot behind him, bracing himself into combat stance, stretching one hand in front of him to take the brunt of the impending collision. He stiffened the other hand into a knife and cocked it back at his waist, ready to skewer either Minnario or Doug when they reached him.

Cursing, I threw myself flat on my belly on the hallway. "Veer right!" I snapped, bringing my Beretta to bear.

Instantly, Doug dodged to the side, Minnario's chair again threatening to fall off with the sudden change of direction. Jagged Nose spotted me and my gun, and he had just enough time to do the eyes-widening thing again before I dropped him onto the floor with three snoozers to the chest.

I scrambled back to my feet as Doug came to a wobbly halt beside the unconscious Filly, his head darting back and forth. "We're alone," Minnario called softly. "But others are coming. Come quickly."

"Thirty seconds," I called back. Stripping off my jacket, I laid it out on the floor beside the hovering desk wreckage, then crouched down and reached to the rear of the desk, shutting off and retrieving one of the supporting thrusters back there. I laid it on top of the jacket and then pulled out the second rear thruster, that end of the desk dropping to the floor with a muffled thud as its support disappeared. I set the thruster on the jacket beside the first, then repeated the procedure with one of the front thrusters, leaving the desk balanced precariously on a single point.

"Now!" the Modhri called, his voice urgent. "Come *now*!"

"Go," I ordered, eyeing the fourth thruster and reluctantly concluding that as the last support for the hovering desk it would be tricky and time-consuming to extricate. Wrapping the sides of my jacket around the three thrusters, I tied the sleeves together and tucked the bundle under my arm.

Doug had disappeared from the intersection as I scrambled back to my feet. Getting a grip on my Beretta, I sprinted down the hallway, passed the reception desk, and charged around the corner into the wider intersecting hallway.

And came to a screeching halt. There were others coming, all right: five Jumpsuits, hurrying toward me from that end of the corridor. A quick look over my shoulder showed four more coming from behind me, as well.

I breathed out a curse, wishing to hell that I'd been a little more circumspect in my approach to the intersection. If I'd seen the patrollers before they saw me, I would have been able to duck behind the receptionist's desk, and with a little luck they might have all charged past into Hchchu's office and missed me completely. Too late for that now.

Which left me facing nine armed opponents with twelve snoozers and fifteen thudwumpers in my Beretta and a pair of badly untenable options. I could open fire here and now, leaving my back open to one group or the other but offering the hope that the cross-fire landscape would encourage them to take out a few of their own number for me. My other choice was to retreat back to Hchchu's office, where I would be trapped with a freshly murdered assistant director, and hope I could hold out long enough to come up with something clever.

Whichever option I chose, I had only seconds to implement it. The Jumpsuits had already picked up their pace as they spotted what could only be interpreted as a suspicious figure with ill-gotten loot in hand. All five of the Fillies I was currently facing had dropped their hands to the grips of their holstered beanbag guns, and the patroller slightly in the lead was already in the process of drawing his. {Halt, Human,} he ordered sternly.

I had just about decided that I had no choice but to have it out right here when a half-dozen watchdogs suddenly appeared behind the Jumpsuits, filtering into our corridor from different offices and cross-corridors. I glanced behind me and saw the same pickup posse closing on the other group.

"Damn," I muttered, turning back to the first group of Jumpsuits. A nice, straightforward plan, and under other circumstances I would have welcomed the Modhri's help.

But not here, and not now. There was no rational reason why a whole bunch of otherwise peaceful domesticated animals would suddenly gather and attack a group of Proteus security personnel. The news of such an event was bound to flash across the station with the kind of speed that only rumors and bizarre news could achieve, certainly long before Bayta and I could find a way off the station.

And even if the patrollers themselves never figured out what had gone wrong with their pets, the Shonkla-raa certainly would. And the minute they realized how and where the Modhri had been hiding aboard Proteus and started singing their siren song to the four-footed walkers, it would be all over. They would have Bayta, and they would have me, and death would be the best either of us could hope for.

There was only one chance I could see to get out of this before it was too late. It would mainly be the un-provoked nature of the impending attack, I judged, that would clue in the Shonkla-raa. Ergo, I needed to come up with some kind of plausible yet obvious explanation for their actions. Something that would fool the Jumpsuits, and might at least give the Shonkla-raa pause.

And I had all of two seconds to pull it off.

The only thing within easy reach was Bayta's reader, tucked into my jacket pocket just in front of my left arm on the outside of my bundle of thrusters. I snatched it out, made a show of quick-punching a half-dozen keys at random, and held it high above my head.

And even as the rest of the patrollers drew their weapons in response, both groups of watchdogs slammed full tilt into them from behind.

It was as impressive a scene of utter chaos as I've ever had the chance to witness. In an instant every Jumpsuit had been knocked to the floor, yelping or screeching with shock, anger, and bewilderment as the watchdogs ran back and forth over their bodies as if they'd all gone insane.

All of them, that is, except one. He was hanging back behind the general pandemonium, standing motionless and gazing steadily at me.

I held my pose for another three seconds, knowing that the more Jumpsuits who spotted the reader and came to the intended conclusion, the better. Then, lowering my arm, I again tapped a couple of keys at random and charged into and through the bedlam and down the hallway. My guide waited until I was almost to him, then turned and loped off, staying just ahead of me.

"Stop the attack and send them back to where they all came from," I ordered the watchdog quietly as he led me around a corner into a cross-corridor. "Have them look shocked and bewildered, like they've just come to their senses and have no idea what just happened. Even better, if you can pull it off, have them look embarrassed or frightened."

The watchdog gave an acknowledging yip and picked up his pace. Ahead, I could see an open service-elevator door off the corridor to the right. My guide gave me another yip and put on a final burst of speed, skidding a little on the floor as he cornered, and disappeared through the open door. With a final glance over my shoulder, I followed.

Doug and Minnario were waiting, the other watchdog panting beside them, when I ducked through the doorway. "Keypad beside the floor-selector panel," Minnario murmured. "Enter the code 33951 and then Floor 201."

I nodded and punched the keys as instructed, relieved that the Filly obsession with nucleics and nucleic locks hadn't extended to their maintenance equipment. Though that was probably because there were too many people using the gear to make something like that practical. "Thanks for the assist, by the way," I said as the door slid shut and we headed up. "But next time, clear it with me first, will you? The last thing we can afford is for the Shonkla-raa to realize—"

"There is trouble, Compton," Minnario murmured. "They have her."

My heart seized up in my chest. "What?" I demanded.

"They have her," he repeated miserably. "They have Bayta."

SIXTEEN :

"They took her from behind," he told me, his voice strained. "There were two of them—there may have been more waiting, but no one else joined in the attack. I'm so very sorry—"

"Forget the sorry," I bit out, forcing back my own anger and fear. Regrets and recriminations wouldn't do anything to help Bayta now. "What did they do? How did they attack? Calm down and think."

"They came from behind," the Modhri said, sounding marginally calmer. "I think they must have been on the same train."

"That, or they had someone waiting at every stop, which is pretty unlikely," I agreed grimly. They probably tailed her from the courtroom, ready to snatch her if and when Emikai got careless.

But I'd changed the game when I broke out of Hchchu's office. Wandek's response had been to abandon his original policy of stealth and secrecy and to send an order for them to move in and take her.

The crucial question was how much the Shonkla-raa knew or suspected. "Who did they attack first?" I asked Minnario. "Emikai or Ty?"

"Emikai," he said. "It was a well-coordinated attack. One of them hit the nerve centers in his back and side, and when those impacts swung him around the other attacker paralyzed his gun arm and then knocked the air out of his lungs with a blow to his chest."

"What about Ty? Did they take him out right away?"

"No, not until after they'd subdued Bayta," he said. "The first attacker grabbed her arms while the second finished disabling Emikai. She managed to kick him twice, but though the kicks seemed to be on target there was no apparent effect."

I nodded. Bayta may not have liked watching my sparring sessions with Emikai, but it was obvious she'd been taking mental notes on where and how to hit a Filly. Unfortunately, the Shonkla-raa had already been way ahead of her. "They probably had their most vulnerable nerve centers moved or overlaid when they had their throat work done," I said. "Emikai warned me about that possibility. What happened next?"

"Once Emikai was down, the second attacker joined the first in subduing Bayta," the Modhri said. "They each took an arm, holding her close so that she couldn't kick them anymore." Minnario's face creased in a frown. "And then, as they started to drag her away, she said something. She shouted, 'To Scotland! To Scotland!'"

I frowned. What the hell was that supposed to mean? "Who was she saying it to?"

"She was facing Emikai at the time," the Modhri said slowly. "But I had the impression she was actually talking to me. It was then that the second attacker seemed to notice Ty and kicked him in the belly. He was disabled and couldn't follow, but could only watch as they took her down the corridor to one of the nearby elevators."

I looked down at Doug and the other watchdog, feeling my stomach curdle. It wasn't enough that they'd taken down Emikai, but they'd kicked a dog, too. Bastards. "Is he okay?"

"How can you think—?" The Modhri broke off. "Yes, he'll recover. So will Emikai, though you haven't asked."

"I haven't asked because I expected them to be more careful with him than with Ty," I growled. "Emikai's an ex-cop, and no one kills or seriously injures a cop unless they absolutely have to. Aside from everything else, it can be bad for your health when the other cops catch up with you." I took a deep breath. "Okay. We've got some good news, and some bad news. The bad news is obvious. The good news is that the Shonkla-raa haven't yet tumbled to the fact that you're here, and that you're inside the watchdogs."

"How do you conclude that?" the Modhri asked. "Because they attacked Emikai first?"

"More precisely because they *didn't* attack Ty first," I said. "They also didn't make sure he was dead or unconscious, which they should have if they'd known you were there and didn't want you monitoring the rest of the proceedings. Bayta tried to help that along by shouting her message toward Emikai instead of Ty. If we're lucky, they'll remain clueless long enough for us to get her free."

"How do we . . . how do we do that?" the Modhri asked.

I frowned at Minnario's face. He wasn't looking good at all. "Modhri, what's happening with Minnario? Is he getting worse?"

"I will hold on as long as possible," the Modhri said. "What did she mean, *to Scotland*?"

"Obviously, that was a message to me," I said, resting two fingers against the side of Minnario's neck. His pulse was slow and thready. "Where are we heading, anyway?"

"The atmosphere treatment and renewal area in the upper domed section," the Modhri said. "Access requires the code you used a moment ago, which means only techs and supervisors should be there. What sort of message would it be?"

"First things first," I said, trying to get my brain working. They weren't going to hurt Bayta, I reminded myself firmly. They wanted to study her, and that would take time. We still had time. "How many walkers do you have aboard Proteus?"

"Four hundred and sixty-eight, all *msikai-dorosli*," he said. "There are also several upper-level Filiaelians and mid-level techs whom I may be able to influence through thought viruses."

"That could be handy," I said. "How often do any of the watchdogs wander off on their own? Or are they mostly locked up in apartments or offices?"

"Occasionally, one is seen out alone," the Modhri said. "But not commonly."

"Can you use thought viruses on their masters to get them to go out for some exercise?" I asked. "We need to get them out looking for Bayta."

"I may be able to do that," the Modhri said. "But I don't think it will be necessary. Give me a little more time, and I'll find her."

"If you're counting on the security system, don't," I warned. "Because our next job is going to be to scramble, cripple, or shut down the cameras, as quickly and thoroughly as we can."

Minnario shook his head weakly. "No need. There are only limited cameras in the upper service areas."

"But there are hundreds of the damn things in the

main part of the station," I countered. "And our absolute next priority is to get Minnario to a medical center. If he doesn't get treatment, and fast, he's going to die."

The Modhri was silent for so long I began to wonder if Minnario had slipped into a coma that even his resident polyp colony couldn't break through. "You care a great deal about other living beings," he said at last.

"One of my many weaknesses," I said shortly. "Can you find me the nearest medical center and the fastest way to get us there? If we can do some of the trip through the upper industrial areas, fine. But if that's going to slow us down, we'll just have to take our chances in the main sections."

"Understood," the Modhri said. "Give me a moment."

He fell silent again. Setting my bundle on the floor, I opened it and started reattaching the thrusters to Minnario's chair. When I finished, it was once again hovering at its usual waist height. "Anything?" I prompted. "Modhri? You still there?"

"I'm still here," he assured me in a raspy voice. "The closest medical center is an emergency node in the next subsector inward, in one of the upper floors."

"How long until we can get there?"

"Not long." I felt the elevator car come to a halt, and drew my Beretta as the doors slid open.

There was no one visible. Doug and the other watchdog trotted out, looked in both directions— "Clear," the Modhri said. "We go left."

I got a grip on the chair's control stick, maneuvered Minnario out of the car, and headed left.

Instead of an actual corridor, with walls and a ceiling and everything, we were in what was simply an extra-wide open space surrounded by industrial equipment. Most of it consisted of dozens of varying-sized tanks, connected by kilometers of rigid pipes and flexible tubing, with occasional readout stations and overhead fans whose sole purpose seemed to be to move the tropical air around instead of actually doing anything to cool it. The watchdogs broke into a fast lope; I adjusted Minnario's chair to match their speed and followed. "How long to the emergency node?" I asked.

"Perhaps ten minutes of walking up here, then a short elevator ride, then three more minutes of walking," the Modhri said.

"Can Minnario hold out that long?"

"I think so." The Modhri hesitated. "But there may be a problem. The emergency node is on the edge of the main administrative part of *Kuzyatru* Station, which is almost certainly now engaged in a frenzied hunt for you. Worse still, there is a security nexus only four doors away."

"That could be a problem, all right," I agreed. "Any progress with the security cameras?"

"No," he said. "I'm sorry, but I have no direct access to patrollers or patroller equipment."

I hissed between my teeth. This just got better and better. "Any chance you can bring Minnario to the node alone? Just do what you're doing right now and tell them you had an accident and get them working on you?"

"I don't think so," he said. "I can talk, but I can't operate his arm and therefore the chair controls. But one of the *msikai-dorosli* may be able to pull me in."

"Is that something they might conceivably do on their own?"

"I don't know," he said. "I've never seen them do anything like that during my time here."

"Well, just because you haven't seen it happen doesn't mean it can't," I said, blinking sweat out of my eyes. "I'll get you down to the right floor, and they'll have to take it from there."

"You mean you'll ride in the elevator?"

"I doubt those paws can handle the buttons." I frowned as something suddenly struck me. "They *can* handle computer keys, though, can't they? *You're* the one who put that message on my computer the night Yleli was murdered."

"Yes," he said. "Their claws aren't designed to handle the necessary pressure needed for the elevator buttons, but they're strong enough to push computer keys."

"I suppose you're the one who took out the medical-dome cameras, too," I said as it all fell into place. "You used Minnario and one of the thrusters from his chair to bend the one upward, while Doug just leaped up and tore the other one off its gimbals with his claws."

"Yes," the Modhri said again. "I was intrigued by the mystery of Building Twelve, and since you had expressed interest in looking into it, I tried to clear the way for you." His breathing caught, halted for a couple of seconds, then resumed. "Unfortunately, before I could get the message to you the Shonkla-raa saw the camera damage, assumed you were responsible, and prepared a trap for you."

"Just as well they didn't see you actually take them out," I said, eyeing Minnario apprehensively. He seemed to be fading fast. "How much farther?"

"Not far," the Modhri said. "But you won't be coming with me."

"I thought we just decided I had to," I reminded him.

"You can enter the elevator, push the proper buttons, and then leave," he said. "The *msikai-dorosli* can take him the rest of the way."

I shook my head. "No good. Like you said, they don't usually go wandering Proteus all by themselves. If someone else gets on along the way and sees a pair of them out for a walk, he'll either call the Jumpsuits or try to corral them himself. Either way, Minnario's likely to die before you get him to the emergency node."

"Then he will die," the Modhri said firmly. "I cannot permit you to put yourself at such risk. Not with Bayta still a prisoner of the Shonkla-raa. You must stay hidden and decipher her last message to you."

"I can do that and get Minnario to the node, too," I said stubbornly.

"Really? Then tell me the meaning."

I grimaced. "I'm working on it."

"And once you've deciphered it, you still face the task of freeing her and making your escape," he continued. "What is *Scotland*?"

"It's a place on Earth," I said, frowning suddenly as a stray thought caught my mind. With my brain tearing itself apart over the image of Bayta in Shonkla-raa hands, I hadn't remembered . . . but hadn't she just been talking about Scotland?

Yes, she had. Two nights ago, when we were lying together in our adjoining cells in the security nexus after Yleli's murder. She'd been talking about the dit-rec drama *The 39 Steps* and commenting about the similarities to my own situation. And in that story, Scotland was the place where Richard Hannay went to get the answers to the mystery.

No—I was wrong. He found answers there, but that wasn't the reason he went. He went there trying to escape.

And in that same conversation, I remembered now, Bayta had also been evasive about what she'd been doing on the room's computer earlier that evening.

The inference was obvious. Somewhere, somehow, she'd set up a plan for our escape.

Only I didn't have the foggiest idea what that plan was.

"Before the attack, after I talked to her, did she do anything?" I asked the Modhri. "Did she say anything to Emikai, or make any calls?"

"She made one call," the Modhri said. "I wasn't looking at her at the time, but I didn't hear her speak to anyone."

A data transfer? "How long was she on?"

"Not long," he said. "Perhaps half a minute."

So it was either a very short data transfer, or else some kind of activation signal. "Do you know if Proteus is set up so that you can access a personal room computer via comm?"

"I assume so," the Modhri said. "I've never actually tried."

"How about sending a pre-stored message?" I asked. "Can *that* be done?"

"Yes, I believe so."

I grimaced. So her last act before being kidnapped had been to send me a message. Unfortunately, if she'd sent it to our room computer, I wasn't likely to be able to get to it any time soon.

Even worse, if she'd sent it to my comm, Wandek was probably reading it right now.

But Bayta wouldn't have been that careless. Not with the way people were always taking our comms. Had she echoed it back to the one I'd just called her from? I pulled out Minnario's comm, but there were no waiting messages. "I need to crack into the station's comm system," I said. "Do you have any of the access codes?"

"No," the Modhri said. "Only senior communications techs and *santra*-class administrators have that access."

I cocked an eyebrow. "Or patrollers?"

He was silent a moment. "I don't know. Perhaps."

It was a risk, I knew. A big risk. But I had no choice. Bayta had sent me a message, and I absolutely needed to find out what that message said. Trying to stifle my sense of misgiving, I punched in Emikai's number.

"It's Compton," I said when he answered. "First of all, are you all right?"

"I am uninjured," he said, his voice dark with anger and shame. "I am sorry, Compton. She was taken."

"I know," I said. "Don't worry, we're going to get her back. I'm told she made a call just after I talked to the two of you. Did you see who she called, or what the signal was, or anything about it?"

"I believe it was a call to the queue," he said. "The part of the system where outgoing messages are stored for later transmission."

"But you didn't see who the message was being sent to?"

"The destination would be part of the outgoing message," he said. "She would only have transmitted a preset code."

I squeezed the phone. "*Logra* Emikai, I need to get a look at that message," I said. "You're an official Proteus Station patroller now. Is there any way you can get access to it?"

"Are you still under suspicion of murder?"

I grimaced. "Probably."

"Then the answer is yes," he said. "If you are a suspect in a major crime, all information concerning you or your associates is open to me, including any message records."

"Terrific," I said. "Get on it as soon as you can. And add in a search for the keyword *Scotland*. Let me know the minute you have something."

"I will," he promised. "Stay safe."

"Bet on it." I keyed off and dropped the comm back into my pocket. "Modhri?"

"Just ahead," he said.

"I see them," I said as I spotted a small bank of elevators. Releasing the chair control, I ran ahead and punched the call button, then returned and finished moving the chair to a halt in front of the elevators. "Just tell them you had an accident, that you hit your head on something," I instructed him. "Do *not* say anything about someone hitting you. Am I going to need an access code to get off this floor?"

"No, only to enter it," he assured me. "The floor you want is 142."

The doors of the middle car opened, and the two watchdogs bounded inside. I followed with the chair, punched in the floor number, and started to turn the chair around to face forward—

Without warning, Doug grabbed my jacket sleeve in his jaws and yanked hard, pulling me off-balance and halfway through the open door. Before I could recover, the other watchdog threw his full weight against my back, sending me sprawling onto the floor outside the car.

"Save Bayta," Minnario said, his voice whispery soft.

I had just enough time to turn around, and not nearly enough time to get my sleeve out of Doug's grip, when the other watchdog leaped back inside and the doors slid closed.

And they were gone.

"No!" I shouted toward the closed door. "No! Damn you—" I broke off as Doug released my arm, and I shifted my glare to him. "*Damn* you, anyway," I snarled, raising my fist in a flash of blind fury.

Doug didn't move, but just stood there looking back at me. For a frozen second I continued to glare at him, my pulse pounding in my throat, my fist shaking with helpless rage.

And then the rage faded, and with another, quieter, curse I let my arm fall uselessly to my side. How could I take out my frustrations on an animal that didn't even know what he was doing?

For that matter, how could I even be angry at the Modhri? He had the same facts that I did, and had simply come to a more practical and less emotion-driven conclusion as to our best strategy.

With a sigh, I climbed back to my feet, wondering briefly if I should try calling another car and following them down. But since the whole idea had been for me to be there to fend off anyone curious or meddlesome enough to interfere with the supposedly stray watchdog, riding down in a completely different car would be pretty useless. "So what now?" I asked.

Doug gave a little woof and settled back on his haunches. "Right," I said with another sigh. "I guess we wait."

Across the passageway from the elevators, tucked in behind some kind of forced-air filter, was yet another monitor station, currently unmanned like all the others we'd encountered. I pulled out the chair, dropped into it, and settled down to wait. Doug sat down again on his haunches in front of me. Then, perhaps knowing better than I did that we were in for the long haul, he lay all the way down, settling his head between his front paws.

I closed my eyes, a wave of weariness washing over me, my mind churning with fear and anger. Beneath the thunderclouds of emotion a colder part sifted through contingency plan after contingency plan, most of them completely impractical, all of them an utter waste of effort given that I didn't even know where the Shonklaraa had taken her, let alone what kind of defenses and safeguards they might have arranged.

And between all the worry and the grandiose plans, I thought about the Modhri.

Why was he helping us this way? True, aboard the super-express I'd had a temporary truce with the mind segment Minnario had been part of. But there had been good and urgent reasons for us to work together there, namely the presence of a shadowy murderer who seemed to be killing passengers at random, including some of the Modhri's own walkers.

But that threat was long since past. Even if it hadn't been, Minnario hardly held the controlling interest in the Modhran mind segment that had already been here on Proteus when he came over from the Quadrail.

Or was that even how it worked? The group mind concept sounded simple enough in theory, with the makeup of each mind segment continually changing as new walkers moved into or out of range, with each new bit of experience and information eventually rippling out to reach every segment as travelers carrying that information moved back and forth across the galaxy.

But the more I thought about the actual mechanics of how such a mind worked, the more tangled the whole thing got. Bayta and I were pretty sure the Modhri had established a new homeland on the Human world of Yandro, and we'd speculated that there was some kind of overall strategic or planning area centered in the mind segment there. But the details of how that actually worked were still pretty vague.

There was another possibility, of course, namely that the Modhri wasn't actually on my side at all, but that this was some elaborate game designed to run us in circles until we dropped. But as I'd already told Bayta, I couldn't for the life of me see any point in that. If the Modhri was working with the Shonkla-raa, Wandek and his buddies could have had us any time they wanted. They could certainly have snatched Bayta while she was sitting at Terese's bedside with Minnario and Dr. Aronobal.

Besides, there was still the fact that if they wanted Bayta under their control, the simplest of all possible solutions was to scratch her with a piece of Modhran coral. Once a polyp colony had formed beneath her brain, they could sing their Modhri siren song and have her just walk into their lab, with no fuss, bother, or questions asked. No, whatever the Shonkla-raa knew about the Modhri in general, they had no idea that he was aboard Proteus.

But that blissful ignorance was about to come to an abrupt end. Even if my improvised explanation for the Modhri's massed watchdog attack had managed to fool them, they were certainly already thinking and wondering. Add to it the soon-to-be-circulating tale of another watchdog miraculously pulling a semiconscious Nemut from an elevator to an emergency node, and that wondering would blossom into full-blown suspicion.

And once *that* happened, all one of them would have to do would be to find the nearest watchdog and hum his siren song. The Modhri might not want to draw attention to himself by activating all four hundred sixty-eight of his watchdog walkers, but I doubted the

Shonkla-raa would be so worried about rocking the boat that far.

Bayta and I might be able to elude a couple dozen Shonkla-raa, or however many were aboard the station. There was no way we could elude them *and* four hundred watchdogs besides. An hour or two after Minnario arrived at the node, the Shonkla-raa would suddenly have themselves a brand-new army.

We absolutely had to be off Proteus before then.

I was still gnawing at the edges of the problem when Minnario's comm suddenly vibrated in my pocket.

It was Emikai. An oddly confused-sounding Emikai. "Are you certain you are under suspicion of a crime?" he asked.

"I was spotted leaving the scene of a murder," I said. "I also shot a *santra* with a couple of snoozers. Either one of those should have done the trick."

"Apparently not," he said. "Your name is not on any of the patroller search-and-detain lists."

I frowned at Doug, who was back on his feet looking alertly up at me. "That's impossible," I said. "You sure you didn't just miss it?"

"I did not miss anything," he said sternly. "Nor did I have to. Your records and Bayta's would have been automatically opened to patroller access as soon as your name was listed. Since those records are still blocked, you are clearly not on the list."

I grimaced, feeling like a fool. Of course Wandek had kept me off the patroller lists. The last thing he wanted right now was for the patrollers to pick me up and hear my side of what had happened in Hchchu's office. "So you got nothing?"

"Not entirely," Emikai said. "Though I could not access individual records, I could search for all messages going through the system at the time she made her call."

"Any torchferry reservations in the mix?"

"No," he said. "Most of the messages were official notifications or internal equipment activations. The only one that struck me as being of interest was a message that had been sent to the laser for transmission to the Tube."

I felt my blood go suddenly cold. Of course. Bayta hadn't just booked us standby passage on the next torchferry, where the Shonkla-raa would undoubtedly be waiting for us to show up. She'd instead sent a message to the Spiders, telling them to come and get us.

Only it wouldn't be ordinary Spiders who arrived on Proteus's doorstep. Ordinary Spiders were genetically incapable of any sort of fighting, and with us trapped in the middle of a Shonkla-raa stronghold, Bayta would have called for someone who could fight.

Which meant she'd called for some defender Spiders.

I stared down at Doug, my stomach hardening into a knot. Back at the beginning of this war, I'd seen a large number of freshly created Modhran walkers take out a whole trainful of Spiders. More recently, on the super-express, I'd seen a single Shonkla-raa freeze a pair of defenders where they stood, while simultaneously taking on three Modhran walkers and Bayta and me and nearly killing all of us. If the Shonkla-raa tumbled to the Modhri's presence on Proteus, not even a group of defenders would have a chance against them.

The Shonkla-raa had wanted Bayta and her symbiotic Chahwyn to experiment on. Now, it appeared, they were going to get a few Spiders as well.

And once they had controlling tones for the Spiders, the Modhri, and the Chahwyn, there would be nothing in the galaxy that could stand in their way. Nothing.

"Compton?"

I shook myself, forcing away that last image. It was a three-hour trip from the Tube to Proteus, with at least two and a half hours left since Bayta's emergency message. We had that long to come up with a plan.

And maybe, just maybe, I had one. "Yes, I'm here," I confirmed. "Are you still willing to help me?"

"In whatever way I can," Emikai promised grimly.

"Shall I have the patrollers launch a search for Bayta?"

I looked at Doug, raising my eyebrows questioningly. He gave a low woof and shook his head side to side. "Not worth it," I told Emikai. "The people who took her will have long since gone to ground. Do you know if Proteus has any docking ports besides the thirty-three big torchliner docking stations around the edge?"

"Yes, there are also over two hundred small service ports scattered around the perimeter of the station," he said. "They are designed to handle maintenance and construction vehicles."

"And as the ports themselves are smaller than the docking stations, I assume the bays they open into are also smaller?"

"Again, correct."

"Good," I said. "Then here's what I want you to do. You'll need to start by going to Sector 25-C and Tech Yleli's old neighborhood."

I told him what it was I wanted him to do. To say he was dubious about the whole thing would have been a serious understatement. "I wish to help you," he said stiffly when I'd finished. "I do not consider it help to be sent on a fool's errand designed merely to keep me out of the way."

"It's not a fool's errand," I assured him. "It is an absolutely vital part of my plan."

"Is it then designed to draw your enemies away from you?"

I took a deep breath. "Look, we don't have time for long explanations. If you don't want to help me, just say so, and I'll do it myself."

He rumbled into the comm. "I will do it," he said.

"Thank you," I said. "Now. I'm guessing Bayta's sent for a transport to come from the Tube to get us. Obviously, it's going to want to avoid all the fuss and bother of the main docking stations, which is why I asked about service bays."

"How will we know which docking station it will arrive at?"

I grinned tightly. That one, at least, was now obvious. "It'll be Bay 39," I told him. "After you dump the package from Yleli's in there, I want you to check up on Minnario. He should be in an emergency node on Floor 142, Sector 16-J, right down the hall from the local security nexus. If he's able to travel, bring him to the docking bay and wait there for Bayta and me. Got all that?"

"Yes," he said. "I trust you will eventually tell me the meaning of all this?"

"If we make it through, you'll get the full explanation," I promised. "If we don't, it won't matter anyway. Get going, and watch yourself."

"You, as well," he said. "Farewell."

I keyed off the comm and looked at Doug. "Well? You know where she is?"

He woofed and bobbed his head. "Good," I said as I stood up. "Let's go get her."

SEVENTEEN :

In theory, now that I knew I wasn't on the Jumpsuits' hunt-and-bag list, it should be safe for me to go back down to the public areas of the station, where there were bullet trains and glideways and all the other conveniences of home.

In actual practice, I had no intention of reentering polite society until I absolutely had to. Wherever Wandek had Bayta stashed, he would be sure to have someone planted in the local security nexus to watch the displays and alert him the minute I showed my face.

And so, with Doug leading the way, we set off across our nice, cozy jungle of pipes, filters, tanks, and high ceilings.

It was slow going. The walkways were designed to give convenient access to the equipment, not to facilitate cross-station travel, and there were a number of times when a path I was following simply dead-ended in a supporting wall or large piece of equipment. At each such T-junction I tried to figure out logically which direction would work best, but I quickly discovered that a flip of a coin would probably do equally well. The Modhri, who I gathered had never had any of his walkers in this particular part of the station, was no better at picking routes than I was.

But he was useful in other ways. Doug was all over the place, scouting ahead, sniffing out the various Fillies on duty and guiding me away from them, and making sure we stayed out of view of the occasional security camera.

Finally, we arrived at a single elevator that had been wedged like an afterthought between a pair of thruster-driven portable extension cranes. Again, Doug's claws weren't strong enough to push the proper floor buttons, but he was able to get up on his hind legs and indicate which ones we wanted. I pressed them, and we headed down. Two minutes later, the doors opened on a narrow, much lower-ceilinged version of the service area we'd just left. A between-floors maintenance crawlspace, I guessed. Doug led the way along a couple more walkways, between consoles and equipment that seemed considerably grimier than the ones upstairs, and we arrived at last beside a horizontal, two-meter-diameter cylinder raised another half meter up off the floor. Its metal surface exhibited the kind of steady vibration that suggested there were one or more fans operating inside. Yet another part of the ventilation system, apparently.

Doug continued on along a narrow pathway paralleling the cylinder. Ten meters later, we reached an outwardly curved wall with a small ventilation grille in it. Doug gave an expectant-sounding woof, and I went up to the wall and pressed my face to the grille.

And felt my throat tighten. Spread out fifteen meters below me were the cedar-covered roofs of a small collection of EuroUnion-style ski chalets. Directly across from my peephole, on the far side of the dome, I could see the wall painting of rugged Alpine mountains.

We were back at the medical dome.

Doug gave a soft, questioning woof. "Sure, why not?" I replied. "With Wandek's planned frame-up no longer pinning me down, he's trying to get back to his preferred approach of stealth and secrecy. But he's also running on borrowed time, and he knows it."

I leaned back and forth around the grille, studying the buildings and surrounding landscape as best I could from my current vantage point. As usual, there were a few Fillies moving between the buildings, but I could also see a couple of figures loitering within view of Terese's old Building Eight. "That's because he has no idea when I'll pop up and try to take her away from him," I continued, turning away from the peephole and looking around the area I was in.

Against one of the side walls I spotted a row of storage cabinets and headed over to check them out. "Or worse, I might manage to get Director *Usantra* Nstroo interested enough to call out the whole Jumpsuit contingent and start hunting them down. Ergo, rather than tuck her away in some anonymous apartment somewhere, he's opted to get right to work figuring out what makes her tick. The only place with the proper equipment is a medical facility; and the only place where a Human patient won't raise eyebrows and unwelcome curiosity is *this* medical facility."

I reached the storage cabinets and opened the first. Inside was a collection of spare valves and fittings, plus a section devoted to replacement control cards. "Unfortunately, Wandek in a tearing hurry means we're in a tearing hurry, too," I said, moving to the next cabinet in line. Flexible ductwork in this one. "It also means we may have to wreck the whole building they've got her in if we're going to make sure they don't get away with any data worth having." I went to the third cabinet and opened it.

Bingo. The entire upper section of the cabinet was crammed to the brim with tightly coiled power cables. "Okay, we're in business," I said, pulling out one of the coils. There was at least thirty meters there, I estimated. Perfect. "Now all we have to do is find a way through this wall," I said, running my eye over the curved metal.

Unfortunately, the only opening I could see that was big enough for me to fit through was currently occupied by the far end of the two-meter cylinder. The one with all the driving fans inside it.

I chewed at the inside of my cheek. I could try working my way around the dome and see if I could find a more obvious way in. Alternatively, I could go down to the public area and just walk in past the receptionist. But the former would take time I didn't have, and the latter would give the Shonkla-raa more warning than I could afford.

I returned to the big cylinder and took a closer look. It was made up of individual two-meter-long segments, either welded together or else connected with some kind of fasteners. I rubbed my fingers along one of the junction lines, brushing off the accumulated dirt. Nothing. I moved to the next junction and repeated the process, then to the next.

Finally, at the fourth junction, I found what I was looking for: a section that was notably shinier beneath the buildup of dirt. Clearly, this part was a replacement that had been added after the original cylinder was installed.

And instead of welds, it was held in place by a set of standard klinckers, probably the galaxy's best compromise between strength and ease of attachment. It was also something my multitool was designed to handle. "Go around to the other side and see if you can spot anything that looks like an access panel—they have to be able to get to the driving fans somehow," I instructed Doug. "I'll start taking this off."

With an acknowledging woof, Doug headed back toward the elevator. Pulling out my multitool, I set to work.

There were six klinckers on this side of the cylinder. I had five of them off when I heard a soft yip from the other side. I finished undoing the sixth fastener, then retraced my steps to the elevator and went around to the cylinder's other side. Doug was waiting at the end by the wall, his head held high in obvious triumph.

There it was: a thirty-centimeter-wide cover panel, situated halfway between the wall and the cylinder section I'd begun loosening. Undoing the four klinckers that held the panel in place, I pulled it off.

Not surprisingly, given the official purpose of the access hole, I was greeted by a blast of warm air from the edge of a spinning fan blade. Blinking against the dust, I peered inside.

One glance was all I needed. The fan was an open design, which meant that once I stopped it I should be able to squeeze myself between the blades. Even better, once I was past the fan the only thing between me and the dome was a fragile-looking grille held in place by four more klinckers.

I looked at Doug. "You're absolutely sure she's in there?"

His woof was about as definitive as a woof could get. "Okay," I said.

There were also six klinckers fastening my target section on this side. I got them off, then worked the now freed section back along the main part of the cylinder until there was an opening big enough for me to squeeze through. Returning to the access panel, I swapped out the klincker tool for the small knife blade and reached gingerly through to the fan's double power cable. Carefully, wondering distantly how much current the fan was drawing, I sliced through both cables.

There was a muffled blue flash, a momentary tingle as some of the rerouted current traveled into my hand and arm instead of down the other wire, and with gratifying speed the fan blades slowed to a stop. I gave the cable one final slice, just to make sure, then turned to Doug. "Here's the drill," I murmured as I started tying my appropriated power cable to the fan housing. "In about two minutes I'll pop open that grating, rappel down through the opening, charge inside, and grab Bayta." I frowned. "She *is* in Building Eight, right? The one where they were keeping Terese?"

Doug woofed and bobbed his head in an affirmative. "While I do that," I continued, "I want you to find some stairs leading to the corridor down there, so that once Bayta and I are out we can sneak back up here. If there isn't any such access, we'll have to split up—you head to Bay 39 on your own, and we'll do the same. Think you can do that?"

Doug woofed again, and with a flick of his tail turned and headed back through the tangle of equipment. I finished tying the cable, slid the coil in through the access panel, then returned to the open section and squeezed through. The opening between fan blades was small, but the thought of Bayta in Shonkla-raa hands was a powerful motivator. A few seconds later I'd made it through and was at the grille.

I had two of the four fasteners off and was starting on the third when Minnario's comm vibrated in my pocket.

I grabbed it, wondering if I dared take the time to get out of the cylinder before answering. All I needed now was to have one of the Shonkla-raa down there hear a Human voice wafting down at him from heaven.

But the minute I entered the dome life was likely to get very hectic indeed. Keying the comm, I pressed it close to my ear and mouth. "Compton," I murmured.

"Emikai," Emikai identified himself, an edge of grim satisfaction in his voice. "We have found her."

I peered through the grille. Nothing out of the ordinary seemed to be happening down there. "Where?"

"A medical storage facility in Sector 18-B," he said. "The patrollers are surrounding the area now."

I felt the sudden pounding of my pulse in my throat. Could the Modhri be wrong about Bayta being in the medical dome below me?

Or had he never intended for me to find her in the first place? Had this whole thing been nothing but a scheme by the Shonkla-raa to get me out of the way while they dragged Bayta's secrets out of her? "How did they find her?" I managed.

"The locator in her comm," Emikai said with even more satisfaction. "Most people who disable their locators do not realize that law enforcers can reactivate them."

I smiled tightly. So actually, they hadn't found Bayta. All they'd found was her comm. An old trick, and a rather childish one at that, but Wandek probably figured that any time he could gain was worth the effort, even if it meant sending Bayta's comm on a trip across the station. "I didn't know that myself," I lied. "Clever."

"Do you want me to join the patrollers in their sweep?" Emikai asked. "I have completed the first part of my errand. I could go to 18-B before I seek out Attorney Minnario."

"No, that's all right," I said. He had better things to do than join the rest of Proteus's Jumpsuits in a wild-goose chase. "I'm closer to 18-B—I'll go. You concentrate on getting Minnario to the bay without being spotted or stopped. Can you alert the patrollers that I'm coming and to hold off their raid until I arrive?"

"I will try," Emikai said doubtfully. "But it may be difficult to hold them back. Filiaelians do not like kidnappers."

"Neither does anyone else," I said. "Tell them I'll be there as soon as I can."

I keyed off the comm and peered again through the grille. All seemed normal down there. Apparently, they hadn't heard me, after all.

And then, the two Fillies I'd seen loitering along the approaches to Building Eight simultaneously strolled away from their posts. Their eyes moved casually around the upper part of the dome as they walked, as if they were merely admiring the mountain painting.

But I wasn't fooled by the carefully crafted nonchalance. They'd heard me, all right, or else the broken fan had clued someone in to the fact that trouble was skulking around up here.

Either way, I was out of time. Wrapping the power cord once around my left leg, I got a grip on it with my left hand, pulled my right foot back, and kicked as hard as I could into the center of the grille.

It popped out with gratifying ease and a clatter that could probably be heard three corridors away. Kicking the coil out of the cylinder, I shoved myself off the lip into the open air and slid toward the deck below.

The two Fillies were already racing toward my landing point, along with three others I hadn't been able to see from my angle. I yanked out my Beretta as I slid toward the ground, lined the muzzle up on the nearest of them, and fired.

The first shot was easy, the snoozer dropping the running Filly into a face-first sprawl and skid on the deck. Unfortunately, shooting while hanging from a rope meant the first shot was the only easy one you got. The gun's recoil threw me into a sudden violent spin, and I wasted my second shot before I was able to nail one of the other Fillies with my third.

And then my feet hit the deck, my bending knees dropping me into a crouch as they absorbed the impact. The remaining Fillies were still coming toward me, but now that I had a stable firing platform I was able to drop them with three quick shots. Dodging through the field of sprawled bodies, I headed toward Building Eight at a dead run.

I was halfway there when the building's door opened and two more Fillies stepped into view. They took a couple of paces toward me and stopped, waiting for me to come to them. I considered giving them a snoozer each, decided to wait until I was closer and could enjoy the thuds as they hit the floor, and kept going.

I don't know what it was that alerted me: an incautious step, a hint of reflection off a window, or just some sixth sense I'd developed during the long months of this war. Whatever it was, I suddenly felt unfriendly eyes on the back of my head, and half turned to look over my shoulder.

All five of the Shonkla-raa I'd just put on the deck were on their feet again, loping silently toward me in an attempt to put me in a pincer that would take me down for good.

And as I skidded to a halt and spun around to face them, the Filly in the lead hurled himself into a pouncing tiger leap straight at me.

There was no time to line up a shot. I ducked to the side out of his path, dodged his flailing arm, and slammed the Beretta's muzzle hard into his side as he passed.

Only instead of feeling the softness of flesh and the slightly flexible hardness of the bone structure beneath it, I felt the muzzle bounce off something hard and unyielding.

Apparently, Wandek had learned from Jagged Nose's encounter with me outside Hchchu's office and had dug up a few sets of snoozer-proof body armor.

The Filly sailing past finished his arc, landing and instantly spinning around for another try. Again slapping his arms out of the way, I jammed the Beretta's muzzle up under his jaw, right where it joined his neck, and fired.

Snoozer rounds were designed to be fired through normal clothing from at least a couple of meters' distance, and putting one directly into his throat this way was probably going to cause a significant amount of damage. But right now, I didn't give a damn. As he gurgled and started to fall, I did a quick two-step around him to put him between me and the other four attackers and started methodically putting snoozers into their unprotected noses.

The old Shonkla-raa might once have been the undisputed lords of the galaxy, but I doubted that many of them had ever done any of their own actual fighting. This bright new generation probably hadn't done any, either, and I fully expected that the sight of my exposed back would be more temptation than the two Fillies standing by Building Eight could resist.

I was right. Even as I dropped the last of the first wave and spun around again, I found the two of them charging full tilt toward me. An extremely vulnerable position, and one which a trained fighter like me could take full and devastating advantage of.

Except that there were two of them, and I was down to a single snoozer.

The thudwumper half of my magazine still had fifteen rounds in it. But killing or maiming would be to take the fight to a new level, and I wasn't ready yet to push things that far.

But while my attackers were Shonkla-raa, they were also normal sentient beings, with all of a sentient being's reactions. Flipping the selector to the thudwumper side of my magazine, I aimed at the floor ahead and just to the side of the leftmost Filly and squeezed the trigger.

Thudwumper rounds weren't nearly as loud as those from larger and heavier-caliber handguns. But the flat crack of the shot, the dull thud of the impact, and the scream of a near-miss ricochet were just as intimidating. I gave the Fillies a quarter of a second to realize I was no longer firing snoozers, then lifted the gun to point squarely at the one whose foot I'd just missed.

His reaction was exactly what one would expect from anyone not in a suicidal frame of mind, and exactly what I'd hoped for. Reflexively, he skidded to a confused halt, leaving his companion to continue their charge alone.

The first Filly came at me like a Quadrail engine, all speed and power and no finesse whatsoever, and I had the brief impression that he hadn't yet realized that his partner had temporarily opted for the better part of valor. Once again, I did a quick sidestep out of his path. But this time, instead of spending a snoozer on him, I did a quick sweep with my leg and knocked his own legs out from under him.

He hit the ground with a grunt and bounded up again, his body armor cushioning his fall enough to keep from having the wind knocked out of him. But if he was expecting me to stick around for another round, he was severely disappointed. Even before his final bounce along the ground I was on my way again toward Bayta's building, keeping my Beretta trained warningly on the other Filly as I sprinted past him. I reached the building, yanked open the door, and went in.

I'd expected to find a state of chaos, and I was right. The receptionist, who was leaning forward talking urgently into her comm, straightened up so fast she slammed herself and her chair into the wall behind her. I strode past her into the main corridor, Beretta held ready as I watched doctors and techs scrambling desperately out of my way or ducking out of sight into offices, labs, and patient rooms. One of the doctors held his ground, apparently with the idea of standing up to me, changing his mind only when I put another thudwumper into the equipment tray beside him. Amid the spray of shattered plastic and glass he joined his fellows in disappearing through the nearest doorway. I continued on, glancing into each room as I passed it, and finally arrived at Terese's room.

There, just as the Modhri had said, I found Bayta.

She was in Terese's old bed, her arms and legs strapped to the sides, her eyes closed, her face pale and drawn. Dr. Aronobal was standing beside her, a hypo in her hand clearly on its way toward Bayta's arm. Flipping my Beretta's selector again, I put my last snoozer into the center of her blaze.

And barely got the gun turned back around as a movement to my left caught the corner of my eye. "Hold it," I bit out, flicking back to thudwumpers.

I'd rather expected Wandek personally to be handling this one. But instead, the lone figure standing silently by the equipment table was my old friend Blue One. "Well, hello there, *Isantra* Kordiss," I greeted him coolly as I took a hasty step backward. "I'd stay right there if I were you."

"And if I don't?" he challenged, matching my move with a more leisurely step forward.

"No, Frank, don't," Bayta said weakly.

Keeping my eyes on Kordiss, I backed across the room. Kordiss stayed put, his eyes on me the whole way. "You all right?" I asked Bayta as I reached her bedside.

"I'm fine," she assured me. "All they've done is taken some blood and checked my brainwaves. Nothing that will tell them anything."

"Lucky for them," I said, risking a quick sideways look at her. Her eyes were open now, half lidded with probably drug-induced fatigue, but they were bright and aware and defiant despite that. "Otherwise, I'd have to kill all of them."

"No, don't," Bayta said earnestly. "Please. I think that's exactly what they want you to do."

"So that they can haul me up on major felony charges and have the patrollers lock me up and leave you defenseless," I said, switching the Beretta to my left hand and starting to undo the strap around her left arm. "Yes, I know. They've already tried that with *Chinzro* Hchchu." I raised my eyebrows at Kordiss. "Whom *Usantra* Wandek murdered in cold blood while I watched."

"Of which claim you have no proof," Kordiss scoffed. "The patrollers are hardly going to take the word of a Human over that of a Filiaelian *usantra*."

"That's the second time you've tried that argument," I reminded him. The strap was turning out to be trickier than it had looked, especially given that I was trying to unfasten it by touch alone. But there was something in Kordiss's expression that warned me not to take my eyes off him. "It didn't hold much water then, either," I continued. "So how come I'm off the patrollers' bad-guys list? *Usantra* Wandek afraid the techs would run their blood tests and conclude *Chinzro* Hchchu died five minutes after the patrollers started packing up his body?"

"Do you really think you can escape *Kuzyatru* Station?" Kordiss asked, almost conversationally. "Because you'll have to kill me to stop me." He cocked his head slightly as if listening. "Along with many others. Do you hear that?"

I heard it, all right: multiple footsteps out in the corridor, heading determinedly this way at a fast walk. "I hear them," I acknowledged. With a final effort, I ripped the restraint free. "But as it happens, I'm not going to have to kill you *or* them."

And as the first of the approaching Shonkla-raa appeared in the doorway I reached into my jacket pocket, pulled out the *kwi* I'd taken from Hchchu's desk drawer, and pressed it into Bayta's newly freed hand.

The Filly in the doorway was the first to go, collapsing without a sound as Bayta fired the *kwi* at him. The second Shonkla-raa in line flailed in sudden disorientation as he tripped over the unexpected obstacle in front of him, and from the sounds of confusion coming from behind him I gathered the rest of the group were slamming into each other like the characters in an old dit-rec comedy. Kordiss himself had just enough time to snarl something and start into a tiger leap of his own before Bayta zapped him to the floor to join his friend.

"Keep them busy," I ordered Bayta as I got her left leg free. Ducking around the end of the bed, making sure I stayed below the *kwi*'s line of fire, I got to work on the right-hand straps.

By the time I finished, two more of the group had strayed into range and view and joined the growing pile of unconscious Shonkla-raa stretched out on the floor. "You up to traveling?" I asked as I took Bayta's arm and helped her off the bed.

"I think so," she said. She staggered once, then seemed to find her balance. "Yes, I'm all right," she said, reaching for the *kwi* wrapped around her hand. "You'd better have this."

"Keep it," I said, shifting my gun to my right hand and taking her arm with my left. "There are a lot of open spaces here, and the *kwi* doesn't have nearly as much range as the Beretta."

"You *do* realize they're still hoping you'll kill one of them, don't you?" she warned.

"Absolutely," I said grimly. "And if they keep this up they might just get their wish. Let's go."

"Wait a minute," Bayta said, pulling back against my grip as I started us across the room. "What about Terese?"

"No time," I said. "Besides, I don't know where she is."

"We can't just leave her here."

"We won't," I assured her, thinking hard. "I'll get you to safety, and then our new everywhere-friend and I will spread out and look for her."

Bayta's forehead creased slightly, probably wondering about this new profession of friendship on my part, possibly also wondering just how far we could push the Modhri on something like this. But she merely nodded. "Do you have a plan?"

"Mostly," I said. "Stay close to me, and shoot anything that moves."

There were four more Shonkla-raa waiting for us outside the room, huddled behind equipment carts in the corridor or lurking in doorways. Bayta and the *kwi* made short work of all of them. We made it through the building, past the now abandoned receptionist's desk, and headed out into the dome.

I'd expected to face more opposition out there, but to my mild surprise no one was moving or even visible. Either the Shonkla-raa were running out of troops, or else Wandek had finally realized that his strategy was overdue for restructuring and pulled back. Bayta and I crossed the dome unhindered and headed past another deserted reception desk into the corridor.

Waiting half in and half out of an open doorway six doors down was Doug.

"Is that *Doug*?" Bayta asked, breathing hard.

"Our native guide, yes," I confirmed, wondering fleetingly why the Modhri wanted us to go to ground this close to the dome. But he hadn't steered me wrong yet, and I was willing to trust him a little farther. Doug ducked back into the room as we approached, and I got us in behind him just as the door slid shut again.

Only then did I discover that what I'd assumed was a standard guest room or meeting area was in fact a maintenance and storage repository. A repository, moreover, with a set of stairs peeking coyly out from behind a tool rack at the rear.

Doug led the way, bounding up three flights, pausing there to give us time to catch up, then heading off through the maze of industrial equipment. Bayta and I followed, weapons still at the ready, until we reached yet another of the small service elevators. "All the way back up?" I asked as I pressed the call button.

Doug woofed a confirmation. The doors slid open and I got Bayta inside. I punched in the authorization code I'd used at the service elevator near Hchchu's office, then the same floor number, and as Doug slipped inside with us the doors closed and we headed up.

Bayta turned to me. "Thank you," she said quietly.

I looked back at her, my eyes flicking across that face I knew so well, my memory flashing with a hundred images of her cheerful, angry, frightened, or determined. I thought about the Modhri, sitting there watching, and about all the other reasons why it was dangerous for a soldier in enemy territory to allow himself to get too close to someone else.

Taking Bayta in my arms, I kissed her.

The first time I'd done this, back on the super-express Quadrail, the kiss had been a half-reflexive, half-furtive expression of relief that she was alive, tinged with guilt that I'd let Muzzfor get as close as he had to killing us both. This time was different. This time, there was no reflex or furtiveness about it. This kiss was one-hundred-percent passion.

And to my slightly disconcerted astonishment, Bayta held me close, giving back every bit as good as she got.

The last time I'd taken this particular elevator ride, with a murder charge hanging over my head and my mind filled with fear for Bayta's safety, the trip had seemed to last forever. This time, with my mind and arms filled with Bayta herself, it was a whole lot shorter.

Still, I wasn't so enraptured that I didn't remember to break off the kiss and snap up my Beretta toward the doorway as the doors slid open.

There was no one there. "Sorry," I said, a bit gruffly, to Bayta. Not because I was, but because I somehow felt I should be.

"Don't be," Bayta said, her own voice serenely calm. "We're going to Docking Bay 39, right?"

"As per your instructions," I said, trying to compose myself. "Good job with that clue, by the way."

"Thank you," she said. "Hadn't we better be going?"

With a flush of embarrassment, I realized we were still standing inside the elevator, my Beretta still aimed at the industrial landscape outside, my other arm still wrapped around Bayta's waist. "I'm waiting on the Modhri," I improvised, dropping my arm hastily to my side as I looked down at Doug. "Well?"

Doug gave a woof and trotted out of the car.

And I could swear I saw an amused grin plastered across his canine snout.

We didn't do a lot of talking during the trek across the station. The whole area was still hot and dusty, there were still scattered bands of techs and random security cameras to be avoided, and I was still not convinced the Shonkla-raa were going to concede this leg of the trip to us without finding some way to make trouble.

But I did make sure, as we walked, that Bayta got the whole story of Hchchu's murder and Wandek's efforts to frame me for it.

She was silent for a long time after I finished. "You really think the Modhri's on our side?" she asked at last.

"If he's not, he's going to way too much effort here," I pointed out. "Unless running people in circles is how the Shonkla-raa get their entertainment, it seems pretty pointless."

"Not impossible," she murmured.

"But unlikely," I said. "As to *why* the Modhri's helping us, I wish I could tell you. Maybe he sees the Shonkla-raa as competition in his drive to conquer the galaxy, and for the moment we're the best tool he has to whack them with. If there's some other deep, dark secret involved . . ." I trailed off as something suddenly struck me. "Oh, hell."

"What?" Bayta asked tensely.

"No, it's okay," I hastened to assure her. "Something just finally occurred to me." I gestured at Doug, busily scouting out the path ahead. "Remember I told you I named Doug and Ty after a pair of actors in dit-rec dramas involving an old mythic character named Zorro? I may not have mentioned that this particular hero ran with a dual identity: harmless upper-class citizen by day, masked defender of justice at night."

"Dual identities," Bayta murmured. "*Msikai-dorosli* and Modhri."

"I was just thinking that," I confirmed. "Either my subconscious has figured out a way to pick Modhran walkers out of a crowd, or as far back as that first security office the Modhri was able to nail me with at least that much of a thought-virus suggestion."

"And you still think he's on our side?"

I hesitated. If the Modhri had infected me, or even just filled my mind with thought viruses, what good were any of my mental processes? I could sit here with my eyes wide open and not even see a trap closing around me.

But if reason and perception were of no use, I still had logic to fall back on. And logic still told me there was no reason for the Modhri to go through all this effort just to betray us.

And maybe, there was one thing more. "Yes, I do," I said. "And I think I can prove it." I looked around us, at the hundreds of places an eavesdropper could be hidden. "Ask me about it later."

The journey took close to two hours, and by the time Doug finally led us onto an elevator I was on my last legs. The heat had long since plastered my shirt against my skin and my hair across my head, fatigue and dehydration had put a small but noticeable shaking into my arms and legs, and overall I felt like something the cat had brought in to play with.

"I hope the ride you called made it through all right," I commented as our elevator headed down. "I don't know about you, but I'm ready for some cool air and a nice, comfy seat."

"It should be here soon," Bayta said as she wearily brushed some stray hairs away from her face. All in all, she didn't look a whole lot better than I felt.

I hadn't had a chance to look up Bay 39's exact location, but from the floor number Doug had had me push it appeared it was nearly at the bottom edge of Proteus's main disk. Once again, the trip seemed to take forever, but finally the elevator came to a halt and opened into another maintenance area. Doug led us through a few more narrow walkways until we came to a pressure door. Holding my Beretta ready, I punched the release, and waited as the heavy door swung open.

Beyond it, exactly as advertised, was Docking Bay 39.

It was a very small docking bay, I saw as we walked inside, smaller even than I'd expected. It was only about sixty meters long, no more than forty wide, with a ceiling that couldn't top out at more than three meters. Rows of equipment and storage lockers lining the walls made the place feel even more cramped, as did the massive hatch that took up most of the bay's far end.

And waiting for us in the center of the room were Emikai, Minnario, and Ty.

"Welcome," Emikai called, lifting a hand to beckon us over. "I am pleased and gratified that you have made it through safely."

"We're kind of pleased and gratified about that ourselves," I assured him. "I presume Minnario has been keeping you apprised of our progress?"

"Yes," Emikai said, with markedly less enthusiasm as he shot a sideways look at Minnario in his hovering chair. Small wonder, since after hearing my impassioned plea in the courtroom that morning he was probably having trouble adjusting to the idea of the Modhri as an ally. "It has been most . . . interesting."

"The Modhri is definitely all that," I agreed, switching my attention to Minnario. "And you, Minnario? You seem to have made a remarkable recovery."

"He was treated most efficiently and professionally," the Modhri confirmed. "There may yet be some lingering symptoms, but he should recover completely."

"Assuming he gets enough to drink," Emikai put in

wryly. "He insisted we stop at four restrooms along the way here for water."

"There should be plenty to drink aboard the transport," I said. "Though he might have to wait in line behind Bayta and me. A few more minutes, and we'll be out of here."

"You may go," Emikai said. "But I will not. Here, among my people, is where I can best fight against this new threat."

"A noble goal," a soft voice said from my left. "A pity that you won't succeed."

I spun around, snapping up my Beretta. Wandek was standing there, half out of sight between a pair of large floor-to-ceiling oxygen tanks. Set into the bay wall behind him was a half-hidden door.

And between Wandek and the door, standing as straight and silent and motionless as a class of about-to-be-graduated Marines, were at least thirty Shonkla-raa.

"And of course," Wandek continued, his eyes glittering, "none of you will be leaving *Kuzyatru* Station."

EIGHTEEN :

For a long moment no one spoke. No one moved. I could feel Bayta's tension to my left, and Emikai's chagrin to my right. On Bayta's other side, Doug had gone utterly still.

Wandek, too, remained still, and it occurred to me that he was probably waiting for me to offer some response. It seemed a shame to disappoint him. "I see you took my advice," I commented into the silence.

He cocked his head. "What advice is that?"

I nodded to the silent Shonkla-raa behind him. "I said that the next time you came after me you should bring the whole crowd."

Wandek smiled. "And now you think you have me?" he asked. "You and your Modhran ally?"

Abruptly, Doug and Ty launched themselves toward him, snarling like rabid dogs, their teeth gleaming in their open jaws.

But before they'd covered even half the distance, a sudden, high-pitched whistle burst out from the assembled crowd, the sound filling the bay. It seemed to cut straight through my ears and head, sending a bone-jarring tingle through my teeth.

And as abruptly as they'd launched themselves into battle, Doug and Ty screeched to a frozen halt.

"You're a fool, Compton," Wandek said contemptuously, raising his voice to be heard over the whistling. "Did you really think I hadn't noticed the curious change in *msikai-dorosli* behavior that has taken place aboard *Kuzyatru* Station since your arrival? Did you think that such careless terms as *everywhere friend* would go unheard and unnoted?"

"You talk a good fight," I told him. "But as you can see, your impressive little organic Modhri whistle doesn't bother me any." I hefted the Beretta. "I seriously doubt it'll stop a thudwumper, either."

"Do you propose to kill thirty of us with your thirteen remaining rounds?" he countered scornfully. "That would be remarkable marksmanship indeed. And as for your friend and her *kwi* . . ." He gestured to my left.

I looked at Bayta, my throat tightening. The Chahwyn part of her operated on a slightly different telepathic frequency than the Modhri did, and its audio response characteristics were also significantly different. The Shonkla-raa's whistle didn't give them the same kind of direct control over her that they now had over the two watchdogs.

But it was close enough for her to feel some of the same effects. Her face was flushed and rigid, her eyes staring unblinkingly at Wandek, her body trembling visibly as the waves of debilitating sound washed over her. With her mind half frozen in battle against the Shonkla-raa's telepathic call there was no way she would ever be able to aim and fire the *kwi*, or even spare enough focus and energy to activate the weapon for me to use.

I turned in the other direction and looked at Minnario. His face was rigid, too, but not with the watchdogs' loss of control or even Bayta's frozen helplessness. Alone of everyone in the room his deaf ears were immune to the Shonkla-raa's siren song, leaving him still free to act.

But his immunity did us no good. He had no weapons to use against the Shonkla-raa, no tools, no special skills. In one way he was as free as I was. In another, he was effectively as helpless as Doug and Ty.

"Okay, I'll grant you the tactical high ground," I said, turning back to Wandek. "But even if I can't take out all of you, I can definitely put a serious dent in your ranks." I lined up the Beretta on his nose blaze. "And I'm pretty sure I'd start with you."

"I don't think so," he said, lifting a hand. Behind him, at the very rear of the group, there was a small stirring of commotion. Something was moving toward the front—some*one* was moving toward the front—

And from behind one of the Fillies Terese German stumbled into view. Before I could move or speak, Wandek grabbed her arm and yanked her roughly over to his side, planting her directly in front of him.

Emikai snapped something vicious-sounding in Fili. Wandek didn't bother to acknowledge the comment. "Well, Compton?" he invited.

"You're an awfully big target to try hiding behind a Human girl that small," I pointed out. "Terese? How are you doing?"

"How do you *think* I'm doing?" she retorted, her voice shaking. "What the fleeking hell is going on here?"

"In a nutshell, these fine folks want to take over the galaxy," I told her. "Their current plan is to do *in vitro* genetic manipulation on unborn Human babies so as to give them enough telepathic ability that they'll be able to control them." I gestured with my free hand toward Doug and Ty. "The same thing they're doing to those two watchdogs right now."

Terese's face had gone white. "No," she breathed. "That's impossible."

"Unfortunately, it's not," I told her. "That's why they have all those other pregnant women stashed away in Building Twelve."

"They have *other* women?" Terese said weakly.

"But you were a more ambitious experiment," I continued. "What they did with you was hire a thug to attack you on your way home that evening, and after you were unconscious they injected you with sperm specially tailored to create the kind of telepathic Humans they've been trying to manufacture here." I cocked an eyebrow at Wandek. "After all, why bother hauling pregnant Humans all the way to Proteus if you can simply rape them on Earth and get the same result?"

"Why, indeed," Wandek agreed calmly. If he was upset at having his most sordid secrets dragged out in the open for everyone to hear, he was hiding it well. "My congratulations on your deduction. You're more perceptive than I thought."

I inclined my head. "You're too kind."

I'd thought Terese's face was as white as it could get. I'd been wrong. "Oh, God," she breathed, her chest heaving with shallow, rapid breaths, her body tensing as she tried uselessly to flinch away from the grip on her arms. "Oh, God. Oh, God."

"So bottom line: your all-expenses-paid trip here was simply so they could follow up on the experiment and see if it worked," I concluded. "Did it, Wandek?"

"We think so," he said. "We'll need to run a few more tests to be certain."

"I'm sure those tests will be exciting to do," I said, a fresh wave of disgust rolling through me. "A shame that you won't be alive to see the results."

"Please," Wandek said contemptuously. "I can see your hands shaking from here, no doubt a result of all your recent strenuous activity. You won't risk Ms. German's life, not even for the satisfaction of killing me."

"I don't care," Terese snarled. "Go ahead, Compton. Shoot him. *Shoot* him."

"Sorry, Terese, but he's right," I admitted, lowering the Beretta. "But don't give up—we're not down yet." I inclined my head to my right. "Emikai?"

"You expect *Logra* Emikai to help you?" Wandek said knowingly before Emikai could reply. "Again, you nurture useless hopes. I'm an *usantra* aboard *Kuzyatru* Station, and he's a patroller in the same locale. He's bound by his own genetics to obey my commands."

"I wondered why you arranged for his reinstatement," I said, nodding as that piece finally fell into place. "I should have known it would be something like that."

"What he arranged, and why he arranged it, are not important," Emikai said, his voice dark and stiff. "A Filiaelian's identity is in his heart, his mind, and his soul. By your actions and words, *Usantra* Wandek, you have forfeited the right to that name."

Wandek spat. {And you think I find sorrow at that loss?} he said in Fili, the first hint of actual anger coloring his voice. {Be assured that the name I carry now will be far longer remembered.} He glared at Emikai another moment, then turned back to me. "*Logra* Emikai's betrayal is to no end," he said, switching back to English. "He carries an expander weapon, which has no capability to kill or even seriously injure."

"I have an enforcement officer's training," Emikai said ominously, taking a step forward.

"Don't try it," I said quickly. "I've seen Shonkla-raa fight. Any one of them could cut you to ribbons."

"So we reach the end," Wandek said. "If you come quietly, Mr. Compton, I promise to spare the traitor and the cripple."

"Who said the negotiations were over?" I countered.

I'd achieved my first goal, that of getting Wandek to admit the truth about Terese's treatment in Emikai's presence. But there was still one crucial card I had to get Wandek to play if we were going to get out of this alive. "*Logra* Emikai's gun may not kill, but I'll bet a beanbag to the throat would put a serious damper on your ability to control the Modhri."

Wandek sniffed. "Perhaps," he conceded. "But he has only eight shots. Even added to your thirteen, that still leaves you woefully short."

"Which will be of great comfort to the thirteen who'll be dead and the eight who'll be slowly suffocating with crushed throats," I said. "You want to call for volunteers? Or shall we pick them ourselves?"

Wandek smiled. "As a matter of fact," he said, "I believe I *can* furnish you with some volunteers."

"Compton," Minnario's voice wheezed.

I turned my head. The Nemut was leaning sideways in his chair, his face and body racked with pain and frustration. "I'm sorry," he said. "I can't . . . stop him. I'm sorry."

"It's not your fault," I said. Out of the corner of my eye I saw the door behind the group of Shonkla-raa slide open.

And a line of watchdogs marched silently into the docking bay.

Beside me, I heard Bayta give an anguished choke. The animals threaded their way between the assembled Fillies, filed past Wandek and Terese, and arranged themselves in a semicircle centered on Bayta, Emikai, Wandek, and me. I waited, also silently, until the door was closed and the last of the animals took his place in Wandek's new shock front. There were twenty of them, I noted, plus Doug and Ty. "There you are," Wandek said equably. "Twenty-two *msikai-dorosli*. One for each of your shots, plus one left to tear *Logra* Emikai's throat from his body." He cocked his head. "Do you still wish to open fire?"

"Twenty of them here in just a couple of minutes," I commented. "That's very quick work. More of that fear and hopelessness thing you tried on me before?"

"I originally assembled them to deal with the Spiders who even now approach *Kuzyatru* Station," Wandek said, eyeing me closely. "But I can bring more, if your plan was to deplete their numbers before the transport arrives."

"Oh, no, I had no such plans," I assured him. "I *had* wondered, though, how you knew which docking bay to come to. They called ahead to confirm their landing-bay assignment, didn't they?"

"As must all ships approaching *Kuzyatru* Station," Wandek said, his voice oddly distant, his blaze mottling. "Fear and hopelessness, you say, Compton. Yet I see neither in your eyes. Do you believe the Spiders aboard the transport can aid you in defeating me? If so, cleanse that hope from your mind. I'm quite certain that the same tone that commands the Modhri and freezes the alien female at your side will do similarly to them."

"Actually, I wasn't counting on the Spiders at all," I said truthfully. "I think you aren't seeing any hopelessness because you didn't let me finish my question."

He frowned. "What question?"

"The one I was starting to ask *Logra* Emikai a minute ago, before you brought in your Parade of the Watchdogs." I raised my eyebrows. "May I?"

Still frowning, Wandek waved a hand in permission. "Thank you." I turned to Emikai. "Tell me, what happened with the errand I sent you on earlier? The one in Tech Yleli's neighborhood?"

Emikai's eyes flicked to me, and for a pair of heartbeats his blaze darkened with confusion.

And then, I saw his face clear as he suddenly got it. "To the right," he murmured. "Two o'clock."

I nodded, my estimation of Emikai going up another notch at his use of that uniquely Human system of orientation, and turned my eyes in that direction.

There they were, just as I'd asked: eight large metal

cylinders, stacked neatly together on their sides between a pair of equipment lockers.

I turned back to Wandek. "Before I forget, *Usantra* Wandek, I want to thank you for bringing Ms. German along," I said, my eyes dipping briefly to the white-faced girl in front of him. "We wanted to get her off Proteus, but I had no idea where to even start looking. This simplifies things immensely."

Wandek snorted. "You spoke earlier of fear and hopelessness," he said. His earlier wariness was gone, replaced by a fresh wave of contempt. "I see now that you speak mostly of bluff."

"Probably," I agreed. "Do you know what I like about Filiaelians?"

The sudden change of topic seemed to throw him momentarily off balance. But he recovered quickly. "Tell me," he invited.

"It's the way our two cultures overlap, complimenting but not duplicating each other," I said. "Take Tech Yleli's funeral, for example. Do you know what Human children birthdays and Filiaelian funerals have in common?" I raised my eyebrows. "Helium balloons."

And swiveling my Beretta to the two o'clock position, I emptied the magazine into the tanks of supercompressed helium.

The bursting metal sounded exactly like a cluster of bombs going off, which was exactly the way Wandek and the other Shonkla-raa reacted. Wandek dropped instantly into a crouch, dragging Terese down with him. The rest of the Shonkla-raa, apparently only now realizing how tempting a target their tight-packed group presented, began to spread out into the main part of the bay where the watchdogs held their stolid vigil. I stood motionless, my empty gun still pointed at the tanks, watching Wandek's face, wondering distantly if this was actually going to work. A wave of coolness washed across my face as expansion-chilled helium mixed with the rest of the docking bay's air.

And then, without warning, Bayta gave a choked gasp, her body sagging like a marionette with cut strings. "Frank—" she wheezed.

It was at that moment that Wandek realized what had happened. With a snarl, he jammed his hand into his tunic pocket and pulled out a small handgun I'd never seen him with before.

But he was too late. In unison, the whole group of watchdogs turned to their Shonkla-raa masters and attacked.

I leaped forward toward the sudden chaos, trying to get to Terese before Wandek got his gun into position. But I had barely started my charge when two of the watchdogs slammed in from opposite directions, nosing their way between Wandek and Terese and shoving them apart. Halfway through their charge, in perfect unison, the watchdog closest to Wandek turned violently into the Shonkla-raa, body-slamming him off his feet, while the other turned more gently but just as insistently the opposite direction to shove Terese into my arms. I grabbed her, spun her around, and shoved her in turn toward Bayta, then turned again to join the fight.

"No!" Minnario shouted over the oddly pitched cacophony of screams and shouts and snarls. "This is *mine*."

And it was.

I'd been on the receiving end of Shonkla-raa hand-to-hand combat, and I knew how strong and cold and deadly they were. Their knife hands flashed as they fought against the watchdogs, jabbing through skin and scale and bone and sending their victims yipping and snarling to the deck to struggle weakly or to lie still in pools of blood.

But for once, all the Shonkla-raa's strength of body and will wasn't enough. Slowly, I backed up toward Bayta and Terese and Emikai, watching in fascinated horror as the watchdogs bled and died and yet systematically tore their way through the enemy ranks. Here and there a gun like Wandek's appeared, but its owner never got more than a single shot before he was taken down, usually by sharp-toothed jaws around his neck.

A few of the Shonkla-raa, mostly those in the rear, recognized the inevitable and made a run for the door. A couple of them actually made it. The rest didn't.

Three minutes later, it was over.

I gave the field of battle one final survey, mostly to make sure none of the Shonkla-raa was still showing signs of life or, more importantly, signs of weapons. Then, exhaling tiredly, I turned back to the others.

Bayta was holding a still white-faced Terese close to her, gently stroking the girl's hair and murmuring soothing words. Emikai looked dumbfounded, his intellect and his genetic programming no doubt locked in a bitter philosophical battle over the slaughter of so many of his *santra* bosses right there in front of him. I wished him luck sorting it all out.

Minnario, in contrast, just looked grimly satisfied. So did the surviving watchdogs, including Doug and Ty, as they moved among the fallen. Probably, like me, checking for survivors and guns.

I walked over to Minnario. "Brilliant, Compton," the Modhri said. "My congratulations."

I shrugged modestly. "A little helium in the room, a little change in air density, and the Shonkla-raa's finely tuned siren song goes straight to hell. Actually, it's a game Humans have played with helium for generations." I waved a hand behind me. "You happy now?"

His eyes drifted across the carnage. "Yes, I am," he said. "You?"

"Mostly, I'm just relieved," I said. "Whenever you're ready, Bayta, call in the Spiders, and let's get the hell off this station."

"And after that, what?" Minnario asked.

I looked him straight in the eye. "I'm going to take them down," I said flatly.

"Alone?"

"If necessary."

He inclined his head. "We shall see."

NINETEEN :

The transport was piloted by a couple of the specialized server-class Spiders who usually ran the Tube's maintenance skiffs. Five minutes after we said our quick farewells to Emikai, Doug, and Ty, we were headed back out toward deep space. A half hour later, the tension aboard finally started to ease.

Their tension. Not mine.

Because of those aboard, I was the only one who understood the enormity of the task facing us.

An unknown number of Shonkla-raa, in unknown locations. All of them endowed with tremendous personal strength and power, not the least of those powers being their ability to control the Modhri and confuse the Spiders. The whole lot of them bent on galaxy domination.

And standing against them, me.

I was resting in my seat with my eyes closed when a subtle wave of air across my face told me I had company. I opened my eyes to see Bayta sink wearily into the seat beside me. "How is she?" I asked.

"Still pretty upset," she said. Her voice was as tired as the rest of her. "But I think she's starting to calm down. A little."

"Don't expect her to get it all sorted out overnight," I warned. "It's not every day you find out you're carrying Rosemary's baby."

"Rosemary's baby?"

"Dit-rec horror drama you haven't seen. Never mind." I nodded toward the front of the transport and the two stationmaster-sized Spiders crouching behind the two pilots. "Anyone ask about the other passengers yet?"

"Minnario looked at them, but didn't say anything," Bayta said. "Terese has other things on her mind."

I nodded. Minnario's restraint was mere politeness, of course. He had to be desperately curious about the Spiders whom Bayta had called into a probable confrontation with the Shonkla-raa.

And if Minnario himself wasn't curious, the Modhri inside him certainly was. Distantly, I wondered what the Modhri's response would be if and when he finally saw a defender Spider in action.

Or if, indeed, he ever did. The Shonkla-raa could already stun defenders into immobility. If they ever found the right tone to take them over completely . . .

"Is this later yet?" Bayta asked.

I frowned. "Come again?"

"You said you'd tell me later why you thought the Modhri was on our side," she said. "Is this later yet?"

"It's close enough," I said. "It was something Wandek said when he was congratulating himself on how they'd figured out you could talk telepathically to the Spiders and how they were going to strap you down until they figured out how you did it. In and around all the gloating, he also bounced several suggestions off me, starting with the thought that you might be a Human/Spider hybrid, then suggesting that you were an unknown alien encased in a Human shell, and finally speculating that maybe you were one of the people who actually ran the Spiders and the Quadrail."

Bayta shivered. "Way too close. With all of them."

"That he was," I agreed. "But that's the point. In retrospect, I can see he was throwing out every possibility he could think of in the hope that one of them would spark a reaction. He didn't really know who or what you were."

"And?"

"Think back," I said. "He didn't know who runs the Quadrail . . . *but the Modhri does*. Remember, back with EuroUnion Security Service agent Morse, when we were trying to beat the Modhri to the third Lynx sculpture?"

"The Quadrail siding," Bayta murmured, her face suddenly rigid. "He saw a Chahwyn."

"And since we know Morse is a deep-cover walker, it follows that the Modhri has surely figured out by now what it was he saw," I said. "Furthermore, by now that information has certainly spread to every mind segment across the galaxy. If the Shonkla-raa don't know who's running the Quadrail, it can only be because the Modhri hasn't told them."

Bayta looked across the transport at the back of Minnario's head. "But why not?" she asked. "Can't the Shonkla-raa force him to talk?"

"Probably, but only if they think to ask the right questions," I said. "In this case they didn't, and the Modhri clearly didn't volunteer it. That also means the Shonkla-raa's telepathy is one-way, by the way—they can implant commands while they're whistling their happy little tune, but they can't read their slaves' minds. Anyway, the point is that if the Modhri's not on the Shonkla-raa's side, he's on ours."

"Or on his own."

"True," I conceded. "But right now, I think that's as good as we're going to get."

Bayta shook her head. "I hope you're right."

"Me, too," I admitted. "But we're safe, Terese is safe, and the Shonkla-raa haven't got you to experiment on. I'm ready to call that enough victory for one day."

For a moment Bayta was silent. "They wouldn't have gotten what they were looking for, you know," she said. "The Chahwyn auditory and telepathic frequencies. If they'd gotten close . . ." She trailed off.

I felt my stomach tighten. "Your symbiont?"

"Would have chosen to die," Bayta said simply.

"Ah," I said, the complete uselessness of the word making my stomach tighten even more. "I mean—"

"I know what you mean, Frank," she said. She hesitated, then reached over and took my hand. "I do understand you, you know. Maybe better than you think I do."

I gazed into her eyes, once again completely at a loss for words. What did she mean by that? *I* understand? Or *we* understand? What was it like, her life with a Chahwyn symbiont inside her, or interwoven with her, or however it worked? Were they truly one being, as she'd described it to me?

If so, what would have been the cost to her for her Chahwyn part to die?

I didn't know. I couldn't begin to know.

But I would fight, and I would die, to prevent her from ever having to find out. "It won't happen," I said. "I won't let it."

"I know," she said. She lowered her eyes. "By the way. That kiss earlier?"

I swallowed. Here it came. "Yes?" I said warily.

"I just wanted to say that I enjoyed it. Very much." Her lips puckered mischievously. "So did she."

I was still trying to find something to say to that when she stood up and crossed back to where Terese was curled up in her seat.

She had resumed her place beside Terese, and I could tell from their head movements that they were talking again in low tones, when Minnario activated his chair and floated back to me. "May I have a word?" he asked.

"Certainly," I said, shifting over to the aisle seat so that I would be closer to him. "I was just thinking about Emikai."

"I'm sure the Shonkla-raa are doing likewise," Minnario said soberly. "I believe he'll prove to be a formidable opponent for them, provided he survives Director *Usantra* Nstroo's investigation. To have had so many *santras* and *msikai-dorosli* slaughtered in his presence may be difficult to explain."

"That shouldn't be a problem," I assured him. "He's going to blame the whole thing on me."

Minnario's eyes widened. "On *you*?"

"Why not?" I said. "I was the one everyone saw waving my reader outside Hchchu's office just before they were attacked by a group of watchdogs. Obviously, I must have used the same gadget against Wandek and his buddies."

"Interesting," Minnario murmured. "Simple, effective, and impossible to disprove."

"Unless someone takes a close look at the watchdogs' bodies," I said with a grimace. "Even for Fillies, I'm guessing that kind of knife-hand engineering is pretty unorthodox."

"*Isantra* Kordiss and the surviving Shonkla-raa should have sufficient rank to discourage any such investigations," Minnario said. "You need not worry about the station's remaining *msikai-dorosli*, either. Now that the Shonkla-raa are aware of my mind segment's presence, they'll certainly realize it's in their best interests to keep the animals alive."

"Ready to be pressed into service should the need arise," I said ruefully. "One more good reason to avoid Proteus Station in the future. I hope Emikai hasn't bitten off more than he can chew."

"Only time will tell," Minnario said. "But he may yet find unexpected aid in his battle."

I eyed him. There was an odd hint of grim amusement about his face. "Is there a joke here I'm missing?" I asked.

"Yes," Minnario said. "But the joke is not on you."

I frowned . . . and then, I got it. "Which one of them is it?" I asked. "No, wait," I interrupted myself. "It's Kordiss, isn't it? Our old buddy Blue One."

"Exactly," Minnario said. "You are amazing, Mr. Compton. Simply amazing."

"Hardly," I said with a snort. "I should have figured that one out hours ago. How else could you have known where the Shonkla-raa were keeping Bayta?"

"How else, indeed?" Minnario said with a nod. "Though I will admit I had a bad moment during her rescue when you threatened him with death."

"Good thing Bayta zapped him with the *kwi* before it came to that," I agreed. "Doubly good, actually, since that meant he missed the party in the docking bay. And the Shonkla-raa even provided the hypo you used to inject a piece of coral into him while he was unconscious in your room. I suppose the coral was hidden in the central cylinder of your chair's thruster array?"

"Correct," Minnario said. "Don't be concerned, though. It's not there anymore."

"I know," I said as another bit of the puzzle fell into place. "All those bathroom breaks you made Emikai stop for on your way to the docking bay. You dumped the rest of the coral into the station's water system."

"Where it will cement itself to the inside of one of the water reclamation tanks," Minnario confirmed. "Thus avoiding the normal purification procedures."

"Thus providing a larger base for the watchdog mind segment," I said, nodding. "*And* for your new ally among the Shonkla-raa."

Minnario's mouth made a wincing motion. "*Isantra* Kordiss is not an ally, not in the way you assume," he said. "He can't be. If the colony settled into its normal resting place beneath his brain, he would react the instant any of his fellow Shonkla-raa used their control tone."

"Oh," I said, frowning. That wrinkle hadn't even occurred to me. "That wouldn't be so good, would it? So where *is* the colony?"

"Interwoven in the tissue around his left optic nerve," Minnario said. "Regrettably, in many ways *Isantra* Kordiss will be of only limited use. I will see what he sees through that eye, but will not be able to access his other senses. Nor will I be able to offer suggestions for him to follow."

I nodded. "He's a spy, but not a saboteur. Excellent. Use him wisely."

"I fully intend for us to do so," Minnario assured me.

"*Us?*" I asked, frowning at the odd pronoun. "I thought you were an *I*."

"I am." Minnario hesitated. "By *us*, I was referring to myself . . . and you."

"You and me," I said, my voice sounding flat in my ears.

Minnario seemed to brace himself. "I've now experienced what it's like to be a slave, Compton," he said, his voice trembling with suppressed emotion. "You can't possibly envision what it's like. To have your mind and heart invaded, to hear the gloating arrogance of your master as he turns your hands to his own purposes. It's the most horrible experience one can possibly go through."

"I can imagine," I sympathized, wondering if he appreciated the true irony here. I personally didn't know what that was like, but the millions of people the Modhri had turned into walkers were living a version of that exact same slavery. The only reason they didn't also get the gloating part was because the Modhri blacked them out when he took them over.

"No, you can't," he countered tautly. "I've had a taste of what will become of me if the Shonkla-raa ever again rise to power." His gaze defocused, his expression that of someone seeing hell itself coming for him. "I can't let that happen. I won't be their slave. Not ever."

An odd sensation formed in the pit of my stomach. Were we really heading where it looked like we were heading? "What exactly are you saying?" I asked carefully. "That you want me to help you take down the Shonkla-raa?"

Slowly, his eyes returned from the terrible future to the only slightly less ominous present. "You misunderstand," he said quietly. "I was designed as a spy, not a warrior. I have none of a warrior's skills or intellect. Even with your help—" He shivered and shook his head. "I could never defeat the Shonkla-raa."

He leaned forward, a sudden new intensity in his eyes. "But you *are* a warrior. I've experienced your battles against me, and I've now seen your battles against the Shonkla-raa. Of all those I've encountered across the galaxy, you are the one who stands the best chance of pushing back this threat."

He drew himself up. "I don't ask for your help, Frank Compton. I instead offer you mine. Completely, totally, unconditionally."

I looked past his shoulder to where Bayta and Terese were still talking quietly together. "Fine," I said. "Let's talk ground rules. I'm in charge. I give an order, you carry it out. I ask for intel, you supply it. Anything I want from you, you give me."

"Accepted," the Modhri said without hesitation.

"And I want to meet the governing body," I added. "Or whatever you call the part of you that makes overall policy decisions. Not that I don't trust your sincerity, but I'd like to see a little more weight behind this offer."

"Also accepted," the Modhri said. "But you need not worry about that. During the two weeks of Quadrail travel after we left the super-express I sent many messages to the segment-prime."

"That's the mind segment based on Yandro?"

Minnario's mouth twisted in an ironic smile. "Yes," he confirmed. "All the components of the Modhri—all the parts that make me what I am—*all* of me recognizes the danger. And all of me accepts your leadership in defeating it."

"Okay," I said, eyeing him closely. A sudden, right-angle turn in my universe . . . and yet, it somehow wasn't nearly as brain-numbing as it should have been. Perhaps on some level I'd already seen where our temporary alliance aboard the super-express and Proteus Station had been going. "For the moment, I can give you a tentative yes. But I'll still want to discuss things directly with the segment-prime."

"Of course," he said, and there was no mistaking the relief in his voice. Had he really been so terrified, I wondered, that I would turn him down? "The segment-prime will speak with you at any time of your choosing."

His misshapen mouth puckered. "And I expect you and Bayta will also need to consult with her masters among the Chahwyn."

I inclined my head. "Touché, in turn," I said. "One final warning." I locked eyes with him. "From this point on, Bayta and I and any other allies I pull into this are off-limits to your recruitment efforts. If it even *looks* like you're trying to get us into touching range of Modhran coral, the deal will be off."

Minnario snorted. "Be assured, Compton, that that's the easiest promise of all. Do you think I'd be foolish enough to risk dulling your capabilities by tainting your thoughts and ideas with my own? I need you—this war needs you—exactly as you are."

"As long as we're clear." I puffed out a lungful of air. This entire conversation, not to mention the deal I'd just made, was skating right on the edge of certifiably insane.

And yet, the more I thought about it, the more sense it made. After all, the kind of infiltration and intel-gathering I had in mind for the Modhri was exactly what he'd been designed for in the first place.

Not to mention the fact that using those abilities against the philosophical descendants of the despots who'd created him rather appealed to my sense of irony. "Okay, then," I said. "Louie, I think this is the beginning of a beautiful friendship."

Minnario frowned. "Excuse me?"

"Nothing," I said. "A classic line from a Human dit-rec drama. *Casablanca*. Not important."

"I will have to view that someday."

"Yes, you should," I agreed. "I think you'd like it."

I had thought that Minnario might take the journey with us back to Earth. But we'd barely reached the safety of the Ilat Dumar Covrey Quadrail station when, stunned and dumbfounded by the fact that his supposed medical transfer to Proteus had actually been some kind of mix-up, he immediately booked passage aboard the next train for his proper treatment center in the Morak Trov Lemanab system. He accepted my thanks for his legal assistance, wished me well in any future problems with the Filiaelians, and headed off into the heart of the Filiaelian Assembly.

And as he traveled, he no doubt pondered this brand-new symptom he'd developed, this recurring problem of persistent mental blackouts.

"Do you think we can trust him?" Bayta asked quietly as she, Terese, and I made our way across the crowded station toward the platform where we'd be picking up our own train back to Venidra Carvo.

"He could have betrayed us," I reminded her. "He didn't. He could have infected us so that he'd have direct access to my allegedly brilliant strategic and tactical abilities. He didn't do that, either. Besides, his reason for opposing the Shonkla-raa rings pretty true."

"Because he doesn't want to be a slave." She eyed me. "I suppose you find that funny."

"I find it ironic," I corrected. "Not necessarily the same thing. And frankly, having now seen the Shonkla-raa in action, I'll take any help I can get."

"I'm not sure my people will accept this," she warned, lowering her voice still further.

"They'll be welcome to voice any objections," I assured her. "Provided they can also offer some practical alternatives."

"Mr. Frank Compton?"

I turned, tensing, my hand automatically reaching for the Beretta, which was already tucked away in a Spider lockbox ready to be loaded aboard our next train.

But it wasn't a Shonkla-raa who was striding toward me, or any Filly at all, for that matter. It was a Halka, tall and regal, dressed in the distinctive tricolor layered robes of the Halkan Peerage. A couple of watchful and tough-looking bodyguards trailed at a respectful distance behind him. "I'm Frank Compton," I confirmed warily. "Do I know you?"

"Senior Ambassador ChoDar of the Halkavisti Empire," he identified himself formally. "No, we haven't met. But I believe we may once have had an acquaintance in common. High Commissioner JhanKla."

I suppressed a grimace. JhanKla and I had met, all right. He'd turned out to be a Modhran walker, he'd tried his best to kill me, and I'd ended up killing him instead. "Yes, the high commissioner and I did meet once or twice, Your Eminence," I conceded.

"Yes, I thought so," ChoDar said. "So very regrettable, his mysterious disappearance aboard that ill-fated Quadrail." He shook his head, chasing the memories away. "But that is the past. Tell me, Mr. Compton, are you and your companions on your way back to our side of the galaxy?"

"Yes, we are," I said, frowning. Given ChoDar's rank and position and how thoroughly the Modhri had penetrated the upper echelons of Halkan society, it was almost a dead certainty that he was also a walker. What was the Modhri up to? "Why? Was there some place in the Assembly you thought I might like better?"

"By no means," he assured me. "As it happens, I too have decided to return to my home. Since we travel the same route, and since you were a friend of High Commissioner JhanKla's, I'd hoped you and your companions would share my Peerage car during the journey."

And then I understood. A Halkan Peerage car was one of the standards of galactic elegance, dripping with luxury, comfort, and prestige. More importantly, Peerage cars were always connected to the rear of whatever Quadrail they were traveling with. Nestled snugly inside, we would be isolated, alone, and away from prying Shonkla-raa eyes. "That's very generous of you, Your Eminence," I said. "But I wouldn't want to impose on your hospitality."

"It would be an honor, not an imposition," he said.

"But I warn you: if you accept, be aware that you won't be able to change your minds after we've left." He glanced around and lowered his voice. "To be honest, I find Filiaelians to be sometimes wearisome. I have therefore requested the Spiders to omit the usual vestibule connector between our car and the rear baggage car of our train."

I smiled tightly. Isolated, alone, away from prying eyes, and now completely separated from the rest of the train by a couple of meters of partial vacuum, a barrier even a Shonkla-raa whistle couldn't penetrate. Unless Bayta and I were willing to be cooped up for the next two months inside a Spider tender, there was no safer way for us to get back to Human space.

The Modhri wasn't just waiting around for me to make up my mind about accepting him as an ally. He was already behaving like one.

"Thank you, Your Eminence," I said. "We would be honored to accept your hospitality."

"I'm pleased," he said. He smiled, and for just a second his face sagged and his eyes flattened with the telltale signs of a Modhran presence. The Modhri's version of a knowing wink? "I look forward to whiling away the hours in pleasant conversation with you. An ambassador, after all, hears many things."

"I'm certain he does." I looked at Terese, who was oblivious to the true nature of the situation. I looked at Bayta, who understood the situation completely and still was far from sure this was a good idea.

"Especially my particular passion of Filiaelian high opera, and those who sing it," ChoDar added. "Are you interested in such things, Mr. Compton?"

"Indeed I am," I said softly. "I look forward to hearing all about it."

TWENTY :

An hour later, as snug and safe as we could reasonably hope to be under the circumstances, we headed out.

It was a potentially stressful situation, given the fact that we were all essentially strangers to one another. But ChoDar was a senior ambassador, and within minutes of our train passing through the station's atmosphere barrier it was clear that his rank and title hadn't just been someone's idea of a last-minute New Year's gift. He started by personally giving us a tour of his car, chattering away genially the whole time. He introduced us to his two guard-assistants, the servitor who handled most of the day-to-day servant work, and his chef. He even allowed us a tantalizing sample of the sauce the latter was working on for our dinner, a Halkan courtesy that was usually reserved for close friends. By the time he showed us to our sleeping compartments even Terese's tension had eased noticeably.

Dinner, two hours later, more than lived up to what the samples had promised. Again, ChoDar was the perfect host, keeping the conversation going and filling in any potentially awkward gaps with highly entertaining stories of his experiences traveling around the galaxy on behalf of the Halkavisti Empire.

After dinner came drinks in the lounge and more stories. Terese seemed to be fading rapidly—not surprisingly, given the stress of her pregnancy plus the hell she'd just been through on Proteus—and I made a point of keeping an eye on her.

Sure enough, midway through my second iced tea her eyes drooped closed, and her body slumped limply in her contour chair.

"Spice-broiled *pipita* often has the same effect on me," ChoDar commented cheerfully, gesturing to the sleeping girl. "Shall I have YhoTeHeu carry her to her compartment?"

"No, she should be all right here," I assured him, going over for a closer look at her. She seemed all right.

On the other hand, we really had no idea what Aronobal and the rest of the Shonkla-raa ghouls had done to her back on Proteus. Tomorrow, I decided, I would take a few skin and blood samples from her, unpleasant though that kind of task was to me, and run them through my reader and its sophisticated sensors.

"She certainly should be comfortable enough," Cho-Dar commented, fondly patting the arms of his own chair. "These chairs are every bit as restful as the sleeping-room beds." He yawned, a Halkan facial gesture that those unfamiliar with the species invariably assumed was an angry snarl. "In fact, if you'll forgive such unhostlike behavior, I feel a small nap of my own coming on."

"No apology or forgiveness needed," I assured him. "In fact, I've been wondering myself how these chairs sleep."

"Do try it, by all means," ChoDar urged sleepily. "We're all friends here, after all. Until later."

He closed his eyes. I waited, and within a minute his breathing settled into the long rhythmic pattern of sleep.

I took a deep breath. "Hello, Modhri," I said quietly.

Even in sleep, ChoDar's face betrayed the slight but distinctive sagging of Modhran control. "Hello, Compton," he murmured back. "A greeting to you, as well, Bayta."

"Good evening, Modhri," Bayta said. Her voice was polite enough, but I could tell she still wasn't happy with this whole cozy relationship.

"Before we turn to other matters," the Modhri said, "be first assured that the Shonkla-raa did nothing of long-term hazard to your companion. My mind segment on the Ilat Dumar Covrey station included two doctors. By the time our train left they had discussed the various medicines and procedures that my Eyes on *Kuzyatru* Station had seen and concluded that she is in no danger."

His mouth twitched. "No additional danger, rather," he amended. "She still carries the same genetic disorders that she had when she first came to the Filiaelian Assembly."

"Yes," I said, feeling a pang of guilt. Which was ridiculous, of course. Bayta and I had saved her from deadly danger out there.

Or had we?

Because we knew now that what the Shonkla-raa wanted was her unborn son. Part of that goal would have been for the boy to grow up into a productive, influential member of Human society. And the simplest way to do that would be to make sure he had a living, healthy mother.

Did that mean that, except for our interference, they would have cured her genetic problems?

But I couldn't afford to think about one young girl's future. Not when the future of every person in the Twelve Empires depended on us.

"We appreciate the information," I said to the Modhri. "If we succeed in our endeavors, we may yet be able to deal with her medical problems."

"We may hope so," the Modhri said. "But now to the business at hand. May I ask how you intend to proceed? Particularly now that you may no longer travel freely through the Filiaelian Assembly?"

"I can travel *through* it just fine," I corrected. "I just can't leave the Tube."

ChoDar snorted gently. "A meaningless distinction, since the Shonkla-raa will not *be* in the Tube."

"Oh, they'll be here, all right," I said, grimacing. "As long as we're here, there will be Shonkla-raa haunting every station and probably every train between here and Homshil."

"Perhaps," the Modhri said. "That will still leave the bulk of the enemy outside your area of operation. And as you're already aware, my own presence in the Assembly is limited to traveling non-Filiaelians."

"True," I said. "But I have a few allies of my own I may be able to press into hunting duty."

ChoDar inclined his head doubtfully. "You'll need more than a few," he warned. "The Assembly is an incredibly huge place."

"But Shonkla-raa throats aren't exactly easy to hide," I reminded him. "Speaking of which, have you spotted any aboard this train? Or are we too far back to be in contact with the rest of your mind segment?"

"No, my other Eyes are spread out sufficiently to maintain a single segment with this Eye," the Modhri said. "I haven't yet seen any Shonkla-raa, though there may be one or more secluded inside first-class compartments."

"They'd do better right now to use agents like Dr. Aronobal who aren't actual Shonkla-raa," Bayta murmured. "We wouldn't be able to identify them so easily."

"Good point," I agreed. "And with the chaos we left back on Proteus, I'm guessing that's all they were able to get on our train in time anyway."

"What then do we do?" the Modhri asked.

"We watch and wait," I told him. "If their agent is clever enough to avoid identification, there's nothing we can do." I cocked an eyebrow. "On the other hand, if we *can* identify him . . ."

ChoDar's head nodded slightly, as a sleeping person might. "We can make him one of my Eyes."

Abruptly, Bayta stood up and strode out of the lounge toward the sleeping rooms.

"My apologies," the Modhri said quietly. "That was insensitive of me."

"That's all right," I said. "She's still getting used to this."

"And you?"

I shrugged. "I was in Intelligence work long enough to know that you sometimes have to deal with one threat at a time. Right now, the Shonkla-raa are holding down the number-one spot on that list."

"And after they're defeated?" the Modhri asked, a

sudden edge of nervousness to his voice. "Will our war then resume?"

"Do you want it to?" I countered.

ChoDar sighed. "I am what I am, Compton. You are what you are."

"Maybe," I said. "Personally, I'm a big believer in the idea that people can change."

ChoDar smiled faintly. "And that, I believe, is the great strength of your people. No matter how powerful the forces arrayed against you, you never give up."

"It's definitely a strength," I agreed. "But it can also be a weakness. I've seen people latch so hard onto a pre-conceived notion that they don't let go even when reality no longer supports it."

"Let us hope that neither of us ever so blinds himself," the Modhri said.

"Indeed," I said. "Anyway, by the time we have all the Shonkla-raa nests identified and located, I'm hopeful that we'll have the capability of destroying them."

ChoDar's breathing changed, just slightly. "You have a plan?"

"I always have a plan," I said, allowing just a bit of smug confidence into my voice. "Nothing I'm ready to share at the moment."

For a moment he was silent. I wondered if he was going to take offense at my going all dark and mysterious on him, especially when we were supposed to be on the same team now.

But he didn't. Maybe he knew that pressing the issue would be a waste of time. Maybe he simply trusted me. "I'll look forward to hearing it when the time is right," he said instead. "Have you any plans for the present?"

"I'll start by sending out word to my various allies from the Spider message center at the next station," I said. "Some of them are a bit tricky to locate, so I'll need to start the process as soon as possible. In two weeks, when we reach Venidra Carvo and transfer to the super-express, I should have pings from all of them and will know where to send their individual orders and search areas. I'll do that, and by the time we reach Homshil we should have preliminary reports from all of them."

The Modhri seemed to ponder that. "Then some of your allies are already here in the Assembly?" he asked. "Otherwise, they will barely have arrived in Shorshian territory by the time we reach Homshil."

"Let me worry about the timing and locations," I said. "For now, all you need to do is keep an eye out for Shonkla-raa agents."

"I will," he promised. "When we reach the next station and you leave the car to deliver your messages, will you wish me to provide escort for you?"

"I'll let you know when we get there," I said. "Fillies in general aren't all that good at distinguishing one Human face from another, and I may be able to just slip through whatever search party they're able to throw together."

"As you wish," the Modhri said. "I'll await your instructions."

"Good." I stood up. "And now, I think I'll turn in. It's been a long and rich day."

Again, a faint smile creased ChoDar's face. "That it has," he agreed. "Shall we let the other two sleep here?"

The other two: Terese, and ChoDar, the body he was currently inhabiting. Even now, hearing the Modhri talk about his current host in the third person could still creep me out. "Fine with me," I said, forcing my voice to stay casual. "As you pointed out, the chairs *are* quite comfortable."

"Indeed," the Modhri said. "Sleep well, Compton."

ChoDar took a deep breath, and the sagging of his face disappeared as the Modhri retreated again into the recesses of the Halka's brain. "You too," I murmured.

My compartment door was open when I arrived. Bayta was sitting on the couch, gazing moodily out the display window at the featureless Tube landscape rolling past. "You heard?" I asked as I sat down beside her.

"Most of it," she said. "Who exactly are these allies you were talking about?"

"The Modhri himself, for starters," I said. "*Korak* Fayr and his Belldic commando squad. Also Bruce Mc-Micking, who's always up for a good fight. One or two others. The Spiders. You."

"Most of whom are nowhere near Filiaelian space right now."

"Well, there's *Logra* Emikai," I reminded her. "He's certainly become an ally. But aside from him, you're probably right. Though you really never know where Fayr might pop up."

She took a deep breath, let it out in a long, silent sigh. "You don't really have a plan, do you?"

"Sure I do," I said. "We draw the Shonkla-raa out of hiding, kill them, then destroy any records they may have left about their procedures."

"Those are goals," she pointed out. "Not plans."

I shrugged. "I'll admit there are still a few details to be worked out. Don't worry, we've got time."

"You really think you can trust the Modhri?"

"For the moment, yes," I said firmly. I might not have a real plan yet, but that one, at least, I had no doubts about. "He helped us on the super-express and at Proteus, and enlightened self-interest should keep him firmly on our side." At least, I didn't add, until we got back to Yandro for my requested face-to-face with the segment-prime.

At that point, things might change. Drastically.

"And once we've destroyed the Shonkla-raa?" she asked. "What then?"

"I have a couple of ideas," I said evasively. "I think we can make it work."

"Make what work? A truce? An armistice? Peace?"

"We'll make it work," I said again.

"All right," she said, her tone suggesting more dutiful acceptance than genuine agreement. "The next stop is six hours away. Do you want me to help you encode the messages you said you wanted to send?"

"No, I can do it," I said. "They're mostly just the preliminary heads-up notes to get Fayr and McMicking ready to move. The more detailed stuff can wait until Venidra Carvo."

"When you *will* have a plan?"

I reached down and took her hand. "It's going to work, Bayta," I said quietly. "Trust me."

She gave me a forced smile. "I always have, Frank," she said, just as quietly.

"Then that's settled," I said, trying for a touch of levity that didn't quite come off. "And now, it's time we both hit the sack. Come on, I'll walk you back to your room."

She smiled, a real one this time. "What, the whole ten meters?"

"A gentleman never considers the distance," I said, standing up and offering her my arm like all the best gentlemen heroes from the dit-rec classics.

A minute later we said our final good-nights, and her door closed in front of me. I waited until I heard the snick of the lock, then went back to my own compartment.

I had a plan, all right, or at least the beginnings of one. One that had a fair chance of success.

The problem was that I was also pretty sure no one on my list of allies was going to like it. Bayta, probably not. The Chahwyn, almost certainly not.

The Modhri, absolutely not.

But the clock was ticking, and we were running low on time. Even as we headed toward Human space at a light-year per minute, whatever was left of the Proteus group would be madly throwing message cylinders in all directions, messages that would travel a thousand times faster than we could. By the time we reached Venidra Carvo two weeks from now, they could very well be ready to make some kind of move against us. By the time we reached Homshil six weeks after that, their entire army could be on the move.

I had until then to finalize my plan. Or to come up with something better.

The first hurdle, at least, turned out to be easy. Six hours later, at the next station, I left the Peerage car along with a trickle of other passengers. Weaving my way through the waiting clumps of Fillies, Shorshians, and others to the Spiders' message center, I added my handful of messages to the queue.

Neither Bayta nor the Modhri liked the idea of me going out all by myself. But I wasn't worried about it. If there were any Shonkla-raa agents aboard our train, I knew there would have been no time at Ilat Dumar Covrey to give them any instructions more complicated or aggressive than to lie low and watch our movements.

And, of course, to report those movements. On my way out of the message center I spotted four Fillies heading toward it. One of them, I had no doubt, would be sending a quick report to Proteus and beyond. But as I expected, none of them tried to interfere with me.

Half an hour later, we were off again.

The next hurdle, unfortunately, wouldn't be nearly so easy. As soon as the Shonkla-raa leadership learned that I wasn't just running for home but was sending off messages along the way, they might well decide that their first priority should be to get those messages stopped.

If they found a way to steal or destroy the messages, we were going to lose valuable time. If they decided they'd rather destroy the messenger, we might lose something considerably more valuable. Me.

The days passed slowly. Most of our waking hours were idled away with conversation, meals, music, and dit-rec entertainment.

And slowly, as I gazed unseeingly at the current dit-rec or stared up at the darkened ceiling above my bed in the middle of the night, I hammered out my battle plan.

It was my one, single focus in life. Every other part of our day-to-day schedule—eating, socializing, exercising, even the occasional evening card marathon—ran almost completely on mental autopilot.

Which was probably why I didn't notice the change that had come over Terese. Not until it was almost too late.

With a final creaking of brakes, the train pulled into Venidra Carvo Station.

"According to the schedule, we have another six hours before the super-express departs for Homshil," ChoDar said as we watched out the lounge display windows at the drudge Spiders detaching our car from the rest of the train. "If you would like to take some exercise around the station during that time, please feel free." He smiled. "I'm accustomed to the close quarters of this car, but others sometimes find it a bit stifling."

"Yes, I think we will take a short stroll," I said, taking Bayta's arm and starting us toward the door. "I should at least go to the message center and see if there's anything waiting for me."

"As should all who are about to embark upon the great silence of that long journey," ChoDar agreed. "If you're willing to wait until YhoTeHeu has prepared the diplomatic bag, perhaps the three of you can travel together." He smiled. "Here in the midst of Shorshian territory, it would be wise for non-Shorshians such as ourselves to stick together."

I smiled at the small joke, a mostly untranslatable play on the Halkan term for *stick*. It was a traditional favorite of Halkas who were relatively new to the oddities of English. "A wise precaution, lest we get stuck," I agreed, making the traditional counterjoke in return. "We would be honored by YhoTeHeu's companionship."

Ten minutes later, YhoTeHeu, Bayta, and I left the car and trooped across the platform toward the stationmaster complex and the Spider message center.

The Shorshic Congregate was the second biggest of the Twelve Empires, a huge place that was nearly the size of the Filiaelian Assembly, and Shorshian pride was right up there with that of their Filly neighbors. The Venidra Carvo station might not be as ostentatious as Proteus, but that didn't mean the Shorshians hadn't done a thorough job of tricking it out. Shops, restaurants, and hotels lined the platforms, tucked in between stands of vibrant flower hedges and the Quadrail tracks that lined the entire circumference of the two-kilometer-diameter station. Some of the buildings were fifteen stories tall, with elaborate facades and typical Shorshic heptagonal windows. The biggest buildings, especially the official ones, were decorated with Shorshic artistic flourishes: pointy anglecrons, undulating wave-shaped sweeplets, and others whose names I didn't know. The overall effect was that of being in a field of underwater thornbushes.

But I didn't have any attention to spare for cultural evaluation. The majority of the travelers milling about the station were Shorshians, but probably a quarter of them were Fillies, earnest, haughty, and well-dressed.

And every one of them who crossed our path got my complete and undivided attention for as long as it took to get a good look at his or her throat.

The good news was that none of the Fillies I saw had Shonkla-raa throats. The bad news was that way too many of them gave our little party the same kind of brief but intense scrutiny that I was giving them.

Most of that attention was innocent, of course. The vast majority of Fillies, even well-traveled ones, never made it to our end of the galaxy. Humans and Halkas were rarities, and it was only natural for them to stare.

Unfortunately, I was pretty sure not all of those eyes were friendly. Even more unfortunately, I had no idea yet which ones were which.

But we had no choice. I couldn't risk giving my collection of messages to any of the Spiders roaming the station, not with Shonkla-raa possibly on the loose. Comms didn't work inside the Tube, and the messages were too long and complex for me to have Bayta transmit them telepathically from one Spider to the next all the way to the message center.

On the other hand we weren't nearly as helpless as we looked. My Beretta was still in its under-train lockbox, of course, but the *kwi* wrapped around the hand I had casually buried in my jacket pocket was already tingling with its activation signal. A Shonkla-raa who tried to freeze Bayta with his control tone would hopefully be too late to keep me from zapping him right off his feet.

And should anyone try the more direct approach, we had YhoTeHeu striding along beside us. Not only was he a combat-trained veteran of the Halkan military's special forces, but he was also *not* carrying a Modhran colony. Here in the weaponless Tube, YhoTeHeu's brawn and my *kwi* should make short work of anything the Shonkla-raa tried to throw at us.

Still, the last thing I wanted was to make a scene here, even if someone else started it. The Spiders might officially control the Tube and the station, but there were also plenty of Shorshic authorities on hand, none of whom would be happy at my use of an unknown weapon knocking their people and guests around. With our superexpress leaving in a few hours, this was pretty much the Shonkla-raa's last chance to keep Bayta and me here on their side of the galaxy.

But either they weren't worried about our departure or else they didn't want that scene any more than I did. We reached the message center with nothing more serious than a slightly bruised shin where I'd misjudged the path of a hard-edged footlocker rolling past me. Three minutes of waiting in line got us to the counter, where I delivered my encoded data chip to the stationmaster Spider on duty. Six lines over, I watched out of the corner of my eye as YhoTeHeu received the chip containing ChoDar's messages and secured it inside his boss's tamper-proof diplomatic bag. We retraced our steps past the Shorshians and Fillies still waiting in line, rendezvoused with YhoTeHeu outside the building, and with Bayta walking between us we started back toward the Peerage car.

We'd gone maybe fifty meters when I spotted two Fillies ahead and to our right, walking in military lockstep, their heads held high, their eyes alert.

And they were heading straight toward us.

Bayta spotted them the same time I did. "Frank?" she murmured.

"I see them," I murmured back, taking her arm and angling us slightly to the left.

I hadn't bothered to inform YhoTeHeu of my course change, and for a couple of steps he kept going in the wrong direction. But we'd only made it another couple before he was back beside us again. [Is there trouble?] he rumbled in Halkora.

"Two Filiaelians right-forward," I told him, scanning the area for more of them. The Shonkla-raa must surely have been able to dig up more than a measly pair of agents to make trouble for us.

They had. Thirty degrees around front from the original twosome were another pair, and a quick glance behind me showed two more coming up slowly but steadily from behind. Another quick sweep showed a second layer, again in pairs, about five meters behind the inner three groups and offset from them. Twelve very obvious potential foes, who now had us neatly boxed in.

Except for the conveniently open area to our left.

[Do they pose a threat?] YhoTeHeu asked in an ominous tone, shifting the diplomatic bag from his right to his left hand.

"They might," I told him, picking up our pace as I gave another careful look to our left. Not a single junior military cadet visible anywhere over there. Either the Shonkla-raa employed the most incompetent henchmen in the galaxy, or they were simply hoping we would think that.

YhoTeHeu was on the same page I was. [They're trying to herd us to the left,] he said, his voice dropping half an octave into the low-pitched command/combat voice I'd sometimes heard from Shorshic military attachés during my Westali days.

"That they are," I agreed, studying the area in that direction. There was a block of buildings over there, including a five-story hotel, two café-type restaurants, an imported-clothing store, and a music/dit-rec shop. On both sides of the building cluster were stands of exquisitely sculpted shear-layered trees and shrubs.

In other words, whether this group preferred to stage their ambushes indoors or out, they'd picked a good spot for it.

I looked back at the Filiaelians coming in from our two o'clock position. Their stride had picked up an almost jaunty air, the cockiness of a pack of wolves who've spotted their prey and are mentally choosing which fork would go best with elk.

Which struck me as a little odd, because of all the Fillies in the ring, that particular pair had the least cause for cockiness. One of them was big and strong and no doubt would be a match even for the specialized Filly combat techniques Emikai had taught me on the trip in to Proteus. But the other of the pair was short and thin, not very muscular at all, and in fact rather delicate and scrawny.

A commander facing weaponless combat typically chooses his biggest and strongest soldiers for the job. A less than impressive perimeter point was practically an engraved invitation to break out, especially when the hunter knew the prey would see the leftward pressure as an obvious trap. If so, it was likely that the Shonkla-raa had placed their best fighters as Scrawny's backup, hoping I would pick Scrawny as the breakout point and thus walk directly into their arms.

Still, they may not have expected YhoTeHeu to be with us. At any rate, we really didn't have any choice. [There are the two, then two behind,] I warned YhoTe-Heu, switching to Halkora in case the Shonkla-raa had been smart enough to send henchmen who understood English after me.

[I see them,] YhoTeHeu said. [I will take the larger of the foremost. I will attempt to push him into the smaller one, entangling them together, then move against the rearmost pair while you finish off the foremost.]

[Accepted,] I said. It wasn't the greatest plan I'd ever heard, but we didn't have a lot of options right now. If we could dispatch our opponents quickly enough, their reinforcements shouldn't have time to reach us before we were clear of them.

At that point, of course, they would still outnumber us. But once we were no longer surrounded, at least they'd only be coming at us from a single direction. [On three we charge,] I said.

[Accepted,] he said. [One, two—]

And even as I started to shift my balance, a slender Tra'ho wearing elaborately embroidered clothing shot past on my left, running like an Olympic sprinter carrying a barrel of gunpowder with a drip fuse burning just a shade faster than he was running. (Stand clearing!) he shouted in mangled Shishish, the ultrasonics in his voice buzzing across my head as I jumped aside to keep from getting run over by the rolling luggage careering along behind him. Directly ahead, the ambling masses of Quadrail passengers spent a precious half-second gawking, then galvanized themselves into a mad scramble to get out of his path. (Stand clearing! I am trying to miss not my train!)

(Stand clear!) another Tra'ho voice came from my right, and a second Tra'ho whipped past YhoTeHeu, moving with the same speed and determination as the first one. He tore past, scattering his own group of passengers, leaving YhoTeHeu, Bayta, and me standing in a narrow corridor of calm between two barriers of rapidly moving Tra'ho luggage.

And with the inspiration born of utter obviousness, I grabbed Bayta's arm and took off after them.

Our Filly opponents realized instantly what we were up to. But it was already too late for them to do a damn thing about it. One of them made a single attempt to get through the obstacle course as we passed and was nearly crippled as a footlocker even bigger than the one I'd tangled with earlier clipped his leg. At that point even the two in the rear, who'd been angling to get into our safe corridor before the two Tra'ho'scej passed, seemed to think better of it and joined the rest of the station in getting out of the way.

But all the rolling luggage in the galaxy couldn't prevent them from glaring at us as we hurried past. Scrawny was particularly good at it, and from the look on his face as we charged past I decided that the sooner we got ourselves back inside the Peerage car, the better.

I made sure we'd left the Fillies comfortably far behind before slowing us down, letting the Tra'ho'seej and their luggage continue their hurried journey by themselves. Ahead and to the left, I caught an unexpected sight: a fellow Human emerging from a beverage shop in the middle of yet another row of buildings.

On second glance, I saw that the figure wasn't so much emerging from the building as it was staggering from it. Clearly, whoever it was had had way too much alcohol, particularly for such a relatively short, slender Human.

A short, slender Human wearing the same color sweater and jeans as Terese had been wearing when Bayta and I left for the message center.

"Oh, hell," I breathed, grabbing Bayta's arm and pointing.

Just as the figure gave one final stagger and collapsed onto the ground.

"Bayta?" I snapped as we broke into another run,

toward the bemused spectators starting to gather around Terese's limp body.

"Two drudges are on the way to take her to the medical center," she panted back. "The Spiders are alerting the doctors now."

[Why is she out here?] YhoTeHeu demanded. [She had no errand to perform.]

"Oh, she had an errand, all right," I snarled, swearing silently over and over to myself. "She had a murder to commit."

His bulldog snout turned sharply to me. [A *murder*?]

"Yes," I said grimly. "Her own."

TWENTY-ONE :

Throughout the ages, countless Humans had fatally overdosed on alcohol, though granted most of them had done so accidentally. The modern era of Quadrail travel, which had opened up whole new vistas of non-Human alcohol products, had added its own numbers to that total.

Still, for the most part, the Shorshic varieties were pretty unattractive to Human taste buds. You had to be seriously determined to kill yourself that way.

Terese hadn't been that determined. But she'd been damn close.

(She will recover,) the Shorshic physician assured Bayta and me as we stood together on the other side of the treatment table. (I've filtered the alcohol from her bloodstream, and have induced the flushing of the remainder from her liver and other tissues. One hour, no more, and she should be recovered enough to travel.)

"Thank you, Doctor," Bayta said quietly.

(My pleasure, as well as my profession,) he said. (The machines will complete the rest of the procedure. I will be at the monitor station should you have any other concerns.)

"One question before you go," I said. "If we hadn't gotten her here when we did, what would have happened?"

A Human doctor, coached in tact and bedside manners, might have hesitated. Not this one. (She would be dead,) he said flatly.

I grimaced. It was the same conclusion I'd already come to. "Thank you."

He gestured a polite farewell and left the room. "Interesting," I commented to Bayta.

"Not the word I would have used," she said soberly. "This makes no sense, Frank. Why would she want to do something like this to herself?" She shot a sudden frown at me. "Or did you just say that for YhoTeHeu's benefit?"

"No, I meant it," I told her. "Or at least I did at the time. Now, I'm not so sure. Rather, I'm not sure Terese herself was her intended target."

"But then—?" Bayta broke off, her throat tightening. "Oh."

"Oh, indeed," I agreed grimly. "I suppose I can't really blame her, either. How would *you* like to suddenly find out that the baby you were carrying was a genetically manipulated monster designed by a bunch of megalomaniacs who wanted to take over the galaxy? You might want to try and do away with it, too."

"No, I wouldn't," Bayta said, an edge of cold fire in her tone. "I'd focus on the ones who had done this to me. To me *and* to the child."

"Good for you," I said. "But you're not a sixteen-year-old who's all alone in the universe. No, I think . . ." I trailed off, frowning, as something odd suddenly struck me.

Normally Bayta was sensitive enough to my voice and expression to pick up on such things. This time, with her full attention on Terese, she missed it completely. "Why didn't she say something?" she murmured, gazing down at the girl's sleeping face. "Why didn't we see it coming?"

"We did," I said. "Or rather, I did. Or rather, I should have."

"You're not making sense."

"Because I'm mad at myself." I took a deep breath. "Think back, Bayta. Terese was at every meal over the past two weeks. She watched every dit-rec with us, played or at least watched our card games, even sat there those two afternoons that ChoDar spent inflicting his music on us."

"Though she didn't actually listen to it," Bayta said. "I noticed she was running her own music through her headphones."

"Which just proves she has a modicum of good taste," I said. "My point is that through all of that her body might have been there, but *she* wasn't. Her heart and mind were a million light-years away."

"She was like that on the super-express, too," Bayta reminded me. "You saw what a private sort of person she is. And as ChoDar said, a single Peerage car can be stifling. There was nowhere she could really get away."

"Of course there was—there was her room," I said. "She could have gone in there any time she wanted to and locked the door. ChoDar probably would even have had MewHijLosFuw deliver her meals there if she couldn't stand the sight of us even that long. But instead she sat out there with everyone else, pretending to be sociable."

"Because she was trying to look normal," Bayta said, and I winced at the ache in her voice. Of all the people in the galaxy, Bayta knew best what it meant not to be what anyone else would define as normal. "She didn't want to draw attention to herself by being antisocial."

"Because she'd already made up her mind what she was going to do the first chance she got," I said quietly. "This was that chance."

"She knew she couldn't get anything from Senior Ambassador ChoDar's drinks cabinet without his or Chef KhiChoDe's permission," Bayta said, nodding tiredly. "And she was probably afraid it would tip us off if she tried."

"That's my guess," I agreed. "Unfortunately, this is going to drastically change our travel plans."

"What do you mean?"

"I mean we can't spend the next month and a half cooped up in the Peerage car," I said. "She may try to kill herself or her child again, and none of us has the necessary medical training or equipment to deal with that if she does."

Bayta's eyes widened. "Frank, we can't ride the regular super-express," she said, her voice low and urgent. "The Shonkla-raa have already tried to get us once."

"I know, but I don't see any choice," I said. "Not unless you want to strap her down in her Peerage-car compartment."

"We could do that," Bayta said. "I mean, no, we can't strap her down. But we could restrain her. We could do *something*."

"And turn the only friends she's got into her jailers?" I asked gently.

For a moment Bayta stared at me. Then, she exhaled a long breath, and her shoulders slumped. "She would hate us," she said, an infinite sadness in her voice. "And once we reached Earth, and we couldn't watch her anymore . . ."

She didn't finish the sentence. But then, she didn't have to. Once Terese was on her own again, she would finish the job she'd started today. One way or another.

"What it boils down to is that we can't physically stop her from destroying her child if she wants to," I said. "So what we need to do is make her not want to anymore. We need to persuade her to your way of thinking, that it's the Shonkla-raa she should be fighting, not herself or her child. And we have to start by forgiving her for this stunt, and to prove we trust her by giving her some space and freedom."

Bayta exhaled a snort. "On a Quadrail filled with Shonkla-raa and their agents?"

"Probably not exactly *filled* with them," I soothed her. "And we'll have a whole bunch of Spiders around to help us keep track of her."

"Spiders who'll be helpless if the Shonkla-raa attack," Bayta pointed out grimly.

"They're pretty much helpless anyway, at least in any serious fight," I said. "Fortunately, I doubt the Shonkla-raa are ready to take it to that level. Not yet."

"I'd hate to count on that," Bayta warned. "After what we did to them on Proteus, they must be pretty angry."

"Actually, if they're that strongly driven by revenge, we can all heave a sigh of relief," I said. "Revenge-seekers are incredibly easy to manipulate to their own destruction. No, I don't think they'll do anything because of two crucial facts. One, they don't know who all our allies are; and two, for all their incredibly smug confidence they're still a pretty small group."

Bayta shivered. "But very powerful."

"True," I conceded. "Lucky for us, it's the raw numbers that matter here. See, if you've got a big army, the simplest way to find out who your secret enemies are is by letting those enemies take potshots at you. You'll lose a few of your own in each attack, but I've known commanders who wouldn't be bothered a bit by that cost as long as it got them what they wanted."

"I see where you're going," Bayta said, nodding slowly. "A small group can't do that, and they've already lost quite a few of their number. If they hit us again, they could lose more, and they can't afford to keep doing that."

"Exactly," I said. "Especially since hitting us won't tell them anything new about our allies. No, for now they're going to be watching and waiting, giving their agents time to figure out who and what we have lurking in the shadows."

For a moment Bayta was silent, and I knew she was thinking about the depressing fact that, no matter how short the Shonkla-raa membership rolls might be, our own list of allies was considerably shorter. "How many compartments will we want?" she asked.

"Ideally, three," I said. "If that's not possible, I suppose you and Terese could bunk together."

There was another moment of silence as she conferred with the stationmaster. "There aren't any compartments available," she said at last. "But there's a long enough request list that the stationmaster is willing to add another compartment car. The three of us can have a double."

"Good enough," I said. "I'll see if YhoTeHeu's still in the lobby. If he is, I'll tell him to wait here with you and Terese while I go tell ChoDar about the change in plans."

Reaching into my pocket, I pulled out the *kwi* and pressed it into Bayta's hand. "I'll leave this with you regardless. Back as soon as I can."

ChoDar wasn't happy with my proposed change of plans. He'd been most pleased with our company, he told me regretfully, and had looked forward to sharing more dit-recs and elegant cuisine with us over the remainder of our journey.

The Modhri inside him was even less happy about it, especially after having sent two of his walkers tearing halfway across the station to give us cover from the Shonkla-raa attack. I thanked him, promised everything would be all right, and told him I would look forward to meeting the members of the mind segment that would be traveling with me.

I didn't mention that I mostly wanted to meet those walkers so that I'd know who I'd be fighting if I was wrong about the Shonkla-raa making a move on the super-express.

The Modhri didn't mention it, either. But he didn't have to. We both knew.

Two hours later, the super-express—all fifty cars of it—pulled out of the station. We rolled up the ramp into the Tube and headed into six weeks' worth of complete isolation.

Normally, the compartment cars were all lined up together at the front of the train, between the engines and the regular first-class coach cars. In this case, at Bayta's suggestion, the Spiders had put our extra compartment car a bit further to the rear, placing it between the first-class dining car and one of the extra storage cars that came with super-express trains. That meant Bayta, Terese, and I could get our meals without having to run the gauntlet of other compartment cars, whose doors might conceal any number of possible dangers, and also avoid putting ourselves on obvious display as we walked through the regular first-class coach cars.

I'd expected the Modhri to have a mind segment aboard, and he did: six walkers, four ahead of us in first class and two behind us in second. ChoDar himself would have been a seventh, but I was informed by a gregarious Shorshian who approached Bayta and me at dinner on the first night out that ChoDar was too far away from the train's passenger sections to link up with the rest of the mind segment.

In some ways, that was a good thing. The Modhri was already planning to send one or two of the walkers back through third class and the baggage cars every day or two, moving them close enough to the Peerage car to link up with the ChoDar mind segment and keep it apprised of events. At the same time, ChoDar's isolation meant that, should things go to hell up here, the overall

Modhri mind would at least have some data on what had happened.

I'd also expected the Shonkla-raa to have some of their number aboard, and I was right about that, too. Within the first two days of travel the Modhri identified one full-fledged Shonkla-raa, enlarged throat and everything, plus four Fillies who were probable Shonkla-raa agents.

One of those four, to my mild surprise, was our friend Scrawny from the Venidra Carvo station. Apparently his failure to corral us back there wasn't being held against him.

Those things I'd expected. What I *hadn't* expected was to walk through the rear first-class car on our third day out and find YhoTeHeu seated there, calmly watching a dit-rec drama on the nearest display window.

In hindsight, I should have anticipated something like that. The Modhri would be unable to protect me if our enemy decided to make serious trouble along the way. He also knew from my confrontation with *Asantra* Muzzfor that I couldn't take a Shonkla-raa all by myself.

Hence, ChoDar's parting gift of a combat-trained fellow fighter. Whatever the Shonkla-raa had in mind, YhoTeHeu might give us the edge we needed.

But as the train continued to click its way down the Tube, and the passengers settled into their own personal routines, that confrontation continued to not happen. The Shonkla-raa himself proved to be the bashful type, seldom leaving his compartment near the front of the train and never when I was out and about. As the days passed, I began to hope that he had strict orders to merely watch us, and that he might remain under his rock all the way to Homshil.

Two weeks into the trip, that hope came to a sudden stop.

It was late at night, and Bayta and Terese had gotten into one of the light conversations that Bayta had been nurturing with the girl ever since our departure from Venidra Carvo. Their talks never seemed to get past dit-recs, food, and clothing, but Bayta was being gently persistent, and in this particular instance I had the feeling that the two of them might be on the edge of something a little deeper. Since it was obvious they weren't going to get serious as long as I was hanging around, I excused myself and headed to the bar end of the dining car.

I was sitting at a rear table, nursing a sweet iced tea and pondering the mysteries of womanhood, when a lone Filly seated with his back to me two tables over pushed back his chair and stood up. I had just enough time to register his oversized throat before he strode casually over and lowered himself into the chair across the table from me. "Hello, Compton," he said casually.

"Hello, Shonkla-raa," I managed, matching his tone as best I could with a suddenly racing heartbeat. "Enjoying the trip?"

He gave a small shrug. His nose blaze, I saw, had subtle diagonal stripes built into the mix of browns and tans. It reminded me somehow of sergeant's stripes. "It has been said that travel broadens the mind," he said. "Would you care to have your mind broadened, Compton?"

Looking furtively around, I knew, would be taken as a sign of weakness and desperation. With an effort, I kept my eyes on the Filly instead.

Besides, I already knew there was no help for me here. Aside from the two of us, the bar's current clientele consisted of two Shorshians having a drinking contest and a pear-shaped Cimma lost to the world in his simmering cup of something hot. None of the Modhran walkers was in the room, which under the circumstances was probably a good thing. The server Spider who was supposed to be behind the bar had vanished, either gone off-duty or else on a resupply trip back into his stockroom, eliminating any chance of bringing Bayta and the *kwi* that was living in her pocket these days.

I was on my own.

"That depends on the kind of broadening you had in mind," I said, easing my knees to the side so that I'd have at least a halfway decent chance of getting my legs out from under the table when he made his move.

He gave a short, amused little whinny. "Calm yourself, Compton," he said. "I haven't come here to destroy you. I could have done that anytime in the past fourteen days. I'm here merely to offer you truth." He cocked his head to the side. "And to seek your advice."

"I'm flattered," I said. "Afraid I'm not feeling very consultative at the moment."

"I can hardly blame you," the Shonkla-raa said, his voice suddenly low and earnest. "After what you and your friends went through on *Kuzyatru* Station, I can well imagine the veil of suspicion and anger through which you see us." He cocked his head again. "That's why I've come here this evening. I wished to set the record straight."

"Very thoughtful of you," I said. This ought to be good. "Go ahead."

"Firstly, I must apologize for the misguided zeal of my companions," he said, still using that solemn, used-marshland-salesman voice. "They jumped to the conclusion that you were a deadly enemy, someone to be destroyed at all costs."

"And I'm not?"

"Not at all," he said. "As I've observed your interactions with the Modhri aboard this train, I've come to realize that you are, in fact, merely a pawn."

"Interesting," I said. "Not very flattering, though."

"You would do well to put your Human pride aside for a moment," he said severely, a hint of the old familiar Shonkla-raa arrogance peeking momentarily through. "We're speaking about warfare and survival."

"No, we're speaking about recruitment," I corrected.

"You *are* trying to talk me into switching sides, aren't you?"

"The premise in your question is flawed," he said flatly. "The Modhri isn't on your side. *You* are on *his*. He's using you, making you as much a tool as any of his Eyes."

"And your side will treat me better?"

He drew himself up. "My side will win, Compton," he said, the earnestness in his voice taking on an edge of darkness. "It's inevitable. We've unlocked the secrets of the Shonkla-raa of old, the ability to tune Filiaelian minds to the telepathic frequencies of all known species."

"Except for Humans, who haven't got any telepathic frequencies," I reminded him. "And your little artificial-insemination program isn't going to change that."

He snorted, his nose blaze darkening. "That program is a pointless toy. But what of it? Do you really think your small cluster of Human worlds can hold out against the might of the reborn Shonkla-raa and the weight of the entire galaxy?"

"Well, when you put it *that* way, I suppose not," I conceded. "But we must be of *some* use to you. Otherwise, why the sales pitch?"

"Your people are of no use," he said with a dismissive sniff. "But you, Frank Compton, are another matter."

He leaned back in his seat, eyeing me thoughtfully. "There's a chapter of your Western Alliance history, two hundred and more years ago, called the War Between the States. You're familiar with it?"

"Of course," I said. "I'm rather impressed that you are."

"One must study the peoples one intends to conquer and rule," he said, waving casually. "Before the conflict began, a general named Robertee-lee was offered the command of the Northern armies. He refused, choosing instead to command the forces of his native South. The war was long and devastating, costly in lives and property, and though Robertee-lee and those under his command fought hard, in the end they were defeated. Am I incorrect?"

"No, that pretty much covers the gist of it," I said. "Your point?"

"My point is that some historians believe that if Robertee-lee had instead accepted the North's offer the war would have been over in weeks, sparing many lives and vastly decreasing the subsequent turmoil and bitterness."

"Ah," I said, nodding. "So you're saying I'm the modern Robert E. Lee, and that if I'll just come over and assist your side with strategy and tactics it'll be over so much more painlessly?"

"Exactly," he said. "But more importantly, Earth and the rest of your people will be safe from the coming chaos."

"At least until you finish beating down everyone else?"

"Not at all," he said. "I'm offering you and your people an alliance. In exchange for your services, we'll leave your worlds and your people strictly alone."

I snorted. "Big offer. Your soldiers of choice are Modhran walkers, and we've managed to keep the Confederation pretty much free of them."

"Which isn't to say we couldn't import all we needed," he pointed out. "Nonetheless, I repeat my offer: if you work for us, the coming war will pass your worlds by. Your people will be free to live their lives as they themselves choose. We would even grant them free run of the galaxy, to roam wherever they wish, with all the rights and privileges we intend to grant our own Filiaelian people."

"Sounds way too generous," I said. "What would their task be in your New Order? Stoking the cremation furnaces or something?"

"They would have no duties of any sort," he assured me. "Only to live in contentment and freedom."

"And all this because of the value of my service to you?" I shook my head. "I have *got* to talk to the Spiders about raising my pay grade."

"Few people understand a warrior's true value," the Shonkla-raa said sagely. "Especially not his allies. Only his enemies have such clarity of vision."

"Probably has something to do with looking down the wrong end of a gun barrel," I said. "This alliance you mentioned. Would you be willing to write a contract to that effect?"

"Of course," he said without hesitation.

A shiver ran up my back. Either he was an extraordinarily good actor, or he fully meant the offer he'd just pitched. Every Filiaelian was brought up to respect legal contracts, and even a soulless Shonkla-raa should at least hesitate before declaring his willingness to commit fraud. "Good to hear," I said lamely.

"But I don't ask for an answer now," he went on. "Consider my offer. Consider also the odds against you, and the potential for destructive vengeance against your people should they join the rest of the galaxy in defying us." He lowered his voice. "And observe, too, the way the Modhri acts and speaks to you. He's not the ally he claims. He has his own objectives, and will pursue them in his own way."

"Don't we all."

He eyed me a moment longer in silence, then stood up. "I'll come to you again at journey's end. At that time, I'll expect your answer."

"I'll be sure to give your proposal every bit of thought that it merits," I assured him. "In the meantime, if I should want to discuss it further, who shall I ask for?"

For a moment he eyed me, and I wondered how good his ear was at detecting Human sarcasm. "I am *Osantra* Riijkhan," he said.

"Nice to meet you," I said. "And while I consider all of your points, you might want to consider a couple of mine. One, the old Shonkla-raa never conquered Earth.

Maybe it was just the fact that we weren't telepathic, like *Usantra* Wandek thought. But maybe there was something else. Something a little more dangerous."

"Such as?"

"I have no idea," I said. "That's why you might want to think about it. Fact number two: even with all their numbers and weapons, not to mention having the whole galaxy under their dominion, they were still destroyed."

"Irrelevant," Riijkhan said calmly. "There were far more peoples and cultures arrayed against us than exist now." He cocked his head. "Another possible consequence of defiance you would do well to remember."

"Oh, I will," I promised softly, my stomach tightening. Those peoples and cultures didn't exist anymore because they'd been obliterated in the Shonkla-raa's death throes. "Do remember, though, that none of those genocided races were around to help me when I killed *Asantra* Muzzfor. I did that all by myself."

His nose blaze darkened. "Yes, the last message from *Kuzyatru* Station included that claim. I don't find it believable."

"That's okay," I said. "Neither did *Usantra* Wandek. Of course, he's dead now, too, along with quite a few of his compatriots."

Riijkhan snorted. "Again, irrelevant," he insisted. "The deaths you speak of weren't a result of any great combat skill in your possession. You defeated them only through the use of a trick."

"Of course I used a trick," I said. "That's what tactics is all about. Coming up with tricks that work."

For a long moment he stared at me. Then, he gave a small shake that began at his head and ran, dog-like, through the rest of his body. "All the more reason for us to hire you," he said. "I'll see you at journey's end, Frank Compton." Turning, he strode from the bar and headed forward toward the first-class cars.

I gave him a thirty-second head start. Then, downing the last of my iced tea, I headed off after him. I had the

Modhri's list of probable Shonkla-raa agents, but it never hurt to check out such things for myself. With luck, Riijkhan would take a moment to consult with his minions, or at least nod to them on his way back to his compartment.

I reached the end of the dining/bar car, punched the release, and stepped through the sliding door into the vestibule. A few quick steps, another tap on the release at the vestibule's other end, and I stepped into the rear of the number-one first-class coach car.

And came to a sudden halt. Standing in a triangle formation facing me at the rear of the car were three of the four Shonkla-raa agents the Modhri had fingered for me, with only Scrawny absent. A few steps behind them, Riijkhan had turned back to face me. "You spoke of tricks and tactics," he said. "I offer you the opportunity to demonstrate." He gestured around at the scattering of closed sleeping canopies around him. "My apologies for not providing you with a proper audience."

Turning, he continued down the car to the end. He punched the release and kept going, disappearing as the vestibule door slid shut behind him.

"And now," the Filly in the center said, speaking softly as if concerned he might awaken one of the sleeping passengers. "Let us see how a Human fights."

"And how a Human bleeds," the one on my right added.

"Sorry to disappoint you," I apologized. "The first rule of tactics is to never take on superior odds." With that, I took two quick steps backward, slapped behind me at the door release, and ducked back into the vestibule.

Apparently, rumors of my courage had preceded me. The door was already closing between us before any of them broke from their stunned paralysis at my unexpected demonstration of cowardice. I caught just a glimpse of them making a mad rush forward as the door finished sliding shut. Taking a half step backward, I waited.

And as the door opened and the first of them came charging through, I snapped a kick into his upper torso.

Emikai had warned me that a professional fighter might have had his heart sac area strengthened against such attacks. It was instantly obvious that this particular Filly, at least, wasn't a professional fighter. He went down like an empty bag, slamming the side of his head hard enough against the floor to show he wasn't faking. The second Filly faltered in his own charge as he stumbled over the obstacle that I'd unexpectedly dropped in front of him. A flash of surprise and malice crossed his face as he threw his arms up to protect his torso and heart sac.

So instead I kicked him in his right upper-leg nerve center, collapsing the leg out from under him.

Desperately, he threw his arms wide, trying to prevent himself from falling by bracing himself against the sides of the vestibule. The maneuver actually succeeded, stopping his fall just long enough for me to cock my leg back and send a kick to his heart sac. He dropped on top of the first Filly and lay still.

Leaving the last Filly goggling at me as the vestibule door closed behind him.

"Unless," I said mildly, "you can find a way to decrease those odds." I lifted my hands into one of the Filly combat stances Emikai had taught me. "Shall we see how you do at one-on-one?"

Apparently, Shonkla-raa minionhood didn't include dying unnecessarily for the cause. With a final look at the two crumpled figures at his feet, he slapped the door release and hotfooted it out of there.

I waited until the door had closed again behind him. Then, keeping an eye on my two downed attackers, just in case, I headed back toward the safety of my room. *Osantra* Riijkhan, I suspected, wouldn't be very happy when he found out how the evening had gone.

Then again, maybe he would.

I didn't say anything to Bayta right away, since she was still talking to Terese and I didn't want to worry the girl. But it was clear from the tension in Bayta's face as I came in that she already knew. Apparently, the Spiders hadn't been as absent during the confrontation as I'd thought.

Bayta didn't say anything, either. But within five minutes of my arrival she found an excuse to leave Terese in their half of our double compartment and to join me on my side, closing the dividing wall between us.

The wall had barely snicked shut when she was up in front of me, her hands gripping my upper arms, her face tight with worry as she gazed into my eyes. "Are you all right?" she asked anxiously.

"I'm fine," I said, reaching up and resting my arms reassuringly on her shoulders. "They never laid a hand on me."

"I meant—" She broke off.

"You mean what am I going to do when we reach Homshil and *Osantra* Riijkhan wants an answer to his recruitment pitch?" I asked, easing her back and sitting us both down on the curved couch that had folded out from the dividing wall as it closed.

"Yes," she said, her voice dark. "He may have more people and resources assembled by the time we get there."

I shrugged. "I'm sure he will. For that matter, he's probably got more resources already on this train. That's what that whole nonsensical attack was all about."

Bayta's lip twitched. "I was wondering about that," she said. "He only sent the agents we already knew about."

"Exactly," I said, nodding. "Well, all except Scrawny, anyway."

"Scrawny?"

"The Filly we were all set to charge through on Venidra Carvo if the Modhri hadn't sent those two Tra'ho'seej to run interference for us," I explained. "Not that he would have been much good in a fight anyway. But you're right. The whole point of that exercise was to give us the illusion that Riijkhan was still being proactive without actually showing us any new cards."

"So he's still here to watch us?"

"That's my guess," I said. "And sneering bravado aside, he might also be a little bit worried. No matter how many minions he's got on hand, the fact remains that he's only one Shonkla-raa, and we've already demonstrated that we can take on lone Shonkla-raa and win. No, unless we push him too hard I think we can assume he'll wait until Homshil before trying anything."

"And then?"

I shrugged. "I don't know," I said. "Maybe I'll take him up on his offer."

Her eyes were steady on me. "You *are* joking."

"There *is* something to be said for getting invited into the middle of your enemy's planning sessions," I pointed out. "But don't worry, I'm not going to change sides."

"He won't be happy about that," she warned.

"He can be as unhappy as he wants," I said. "By the time the train reaches Homshil Station we'll be long gone."

Bayta frowned. "We'll be—? Oh," she interrupted herself, her forehead smoothing. "A tender?"

"Exactly," I said. "One of the messages I sent from Venidra Carvo was to the Homshil stationmaster. About half an hour out from Homshil a tender is supposed to pull alongside and set up a—what did the defender call the thing the last time we did this? That portable airlock thingy of theirs?"

"A side-extendable sealable passageway," Bayta supplied.

"Right—that," I said. "The three of us—you, me, and Terese—will slip out the door into the tender. By the time the super-express hits the Homshil atmosphere barrier, we'll already be past the station and on our way to Yandro."

A small shiver ran through her. "You still want to go there?" she asked quietly.

"Not really," I admitted. "But I don't see any other option. We need to know how far the Modhri's prepared to go to get out from under the collective Shonkla-raa thumb. If he's willing to sign on to my plan, great. If he's not . . . well, we'll deal with that if and when it happens."

"A plan you haven't yet told me," Bayta pointed out.

I gazed into her eyes, torn by indecision. How much should I tell her? How much could I afford to tell her? "The basic plan has two prongs," I said. "The first part is to try to drop the Modhri out of the equation. If we can do that, the Shonkla-raa's list of allies instantly drops by a factor of about a million."

"All right," Bayta said slowly. "But how are you going to do that? Persuade him to send all his walkers into hiding?"

"That's one possibility," I said. "I'm hoping to find something with a little more staying power, though."

"Such as?"

"Still working that out," I lied. "Anyway, once he's out of the picture, all we need to do is raise ourselves an army."

Her face suddenly became very still, and it didn't take any great insight on my part to guess she was thinking about the Chahwyn's defender Spiders. A few of them might be of great assistance in this confrontation with the Shonkla-raa.

An army of them would change the face and tone of Quadrail travel forever.

"And since there's only one species we know the Shonkla-raa can't control," I went on before she could say anything, "that means our army will be composed of us lowly Humans."

Her eyes did a quick double-take, and some of the fresh tension lines faded. But only some of them. "*Humans?*" she echoed.

"Yes," I confirmed. "Ironic, isn't it? After being looked down on by pretty much everyone else for the past thirty-odd years, we're going to be the ones who come charging over the hill to save the day."

"You really think . . . ?" She trailed off, her usual impassive expression dropping back over her swirling uncertainties.

"It'll work, Bayta," I said. I took her hand and squeezed it, savoring the warmth and strength as she squeezed back. "We'll make it work."

She took a deep breath. "I hope so," she said quietly.

"It will," I said. With an effort, I looked her straight in the eye. "Trust me."

TWENTY-TWO :

The rest of the trip was uneventful. We kept busy with the usual diversions: dit-recs, games, music, and of course the consistently superb food and drink. Unlike many of the first-class passengers, Bayta and I also made regular use of the exercise equipment, visits that served the dual purpose of helping us work off the calories as well as giving Terese a few precious hours of solitude. Bayta was always a little nervous about leaving the girl alone that way, but as long as she made sure there was at least one Spider watching over the girl she was able to keep her concern mostly in check.

Through it all, I kept waiting for Riijkhan to make a return appearance. But having had his say he apparently saw no need to underline his point and went back to spending the bulk of his time in his compartment.

Scrawny likewise spent the rest of the journey making himself scarce. Riijkhan's other three minions, in contrast, seemed to be everywhere, dogging my steps, throwing furtive glances in my direction, and otherwise doing the stuff you apparently learn in Shonkla-raa minion school.

For a while I tried watching them, hoping I could

catch the subtle signs of recognition between them and the unknown agents I was still sure Riijkhan had aboard. But after a couple of weeks I gave up the effort. These three clearly had no clue who the rest of the team members were, and with Riijkhan not giving me the chance to watch his own reactions the hidden agents were likely to stay that way.

Bayta didn't seem to be having much luck with her chosen project, either. Terese's barriers were slowly coming down, but while she was willing enough to talk to Bayta their conversations still tended to be rather superficial.

But at least the girl was talking. More importantly, there were no repeats of her earlier suicide attempts, even with her method of choice easily available in any of the train's bars. Maybe her close brush with death had made her realize that there were better solutions to her problems.

Or perhaps she simply realized that the Spiders were watching her even when Bayta and I weren't.

Our surreptitious exit from the train came off perfectly. The tender pulled close beside the super-express and extended its airlock to our car door, and Bayta, Terese, and I slipped through. By the time the super-express rolled to a stop at its designated platform, just as I'd predicted, we were riding up the station slope to the atmosphere barrier and heading back into the main Tube.

After the luxury of Quadrail first class, and even more so after the hyper-luxury of the Halkan Peerage car, a Spider tender was a big step down. I watched Terese's face as she looked around at the plain, open compartment: twin bunks at each end, a simple half-bath cubicle in the middle, and a compact food prep/storage area. It didn't take a genius detective to see that she was seriously underwhelmed by our new accommodations.

Fortunately, it was only a few hours from Homshil to Yandro at the tender's enhanced speed, which meant she wouldn't have to endure the Spartan accommodations for long. Even more fortunately, even if Riijkhan and his buddies guessed we were headed for Yandro, they could lie in wait for us forever at the station without ever spotting us.

Because Yandro, unlike any other system in the entire galaxy, had *two* Quadrail stations.

It was the result of a deal Bayta and I had made with the Chahwyn and Spiders nearly two years ago. We'd identified Yandro's Great Polar Sea as the Modhri's new homeland, and we needed a clandestine staging area to assemble an attack force without tipping off the watchers he had manning the transfer station. Hence, this little back door, which we'd funded with the help of Bruce McMicking and a trillion dollars I'd blackmailed out of the coffers of McMicking's industrialist boss Larry Cecil Hardin.

That attack had succeeded in destroying every shred of coral the Modhri had in that area. At the time, I'd naively concluded that that was the end of it, and that all we had left to deal with were the thousands of decorative coral outposts and millions of Modhran walkers scattered around the galaxy.

Only in recent months had we discovered that the Modhran homeland might be down but was far from out. Somehow, somewhere, he'd managed to stash away a lot more of his coral elsewhere on Yandro.

And now we were going to that same homeland, to face the segment-prime that we'd hit so hard and with such devastation.

I could only hope the segment-prime wasn't the type to hold a grudge.

Seven hours after leaving Homshil, we pulled into Yandro's second station.

The place was just the way I remembered it: a barely noticeable wide spot in the Tube with a single siding, a single hatchway leading out into the vacuum of space, and a handful of service buildings scattered around. If any passengers even spotted it as their train roared through, they would naturally conclude it was some sort of maintenance area.

Two Humans were waiting near the hatchway as the tender door irised open and Bayta, Terese, and I stepped out. One, an older woman with pure white hair, was stretched out on a sort of mobile recliner, her eyes closed, her chest rising and falling with the slow rhythm of sleep. Our sector-prime contact, presumably, once again by prearrangement via my messages from Venidra Carvo. The second Human, a male, was standing beside her with his back to us. Beyond the hatch, a pair of Spiders stood motionlessly. "Modhri?" I called as we approached the Humans.

"Yes," the man confirmed, turning around to face us.

And as Bayta jerked to a stunned halt, I felt my eyes widen.

Because the man wasn't just the old woman's nurse or attendant. He was EuroUnion Security Service agent Ackerley Morse. A deep-cover Modhran walker, who also happened to hate my guts.

And his presence here was most certainly *not* by prearrangement. At least, not *my* prearrangement.

"Hello, Compton," he continued, his voice calm as he nodded to me. "And to you, Bayta," he added, nodding to her as well. "It's been a while."

"Indeed it has," I managed, flicking my eyes quickly across his clothing in search of a concealed weapon. If the Modhri had in fact lured Bayta and me here in order to kill us, they couldn't have picked a better tool than Morse.

Trained agent that he was, he picked up on my visual frisk. "Oh, relax," he said, his tone in that irritating range between chiding and amused that I especially hated. "You must remember that even this little side door has the complete set of Spider weapons sensors." He nodded at the two Spiders standing in the background. "*And* the complete set of weapons enforcement specialists."

I focused on the Spiders for the first time, a chill running through me as I spotted the pattern of white dots across their spheres. Only stationmasters and defenders had such patterns.

And here, where no one came except by invitation, there were no stationmasters.

Once again, Morse read my glance and its significance. "Yes, they're defenders," he confirmed. "Or so I assume. If you'd like, I could pick a fight with one and find out for certain."

"No, that's all right," I said. "Try not to take this the wrong way, Morse, but what the hell are you doing here?"

"I'm part of the Modhri delegation, of course," he said, his civilized voice turning slightly brittle. "One of his representatives to these negotiations."

"Really," I said, not trying to hide my skepticism. Having a group of walkers spread out over a super-express or a Filiaelian space station could be very handy. Having a group of them at a conference was completely superfluous. "Are you expecting her to seize up and die or something?" I added, nodding toward the sleeping woman.

"No fears," the woman murmured, her eyes still closed. "This Eye is healthier than she appears."

Her hand lifted limply, gesturing toward Morse. "But Agent Morse is no longer merely an Eye. He is something new."

I eyed Morse. "I can hardly wait to hear this."

"Oh, you'll like it," Morse promised. "I'm now—" He paused, his eyes turning again to Bayta. "Actually, I'm now the Modhran version of you."

I stared at him . . . and then, abruptly, it clicked. "You mean you're *aware* of him?" I asked disbelievingly.

"Not only aware, but in something of a partnership," Morse said dryly. "And I must say, Bayta, that it's given me a much greater appreciation for the way you've had to live your life."

"Wait a minute, wait a minute," I said, feeling like I was still two steps behind. "You're in a *partnership*? With the *Modhri*?"

"Correct," the old woman said. "I have pledged to Agent Morse that he will have autonomy in all his actions, and that I will communicate with him but not control or influence him."

I eyed Morse. "And you're guaranteeing this how?"

"The same way anyone ever guarantees anything," Morse said. "He's given his word."

"His word," I said flatly.

"Like the word you gave him that you'd help his war against the Shonkla-raa," Morse said pointedly. "Plus I know now how to spot the signs that he's cheating."

"Interesting experiment," I said. "And we're doing this why?"

Morse snorted. "Why do you think?" he demanded. "You've stated over and over that you don't think the Modhri can survive without taking over everything in sight. This—me—is to show that he can."

"Really," I said, studying his face. Certainly there were none of the subtle signs of Modhran control that I was familiar with. "Well, as a good-faith gesture, I'll admit it's impressive."

"It's more than a gesture," the woman insisted. "It's a step toward my future."

"Is it?" I countered, gesturing at the old woman. "What about her? You haven't told *her* what she's carrying inside her, have you?"

The woman's lip twitched. "It was deemed that she would be unable to accept the truth," the Modhri said reluctantly.

"He's got that right," Morse put in gruffly. "I can tell you it was a hell of a surprise to have my mind suddenly talking back to me. Thought I'd finally gone round the bend."

"I can imagine," I said. "But if you're the Modhri's future, it does rather bring up the question of what happens to the Modhri's past. What happens to all the walkers like her who *can't* handle the shock?"

"What do you wish me to do?" the Modhri countered. "Order the colonies within all of those Eyes to die?"

"And if I gave you that order?"

The woman's face tightened. "Don't ask me to do that," she warned, her voice dark and grim. "Don't ever ask me to do that. Ever."

"Take it easy," I said, thrown a little by the Modhri's reaction. "And watch your tone. You've agreed to follow my orders, remember? Besides, none of your individual colonies are of lasting importance."

"Don't ever ask such a thing of me," the Modhri said again.

"Don't push it, Compton," Morse warned quietly. "You know what happens when a mind segment starts losing pieces."

I grimaced. I did, too. It was the loss of two of his component parts to the murderer on our first superexpress that had pushed that mind segment into making an alliance with me in the first place. "I understand your feelings," I said. "But this is war. The odds are very high that some of us won't live through it. Possibly none of us. You say you'll follow my orders. But will you still say that when your walkers start dying and your mind segments feel their lives slipping away?"

"Compton, what the hell are you doing?" Morse asked. "You trying to kink the whole deal?"

"I'm trying to make sure he's fully counted the cost," I said. "The Modhri is like a wolf. He's predatory, driven to grow and take over everything around him. That could make him an unreliable ally, especially if he's going to argue every order on the grounds that it could hurt a little."

"Compton—"

"It also makes him an unpleasant friend," I continued.

"You'd have a hard time finding people who would want a wolf living with them. You'd never know when something would set it off, and you'd suddenly be turned into lunch. Or a mindless puppet, rather."

"I am what I am," the old woman said, the sadness in her voice even more pronounced. Clearly, the Modhri was wondering if I was having second thoughts about our deal. "I am what I was created to be."

"And if you're talking about me, I have no problem with our current relationship," Morse added.

"I understand that," I said, nodding. "But you're an extraordinary person. Most people, as I say, wouldn't live with a wolf." I raised my eyebrows. "But a lot of people are more than happy to share their lives with a loyal, trustworthy dog."

I looked back at the old woman. "Tell me, Modhri. What would you do if you were offered the chance to change from a wolf into that loyal, trustworthy dog?"

Her forehead wrinkled. "I don't understand."

"You said you were the way you were created," I told him. "So are all the rest of us. But none of us has to stay that way. We can change. *You* can change. The question is whether you're willing to do so."

For the first time the woman's eyes opened. "How?" she asked.

I braced myself. The next thirty seconds would make or break this whole deal. "You invite in the Abomination."

"The what?" Morse asked, frowning. "What the hell is—?" Abruptly, he broke off. "Oh," he said in a suddenly subdued tone.

"What's an Abomination?" Terese asked.

"It's exactly what I just said: a calm, loyal dog to the Modhri's wolf," I told her. "Modified coral, modified walkers. They actually call themselves the Melding— *Abomination* is the Modhri's term." I frowned at Morse as something suddenly hit me. "In fact, now that I think about it, the Melding is exactly the same format that the Modhri's running with Agent Morse right now."

"It would change me," the old woman said, her voice trembling now. "I would never again be the same."

"Yes, that's true," I said, putting all the soothing confidence and sympathy into my voice that I could. "And I understand that change can be frightening, especially a change of this magnitude. I also know you fought the whole idea of that change once before."

"You were there," Morse murmured.

"Very much so," I agreed. "But the situation's changed. It's no longer a choice of living as the Modhri or living as the Melding. It's a question of living free or as the Shonkla-raa's slave."

The woman shivered. "It can't work," she murmured tautly. "It would change me. It can't work."

"Yes, it can," I assured the Modhri. "It will. The Melding's a cooperative partnership, which is what you've stated you want to be."

"And the Melding coral isn't truly alien to you," Bayta added quietly. "It's only a modification of what you already are. The change won't be nearly as large or as terrible as you think."

"But whatever the change, it will be permanent," the Modhri said.

"Probably," I conceded, watching the old woman's face. The Modhri was teetering on the edge, fear and hope pulling in opposite directions.

I braced myself. Time to play my final card.

"There's one other thing to consider," I said. "Bayta's right about the Melding coral being similar to yours. But it's not identical, and as a result the people in the Melding run on a slightly different telepathic frequency than you do." I paused, waiting for the Modhri to find the obvious conclusion for himself.

Morse got it first. "The Shonkla-raa may not be able to control them," he said, an edge of cautious excitement in his voice. "*Or* to control us once we've combined with them."

"That's my hope," I said, nodding. "Now, it may be that the Shonkla-raa will still be able to affect the Melding the same way they do the Spiders and Bayta, which pretty much freezes them in confusion. But having your Eyes standing around like statues instead of actively shooting at us will go a long way toward making you useless as a weapon."

"Agreed," the Modhri said. The fear was still in his voice, but the hesitation was gone. He was doing this to get out from under the Shonkla-raa's thumb, and any step in that direction was a good one. "I accept your offer. How do we proceed?"

"We start by bringing the same offer to the Melding," I said. "Bayta and I will do that. While we're gone, I suggest you send some of your Eyes to Homshil, Jurskala, and other major Quadrail centers in the area. The more mind segments who get the word, the faster we'll be able to get the whole Modhri community up to speed on the plan."

"You think that's wise?" Morse asked. "The more we spread the word, the easier it'll be for some wandering Shonkla-raa to grab an Eye at random and find out what we're up to."

"Let them," I said as casually as I could manage. I was, in fact, counting on the Shonkla-raa doing that very thing. "Knowing that we're going to alter the Modhri's character won't do them a damn bit of good until they know what direction that alteration will take."

"Because they can't adjust their control tone and telepathic frequency until they know what ours will be," Morse said, nodding. "They might be able to adjust long-term, but not short-term."

"And with luck, short-term is all we'll need," I agreed. "As for you, I'm thinking I'd like you to come along with Bayta and me. Ride shotgun, and all that."

Morse's forehead creased. "Are you sure? I'm as vulnerable as anyone else."

"In theory, yes," I said. "But as far as I know, the Shonkla-raa have never tried their bag of tricks on a Human walker before. You might surprise them."

"Or I might not," Morse warned.

"It's worth the risk," I said firmly.

"You're the boss." Morse's eyes flicked to Terese. "Or I could let you two go and I could escort Ms. German back to Earth."

"Yes, let's do that," Terese spoke up before I could answer.

"Sorry," I said, shaking my head. "We know the Shonkla-raa still want you, and we also know they have some sort of force on Earth that hunts for pregnant women to exploit. We can't risk you going back yet."

"And how is that *your* decision?" Terese demanded.

"Because right now we're the only ones who can protect you," I said.

"Is it me you care about?" she shot back. "Or this?" She jabbed a finger toward her belly.

"We care about you both," I said.

"Yeah, that's what Aronobal said, too," she said acidly. "My life isn't your business, Compton, and I'm done with this." She gestured to Morse. "You—take me back to Earth. Now."

"I'll be happy to take you back to the Terra Quadrail station, if that's what you want," Morse said gravely. "But as you just heard, I have other important duties I need to perform. I can't take you all the way to Earth."

"Fine," Terese said. "I can get back on my own."

"Of course," Morse said. "But Compton's right. Once our protection is removed, the Shonkla-raa and their agents will have little trouble taking your child."

Terese snorted. "They can have him."

"And since he's not yet developed enough for them to risk removal," Morse continued smoothly, "they'll need to take you along with him. And to keep you for several more weeks."

"Until they think it's safe enough for them to cut you open and take him out," I added.

Terese swallowed hard. "You're just trying to scare me."

"We're trying to give you the realities of the situation," Morse said. "Staying with Compton and Bayta may be uncomfortable for you. But it won't be nearly as uncomfortable as being in Shonkla-raa hands again."

Terese looked like she was ready to chew sand. But she just sighed. "Fine," she muttered. "Whatever."

"So it's settled," I said. "Bayta, Terese, Morse, and I will head out to talk to the Melding, while you send some Eyes to play Paul Revere."

"And then?" the Modhri asked.

"I'll let you know once I've talked to the Melding," I said.

"You must have some thoughts," the Modhri persisted.

"I have a few," I said. "It would be best if we didn't discuss them just yet."

"Compton—"

"No, he's right," Morse said. "The Shonkla-raa can't freeze him and demand he give up state secrets. They can do that with us. The less we know, the better."

"Exactly," I said. "Bayta, we'll take the tender back to Homshil and pick up a regular train."

"I suppose this Melding's halfway across the galaxy," Terese said sourly.

"Not nearly that far," the Modhri assured her. "They're in an unspecified system near Sibbrava in the Cimmal Republic. Approximately a ten-day journey from here."

Terese stared at the old woman. "You already *know* where the Melding is? I thought they were a big fat secret."

"I know only the approximate area," the old woman said. "Not the precise location."

"The Modhri knows a great deal about the galaxy," I said. "It's one of the things that makes him such a useful ally. Bayta, get the tender fired up, and let's get moving."

The last couple of weeks aboard the super-express had seen a slow but steady opening up of Terese's defenses, at least toward Bayta. That relaxation of tension had faltered a bit during the seven-hour trip to Yandro, but I'd put that down to Terese's very reasonable annoyance at being hauled out of her comfortable surroundings and loaded aboard a Spider tender.

Now, as we left the hope of a quick return to Earth behind and headed back toward Homshil in that same tender, I discovered her walls had once again gone up.

A logical, rational person would have blamed me. Terese, who was neither, blamed all three of us.

I was used to it. Morse didn't seem to care very much one way or the other.

Bayta was devastated.

She tried to hide it, of course. But I could tell. She'd worked so hard to get Terese to open up, and to be a friend to her, that she couldn't help but take the teenager's rejection personally.

What I *wasn't* expecting was that Bayta apparently didn't blame me for messing all that up.

That worried me. Bayta and I had been through enough that I expected her to trust me. But Terese's current situation *was* my fault, at least partially, which should realistically have given rise to at least a little annoyance or frustration on Bayta's part.

Only it hadn't. Which strongly implied that she'd figured out what I was up to.

And that didn't just worry me. It scared the living spit out of me.

Because sure as God made little gray sewer rats there would be Shonkla-raa aboard the train we would be boarding once we reached Homshil. I had no idea how well versed they were in the subtleties of Human psychology, but if they sensed any anomalies in Bayta's behavior my entire plan could come crashing down around us.

But there was nothing I could do. Not with Terese glowering across the tender where she could listen in on any conversation Bayta and I might have. I would just have to carry on as if nothing was wrong and hope the Shonkla-raa misinterpreted whatever data they managed to collect.

There hadn't been any way for Bayta to set up our new travel plans from the secret Yandro station. But I'd spent some time with the Quadrail schedule and had concluded we would have less than two hours to wait before the express train I wanted arrived at Homshil.

For once, my timing was dead on. An hour and forty minutes after we stepped off the tender at Homshil we were on our way to Sibbrava.

I'd hoped that our little side trip to Yandro might throw Riijkhan off the scent. No such luck. He hadn't managed to score a compartment this time, but when I escorted Bayta and Terese to the dining car for our first meal of the trip I spotted him right there in the middle of the first-class coach car.

Fortunately, sitting seemed to be the only thing he wanted to do at the moment. That, and staring unblinkingly at us as we walked past.

Bayta spotted him, too, but limited herself to a single emotionless glance in his direction before turning her eyes away. Terese, equal opportunity grouch that she was, uncorked a defiant glare that was impressive even by her standards.

Morse was waiting for us, having come in on his own from the second-class car just behind the dining car, the closest place Bayta had been able to get him a seat. "Any trouble getting in here?" I asked him as we sat down at his table.

"None," he assured me. "A first-class ticket gets you into first-class territory even if your seat is in second. What news from your end of the world?"

"Riijkhan's aboard," I said. "I didn't spot any of his original entourage, though. He may have split them off to cover the stations between Homshil and Earth."

"If he did, he didn't split all of them," Morse said, his eyes flicking briefly to his left.

Under cover of pushing Terese's fork and spoon closer to her, I looked in that direction. Seated with two other Fillies, trying to look inconspicuous, was a familiar face. "Well, well—our old friend Scrawny," I commented, returning my attention to Morse. "At least with him we don't have to worry about getting ambushed in the still of the night."

"Don't be too sure," Morse warned. "He could be a genetically enhanced fighter who's deliberately chosen to look non-threatening."

"There's that," I conceded. "Well, it wasn't like we weren't going to keep an eye on him anyway. What exactly does that *we* consist of, by the way?"

"There are eight Eyes in first, plus another six in second," Morse said. "Bearing in mind, though, that the latter group would need Spider permission to come into first-class territory if we need them." He looked at Bayta and raised his eyebrows invitingly.

Bayta grimaced, but nodded. "If you need them, they should give the Spiders the password *filigree*."

"Filigree," Morse repeated, nodding. "Got it."

A server Spider came up, and we gave our dinner orders. "So what's the rest of the plan?" Morse asked after the server had gone. "Specifically, what happens when we hit Sibbrava?"

"We get off and grab another tender that hopefully will be waiting for us," I said, glancing reflexively at Scrawny and his dinner companions. Quadrail dining cars were acoustically designed to keep table conversations confined to those immediate environs, but checking for possible eavesdroppers was a habit trained security types like me found almost impossible to break. "We take a quick trip to the Melding's secret location, present our case, and if we're lucky an equally quick trip back to Sibbrava with some new passengers and a few crates of additional cargo."

"And if they politely decline to join in the fun?"

"They won't," I said. "The essence of the Melding is about nurturing and cooperating with others. They consider the Modhri a somewhat dysfunctional member of the family, and want to help him." I made a little hand gesture. "No offense."

"None taken," Morse said, his voice more grim than offended. "I'm more concerned about . . . the point is, Compton, that I'm starting to wonder if this is really the right time to be turning the Modhri into a lapdog. Seems to me that the wolf version is exactly what we need right now."

"One: I said *dog*, not *lapdog*," I reminded him. "Big difference. Two: you heard what I said about the Melding's possible frequency shift."

"And I'm thinking that's a crock," Morse said flatly. "It's the same coral, the same polyps, the same sense of hearing with everyone. I don't see how the Eyes' attitude or whatever can make two sticks' worth of difference."

"Is that you talking, or the Modhri?" I asked.

"It's me," Morse growled. "But the Modhri's not so sure, either."

"You tell the Modhri he needs to remember who's wearing the leader hat here," I said. "And you both need to trust me."

"The Modhri does." Morse's eyes flicked to Bayta. "I gather Bayta does, too."

"And you?"

He looked me square in the eye. "Not so much."

"That'll change," I promised him. "Sooner or later, that'll change."

I hoped to hell I was right.

TWENTY-THREE :

The ten-day trip from Homshil to Sibbrava translated, in this case, to ten days of watchfulness, dit-recs and cards, meals and drinks, and, as it turned out, unnecessary anxiety.

Every time I left our compartment I expected Riijkhan or one of his friends to make some sort of trouble. But nothing of the sort ever happened. As far as I could tell, the whole Shonkla-raa community could have decided to give up and go away.

Which just meant that what they were *really* doing was gathering their strength for some seriously massive attack.

I could hardly wait.

We reached Sibbrava and the four of us transferred to another of the Spiders' modified tenders. Three and a half hours later, we pulled into the unfinished station in the still unnamed Cimmal system where the Melding had set up their new home.

A long-range service vehicle, also modified for Human use, was waiting at the hatchway for us. With a service Spider at the controls, and a defender Spider standing beside him, we headed out into space.

With a near-Earth-type planet beckoning invitingly from the inner system, plus any number of moons and large asteroids available for warren habitats, my assumption had always been that the Melding's leaders had moved inward from the Tube. It was something of a surprise, therefore, when our transport instead turned outward, toward the vast emptiness of the outer solar system.

In retrospect, though, it made sense. Quadrail Tubes typically touched their client systems far out in the local sun's gravity well, putting ninety-nine-plus percent of the useful real estate on the inward side of the line. The handful of hardy knowledge-seekers who might go in the other direction would never even spot a lone, silent ship drifting through all that blackness.

Or in this case, six ships: six old survey/sampling vessels, Cimman design, probably leftovers from the system's initial exploration sweep. The ships were linked together by wide transfer cylinders, with an industrial-sized fusion generator trailing along behind the whole thing like a pet dog on a leash.

Docked beside one of the ships in the cluster was a torchferry, presumably the vehicle the Melding used to get back and forth to the Tube when necessary. None of the other ships' docking ports had the glowing red outlining that would indicate it was receiving guests, but our Spider seemed to know where he was going. He maneuvered us alongside the ship on the opposite side of the cluster from the torchferry, and I felt the slight tremor as the docking collars engaged. "Okay," I said, as our engines went silent. "You all sit tight. I'll go in and make sure everything's okay."

"No," Morse said, his voice tight. "We go together."

"Morse—"

"They want to see all of us," he said. "Might as well go in together and get it over with."

Back when Bayta and I first sneaked Rebekah off New Tigris and out of the Modhri's hands she'd said there were about three hundred of these Melding people. From the size of the crowd gathered in the shuttle hangar bay as we walked inside, it looked like the whole crowd had come out to greet us.

And not all of them had friendly looks on their faces. Not even most of them.

I cleared my throat. "Hello," I called, my voice echoing strongly in the hangar despite all the people gathered there. "I'm Frank Compton."

"We know who you are," a Jurian in the center of the front row said. "We know who all of you are." His gaze swept over us, settled on Morse. "Why are you here?"

"We need your help," I said. "The Shonkla-raa have revived—"

"Why are you here?" the Jurian repeated.

Only then did I realize he wasn't talking to me. He was talking to Morse. Or rather, to the Modhri inside Morse.

I shifted my attention to Morse. He gave a little nod, as if giving silent permission to an unspoken question.

And abruptly his face sagged subtly as the Modhri took over his body. "To see if I can be changed," he said.

"And if you can?" the Jurian asked. "Will all of you— the entire Modhri—accept this change?"

"Why can't they just make him?" Terese murmured from beside me, her usual shoulder-chip attitude momentarily eclipsed by the eerie gravity of the moment. "They've got to have hundreds-to-one odds on him."

The Jurian had good ears. "We won't impose our will on anyone," he said, his eyes flicking briefly to Terese before returning to Morse. "Will all of you accept this change, Modhri?"

Morse braced himself. "I won't hide from you that I fear this." He looked at me, as if seeking reassurance. Or else reminding himself what was at stake. "But more frightening is the thought of being a slave to the Shonkla-raa," he added. "Yes. All of me will accept the change."

The Jurian nodded. "Then open yourself," he said. "Do not resist. Open yourself to us, and allow us to bring forth the person that you can be. The person you were perhaps meant to be."

I don't know what I was expecting. Something dramatic, I suppose, something in line with life-changing events in the dit-rec dramas I'd watched over the years. But there was nothing of the sort. Morse's head twitched back a bit, more like the precursor to a sneeze than anything else.

And then, he turned to me, a look of utter bewilderment

on his face. "I'll be damned," he said, the same bewilderment in his voice.

"What?" I asked, reflexively shifting my feet into combat stance. "What happened."

"This," Morse said, waving a hand vaguely around him. "You ever wear glasses, Compton?"

I frowned. Did incorporating the Modhri with the Melding cause the former to go suddenly senile? "Sure, when I was a kid," I said. "Most doctors won't work on your eyes until you've stopped growing."

"I remember the first day I got my glasses, when I was eight," Morse said, his eyes sweeping the room but not really focusing on anything. "I hated the thought of wearing the things, so I'd been faking it for at least four years. You know what the first thing was I discovered?"

"That the things pinched your nose?"

"No." He gestured. "That trees have leaves. All the way to the top. Individual leaves. And I could see them."

He smiled. "I can see clearly now, Compton. Or rather, the Modhri can."

"I'm happy for you both," I said cautiously. It couldn't be this easy. It couldn't possibly be this easy.

Only, apparently, it was.

"We need to get you and your people to Yandro as quickly as possible," Morse went on, the sense of awe in his voice giving way to brisk professionalism. "Compton, I saw five tenders at the station back there—are those for us to use? Four per tender would mean twenty of them could go now, plus as much coral as they can squeeze in—"

"Whoa, whoa," I cut him off. "Let's pause for a minute and think this through, shall we?"

"What's to think through?" Morse countered. "You were right. It works. We need to get some of this coral to Yandro and start getting the segment-prime up to speed."

"Don't dampen his enthusiasm, Compton," the Jurian said. I'd never heard a Jurian sound chiding, but this one managed it. "For the first time he sees what he's been missing. He's eager to share this discovery with the rest of himself."

"Yes—the leaves on the trees, and all that," I said, thinking fast. I'd expected the trip from the station to the Melding's hideout to take considerably longer than the three and a half hours it actually had. If we started back now, my timing was going to be dangerously off the mark. "But that doesn't mean charging blindly ahead," I went on. "There are logistics to consider— how much coral, who goes, what happens to everyone who's still here. Once we get to Yandro, what then? Does everyone head inward to the planet for direct contact with the Modhran coral, or does the segment-prime send some Eyes out to meet with the Melding?"

"Good questions, all," Morse said, his forehead creasing. "And all of them except the ones about numbers and coral tonnage can be worked on en route."

"And besides that, I'm tired and hungry," I said.

"Two issues I believe we can solve," the Jurian said gravely. There was movement at one side of the group.

And our old friend Rebekah Beach stepped out into view.

It had been less than six months since Bayta and I had said our final good-byes to her back at the unfinished Quadrail station. But even in that brief a time, the girl had undergone a dramatic change. She was noticeably taller, as generally happened with ten-year-olds. She'd also cut her hair into a shorter style, one that suited her face better than the old one had.

But more impressive than her physical changes was the new air of calmness and maturity that hovered around her. Back when we'd been running from the Modhri, Rebekah had tried very hard to be all grown up, to face the danger and uncertainties as best she could. But those efforts had been only partially successful, like a set of ill-fitting clothes she'd hastily thrown on.

Now, after only a few months, I could see her wearing those adult attitudes and responsibilities like a tailored suit.

Back then, I'd wondered whether the Melding colony within her had cheated her out of her childhood. Apparently, whatever forces were at work in her were well on their way to depriving her of her teen years, as well.

Which, as I remembered back to that period in my own life, wasn't necessarily a bad thing.

But despite all that maturity wrapped around her, I could see a hint of the excited child shining in her eyes as she saw Bayta and me.

Not that that kind of excitement was solely the province of ten-year-olds. I was still only halfway through my observation and analysis when Bayta broke from my side, hurried forward, and attacked the girl with a huge bear hug.

"Rebekah will take you to a room where you may rest," the Jurian continued. "Meanwhile, we'll prepare food for you."

I inclined my head to him. "Thank you."

"Any idea how long this nap of yours is going to take?" Morse asked.

"A few hours," I said. "Maybe more. It's been a long time since I felt genuinely safe, and I've got a lot of sleep to catch up on." I turned back to Bayta and Rebekah, who had now disengaged from their hug and were talking softly together. "Whenever you're ready, Rebekah," I added.

The girl gestured to a line of unoccupied floor that had opened up through the crowd behind her. "This way," she said. Her eyes shifted to Terese. "Would you like to come with us, too, Terese?"

"That's okay," Terese said. "I'm not very tired."

"Could we talk, then?" Rebekah persisted.

The question seemed to take Terese by surprise. "About what?" she asked suspiciously.

"Nothing special," Rebekah said, her air of calmness faltering a bit. "Just about . . . things." She hunched her shoulders. "There isn't anyone else aboard even close to my age. I just thought we could . . . just talk, that's all. Or maybe listen to music. There isn't much Human music here. Do you have anything modern with you?"

"Some," Terese said. Her voice was still wary, but I could hear her warming to the idea of having some company that wasn't Bayta, Morse, and me. Especially that wasn't me. "You like Adam Pithcary?"

"I don't think I've ever heard him," Rebekah said. "But I'd like to. Come on, we'll show Mr. Compton to his room and then we can go to mine. Wait'll you hear my player—it's really good."

She took Terese's arm, and the two of them headed toward a door in the hangar's rear. It looked a little odd, the little girl leading the teenager, but somehow seemed both right and proper given their different personalities. Bayta walked behind them, hanging back to give them some space, and I dropped into position a couple meters still farther to the rear.

We were walking down a beautifully decorated corridor when Morse caught my arm. "We need to talk," he murmured.

I slowed down, letting Bayta and the two girls gain some distance on us. "What about?" I asked, turning to face him.

"About why you're stalling," he said, his eyes digging into my face like twin entrenching tools. "You just ate three hours ago, and you can sleep all you want on the way back to Yandro."

"I already told you I don't sleep well when I'm in danger," I reminded him.

"That's a bloody load," he bit out. "And you know it." He leaned in a few centimeters closer, getting right up into my face. "What are you up to, Compton?"

I considered introducing him to the deck, decided that a public scuffle wasn't really what we needed right now. "I'm trying to win a war," I said instead.

"Are you?" he countered. "You do realize, don't you, that every hour you stall us out here gives the Shonkla-raa an extra hour to bring in more of their numbers."

"It also gives them another hour to scatter frantically to the four winds looking for us," I said. "Remember, they have no way of knowing how far we were going to go once we left Sibbrava."

"You sure about that?" he asked darkly. "I understand *Osantra* Riijkhan offered you Earth's safety in exchange for your help."

In other words, had I betrayed him and the Modhri when they weren't looking? "Yes, he offered," I said. "I didn't say yes."

"You also didn't say no."

I sighed. How many times was I going to have to go through this? "Look, Morse. If you get taken by the Shonkla-raa, what's the first question they're going to ask you?"

"I thought you weren't even sure that they could take control of Human Eyes."

"Indulge me," I said. "Assuming they can, what's their first question going to be?"

"Where can I get one of those lovely English accents?" he suggested sarcastically.

"That's question two," I said. "Question one will be 'What's Compton's plan?' Am I wrong?"

His lip twitched. "No."

"And since you would then have to tell him, it follows that it's best if you don't know my plan," I said. "Is this starting to sink in?"

He glared at me another few seconds before pulling his face back to a civilized distance. "So I gather this delay is part and parcel of your plan?"

"This delay is because I'm tired and hungry," I said, emphasizing each word.

"Sure." He grimaced, the last remnants of his glare fading away into a sort of unhappy watchfulness. "I hope you know what you're doing."

"I always know what I'm doing," I told him.

"Are you always right?"

"Of course," I said. "Aren't you?"

He grimaced. "Fine. Go enjoy your rest. I'll go see if I can help get the coral packed for transfer."

He turned and headed back toward the hangar. Bayta and the girls had disappeared, but as I continued on down the corridor I spotted Bayta waiting for me outside one of the doors. "This our Fortress of Solitude?" I asked as I walked up to her.

"Our what? Oh—right." She touched the control to open the door. "Yes, this is where Rebekah said we could rest. She and Terese are another three doors down, if you wanted to check on them first."

"They'll be fine," I said, gesturing her into our room.

The room was bigger than I'd expected, with a single large bed, a washstand with running water, and a couple of comfortable-looking chairs. From the marks on the floor, I guessed it had been an analysis room, with most of the current empty space originally filled by lab tables and equipment racks. "There's a food locker over there with ration bars, in case you wanted something to eat before they get a proper meal prepared," Bayta said as the door closed behind us.

"No, thanks," I said, crossing to the bed and lying down. "I mostly just wanted some breathing space."

"And to give Rebekah time to talk to Terese?" Bayta asked.

I nodded. "Terese desperately needs someone new to talk to. I was hoping the two of them might click."

"But that's not the real reason for the delay, is it?" Bayta said, coming over and standing beside the bed.

I shook my head. "No."

Morse had pressed me for more. But Bayta wasn't Morse. "Okay," she said. For another moment she stood looking at me. Then, to my mild surprise, she lay down on the other side of the bed.

And to my even greater surprise she proceeded to slide up beside me.

Close beside me. Way closer than she needed to.

"It's not going to work, you know," she said quietly. "The Melding may be able to adjust the Modhri within Agent Morse, but they can't possibly have enough coral to do the same to the segment-prime."

"I know," I said. "Fortunately, we have another source of Melding coral."

She lifted her head and frowned at me. "What do you mean?"

"At least, I'm pretty sure we do," I said. Sliding over the last few centimeters that separated us, I slid my arm behind her raised head. "How much do you know about how the Melding came to be?"

She continued frowning at me, her head raised, and for a few awkward seconds I wondered if she was going to respond to my smooth move by simply not lying back down. But then her expression changed, and she lowered her head back to the pillow and across my arm.

And then, to my surprise, she rolled up onto her side toward me, resting her body right up against mine. "It still won't work," she murmured, her breath warm on my cheek.

My first flash reaction to this unexpected intimacy evaporated into the cold reality of her words. "Sure it will," I said, crooking my arm at the elbow and bringing my hand up to rest on her shoulder. "We're already well on our way."

I felt her give a small shake of her head. "They won't give you the coral," she said. "Not without safeguards."

I pursed my lips. So she *did* know that it was the Chahwyn who had bioengineered the Melding coral in the first place. Or if she hadn't known she'd deduced it, just as I had. "They don't have any choice," I said firmly. "Not if they want the Modhri to be a reliable ally."

"They won't believe he *can* be that ally," she said. "They'll be afraid he'll overwhelm the Melding, no matter how much coral they deliver. They'll instead want to keep producing the coral until they're sure they have enough to make it work. Only they never will."

I grimaced. Unfortunately, she had a point. No matter how fast the Chahwyn created their Melding coral, the original Modhran coral would also be reproducing, sitting there in its cold-water habitat on Yandro. The Chahwyn would be racing a moving goal line, without ever knowing exactly where that goal line was. "The situation is different now," I reminded her. "The Modhri is willing to change. In fact, if Morse is any indication, once he sees what the Melding offers, he'll be downright eager to change."

"They don't trust him," Bayta said. "They'll never trust him. They'll go with their alternate weapon."

I felt my stomach tighten. "The defenders aren't an alternate weapon," I said. "They're a self-springing trap."

"I know," Bayta said. "But they don't understand that. And they won't. Not until it's too late."

"Then we'll have to find a way to explain it to them."

She gave a wry little snort. "I don't think your usual tools of persuasion will be of much use this time."

"Don't count me out yet," I warned. "You'd be amazed how many of those tools I have up my sleeve."

She shook her head again. "I know the Elders. Once they've made up their minds, they won't change. They're probably already working on creating new and better defenders to send against the Shonkla-raa."

She breathed out a long, weary sigh. "And whoever wins that battle, freedom will disappear from the galaxy."

"Well, at least the defenders aren't lusting after power, the way the Shonkla-raa are," I said, searching for something positive to say. "I suppose that's something."

"The Shonkla-raa want power," she said. "The defenders will calmly and unemotionally take it whether they want it or not. I don't see a lot of difference."

I pursed my lips. "There *is* an alternative," I reminded her. "The one you suggested aboard our first super-express. You told me we could destroy the Thread, dis-integrate the Tube, and end the whole thing."

"Yes, we could probably do that," she said, a deep sadness in her voice. "Only it wouldn't help. The Shonkla-raa, or the defenders, would still control the people they happened to be among when the Quadrail collapsed."

Which was pretty much the same conclusion I'd come to the first time she'd offered this approach. "You're right, that doesn't really gain us anything," I agreed. "In fact, it might make things worse. If someone ever fig-ured out a way to beat back the Shonkla-raa, without the Thread and Quadrail there wouldn't be any way for them to share that information with the rest of the galaxy."

For a long minute we just lay quietly, our bodies still pressed close together. Gently, I stroked her shoulder; hesitantly, almost unwillingly, she lifted her arm and laid it across my chest. "Tell me something," I said at last. "In any of your discussions with Terese, have you ever found out who exactly she is?"

Even without looking, I could sense Bayta's frown. "What do you mean?"

"Well, for starters, she says her name's Terese Ger-man, but we don't know if that's true," I said. "More importantly, why did the Shonkla-raa pick her to be the host for their little Trojan Horse invader? The Modhri usually shoots for top political, industrial, and military targets. Is that the Shonkla-raa approach, too? If so, what exactly does Terese bring to that table?"

"I don't know," Bayta said, her voice thoughtful. "She's never mentioned any family to me. Maybe it was just her genetics that made her a good host for their ex-periment."

"Then why were there all those other women in Build-ing Twelve?" I countered. "Did they all have Terese's unique biochemistry? Besides, I can't see the Shonkla-raa limiting themselves any more than they had to. No, there's something about Terese we don't know."

"Do you want me to go ask her?"

"If she hasn't volunteered the information by now, I doubt she will," I said. "But she might tell Rebekah, especially if Rebekah asks her nicely. Tell me, are you on friendly speaking terms with the Melding these days?"

"Am I—?" She broke off, and I could feel her shoulder stiffen under my hand. There were at least two different levels of outrageousness in what I'd just suggested, and she was clearly trying to catch up. "I can't communicate directly with them," she said after a moment. "Even if I could, I'm not sure Rebekah would agree to do it."

"I'm not asking her to betray her new friend," I said. "What I want isn't even secret. Terese's data is on file *somewhere* on Earth—theoretically, we could go dig it out any time we wanted. But that would take time, and time is something we have limited quantities of."

I could practically hear the question spinning around in her brain: if we were that critically short on time, why were she and I still lying here side by side instead of helping Morse and the others load coral aboard our transport? "I suppose," she said instead. "I'll go talk to one of the others."

"That's all right," I said. "My idea—I'll do it. If any heat comes from either Terese or the Melding over this, I should be the one on the receiving end." I touched the arm lying across my chest. "I suppose you'll have to take this back."

"Okay," Bayta said, making no attempt to move her arm. "You need to do this right now?"

The bed really *was* pretty comfortable. "A few more minutes shouldn't hurt."

I'd set up this needing-to-rest thing mostly as a pretext to stall our return to the Tube. But it was quickly clear that Bayta really *was* exhausted, more so than I'd realized. We hadn't been lying there together more than three minutes when her breathing slowed into the rhythm of sleep.

Apparently, I wasn't in much better shape. Within a very few minutes, I drifted off to join her.

I woke an hour later with that heavy, groggy feeling of having had a too-short nap on top of a still massive sleep deficit. Sometime in that hour Bayta had rolled over to face away from me, but her back was still snugged up against my side. I managed to extricate my arm from beneath her neck without waking her and slid out of my side of the bed. A minute later I was walking back down the corridor toward the hangar.

The earlier crowd had long since dissipated, but there was a lone Melding member—a Pirk male—waiting by the docking collar leading into our transport. I approached him warily, but like the other Melding Pirk Bayta and I had run into once before this one had none of the overwhelming odor that emanated from most members of his species.

"Compton," he greeted me gravely. "You are rested?"

"Enough," I said. "I need a favor. Two favors, actually."

He inclined his head. "Speak."

"I need to know who exactly Terese German is," I said. "Not her name, but who she's related to, or under the protection of, or whatever it is that drew the Shonkla-raa's attention to her. I assume Rebekah's still talking to her—maybe she can ask her."

"This knowledge is necessary to your war effort?"

"Probably," I said. "I'm not absolutely sure, but probably."

The Pirk nodded. "Then Rebekah will ask her."

"Thanks," I said. "Subtly, of course, and without telling Terese that it was me asking."

The Pirk smiled faintly. "Rebekah has heard all about

Terese's feelings toward you," he said. "Rest assured, she will know how to ask the question."

"Thanks," I said again. "The other favor is that I'd like one of the people who are coming back to Yandro with us to ride on the regular Quadrail along with Bayta, Terese, Morse, and me."

A flicker of surprise crossed the Pirk's face. "I assumed you would be traveling on the Spider tenders along with us."

"Unfortunately, there are a couple of other errands I need to deal with along the way that have to be done at the normal stations," I told him. "Arriving there by tender would draw more attention than we can afford. Oh, and along with one of your members, we'll also want to take some of the coral."

For a few seconds he gazed at me, and I had the sense that the whole Melding was being brought in to consider this one. "What are you planning?" the Pirk asked at last.

My mind flicked back to Morse's earlier questioning of my motives and loyalties. "The less you know, the better," I said, trying the same argument I'd used on him.

The line hadn't gone over very well with Morse. It didn't do any better with the Melding. "Unacceptable," the Pirk said flatly. "In our estimation, the risks of knowledge far outweigh the risks of ignorance."

"I'm sorry you feel that way," I said. "But I'm the one in charge, and my decision stands."

"The Modhri may have accepted your leadership," the Pirk said. "But the Melding hasn't yet done so. What if we withdraw from this action?"

"Then you'll lose your only chance of bringing the Modhri back to the light," I said. "Without me, I doubt the Modhri will be willing to join with you, and without that joining he'll be left the way he is now. His mind will stay broken and limited, without the ability to interact with others in any civilized way." I cocked an eyebrow.

"Are you willing to have that on your collective conscience? That you could have redeemed him, but chose not to?"

"Your argument is flawed," the Pirk said evenly. "The choice is not simply one of showing the Modhri the way, but also of risking our own survival."

"Your survival is already forfeit," I said bluntly. "Morse knows where you are. If the Shonkla-raa win, sooner or later they'll drag that information out of the Modhri and come after you. The only way any of us will live through this is to join forces and take them down."

"Under your leadership."

"Yes."

There was another moment of silent inter-Melding communication. "Very well," the Pirk said. "Rebekah will travel with you."

I felt a sudden tightening of my throat. *Rebekah?*

"Is that a problem?" the Pirk asked, eyeing me with an uncomfortable intensity. "Surely her participation in a few simple errands pose no threat to her."

I grimaced as I realized how neatly I'd just been had. And by whom. "This is Morse's idea, isn't it? He told you that I might be willing to put some random Melding member at risk, but would never take a chance like that with Rebekah."

The Pirk inclined his head in acknowledgment. "Agent Morse is far more versed in such things than we are," he agreed. "That was indeed his reasoning."

"Oh, you and the Modhri are going to make a great team, all right," I said sourly. "Fine—Rebekah it is. How soon before the coral is loaded aboard the transport?"

"Another two hours," he said. "I thought you also wanted to share a meal with us before you left."

"I do," I said. "I just wanted to get some idea about our timing. I'm going back now to get a little more sleep."

I left the hangar and headed back toward our room, fuming the whole way. Morse had called it, all right, damn him. He was right about Rebekah being the one person aboard whom I would hesitate to put at risk.

Now, thanks to him, I was going to do exactly that.

And there was nothing I could do about it. Events were already in motion, events I could do nothing to stop or even slow down.

Bayta was still sleeping when I reached the room. For a moment I stood beside the bed, gazing down at her, a sense of guilt flowing over me. Here I was worrying about Rebekah when I should also be worrying about Bayta. After all, she would be in as much danger as any of the rest of them.

But then, Bayta was already squarely in the Shonklaraa's crosshairs. She would be in danger no matter where she was.

It was complete and utter rationalization, of course. But right now, rationalization was all I had.

Sighing, I lay back down beside her. This time, it took me considerably longer to fall asleep.

TWENTY-FOUR :

Terese was ecstatic at the thought of Rebekah joining our little group on the trip back to Yandro. I was a little taken aback by her enthusiasm until I discovered that Rebekah had promised her that the two girls could share a compartment, which meant Terese would have ten glorious days without having to look at either Bayta or me except at mealtimes.

I wasn't happy about that. Neither was Bayta. But it was clear that this was the deal the Melding was offering, and I could take it or leave it.

We took the transport back to the unfinished station, where the twenty volunteer members of the Melding plus all their coral were distributed among the five tenders we'd seen parked there earlier. The Spiders had meanwhile brought in a sixth tender, which was soon loaded with the five members of my group and the three small crates of Melding coral that I'd asked for.

We gave the other tenders a three-hour head start, which I hoped would be sufficient to slip them past whatever observation net the Shonkla-raa had set up between us and Yandro. Then, with Terese and Rebekah chattering together like a couple of kids—which, of course, they were—we headed out.

We arrived at Sibbrava three and a half hours later. Once again, I'd timed things carefully, and the express train I'd been aiming for was no more than ten minutes out.

Unfortunately, aside from the double compartment that the Spiders routinely held in reserve whenever Bayta and I were in the area, the rest of the compartment car was booked solid. Apparently some major medical conference had just ended, and the first- and second-class sections of the express were bulging with Jurian, Halkan, and Belldic doctors. The latter group, according to the Spiders, had taken three double compartments all by themselves, using the fold-down upper berths as Bayta and I had with Terese to pack themselves two per compartment and four per double. I made a mental note that if I wanted to order any Belldic cuisine on this trip, I'd better grab it quick before everything got snatched up.

Back when we'd left Shorshic space for this end of the galaxy the Spiders had been able to add another compartment car to the train. Unfortunately, here at Sibbrava there was neither the time nor the car available for such a modification. That left half our reserved compartment for Terese and Rebekah, and the other half for Bayta, with ordinary first-class seats for Morse and me.

Bayta didn't like that a bit, and offered several times to share her side of the compartment with me. Each time I gently but firmly refused. It wasn't the arrangement I would have picked, but there were certain tactical advantages in having Morse and me separated from Bayta, but still in communication with her via Rebekah and the Modhri/Melding consciousness that she and Morse now shared.

I was careful not to point out that it also gave me a freedom of movement that I wouldn't have if I was cooped up in a compartment with her.

We boarded, I got Bayta and the girls settled, made sure the crates of coral were secure, then headed back to the first-class coach car. Morse had found our seats, which had started out in opposite rear corners, and had moved them across the car to a spot where we could keep an eye on our fellow passengers and both the front and rear doors. He also gave me a quick head count on our current allies: two walkers in our first-class coach car, one of whom was among the crowd of Jurian doctors returning from the conference, plus eight more in second class who hadn't been able to find seats in first.

The first day passed uneventfully. I kept an eye out for Riijkhan or any of the other Shonkla-raa whose acquaintance we'd already made, but I didn't spot any of them. I did see a Filly who looked remarkably like our old friend Scrawny going into one of the compartments when I went forward to escort Bayta and the two girls to dinner. But later that evening, when I got a closer look, I realized it wasn't him.

I'd expected to sleep badly that first night, stuck out in the open in a coach car. But to my surprise, I actually slept soundly and straight through. It wasn't until I woke up in the morning that I recognized what my subconscious had already concluded: that the Modhran mind segment in our compartment was on guard, keeping close watch on Morse and me. The only way for the Shonkla-raa to short-circuit that watchfulness would be to take control of the walkers, and for that they would have to use their very obvious and distinctive control tone. I already knew that tone, and it was highly unlikely that I would sleep through it.

The second day also passed without incident. Morse periodically fed me updates from the Modhri, and on my frequent visits to the girls' double compartment Bayta gave me similar reports from the Spiders. There were several Fillies aboard, with five in particular that I tagged as possible Shonkla-raa. Unfortunately, all five wore the high collars of the *bishreol remak*, a Filiaelian medical sect, and none of us were able to get a proper look at their throats.

Still, if they *were* Shonkla-raa, they were keeping their heads down. As the train settled down for the night I began to wonder if the enemy was still on their watch-and-wait game.

Late afternoon on the third day, the watchful waiting came to an abrupt end.

Morse and I had gone to the bar for a pre-dinner drink, and were in the middle of a quiet conversation on general strategy and tactics when he suddenly stiffened. "Uh-oh," he murmured. "Here we go. One of our possible Shonkla-raa in first has just announced that there's going to be a birthday celebration in the dining car in ten minutes, and the guest of honor is offering a certificate good for ten thousand free Quadrail light-years to everyone who shows up and offers a toast."

"Nice," I said, grimacing. Ten thousand light-years was the equivalent of a week's journey. Even ultra-rich travelers who thought nothing of dropping hundreds of thousands on first-class Quadrail tickets weren't likely to pass up a freebie of that magnitude. "They taking him up on it?"

"What do you think?" Morse said grimly. "They're currently making a mad dash—a civilized mad dash, but a mad dash nonetheless—for the rear door. Do you want the Modhri to keep his two Eyes in there?"

"No, better let them go with the rest of the crowd," I told him. The fewer potential obstacles to what was about to happen, the better. "Let's head back and see what the Shonkla-raa have in store for us this time."

We were nearly to the bar's exit when the leading edge of first-class passengers appeared, heading past toward the dining half of the car. Rather than try to swim upstream against them, we stayed where we were. The last of them passed, and Morse slipped through the opening into the corridor. "You coming?" he asked.

"Go ahead," I said. "I'll catch up."

A frown flicked across his face. But he nodded and disappeared around the corner as he headed forward.

I turned and hurried back to the server Spider behind the bar counter. "Relay," I said quietly toward the expressionless gray globe hanging from its seven legs. "Now is the time for all good men to come to the aid of their country. Repeat: now is the time for all good men to come to the aid of their country. Acknowledge."

The Spider hesitated, then dipped his globe in response. "Acknowledge," he said in his flat voice. Nodding, I turned and hurried back across the bar and down the corridor to the vestibule. I popped the door, crossed the vestibule, popped the far door, and stepped into our coach car.

Morse was waiting for me about twenty meters in, his posture unnaturally stiff. Standing with him were three of the five Fillies we'd tentatively tagged as Shonkla-raa.

Only it wasn't so tentative anymore. They'd thrown open their high-collar *bishreol remak* disguises, revealing the telltale Shonkla-raa throats.

And filling the car was the high-pitched whistle I'd heard way too many times recently.

"There you are," one of the Shonkla-raa said conversationally as I stopped just inside the vestibule door. "Please, come in. The party's just getting interesting."

"I'm sure it is," I said, looking around as I walked slowly toward them. The promise of free Quadrail travel had cleared out the car, all right. Aside from us, the only two passengers still here were a Cimma with his back to us, who seemed to be thoroughly engrossed in the dit-rec drama playing on the display window in front of him, and a thin, elderly Human male sleeping in his chair, a furry blanket on his lap and a matching pillow tucked behind his head. I couldn't tell if his chair's music player was running, but if it was I had no doubt that the free travel announcement had missed him completely.

In fact, if the volume was high enough, there was a good chance that whatever unpleasantness the Shonkla-raa were about to unleash would also go unheard. "You realize we *were* expecting something like this, don't you?" I said, turning my attention back to the Shonkla-raa.

"For whatever good that preparation has done you," the Shonkla-raa said, looking around the empty car. "Amazing, isn't it, how easily manipulable the peoples of the galaxy are?"

"Oh, I don't know," I said. "I see two who managed to resist your bribe attempt."

The Filly snorted. "Not because of any integrity on their part, I assure you. I have no doubt we would be completely alone right now had they been physically able to hear our offer."

"Maybe," I said, stopping a couple of long strides short of their little group. "Though considering your preferred method of attack *physically able to hear* is an interesting turn of phrase. Might turn out to be a significant metaphor, too."

"You may cling to such hopes if it pleases you," the Shonkla-raa said, his eyes flicking to the sleeping man. "But rest assured that if that Human was a Modhran Eye, all the music in the galaxy would not protect him from our call. He, too, would be standing here with us right now." He gestured toward Morse. "As is your former ally."

I grimaced as I studied Morse's face. So much for the

hopeful theory that Human walkers might require a different command frequency. He was clearly locked up, tight as a drum and ready to dance to the Shonkla-raa's tune. "That's one for your side, I suppose," I conceded. "By the way, where's *Osantra* Riijkhan? He always struck me as the sort who'd never miss an opportunity to gloat."

"Unfortunately, our guess was slightly incorrect as to where these supposed new allies of yours were located," the Shonkla-raa said. "*Osantra* Riijkhan was caught out of position and unable to join us in time. The honor of your final defeat has thus come to me."

"Well, don't go counting your chickens, because I'm not yet ready to hand over my sword," I warned. "Regardless, it's considered a basic courtesy for the challenger to offer the challenged his name."

The color of the Filly's blaze was fluttering a little, probably from all the Human cultural references I was throwing at him. But his voice was clear and steady enough. "Forgive me," he said, inclining his head. "I am *Isantra* Yleli."

I stared at him. "*Yleli*?"

"I'm pleased you remember his name," Yleli said, clearly enjoying my bewilderment. "Yes, the late Tech Yleli was one of my kinsmen." His blaze darkened. "That was why we knew his murder would be the ideal bait to draw you and the alien woman Bayta into our *Kuzyatru* Station trap."

A shiver ran up my back. I'd known how ruthless the Shonkla-raa were. But this was a level of cold-bloodedness far beyond anything even I had expected.

And I'd deliberately brought Rebekah into reach of these people. Rebekah, Terese, and Bayta.

But there was still a chance. I had to hold on to that. "I'm constrained to point out that his murder, convenient though it might have been for you, didn't exactly result in a Shonkla-raa victory. As I recall, it ended in a rather resounding Shonkla-raa defeat."

His blaze went considerably darker this time. "They were careless," he said stiffly. "We won't make that mistake again."

"Of course not," I said. "But thank you for the demo. I imagine you'll want to settle back in under your rocks before the rest of the passengers finish toasting the birthday boy and come trooping back."

"There's no hurry," Yleli assured me. "It is, after all, a very long and complicated toast. And the demo is far from over." He gestured to one of his two companions.

The other nodded silently and turned, heading forward toward the compartment car. He reached the vestibule, popped open the door, and stepped inside.

I tensed. The instant the door closed behind him, his contribution to the control tone holding Morse in place would be cut off. That would leave just the other Shonkla-raa still broadcasting. If I could get to him before Yleli could pick up the slack . . .

But Yleli was already a step ahead of me. The vestibule door was still sliding closed when he raised his own voice in the whistling control tone. "What now?" I asked, wondering if I could get him to stop whistling and explain or gloat some more.

But again, he was smarter than that. He ignored the question, keeping up his part of the siren song. Grimacing, with nothing else I could do, I settled in to wait.

The seconds stretched into minutes. Morse's face changed once during that time, lines of puzzlement or concern rippling briefly across his face. But if Yleli noticed, he didn't bother to ask about it. To my right, the Cimma snuffled a couple of times, and I realized he'd fallen asleep with the dit-rec drama still playing in his chair's sound system. Maybe he'd been asleep all along. Behind me, the old man gave a wet-sounding snort of his own and shifted a little in his own journey through dreamland.

And then, after about three minutes, the vestibule door opened again and Terese stumbled into view, her face ashen white. Behind her was Rebekah, her eyes as glazed in their own way as Morse's, walking toward our little group like a person in a slow-motion dream.

Behind them, her eyes not nearly so glazed, her expression a mixture of fear and determination, her arm held firmly in the Shonkla-raa's grip, was Bayta.

"You said earlier that was one for our side," Yleli said as the newcomers came up behind him. "I believe this is now *four* for our side."

I studied Rebekah as she and the others came to a halt. The impression I'd first had of her as a sleepwalker was still holding. Her movements were slow and reluctant, and I noticed that she took an extra step after the Shonkla-raa came to a halt, as if she was slightly out of synch with her new masters' commands. Maybe that was the Melding itself, or possibly her polyp colony plus the inertia of the extra coral tucked away in the compartment.

Still, the fact that Rebekah *was* moving, albeit slowly, didn't add up to much of a victory for our side.

Not that I was going to admit that to Yleli. "Looks more like three and a half to me," I said. "Or maybe two and two halves. Rebekah doesn't look like she'd be of much use in a fight, and you're barely getting Bayta to walk."

"I admit your new allies are a challenge," Yleli said. "But have no fear. We'll have them under full control soon enough." He half turned to look at Bayta. "As for Bayta, a bit of study on her and we'll soon have her people's command tone, as well."

"Not likely," I said. Out of the corner of my eye I caught a double flicker of subdued light from the Tube wall outside the display window on that side. "I also seriously doubt that Rebekah and her Melding cohorts will ever be of any practical fighting use to you." I gestured at her. "You might as well attack Buckingham Palace with a bunch of stick puppets. In fact, let's give it a try." I started forward, veering to the side to avoid Yleli and Morse, and headed toward Rebekah.

The sheer unexpectedness of the move apparently caught Yleli by surprise. I got to within two steps of Rebekah before he took a quick step to his side, putting himself between her and me. "Stop!" he ordered, his hands snapping up into their stabbing configurations.

"What's the problem?" I asked, stopping as ordered and forcing my hands to stay at my sides. The last thing I wanted right now was to give him even half an excuse to attack me. "You think you can control her well enough to fight? Fine. Prove it."

"Move back," Yleli said, all trace of his earlier mocking levity gone. He'd probably heard enough of my exploits from the Proteus survivors to know that even the most casual move on my part should be viewed with suspicion.

So had his two friends. Even as I obediently took a step backward they circled around Morse and the women to flank me. "You have the wrong idea," I said mildly.

{Remove him to the baggage area,} Yleli said, his voice all icy business now as he switched from English to Fili. {Secure him there—we may yet have need of him alive. When you return we'll transfer the coral to our compartment for closer study.} One of the other two Shonkla-raa acknowledged, and they both started toward me.

And at that moment, the vestibule door behind them at the forward end of the car slid open and a dozen Bellidos streamed in, chattering away among themselves, the soft plastic status guns in their shoulder holsters bouncing rhythmically against their sides as they walked. The whole Belldic doctor contingent had apparently decided to head en masse to the dining car for an early dinner.

One or two witnesses apparently weren't a problem for Yleli, given that he hadn't bothered to completely clear out the coach car before confronting us. But even a Shonkla-raa had to hesitate at the logistical challenge of killing and disposing of this many beings. He snapped a quiet order that stopped his two buddies in their tracks, flashed me a warning look, then went as still as a hunter in a duck blind as he watched the line of doctors strolling toward us.

Not that the Bellidos themselves showed the slightest awareness that anything unusual was unfolding in front of them. A couple of them glanced incuriously at our group, then returned to their conversations. A couple of others looked around and at the ceiling, frowns briefly crossing their striped chipmunk faces as they tried to locate the source of the command tone whistle filling the car.

But the sound had no medical ramifications, and their interest was idle and brief, and they too quickly turned their attention back to their colleagues. The leading edge of the stream reached us and split, each conversational group turning left or right at random, avoiding the motionless clump of humans and Fillies as they continued on their way in their quest for food.

And then, in front of me, I heard Yleli catch his breath.

Perhaps he'd belatedly realized that the Bellidos' casual traffic pattern had flanked himself and his companions. Perhaps he'd suddenly noticed that the soft plastic guns bouncing at the doctors' sides no longer had their long plastic barrels. {Alert!} he snapped.

But he was too late. As he brought his hands up into combat position, I threw myself forward and down, dropping onto my side on the floor and aiming a kick at his knees. Reflexively, he turned his eyes back to me, simultaneously dancing back to get out of kicking range.

As he did so, the two Bellidos passing us pulled nunchakus from beneath their tunics and whipped them with crushing force across his throat.

And pandemonium erupted.

I rolled up and leaped back to my feet as the rest of the Bellidos charged to the attack, their nunchakus whipping with devastating force across the other two Shonkla-raa's heads, arms, and torsos as I tried to get to

Bayta and the two girls. But Yleli was faster than I was. He slashed viciously at one of his two attackers and then jumped into my path, his other hand jabbing at my gut. I managed to twist out of his way in time, but the movement cost me my balance and I went crashing back onto the floor.

Yleli leaped at me again, aiming a kick at my head, but even as I ducked out of the way he staggered as a nunchaku slash caught his other knee. With his supporting leg under attack, he was forced to drop his kicking leg prematurely back to the floor. The other Bellido was already swinging his nunchaku at Yleli's head, but the Filly managed to drop into a crouch in time, leaving the flail to whip harmlessly through the air above him. Before either of the Bellidos could recover for another attack Yleli shoved himself off the floor, again diving at me.

I was caught flatfooted, on my way back up to a standing position but not quite there yet. Desperately, I tried to throw myself to the side, knowing the move would again cost me balance and mobility but not having any other real options.

But I was too late. Yleli was hurtling toward me, his arm held rigidly in front of him like an organic spear. One of the nunchakus whipped past, slamming into his back hard enough to crack bone but doing little to alter his direction or speed. There was a blur of motion at my right.

And Morse's body slammed sideways into Yleli's shoulder, knocking him off-target and sending both of them sprawling onto the floor.

Somewhere in all that nunchaku flailing, while I'd been preoccupied with my own troubles, the Bellidos had managed to silence both of the other Shonkla-raa command tones.

I hit the floor and rolled back up to my feet. Morse was still on top of Yleli, trying to pin him down. But like all the rest of the Shonkla-raa I'd run into, Yleli had been genetically modified for strength. With a single violent shove he threw Morse half a meter into the air to crash down onto the floor beside him and started to scramble to his feet.

His eyes were glittering death in my direction when two nunchakus caught him one final time, one of the flails slamming again into his throat, the other hitting hard enough to splinter bone at the back of his skull. He sprawled face-first onto the floor.

This time, he didn't get up.

I looked around, gasping in vast lungfuls of air. All three Shonkla-raa were down, all of them quite dead. Four of the twelve Bellidos were also down, one of them probably also dead, the other three making the small sounds and movements of the seriously wounded. The Bellidos still on their feet were gazing warily at the three dead Fillies, but I could see them starting to slowly come down from their adrenaline-driven combat frenzy. As I stumbled over to where Morse was lying on the floor, four of the Bellidos headed over to check their wounded. Across the room, a horrified Terese and a grim-faced but steady Rebekah were clinging to each other. Bayta was nowhere in sight.

The whole deadly melee, I estimated, had lasted less than thirty seconds.

Morse was starting to stir by the time I reached him. "You okay?" I asked, offering him a hand.

"Mostly," he said, his voice dark as he pushed himself up into a sitting position. "Bloody *hell*, but that was weird."

"Which part?" I asked, looking over at the wounded Bellidos. One of the others had retrieved the LifeGuard medical kit from the front of the car and was hurrying back with it. As he did so, the forward vestibule door opened, and Bayta entered, lugging the LifeGuard she'd retrieved from the compartment car.

"All of it," Morse said, grunting as he carefully stood up. "Mostly the takeover. I knew about it from the Modhri, of course. But it's one thing to get someone else's memory of something and quite another to experience it yourself."

"You heard about this from the Modhri?" one of the Bellidos asked, his eyes on Morse as he came up to us.

"Yes, he did," I said, gesturing. "Morse, meet *Korak* Fayr, commando major of the Bellidosh Estates-General."

"Currently gone rogue, running a private mission to destroy the Modhri," Fayr added, still eyeing Morse closely. "And you?"

"Fayr, meet EuroUnion Security Service agent Ackerley Morse," I continued the introductions. "Formerly a deep-cover Modhran walker, currently part of *my* private mission to destroy the Shonkla-raa."

"Pleased to meet you," Morse said, nodding.

"Not certain I can say the same," Fayr said shortly. "Your message, Compton, said that the Modhri had gone neutral in this new war. It said nothing about working with him."

"Because at the time I wasn't sure he'd be willing to actively come onto our side," I told him. "Now I am."

"Your evidence?"

"Well, if the Modhri was on the Shonkla-raa's side, I bloody well wouldn't have stopped Yleli from killing Compton," Morse said. "Especially at the cost of a cracked rib."

I frowned. "You have a cracked rib?"

"Feels like it," Morse said, gingerly indicating a spot on his lower left side. "We'll find out for sure when one of those LifeGuards is free."

I looked over at the injured Bellidos. "How are they doing?" I asked.

"Two will survive," one of the other commandos said over his shoulder. "One is questionable. All three need medical attention."

"Will you need a doctor?" I asked. "For once, there are plenty of them aboard."

"We can deal with our injured by ourselves," the Bellido said. "Once the LifeGuard has finished stabilizing them, we'll need to get them to our compartments."

"We can help with that," I said, pulling out the gimmicked reader that Larry Hardin had given me two years ago when he'd hired me to figure out how to take over the Quadrail system from the Spiders. The disguised data chip that turned the reader into a high-tech scanner was already loaded. "Bayta, there should be a pair of defender Spiders out on the compartment car roof. Give them a whistle and have them pull up the tender they brought along with them. There are a couple more defenders riding inside that can help carry the injured."

"It's on its way," Bayta said. There was a stiffness in her voice, a coldness that was no doubt due to me not having told her about my Belldic hole card in advance.

But the anger would fade. She knew as well as Morse did that I couldn't risk giving out details to anyone the Shonkla-raa might have interrogation access to. "As soon as it's in position, have them extend the airlock," I continued as I stepped over to Yleli's limp body. "Better make it to the compartment car door," I added, glancing at the back of the sleeping Cimma's head. "We don't want anyone else noticing."

"What are you doing?" Morse asked as I lowered my reader to within a few centimeters of the top of Yleli's head and began tracking the device downward.

"Looking to see what other work they had done besides the knife hands and the oversized throats," I told him. "Some of the normal Filiaelian nerve centers are still in their standard locations, but some of the others have been moved. I want to know which ones, where they went, and the locations of any other vulnerable spots."

"And whether we can count on all Shonkla-raa having the same spots," Fayr said, nodding understanding. "Hence, you choose to take out three at once."

"The numbers were Yleli's idea," I said. "But I was pretty sure he wouldn't do this all by himself. We think there are two more of them, by the way, back in the dining car pretending to toast someone's health. Let's try to get this done before they realize something's gone wrong up here."

"It's too late," Morse said grimly. "They already know . . . and they've killed all the other Eyes."

"What?" Bayta asked sharply.

"He's right," Rebekah said quietly. Her voice, unlike Morse's, held only sadness. "They're all gone."

"Take it easy," I said, finishing with Yleli's scan and heading over to the next body. "The other walkers are probably just fine. You can't detect them because they're all out of range."

"How can they be out of range?" Terese asked. "Rebekah told me one of their group minds can cover a whole train."

"It can," I said, starting my second scan. "But at the moment we're actually *two* trains. As soon as I got in here, the two defenders I mentioned unsealed the rear vestibule and unhooked the car, and we were pulled away from the rest of the train. The rest of the people back there won't have noticed anything because there's another engine pushing them along from the rear. But the point is that we're currently a couple of kilometers out in front."

"So that if the Shonkla-raa ask the Eyes what's going on up here they won't be able to tell them anything," Morse said, nodding. "And even if they did suspect something, there isn't a bloody thing they can do about it. Not from way back there."

"Exactly." I looked at Bayta. "It was my idea for the defenders not to tell you," I added, bracing myself for her reaction.

But there wasn't one. She merely nodded silently, in understanding or forgiveness, and let it go.

"But they'll know soon enough," Rebekah warned.

"Even if they assume the Shonkla-raa killed Mr. Morse and me, sooner or later they'll want to get back in here. What happens when they find out they can't open the vestibule door?"

Abruptly, Bayta caught her breath. "They'll use their command tone to freeze a server and try to use his leg to pry it open," she said. "They're doing it right now."

"Damn," Morse muttered. "What about the people in the car? Did they get them all out?"

"I don't think so," Bayta said, her eyes narrowed in concentration. Two kilometers was also a long stretch for her particular brand of telepathic communication, even given the higher number of Spiders in the train back there and the incoming tender that could function as a relay point. "No, the people are still there."

"That tears it," Morse said. "We've got to get back there and reconnect. If they get that door open now, everyone in the car will asphyxiate."

I hissed between my teeth. I'd hoped to have the wounded Bellidos to their compartments and the dead Shonkla-raa safely tucked away in the tender before we reconnected. But Morse was right. If we delayed any longer, a lot of people were going to die.

But I could still make this work. Maybe. "Bayta, tell the defenders to start the reconnection procedure," I ordered. "And send the tender back to the rear—we don't want the Shonkla-raa having access to it. Fayr, can you get your wounded back to your compartments?"

Fayr gestured questioningly at one of the other commandos. "We shouldn't move them any farther yet than absolutely necessary, *Korak*," the other Bellido warned. "The narrowness of the vestibule in particular will be dangerous to them."

"Understood," Fayr said "Move them to the front of the car. We'll make our stand there."

He looked at me as if daring me to argue the point. But I just nodded as I moved to the final Filly. "Sounds good," I said. "Let me finish this scan and I'll help you move some of the chairs. Might as well make them come at us one at a time."

"Good idea," Fayr said, looking around the car as his men started moving their injured to a section of floor near the front vestibule door. "What about them?" he asked, nodding toward the two sleeping passengers.

"Leave them," I said. "If we wake them up, they'll just be inconvenient witnesses that the Shonkla-raa will have to kill. No point making this any more of a bloodbath than it has to be."

Fayr eyed me closely. "Such words imply you expect the Shonkla-raa to win."

"Well, they sure as hell have the numbers," Morse said darkly as he unfastened one of the seats from the floor and began moving it toward where the Bellidos were setting up shop. "All of us together—*with* the element of surprise—barely took down three of them who weren't expecting trouble. They've got two more back there, plus ten Eyes."

"Eleven, counting you," Fayr said pointedly.

Morse grimaced. "Good point," he conceded. "Maybe you'd better take me out of the equation right now."

"One walker more or less isn't going to make that much difference," I said grimly. "Especially one with a cracked rib or two. Besides, numbers or not, we still have the edge in weaponry."

"So we do," Morse said, frowning at the nunchaku in Fayr's hand as he passed the Bellido on his way to another seat. "How in hell did you get those aboard, anyway?"

"Quite openly, in fact," I told him. "All they are is a pair of status gun barrels, filled with water and sealed with pressure-threaded caps, then tied together with the guns' decorative tassels."

"Interesting," Morse said. "The ESS experimented with stuff like that on occasion. But I don't think they ever came up with anything nearly this effective."

"You really have to be a Bellido loaded with status

guns to get away with it," I reminded him as I finished the final scan and put the reader away. "Let me know when you're in contact with the rest of the mind segment, will you? It might be useful to know how the Shonkla-raa are lining up before they pop that door."

"Bear in mind that if we can spy on them, they can also spy on us," Fayr pointed out as he pushed another of the seats toward the barricade Morse and the others were putting together. "And if you don't feel like disabling Agent Morse, you should at least order him to stand well away from us." He turned to look at Terese and Rebekah. "And the female walker should go with him."

I grimaced. The last thing any of us wanted was to have an enemy operative in our midst, and Rebekah qualified almost as much as Morse did.

On the other hand, Rebekah's polyp colony was the modified Melding variety, which I'd already seen wasn't quite as firmly under Shonkla-raa control as Morse's standard Modhran colony.

Moreover, we already knew the Shonkla-raa wanted to get hold of both Rebekah and her crates of coral. If I put Rebekah on the enemy side of the car, the Fillies might decide to grab her and call it a day. I couldn't risk that. "Morse can go away," I told Fayr. "But Rebekah will stay with us. Bayta and Terese can hang on to her and make sure she doesn't cause any trouble."

"That's dangerous," Fayr warned. "Particularly since Bayta will be helpless once the control tone sounds."

"Specifically, she'll mostly freeze in place," I said. "If she's already got her arms locked around Rebekah, they should stay that way. And Terese will be there to help, too."

"We'll keep her from making trouble," Bayta said quietly.

Fayr still looked dubious. But he nevertheless nodded. "Very well," he said. "But Morse leaves."

"No argument," I agreed, catching Morse's eye and

pointing him toward the back corner near the Cimma. "Over there, Morse, if you please."

"Let me help you finish the barrier first," Morse said, heading for another seat.

"I'd rather you move away from us," Fayr said tartly before I could answer. "We don't know exactly when you'll be fully under Shonkla-raa control."

"It won't be until they get in here with their damn command tone," Morse said. But he obediently passed by the chair he'd been heading for and retreated to the car's rear corner near the Cimma.

The rest of us were just putting the final touches on the barrier of chairs cutting across the front third of the car when Morse reported that his Modhran colony was once again in contact with the walkers behind us. I told him to inform the Shonkla-raa that we were on our way back, that we would let them in once the train had been reconnected, and to please stop trying to jimmy open the vestibule door.

But my effort was for nothing. The Shonkla-raa had apparently instructed the Modhri to keep quiet, which meant none of the walkers could speak without a direct question or invitation from their new masters. Unfortunately, that left us with no option but to try to get the train back together before they succeeded in forcing open the door.

Morse also informed us that the planned assault line would be five walkers, followed by one Shonkla-raa, followed by the remaining walkers and the other Shonkla-raa. A nicely logical arrangement, I decided, giving them the maximum level of control while allowing the thrust of our counterattack to fall on the walkers instead of their masters.

For all of their arrogance and megalomania, the Shonkla-raa unfortunately weren't stupid.

Bayta was even less use, info-wise, than Morse and the Modhri. As I'd told Fayr, the tone that controlled the Modhri also paralyzed and dazed Spiders, effectively knocking them out of the telepathic communications network. Bayta could sense the overall physical state of the Spider that the Shonkla-raa were using to pry open the door, but that was about it.

The defenders on the roofs of both cars were unaffected, though, and Bayta was able to keep tabs on the reconnection procedure. By the time the cars had been locked and the vestibule reattached all of us except Morse were standing ready behind the barrier of chairs. Bayta and Terese were holding tightly on to Rebekah as I'd ordered, all three women pale-faced but clearly determined not to give up without a fight. I stood in the middle of the line of Bellidos, the *kwi* tingling in my hand as I pointed it toward the vestibule door.

The door slid open, and as the command tone burst out into the car I saw a line of figures in the vestibule behind a big Halka glowering at me from in front. Aiming at his torso, I opened fire.

The standard military strategy when you're clustered together against incoming fire with no cover is to get clear of the choke point as quickly as possible. But the walkers didn't do that. They instead stayed right where they were, huddled behind the Halka.

And to my bewilderment, the Halka wasn't moving, either. Especially he wasn't falling. He was still standing upright, apparently immune to the *kwi*'s effect.

I put two more shots into him before I belatedly realized what was going on. The Halka wasn't one of the walkers, but was simply some first-class passenger who'd been grabbed and forcibly planted at the front of the line. My first shot had indeed rendered him unconscious, but the walkers behind him were holding or propping him up to act as a living shield.

I got off one final shot, trying to aim past the Halka's bulk, before Bayta succumbed to the tone and the *kwi* went silent.

And the walkers finally made their move.

"Bayta!" I snapped, uselessly squeezing the *kwi*'s trigger

as the walkers began to file into the car, the first one in line casually and uncaringly dropping the unconscious Halka off to the side out of their way. "Bayta! Defenders! Anyone!"

But Bayta was already helpless, her arms frozen around an equally frozen Rebekah, and the defenders on the roof couldn't hear me though the haze swirling through Bayta's mind and from hers into theirs. Swearing under my breath, I dropped the *kwi* back in my pocket and picked up the nunchaku I'd borrowed from one of the injured Bellidos.

I'd half expected the walkers to come charging in screaming at the tops of their lungs like Viking berserkers, hoping to overwhelm us with sheer momentum. But the Shonkla-raa in charge of this particular mob were more subtle than that. The walkers strode stolidly into our car in a complete silence that accentuated the whistling from the Filly behind them. The line moved to the center of the car, staying well clear of our barricade and weapons, and neatly spread out to both sides as the second wave marched in behind them. The second group similarly fanned out into a battle line. As they arranged themselves, Morse, standing stiffly in his corner, moved up to join one end of the first battle line.

The two Shonkla-raa themselves, I noted cynically, stayed a good five paces behind the walkers, where they were even more out of range of our nunchakus.

"Nice," I complimented them, mostly just to get in the first word. "You do children's parties, too?"

Deliberately, the Filly on the right lowered his gaze to the three dead Shonkla-raa still sprawled on the floor where we'd left them. Then, he looked up at me and gestured to his companion. I tensed, but the other Filly merely took a step backward, and I could hear him crank his command tone volume up a couple of notches. "Impressive, Compton," the first Shonkla-raa said, his voice calm but icy cold. "Once again, we seem to have underestimated you."

He waved a sweeping hand across the silent rows of walkers. "Yet at the same time you continue to underestimate us. Tell me, what did you think you would gain?"

"Information, of course," I said. "That's the key to all successful wars."

"And what have you learned?" the Shonkla-raa countered. "That your new ally"—his eyes flicked to Rebekah—"is as vulnerable to us as the Modhri? That your ally Bayta and her Spider friends are no threat to us?"

"But you can't control them," I pointed out. "As for Rebekah, you don't have nearly as good a grip on her as you might like. I watched the way she moved when Yleli and his buddies brought her in. It was like watching someone walk through knee-deep water. I daresay she and her friends aren't going to do you much good as soldiers."

"And you think to neutralize our hold on the Modhri by joining him with this Melding?" the Shonkla-raa scoffed. "A futile hope, Compton. You have neither the time nor the resources for such a move."

"How do *you* know?" I countered. "Because Morse says we don't?"

The Filly's eyes flicked to Morse. "We're well aware that you don't tell Morse everything," he said. "We've already concluded that you showed him only one of the Melding's many bases and only a fraction of the available coral."

He was right on that one, anyway. Or at least half right. Not that I was going to tell him that. "So given that you don't know how much Melding coral we have, you can't be banking on that to stop us," I said. "Ergo, you must be banking on our supposed lack of time. But since you don't also have any idea when we started this whole operation, that's also just a guess on your part."

"You did not begin this operation until you escaped from *Kuzyatru* Station," the Filly said flatly. "But even if you had, your timing would be irrelevant. The Shonkla-raa are on the move, faster than you can possibly imagine.

Within weeks at the most your small rebellion *will* be broken."

"Very impressive," I said. "Also carefully and conspicuously vague. How can you proclaim your victory when you don't even have the full list of your opponents?" I gestured to Fayr and his commandos beside me. "For example, *Korak* Fayr here. As I said, every successful plan requires information, and you don't have enough of it."

The Filly's blaze lightened. "Clever, Compton," he said. "You seek to provoke me into speaking about our plans, knowing that whatever else happens today—whether you die or whether we choose to let you live—that Bayta and the Melding female Rebekah will certainly be taken alive. You hope they will find a way to pass any information that you glean to the Spiders or the Modhri or Bayta's people."

I shrugged. "It was worth a try."

"It was indeed," he said, eyeing me closely. "I will confess in turn that I thought *Osantra* Riijkhan was showing unnecessary caution in trying to bring you to our side. I see now why he thought you worth recruiting."

"It took you this long to figure that out?" I asked. "I thought Proteus Station alone would have been a sufficient résumé."

The Filly's blaze darkened. "You were lucky."

"Call it luck if you want," I said. "The fact is that I've demonstrated a knack for killing Shonkla-raa. As you pore over your maps of the galaxy, I suggest you add that into your calculations."

The blaze went even darker. "Indeed," he said softly. "And you convince me. *Osantra* Riijkhan's hopes notwithstanding, I think it best that your life ends today."

"You're welcome to try," I said, stepping back from the barricade to where Bayta and the two girls huddled together in their frozen clump. "But let me add one other factor into your considerations."

Abruptly, I flipped the nunchaku around in my hands

and looped the cord around Bayta's neck. "You're not going to be dissecting or otherwise studying Bayta," I said into the suddenly rigid atmosphere as I held the cord against her throat. "And she is most certainly not going to die in your hands. If I die, she's dying with me."

Maybe the Shonkla-raa really thought his troops could get through the barrier and the waiting commandos before I could carry out my threat. Maybe he'd simply had enough talk for one day and decided it was time to move on to the main event. Whichever, the eleven Modhran walkers standing in parade formation abruptly started forward, eight of them moving ahead of the others.

The intent was obvious. The front eight were to hurl themselves over the chairs and onto each of the Bellidos, dying or being incapacitated in the process but hopefully pinning down their targets long enough for the remaining walkers to move in for the kill. A simple, straightforward strategy, and one that the Shonkla-raa had the numbers to actually pull off.

But as the walkers moved forward, the old man curled up in his chair behind the Shonkla-raa opened his eyes.

For maybe two heartbeats he gazed at the scene in front of him. Then, sliding silently out of his seat, he headed toward the rearmost of the Fillies, curving back around to his rear to stay out of both Fillies' peripheral vision. His hands dipped into his jacket as he headed forward and emerged with a pair of small handles. I caught a subtle glint of metal wire from between them.

And as he reached the rearmost Filly, he flipped the garrote wire over the other's head and brought his hands together, simultaneously spinning a hundred and eighty degrees around to turn back-to-back with the Filly. The alien gave a choking gasp, his hands clutching uselessly at his throat as he was forced to bend over backward, his command tone cutting off as the garrote paralyzed his voice box.

The second Filly spun around, sheer stunned surprise freezing him for a fatal half second. Still hanging on to the handles, the old man twisted himself up off the floor, the movement tightening the wire even more around the Filly's throat, and snapped a devastating side kick into the other Filly's throat.

And as the whistling command tone went silent, all eleven Modhran walkers spun around in unison and charged.

The Shonkla-raa didn't have a chance. By the time Fayr and his commandos made it to the scene the walkers had the Fillies on the floor, pinning them with sheer weight of numbers. All that was left for the Bellidos to do was beat the Fillies repeatedly across their heads and throats until both were finally dead.

I didn't bother to join in the melee, but stayed behind with the women, helping Bayta and then the two girls to their feet as I watched the carnage. "What happened?" Terese breathed as I got her upright, peering uncertainly over the chairs that had been blocking her view.

"Like he said earlier," I told her. "They underestimated me." I gestured to Bayta. "Shall we?" I invited.

She nodded, her eyes steady on the scene in the other part of the car, a grim but wry awareness coming into her expression. She still didn't like being left in the dark as to my intentions, I knew, but I could also tell she was starting to see the black humor inherent in my methods. "We should at least say hello," she agreed.

"My thoughts exactly," I said, weaving us through the barrier to where the Modhran walkers and the old man were climbing warily off the dead Shonkla-raa and getting back to their feet. Two of the walkers were limping, but otherwise didn't seem to have been badly damaged. "Nicely done," I said. "Introductions, I believe?"

"If you think it necessary," the old man said.

His face was still wrinkled, his hair still gray, his hands still wizened. But his stance was straight and limber and combat-ready, and his eyes were no longer those of the aged. "*Korak* Fayr, I know by sight," he continued, nodding to Fayr. "And I expect Agent Morse is smart enough to have figured it out."

"I'm flattered," Morse said, some of Bayta's wryness in his voice. He hesitated, then held out his hand. "I've heard rumors of your existence and talents, Mr. McMicking. And may I say, I'm very pleased to have you on our side."

"You flatter me in turn," Bruce McMicking said as he took Morse's proffered hand. "I look forward to finding out whether your side is indeed the one I'm on."

TWENTY-FIVE :

Cleaning up the aftermath was going to take some time. To be on the safe side, I had Bayta instruct the defenders on the roof to uncouple the vestibule again to make sure no one wandered in on us.

Not that that was likely. According to the Spiders, the Shonkla-raa had handed out a whole stack of genuine-looking Quadrail travel certificates, and the usual occupants of our car were currently locked in a boisterous competition with each other over who could come up with the longest and most elaborate birthday toast.

The first order of business was to get the injured Bellidos back to their compartments for treatment. Fortunately, by the time Fayr's medic decided they were stable enough to move, the defenders had gotten the tender attached and several of them had come through to our train. Under Bayta's direction, they carefully lifted the injured commandos, two Spiders per patient, and eased them through the forward vestibule to the compartment car.

The five Shonkla-raa weren't treated nearly so gently. With Bayta busy supervising the Bellido transfer, the defenders merely picked up the dead bodies like so many sacks of grain and lugged them back through the airlock to the tender.

I'd worried a little about how the Modhri was going to deal with the walkers the Shonkla-raa had hijacked. But that part, at least, was quickly and efficiently taken care of. By the time the defenders arrived all but one of the walkers had settled into the empty seats and gone to sleep, snoozing away even as Fayr and I started moving the chairs back to their original positions.

The single exception was interesting in its own right. That particular walker, a Juri diplomat, ended up standing to one side, his beak half open and his claws picking restlessly at his clothing as he gazed in horror-edged fascination at the procedure. Midway through the Bellidos' medical transport, Morse walked over to him, and the two of them spent the rest of the cleanup time in low but earnest conversation.

Apparently, the Modhri had decided that this particular walker, like Morse himself, was ready to hear the whole truth.

I hoped he was right. The last thing we needed was high-ranking officials going around the galaxy screaming about enemies, conspiracies, and dit-rec horror drama pod people.

Still, if he was going to go that route, he was at least holding it together for now. Morse was still talking with him half an hour later when we finally reattached the rear vestibule, and by the time the first passengers started trickling back all of the Juri's more overt signs of bewilderment had faded away.

Maybe Morse had convinced him of the danger the galaxy faced, and how a fully-aware walker could help in that war. Or maybe it had simply occurred to the Juri that a diplomat with a tap into what the other side was thinking could have a very bright future.

Now that the Shonkla-raa trap had been sprung and disarmed, Bayta pressed for us to leave the train at the next stop and take a tender the rest of the way back to

Yandro. But I vetoed that. I assumed a new contingent of Shonkla-raa would show up somewhere along the way, if only to help guard the prisoners they were expecting to have gained, and their reaction to our uncaptured presence could be instructive. Further attacks from such a mop-up group were unlikely, I assured Bayta, at least not until they had some idea of what had happened to their fellow conquerors. Besides, with Fayr's commandos and McMicking still available as surprise wild cards, we would always have an advantage they wouldn't know about.

I did, however, instruct the Modhri to get all his walkers except Morse off the train at the next stop and to make sure no others got on. If, contrary to all expectations, the newly arrived Shonkla-raa decided to make trouble, I had no intention of supplying them with extra bodies.

It all went off pretty much as I'd expected. At the next station, Minchork Rej, I watched through Bayta's display window as our walkers casually moved off, bound for other trains, where the Shonkla-raa hopefully wouldn't be able to track them down for interrogation. A minute after the last one vanished into the crowds, another train pulled up a few tracks over and a group of passengers debarked, a handful of them heading toward our train. Two of them were Fillies.

One of the Fillies was *Osantra* Riijkhan.

"I'll be in the bar," I told Bayta, stepping away from the window and heading for the compartment door. "Lock up behind me."

"You think that's a good idea?" Bayta asked, her tone making it clear that she personally did not.

"I want to see his reaction when he finds we're here and his friends aren't," I said. "Don't worry, he's too smart to make trouble."

"What if he isn't?"

I grimaced. She had a point. I hadn't yet seen Riijkhan truly furious, and furious people often did stupid things.

"If you feel the local Spiders go blank, go get Fayr," I told her. "Otherwise, you and the girls stay put."

The train had long since left the station, and I was halfway through my second iced tea, when Riijkhan arrived at the bar. I raised a hand to catch his attention and beckoned him over. He gazed at me for a couple of seconds, then wove his way through the other tables and sat down across from me. "I'm pleased to see you," I said, nodding as I lifted my glass to him. "I was starting to think you'd miss out on this whole operation."

"Only the most interesting parts, I'm afraid," he said, a formal stiffness to his voice. "Once again, we seem to have underestimated you."

"It's been a common theme throughout my life," I said. "Ready to give up yet?"

"Hardly," he said. "And while you continue to deplete our ranks, you will also eventually run out of allies with which to surprise us." His blaze darkened. "And unlike you, we have ways of adding to our numbers."

"What makes you think I can't do the same?" I countered. "For that matter, what makes you think I had any allies here at all?"

"Please," Riijkhan said scornfully. "I know you like to speak of yourself as a strong and nearly legendary warrior. But it strains all logic and credibility to suppose you could single-handedly defeat five Shonkla-raa and their Modhran allies."

"Their Modhran tools," I corrected. "And of course I didn't do it single-handedly. Bayta and I worked together. Just as we did when we destroyed the Modhri mind segment on Quadrail 219117."

"Don't insult my intelligence," Riijkhan bit out, his eyes flashing. "You destroyed the Shonkla-raa with the aid of a group of Belldic commandos and a disguised Human."

I suppressed a grimace. So Riijkhan *was* mad enough to do something stupid. Or at least to say something stupid. "So the Cimma diplomat pretending to be asleep was one of yours," I said. "Yes, I thought so."

"You most certainly did not," Riijkhan said, his voice stiff. Maybe he'd belatedly realized the foolishness of having let that slip. "Otherwise you would hardly have tolerated his presence after *Isantra* Yleli left him behind."

"Actually, I was mostly amused by the fact that his presence meant Yleli wasn't at all sure he and the others would live through the whole experience," I improvised. "That doesn't speak well for your side's confidence."

"Merely a reasonable precaution," Riijkhan said. "Like your having a harmless-appearing agent there as well."

"Except that my precaution was also able to fight," I reminded him. "Yours could only provide you with a postmortem report. I'll ask again: are you ready to give up? It's still not too late for you to retreat back to the Assembly and focus your efforts on taking over some backwater world there instead of trying for the whole galaxy."

A server Spider stepped up beside us. "Your order?" he asked in his flat voice.

"I'm good," I told him. "*Osantra*?"

"Nothing," Riijkhan said shortly. "You speak of retreat, Compton. Shall I tell you something about your employers, something that might well cause you to retreat from *your* current path?"

"By all means," I said encouragingly as the Spider moved away and headed toward one of the other tables. "Let's hear it."

Riijkhan hitched himself a little closer to the table. "Bayta's people, the ones who've hired you to destroy us," he said. "They won't permit you to live beyond the point where your usefulness to them ends."

I clucked reprovingly. I'd expected something a little more inventive from him. "Again with the defeatist attitude," I warned. "Because the point where I'm no longer useful is the point where the Shonkla-raa have ceased to exist. Do you even understand the concept of troop morale?"

"I never said you would win," he growled, clearly starting to get angry again. "I said you would be eliminated once you are no longer useful to them. Whether or not we die, you certainly will." He leveled a finger at me. "And I tell you right now: for you, death will come from a completely unexpected direction."

"You mean you won't get to do it?" I asked. "How disappointing for you."

He exhaled, very slowly, his eyes locked on mine, as his pointing finger stiffened into a knife. "Don't think I couldn't," he said, his voice almost too soft to hear. "I could lean over this table and stab you through your heart before you or any of your allies could even begin to stop me."

"Then why don't you?" I asked, subtly adjusting my grip on my glass. The dishes and flatware used aboard Quadrail trains were specifically designed to break apart under stress and therefore be useless as weapons. But if push came to shove, half a glass of iced tea thrown into Riijkhan's eyes might still gain me a crucial fraction of a second. "Because you know that a few seconds later you'd also be dead?"

"The sacrifice might be worth it," he said. He exhaled again, and his blaze lightened as some of the emotion passed. "But one does not kill one's allies, and I still believe you may be persuaded to become such."

He pushed back his chair and stood up. "When Bayta's people try to kill you, come and see me," he said. "Assuming, of course, that you survive the attempt."

"I appreciate the offer," I said. "I'll see you around, *Osantra* Riijkhan."

"Perhaps." He inclined his head toward me. "Perhaps not." Turning, he left the bar.

For another minute I stayed where I was, sipping at

my tea and trying to get my pounding heart under control. I'd been pretty sure the meeting would go exactly the way it had, but there was always the chance that even someone like Riijkhan would give in to the passion of the moment.

A Shorshian walked past my table, and as the breeze of his passage washed over me I caught the aroma of French onion soup. Glancing to my left, I spotted an elegant, turbaned Sikh sitting at the next table, prodding carefully at the steaming bowl with his spoon, waiting patiently for it to cool down.

I turned away again, carefully suppressing a smile. I'd told Bayta to get Fayr, not McMicking, in case of trouble, mainly because at the time I'd had no idea what McMicking looked like.

And if iced tea in the face would have slowed down Riijkhan's attack, I could only imagine what the effects of a bowl of steaming French onion soup would have been.

The rest of the trip passed without incident. Riijkhan kept to himself, though I did spot him once with the thin Filly that I'd briefly mistaken for our old friend Scrawny. Apparently, Shonkla-raa agents came in all shapes and sizes.

At Homshil Bayta, Rebekah, Terese, Morse, and I transferred again to a waiting tender, leaving McMicking and Fayr's team to continue on in their roles for another few stops, or until the Shonkla-raa lost interest in that particular train and moved on.

We arrived at the secondary Yandro station, to find that the Melding members who'd traveled the whole way via tender had arrived safely and were waiting for us. They'd been there long enough that they'd had time to set up something of a campground off to the side, complete with a Spider space heater and a circle of seats made up of the coral crates they'd brought with them. I half expected to find them singing folk songs and grilling sausages on thorn-twig spits, but they were making do with ration bars and bottled water. If there was any singing going on, it was happening mentally, via their group mind connection.

Behind them, monitoring the whole thing at a watchful distance, were four defender Spiders.

We filed out, to find that one of the Melding, a tall Tra'ho wearing the multiple earrings of the upper class, had left the group and was waiting by our tender. "It is good to see you alive and well," he said gravely, nodding to each of us in turn. "Rebekah had already informed us of your successes in matters of intrigue and combat, Compton, but I confess that many of us thought it more a result of luck than of skill. I am pleased to learn otherwise."

"Nice to be appreciated," I said, looking around the largely empty station. "Though no one in this business turns up their nose at luck if it happens to come our way. Where are our hosts?"

"There," the Tra'ho said, waving back toward the defenders.

"Not them," I said. "I was expecting other visitors." Actually, I was expecting a hell of a lot more than just that. "Bayta, you want to ask them?"

There was a moment of silence as Bayta spoke telepathically with the defenders.

And then another moment. Then another. "Bayta?" I murmured. "What's going on?"

"They're not coming," she murmured back.

I stared at her. The Chahwyn had a crucial role to play in this whole grand scheme. If they were suddenly backing out, we were finished. "This is no time for any of us to lose our nerve," I murmured back, taking Bayta's arm and moving us a few steps away from the others. "We need them."

"I know," Bayta said. "But once they've made up their

minds . . . I'm sorry, Frank. I warned you. They've made up their minds, and there's nothing I can do."

I looked over at the four defenders, standing motionless behind the Melding. "I want to talk to them," I told Bayta. "Now."

She shook her head. "The defenders won't take you there."

"Then you do it," I said. "You can control these trains. We get back on the tender, and we head to Viccai."

I felt her arm stiffen in my hand. "Frank, I can't do that."

"You did once," I reminded her. "And the stakes are a hell of a lot bigger now than they were then."

"I know," she said. "But they're not going to change their minds."

I looked over at Rebekah and Terese. During the past few days, beginning after the failed Shonkla-raa attack, I'd noticed a subtle change in their relationship. The two girls were still friends, but the sight of Rebekah frozen in the Shonkla-raa's mental grip had apparently awakened some deep maternal instincts in Terese that even the baby she was carrying hadn't succeeded in doing.

And the dagger-edged look Terese was giving me right now said that whatever the problem was, I'd better find a way to fix it. "You say they aren't going to change their minds," I said. "Is that a fact or an opinion?"

Bayta sighed. "A fact."

"Good," I said. "Because the only way you can know that for sure is if you're in communication with them right now. So where are they?"

She hesitated. "There's a tender a little ways down the Tube," she said. "One of the Elders is there."

I looked past Terese and Rebekah. This station was much smaller than most, with the atmosphere barrier that defined the edge no more than half a kilometer away.

And now that I was looking, I could see the faint

reflection from the globes of a group of Spiders waiting motionlessly just inside the barrier. More defenders? Or were they just the relay that was allowing Bayta's telepathy to stretch down the Tube to the Chahwyn hiding down there?

Either way, unless there was a line of Spiders strung out all the way to Viccai, Bayta's telepathic limit meant the Elders' tender couldn't be all that far away. "Fine," I told her. "If you won't drive me, I'll walk."

Bayta twitched with surprise. "*What?*"

"If they won't come to me, I'll have to go to them," I said, letting go of her arm. "Let me get the big oxygen tank from the tender and rig up a harness for it."

"Wait a minute," Bayta said, grabbing my arm as I started to walk away. "This is crazy. You don't even know how far away they are."

"They can't be very far, or you wouldn't be able to communicate with them," I reminded her, trying to pull her hand off my arm. "Don't worry, I'll be all right."

But for once, my assurances weren't enough. Neither was my strength. Bayta held on grimly, her fingers tightening against my attempts to pry them free. "No," she said, her voice starting to tremble. "Frank, this is suicide."

I frowned at her, the unexpected word echoing through my mind. Reckless, maybe. Useless, probably. Stupid, almost certainly.

But suicide? How on Earth could a short walk down the Tube be suicide? As long as I kept an eye on the oxygen tank's gauge, I would know when to turn around and head back.

Unless there was something else about to go down out there. Something that would be best handled in the dark loneliness of an empty Tube. Something that Bayta either knew or else strongly suspected.

I looked at the cluster of Spiders by the atmosphere barrier, Riijkhan's words echoing through my mind. Had he been right? Had the Chahwyn decided they no longer needed me? The only way that could happen was if they'd found someone or something that could take my place.

Or if for some reason I'd suddenly become a liability instead of an asset.

"You're right," I said, turning back to Bayta. "So just in case I don't return, I guess I'd better make sure Morse and the Modhri know everything about my plan." I looked her squarely in the eye. "And about everything else." Firmly but gently, I pulled her grip from my arm and beckoned to Morse.

"Wait," Bayta said.

I waited as her eyes became unfocused, and I counted out ten heartbeats before she finished her silent communication. "The Elder will see you," she said with a sigh. "The defender will take you to him."

Out of the corner of my eye I saw one of the defenders detach himself from the Melding and head toward us. "I'd prefer you take me," I said.

Bayta shook her head, a short, choppy movement. "He won't let me," she said. "Only you and the defender."

The dark loneliness of an empty Tube . . . "Okay," I said. "Whatever."

Morse came up to us. "What's the trouble?" he asked.

"No trouble," I said. "The Chahwyn want to talk to me. Probably just a glitch or two that need ironing out."

His eyes flicked to Bayta, back to me. "Sounds good," he said. "I'll go with you."

"I don't think you're invited," I said.

"I don't think I care," he countered. "If we're going to be allies, we have to trust each other."

"You can trust me," I said.

"*You*, yes," he said pointedly. "But so far, only you." He looked back at Bayta. "Make sure they know that," he said gruffly. "The Modhri and I trust Frank Compton. No one else."

"They know," Bayta said quietly.

"He's also the best excuse for a strategist that we've got." Morse's eyes flicked to the approaching defender, then back to me. "And whatever strategy you're working now, good luck with it."

"Thanks." I gave Bayta the most encouraging smile I could, then turned to the defender. "Let's get to it," I said, gesturing him to the tender.

The typical cruising speed for a Quadrail was roughly a hundred kilometers per hour relative to the Tube, which translated to a light-year per minute relative to the universe at large. Usually tenders could pull a slightly better speed even than that.

On this trip, though, the defender telepathically operating the controls didn't seem in any hurry to build up speed. We rolled along the track toward the end of the station at an almost leisurely pace, no faster than the average Olympic distance runner would do. We angled up the slope and through the atmosphere barrier into the main Tube, at which point we slowed to little more than a fast walk.

It was quickly clear why we weren't bothering to pick up speed. Less than thirty seconds after leaving the station, we rolled to a stop. "They are waiting," the defender said, lifting one of his metallic legs and gesturing toward the door.

"Do I at least get an oxygen mask?" I asked, eyeing the door dubiously. Centuries of Quadrail travel and the slow but constant leakage through the atmosphere barriers of a thousand stations had left enough pressure throughout the entire Tube system to protect me against the more serious physiological effects of decompression. But there wasn't nearly enough air out there for actual breathing.

I was still contemplating the unpleasant possibilities when the door opened, bringing with it a gust of slightly stale air. I stepped outside and found myself in a siding, one of the small service areas the Spiders had stashed at various places off the main Tube. Behind my tender—or in front of it, depending on how you looked at it—was another tender, this one with two defenders flanking the door. I walked over to it, veering a little ways outward so that I could see behind it, mostly out of idle curiosity as to whether there might be more defenders hanging around back there.

There weren't any defenders, at least none that I could see. What *was* there was an entire train's worth of tender cars, at least fifty of them plus a pair of engines at each end, nearly filling the rest of the siding track. Either the Chahwyn had indeed brought the modified Modhran coral that I'd asked for, or else we had one hell of a mass migration going on here.

I was still staring at the train when the Chahwyn tender's door irised open. "They are waiting," one of the defenders said.

"Right," I muttered. Squaring my shoulders, I stepped inside.

A single Chahwyn was seated in a chair at the far end of the car, his typically pale skin looking even paler today. The cat-like whiskers above his eyes were undulating in a way that I would have attributed to a restless breeze had there been any restless breezes around. Two more defenders flanked his seat, and I had the itchy sensation of a pair of attack dogs sizing me up. "Be seated, Frank Compton," the Chahwyn said, gesturing toward a chair half a dozen meters in front of him.

"Thank you," I said, crossing to the chair and sitting down. "Do I have the honor of addressing an Elder of the Chahwyn?"

"You do," he said. Like the other handful of Chahwyn I'd met over the past two years, this one had a fluid, melodious voice.

But I could also hear an edge of tension beneath the music. Something was definitely wrong.

"Glad to hear it," I said. "I see you've brought the coral I asked for. When can I arrange delivery down to Yandro?"

"There will be no delivery," he said. "Your plan has been rejected."

"Really," I said, keeping my voice neutral. "Why?"

"Your assumptions and calculations have been reexamined by the assessors," he said. "It has been concluded that there is insufficient coral to carry out your plan."

"With all due respect, your assessors are wrong," I said. "They're assuming we need enough modified coral to overwhelm a Modhri who's actively resisting the change. But as I made clear in my message, that's no longer the situation. Not only is the Modhri desperately eager to cooperate with us, but if Morse's colony is any indication the segment-prime will quickly realize the change is to his benefit and accept it with open arms."

"You assume in turn that Morse is telling the truth," the Elder countered. "You assume that the Modhri will indeed see the Melding change as a gain to him and not as a loss."

"First of all, anything that keeps the Modhri from becoming a Shonkla-raa slave counts as a gain," I said. "Second, I know Morse, and I know how Humans behave when they're lying, and he wasn't."

"Perhaps his Modhran colony was lying to him."

"I don't think so," I said. "In fact, if Morse's current arrangement is anything like the one Bayta has with her Chahwyn symbiont, I doubt he and the Modhri *can* lie to each other. And third, since when is this just *my* plan? This has been *your* plan, too, dating back to at least when you started working on the Melding coral."

"Our involvement in that project is a secret," the Chahwyn said stiffly. "You're not to speak of it with anyone."

"Oh, please," I scoffed. "You really think the Modhri isn't going to put two and two together now that he's actually in communication with the Melding? There's no way he's not going to figure out that you're the ones who created them. Or that your ancestors were the ones who created *him*, back when the original Shonkla-raa were running the galaxy."

There was just the briefest of hesitations. "We believe the Modhri already knows of our role in his origin," the Chahwyn said reluctantly.

"So there should be no problem," I said. "In fact, I daresay that makes it even more likely that he'll gladly accept this new direction. Who else but your creators would know how to make you better than you already are?"

"Perhaps," the Chahwyn said. "But the point is moot. As I have said, the plan is changed. And with that change, your services are no longer needed."

I stared at him. The Chahwyn were firing me? *Again?* "Just like that?"

"Just like that," he said. "Instead of you and the Modhri, we shall send the defenders to fight against the Shonkla-raa."

"They can't," I said as patiently as I could. "Don't you read our reports? The Shonkla-raa command tone freezes them like statues."

"That problem will soon be solved," he said. "We have a variant in development that will be immune to that tone."

"And exactly how soon do you expect to have this miracle defender up and running?" I countered. "How soon after that will you have built up the numbers you need? How soon after *that* will you get those numbers deployed?"

"We believe we have sufficient time."

"No, you don't," I said bluntly. "The Shonkla-raa are on the move, Elder of the Chahwyn. This is no time to go back to square one for a whole new battle plan."

"Nevertheless, that is our plan," the Chahwyn said. "And with you no longer under our guidance and protection, we must ensure that you will not leak its substance to the enemy. You will therefore be taken to Viccai—"

"Wait a minute," I cut him off. The insanity here was coming way too thick and fast. "What's this nonsense about me leaking the plan? Since when have I leaked *anything*?"

"You were seen speaking with the enemy on the Quadrail from Sibbrava," the Chahwyn said, his melodious voice gone flat and stern. "We fear you may speak with them again. We cannot risk that."

"That's ridiculous," I protested. "Talking with the Shonkla-raa doesn't mean a thing. Hey, I talked with the Modhri all the time back when we were still enemies. That's part of warfare, one of the ways you gather intelligence and work out trades."

The Chahwyn's whiskers twitched. "The decision has been made. You will be taken to Viccai, where you will remain for the duration of the war."

A chill ran up my back. *Frank, this is suicide,* Bayta had said. Had she known this was what the Chahwyn had planned for me?

No, of course she hadn't. If she had, she would surely have said something more concrete, something to warn me off. All she'd had was a feeling, some sense of this grim new insanity that had apparently overtaken the Chahwyn.

But it didn't make any sense. All I'd done was talk to Riijkhan. I hadn't made any deals with him, or told him any of my plans, or given him intel on our allies. More importantly, I'd just repulsed two separate Shonkla-raa attacks. If that didn't show I was on the Chahwyn side, nothing would.

Unless it wasn't my talking to Riijkhan that the Chahwyn were concerned about. Maybe it was my listening to him.

What had Riijkhan said to me? More importantly, what had he said that might have thrown the Chahwyn into this insane mental tailspin?

Whatever it was, whatever the Chahwyn thought they'd heard, there couldn't be very much of it. Sitting in the Quadrail bar, Riijkhan and I had been encased in the usual acoustical bubble that prevented outsiders from eavesdropping.

But there *had* been a moment when that bubble had been breached, I remembered now. The point where the server Spider came by to ask for our orders.

And as I thought back, that breach had occurred right as Riijkhan was offering to tell me something terrible about my employers.

A dramatic buildup that had been followed by a big fat lot of nothing. As the Spider left, Riijkhan had merely trotted out the traditional vague threat that my allies would eventually turn on me. It was such a tired old ploy that I hadn't given it a second thought.

But the Spiders had apparently reported Riijkhan's question to the Chahwyn, who were obviously taking it very seriously. Which implied in turn that there was one hell of a secret lurking somewhere in the Chahwyn's collective closet.

And if I didn't do something fast, that secret was about to get me exiled from the entire war. Which was no doubt exactly what Riijkhan had been angling for in the first place.

"If you take me off the field, you will lose," I said as calmly as I could. "The Shonkla-raa will take over the galaxy, they'll track you down, and they'll destroy you."

The Chahwyn lowered his eyes. "There are worse things than death."

"Sure there are," I said acidly. "Slavery is one of them. Watching your friends being murdered is one of them. Having some deep dark secret become common knowledge isn't."

His eyes snapped up, his whiskers flattening. "So we were right," he said. "The Shonkla-raa *did* tell you."

If I'd been smart, I would have just said no: straightforwardly, honestly, passionately, with a little righteous bewilderment thrown in.

But I'm never that smart. My brain is that of a truth-seeker, my training that of a professional investigator, my personality that of a damn the torpedoes, full speed aheader. Even as I opened my mouth, my mind was sifting the problem, sorting like heat lightning through everything I knew about the Chahwyn, the Shonkla-raa, and the universe at large.

What could a Shonkla-raa tell me that the Chahwyn wouldn't want me to know?

I'd heard a little of the story during my one visit to Viccai. Four thousand years ago, the Shonkla-raa had discovered the quantum filament the Chahwyn called the Thread and figured out how to use it for interstellar travel. Over the centuries they'd learned how to ravel off pieces that could be used to link all the inhabited and inhabitable systems together. Once widespread interstellar travel was possible, the Shonkla-raa had built huge warships and sent them out on a systematic subjugation of all the other peoples of the galaxy. Along the way they'd used their skills at genetic manipulation to create the Chahwyn and various other servant races. When the inevitable revolt finally came, the Shonkla-raa had forced the Chahwyn to create the Modhri as a last-ditch, fifth-column-type weapon that they'd hoped to use against their enemies.

Only the end came before the Modhri could be deployed. The Shonkla-raa were destroyed, the surviving races were crushed back to pre-spaceflight levels, and the Modhri was lost and effectively gone dormant. Three centuries after the dust had settled, the Chahwyn had stumbled on caches of Shonkla-raa tech and had used the genetic equipment to create the Spiders and, through them, the Quadrail, wrapping their Tubes around the sections of Thread. When Modhran coral was found and began to spread across the galaxy, the Chahwyn had countered by again using the old Shonkla-raa equipment, this time to create the Melding in hopes of turning the Modhri from a single-minded conqueror weapon into something calmer, more civilized, and less threatening to the galaxy at large.

And as the history lesson flashed across my mind, so did something more recent: the image of the defenders aboard the Sibbrava Quadrail, carefully carrying the injured Belldic commandos to their compartments but merely lugging the dead Shonkla-raa back to the tender like sides of beef.

I'd made sure to take scans of the bodies, hoping to wring out a few secrets about Shonkla-raa physiology that I could use against them. Surely the Chahwyn would want to do the same, and would thus make sure to take special care of the bodies until they could be examined.

Unless there was no need for them to study the bodies. Because they didn't need to know how Shonkla-raa physiology differed from that of normal Filiaelians.

Because they already knew what all of those differences were.

I should have kept it to myself. But I'm never that smart. "You lied to me," I said quietly. "You told me the Shonkla-raa created you. That they gene-manipulated God only knows what creatures into the Chahwyn to be their servants.

"Only they didn't, did they? The Shonkla-raa didn't create you.

"*You* created *them*."

Silently, with the finality of a sealing tomb, the car door irised shut. "Yes," the Elder said, his melodious voice resonating with infinite sadness. "And with that knowledge, you must never be permitted to speak with anyone, ever again."

TWENTY-SIX :

The two defenders started toward me. "What are you going to do?" I asked.

"You cannot be permitted to share that knowledge with anyone," the Chahwyn repeated. "We will take you to Viccai—"

"No, I know that part," I interrupted, watching the approaching Spiders and trying to figure out what the hell I was going to do if this didn't work. I knew something about Shonkla-raa, but I had no idea where defender weaknesses were. If they even had any. "I meant what are you going to do once I'm gone and Bayta and Morse have quit and the Modhri goes back to fighting on the side of the Shonkla-raa?"

"I have already told you our plan," the Chahwyn said.

"You haven't got a plan," I said flatly. "You have a repeat of history. Shall I tell you why your ancestors created the Shonkla-raa in the first place?"

The defenders reached me, each shifting to a four-legged stance and lifting three legs toward me. "You created them to be your protectors," I said. "As you've pointed out countless times, you Chahwyn can't fight. So you created a group of beings that could, enhancing their telepathic abilities so you could more easily communicate with them."

The defenders paused, their legs hovering in midair like a mobile cage waiting to come crashing down around me. "Do I have to remind you how well that worked out?" I added.

"It will be different this time," the Chahwyn said. "We have better control of the defenders than we ever had with the Shonkla-raa."

"No you don't," I said. "Maybe they're obeying you right now, but I don't doubt the Shonkla-raa did the same at the beginning. The problem wasn't your engineering, but with the philosophical basis of the whole project."

The Spider legs were still hovering over me. "Explain," the Chahwyn said.

"What you did then—what you're doing now—is creating independent beings with intelligence, strength, and the ability and desire to compete and fight," I said. "Sooner or later, the defenders will inevitably conclude that they can do a better job of running things than you can."

"They will obey us," the Chahwyn insisted.

"Not when they feel the need to break the rules you've set for them," I told him. "As a matter of fact, they've already started. Back on the super-express from Homshil I needed to get my Beretta from its under-train lockbox. A regular Spider would never have allowed such a thing. But the two defenders you'd sent saw that it was necessary, and they got it for me. Reluctantly and under protest, but they did it."

"But they're bred for loyalty," the Chahwyn insisted, his voice almost pleading. "How can they defy us and our laws?"

"Because that's what *inevitable* means," I said. "Power corrupts, one way or another. That's all there is to it."

"The defenders are Spiders. Their essence is taken from our own flesh."

"But then heavily modified," I reminded him. "I'm sure your ancestors were using similar logic when they picked Filiaelians to use as their Shonkla-raa template. They'd probably seen how Filly soldiers could be genetically engineered for loyalty, and figured that would guarantee their new protectors' compliance and cooperation."

"Then why didn't it?"

"Because just like your defenders, the Chahwyn designers were forced to tweak the formula," I said. "The way the Fillies engineer their soldiers' loyalty is by sacrificing some of their initiative, intelligence, and motivation. We got a taste of that with *Logra* Emikai, when the simple fact that a Shonkla-raa was also a Filiaelian *santra* meant Emikai couldn't take any action against him.

Filly soldiers are even worse—good fighters, but in some ways not much better than ants in an anthill. That kind of strategy requires huge numbers, something your ancestors couldn't come up with. So instead they were forced to make each individual Shonkla-raa smarter and more independent."

I gestured to the two defenders still frozen in their mousetrap positions. "You've done the same thing with the defenders, and it's going to lead to the same end result."

The Chahwyn gave a noiseless sigh. "Your reading of history is accurate," he admitted. "Yet we have no choice but to try."

"Sure you do," I said in my most encouraging voice. "You can close down the project, deploy the defenders you already have for the protection of Viccai, and let me take out the Shonkla-raa."

"With the aid of he who was once our sworn enemy?"

I frowned at him . . . and then, abruptly, I realized what this whole confrontation was really all about.

The Chahwyn knew perfectly well that they were playing with fire. They knew that the last time they'd tried this they'd failed spectacularly, to the tune of the devastation of thousands of worlds and the wholesale slaughter of dozens of races. They'd seen firsthand what the Shonkla-raa could do, and were utterly terrified by this new resurgence.

But they were just as terrified at the thought of deliberately making the Modhri into something smarter, more patient, more competent. Terrified enough that they would rather cross their extendable fingers and hope that this time the protector plan would work.

Their minds weren't made up, the way Bayta had thought. Or rather, the way this Elder had tried to make it appear to her. They were divided and paralyzed with indecision, seeing nothing but death and destruction at the end of all possible paths and afraid to move in any of them. I was here not to batter myself against a mono-lithic stone wall, but to give them a good reason to choose my proposed path over all the others.

Whether my way was the best, I couldn't say. But I was pretty sure I could prove all the alternatives were worse.

"Yes, I'm willing to work with the Modhri," I said. "For two reasons. First, unlike the Shonkla-raa, the Modhri is highly vulnerable to attack. You can walk right up to his coral outposts and destroy them, and if you don't mind slaughtering a whole bunch of innocents you can walk right up to his walkers and destroy them, too. That vulnerability makes him far less likely to start anything grandiose."

"Yet for two hundred years he has been trying to con-quer the galaxy."

"Because that's what you designed him to do," I coun-tered. "That's all he *could* do. But that's about to change. By combining him with the Melding, you're opening him up to new possibilities and options, new ways of dealing with the universe around him."

"Yet you've already said that intelligence and initia-tive leads to competition and the desire to rule," the Chahwyn said.

"I also said that will be limited by his vulnerability," I said. "But you're also assuming that on some level he *wants* to be our opponent. It's my considered opinion that he doesn't."

"What then *does* he want?"

I raised my eyebrows. "He wants friends."

For a long moment the Chahwyn just stared at me. "Friends," he repeated at last, his voice flat.

"Yes," I said. "You don't understand, because you Chahwyn are never really alone. But the Modhri is. He always has been."

"He has a multitude of mind segments."

"All of which are essentially him," I reminded him.

"He's never had any friends, only enemies and potential enemies. He's never had anyone outside himself to trust, or who trusted him. Until now."

"We do not trust him."

"That's okay," I said. "I do."

Another silence settled into the car like fine grains of dust. "Let me offer you a deal," I said into the gap. "Give me the Melding coral and let me try things my way. If I fail, you can always fall back on your defender plan."

The cat whiskers twitched. "Even a short delay could prove fatal."

"Perhaps," I said. "But if you do head down that path, it will permanently alter the tone and texture of your people, the Quadrail system, and the galaxy. Personally, I like the Quadrail and the Spiders just the way they are. I don't want to see them ruined."

"Even at the cost of defeat?"

"There won't be a defeat," I said. "My plan *will* work."

I gestured around me. "And the time here isn't quite as critical as you think. Even if the Modhri and I fail, you can always shut down the whole Quadrail system, boxing up the Shonkla-raa on whatever planets they currently happen to be in. That should give you enough time to build up your defender force."

The Chahwyn's shoulders did a strange hunchy thing. "That assumes the Shonkla-raa won't learn the secret of the Thread."

I grimaced. That was a big, dangerous *if*, all right. If the Shonkla-raa ever realized that the Thread hidden inside the Coreline was the key to the Quadrail's faster-than-light travel, and that the Tube and the trains were just window dressing, then shutting down the system wouldn't even slow them down. All they would have to do would be commandeer a few of the big defense ships that guarded each Quadrail station in the Filiaelian Assembly, wreck the Tube to allow them to get close to the Thread, and they'd be free to travel any place the Thread went. "Hopefully, they won't," I said. "Or if they do that, they'll have their own reasons for sticking to the train system. At least for a while."

I stood up, being careful not to bump into the metallic legs still half birdcaged around me. "All the more reason why we need to get this show on the road," I continued. "Let me get this coral to Yandro and start the Modhri on his path to civilization."

I started to ease past the defenders' legs. But the legs shifted positions, once again blocking my path. "You cannot return to the others," the Chahwyn said quietly. "I've already said that."

I clenched my teeth. What part of *vital to the cause* didn't he understand? "How about a compromise?" I suggested.

"What kind of compromise?"

I gestured to the two defenders. "You send Sam and Carl here with me," I said. "If I ever start to tell anyone about your deep, dark secret, they have my permission to tear my head off."

The whiskers twitched a few times. "That may be acceptable," the Chahwyn said cautiously. "I shall pass the suggestion on to the others."

I shook my head. "We don't have time for a round-table committee discussion. You're the Elder on the scene. You have the facts. You make the decision."

The twitching whiskers started twitching a little harder. Then, abruptly, they stopped. As they did so, the two defenders lowered their upraised legs back to the floor. "Very well," the Chahwyn said. "The defenders will go with you. They will stay with you at all times. If you speak of this matter, they have been given orders to end your life."

The whiskers twitched one final time. "And they will also end the life of any you have told. Is that acceptable?"

I felt my stomach tighten. Bayta, certainly, would want the details of what had happened out here. So would Morse. Whether the Elder had specifically planned it that way or not, he'd now pretty well guaranteed I wouldn't say a single word about my visit to either of them. "It is," I agreed reluctantly.

"You may return to the station," he said. "The coral will follow."

"Thank you." I started toward the door, then paused. "One other question," I said. "Why did you make the Shonkla-raa throats so big? You surely weren't thinking ahead to Modhran command tones, were you?"

"Not at all." The Chahwyn gave a little sigh. "They were given large throats so that they could sing. We very much loved their music."

I probably should have made some sort of comment to that. But for once, I couldn't find anything to say. Inclining my head to him, with my new watchdogs tapping along at my heels, I headed back to my tender.

I'd half expected the entire group to be anxiously waiting for me when the tender slowed to a stop at the Yandro station. But only Bayta was standing by the door as it opened, her face still pale but with only a little of her earlier tension still showing. Clearly, she'd already learned from the Spiders that I was coming back alive.

She'd also obviously already guessed that the meeting hadn't been an entirely friendly one. The sight of my new watchdogs could only emphasize that. "These are the guards I'm told we've been assigned?" she asked, giving the defenders a dubious look.

"These are they," I confirmed as I glanced around. The Melding was still sitting together around their pseudo campfire, and I could see that Terese and Rebekah had joined them. Morse, though, was nowhere to be seen. "This is Sam; I'm calling this one Carl."

"I assume the names have a meaning," she said.

"They're from a dit-rec drama called *Casablanca*," I

explained. "Sam and Carl were two of the hero's employees."

"I suppose that makes you Rick?" Morse asked, coming around the side of the tender and striding toward us.

"I did always like his hat," I agreed, looking past Morse's shoulder. There was nothing in that direction but more empty station. "Communing with nature?"

"Communing with my colony," he corrected. "I suppose that makes me Major Strasser?"

"I can see some similarities," I said, frowning. "What is there for you and your colony to commune about?"

"We're still sorting through the changes that the Melding has made in my colony's attitude and our relationship," he said.

"What sort of changes?"

"For one thing, we can disconnect a bit from the overall mind segment," he said. "Not completely, not the way I assume Bayta can detach from the Spider network. But at the same time, interestingly enough, my colony and I actually seem to have become a little closer."

"That sounds like the way Rebekah described her relationship with her symbiont," Bayta said.

"Which, I believe, was the whole idea," Morse said. "To make the Modhri more like the Spider and Chahwyn setups, with more individuality for the members but with the best aspects of the group mind still there." He shook his head. "But it's definitely going to take some time to sort out."

Bayta cocked her head suddenly to the side. "Can he move?" she asked.

"What do you mean?" Morse asked.

"I was thinking about the Modhran colony Minnario planted in *Isantra* Kordiss," she said. "The polyps were supposed to attach at his optic nerve, where the Modhri could tap into his vision but not control him."

"Right," Morse said, frowning as he probably only now

accessed that tidbit from the Modhri mind segment. "Otherwise, when the Shonkla-raa fired off their magic whistle Kordiss would go marionette on everyone and they'd figure out what we'd done to him. Am I understanding it correctly?"

"Perfectly," I confirmed as I realized where Bayta was going with this. "What Bayta's saying is that if your colony can move to your eyes or ears and away from the motor nerves, then it won't be able to take over *you*, either."

"Bloody hell," Morse breathed. "You know, that never even occurred to me. Hang on—I'll check."

"That's why Bayta and I are the ones running this zoo," I murmured, giving Bayta an encouraging smile. "We think about things like that. Good call, Bayta."

She didn't smile back.

Morse shook his head. "Sorry, but it's no go," he said regretfully. "Once the colony's in place, it anchors itself and can't be moved. Even if we could get it loose, it's really too big to do any serious traveling. Nice thought, though."

"Yes, it was," I said. "Might be worth mentioning to the segment-prime for future reference."

"I already have," Morse said. "So what's the story with the Chahwyn?"

"They've got a trainload of Melding coral on the way," I told him. "Once it's here, we'll ship it down to Yandro proper. Hopefully, there will be enough to give the whole segment-prime this new and improved outlook on life." I cocked an eyebrow. "Assuming he still *wants* this new outlook."

Morse smiled tightly. "You mean the chance to go from an old black-and-white dit-rec drama to full-blown colored 3-D?" The smile faded. "You have no idea what it's like for him, Compton. The Chahwyn should have put him together that way in the first place."

"I'm sure they'd have liked to," I said, watching Sam and Carl out of the corner of my eye. "But I don't think the prospective owners were interested in their new weapon having any bells and whistles."

Morse snorted. "Point," he growled. "So what's next on the big master plan?"

"We take Terese back to Earth," I said. "And we start raising an army."

His eyes widened. "An army? Where the hell from?"

"Given that the whole Terran Confederation is at risk, I think it's time we brought the UN into play," I said. "After we drop off Terese, we'll go have a chat with Deputy Director Biret Losutu."

"*Director* Biret Losutu, you mean," Morse corrected. "Director Klein stepped down six months ago and Losutu took his place."

"Ah," I said. I hadn't realized I was that out of touch with Earth's current events. "Congratulations all around. Anyway, we bring Losutu up to speed and see what he can do about raising a quiet army."

"How quiet?"

"Very quiet," I said. "Because after that, the plan is to lure the Shonkla-raa to Earth."

Morse's eyes bulged. "You want them on *Earth*?"

"It's the best place in the galaxy for a showdown," I pointed out. "Thanks to all those restrictive coral-import laws there aren't any Modhran outposts there for them to use, and therefore only a handful of Eyes. Though I suppose you know the numbers better than I do."

"No, you're right, there aren't very many," Morse acknowledged, his forehead wrinkled in thought. "Maybe a thousand, spread out over the whole planet. How exactly do you intend to lure them in?"

"By messing with whatever Riijkhan's grand scheme is for the Confederation," I said. "He essentially promised me he would keep his hands off Earth if I would join them, which undoubtedly means he's already got some alternate plan under way. We find that plan, we start raining bricks down on it, and hopefully he and his buddies will come charging in to make us stop."

"Okay," Morse said doubtfully. "Sounds bloody iffy, if you ask me."

"But I'm the boss?" I suggested.

"You're the boss," he agreed. "I suppose we can work out the actual details later."

"Exactly," I said. "Do me a favor, would you, and go tell Terese that she's going home?"

"You don't want to give her the good news yourself?"

"She tends to glower whenever I get near her," I explained. "Which tends to obscure her other expressions and emotions."

Morse's lip twitched. "In other words, you also want me to try to figure out how she really feels about going back."

"Exactly," I said. "There's a lot we still don't know about her. More is always better."

He nodded. "I'll take care of it."

He headed off toward the Melding circle. "He doesn't know who she really is?" Bayta asked quietly.

I shook my head. "I asked Rebekah to keep it quiet for now."

"I didn't know she could do that."

"Keep things private from the rest of the Melding?" I shrugged. "Apparently so. Not really surprising when you think about it. After all, you and I have kept secrets from the Spiders and Chahwyn."

"Yes, we have," Bayta said, her voice gone odd. "They've also kept a few from us."

I winced. "Bayta—"

"It's all right, Frank," she said. Her voice still held some tension, but there was nothing but warmth and trust in her hand as she wrapped it gently around mine. "I just don't like not knowing everything that's going on. But I understand that's how it has to be."

"I appreciate that," I said, searching for a way to change the subject.

For once, even if unknowingly, the Chahwyn came to my rescue. At the far end of the station, the long train of tenders I'd seen at the siding popped through the barrier and rolled down the slope toward us. "But right now, we've got work to do," I said, squeezing Bayta's hand and then letting go. "Let's get the defenders organized and start unloading some coral."

I'd assured the Elder that the Modhri would accept the Melding changes with open arms. The Elder had countered with the ominous possibility that the Modhri might be lying about that, for whatever presumably nefarious reason.

Only one of us would prove to be right. But neither of us would know which, not for a good, long while. The Modhri had managed to rent, buy, or otherwise finagle the presence of Yandro's entire fleet of spacegoing vessels—all eight of them—but even at top speed those ships and their cargo of Melding coral would take over ten days to get to Yandro. After that would come whatever time the Modhri needed to adjust to the new coral and his new life, aided by the rest of the Melding members who were going down to the planet to help guide him through the transition. Once everything was settled, the new improved Modhri could have one of his Eyes laser a message to the station to confirm that he had adjusted, after which a message cylinder would be sent to wherever Bayta and I and the others happened to be at the time. I was guessing all of that would take at least another two weeks, and possibly longer.

"All I'm saying is that I don't think we can afford to wait that long," Morse argued as we watched the defenders and some of the stronger Melding members lugging crates from the tenders to the open hatchways where the commandeered torchyachts and cargo transports were docked. "I think we need to assume the acclimation will work and get started right away."

"What do you suggest?" I asked.

"We know Yleli and his friends had me under full

control back on the Sibbrava train," he said. "But we also know that they had only partial control of Rebekah. What was the difference between us?"

"You're the Modhri," Rebekah said as she and Terese wandered over to us. "I'm the Melding."

"Except that by then I was also part of the Melding," Morse pointed out. "Had been since we touched down on that colony of yours."

"It has to be the polyp colonies," Bayta said. "Yours is original Modhran. Rebekah's is the modified Melding version."

"Exactly." Morse looked at me. "Back before we went out to the Melding's place you had the Modhri send Eyes to Homshil and some of the other stations to alert passing mind segments about the new alliance. I'm thinking maybe we should send each of those messengers a lump of Melding coral so they can—" He waved a hand. "*Inoculate*, I suppose, is as good a word as any. Inoculate all the passing Eyes against Shonkla-raa control."

"How's that going to help?" Terese asked, frowning. "Rebekah told me it took weeks or months to grow one of those colonies."

"That's if you start with a polyp hook from a casual touch of the coral," Morse said. "If you scratch someone—I mean a really decent scratch—then enough polyps get in to quickly form a colony."

"You're kidding," Terese said.

"No, he's right," I said, wincing with distant memories. "We had a whole trainload of people turned in just a few hours by a handful of determined Eyes with a supply of coral." I looked at Bayta. "What do you think?"

For a moment her eyes unfocused as she communicated with the Chahwyn, who was apparently still back at the siding. Probably waiting to see if I'd be obliging enough to provoke Sam and Carl into killing me. "It sounds reasonable," she said slowly. "I don't know how we'd go about testing it, though."

"I do," Morse said.

And before I could do anything but stare in astonishment, he strode to the nearest crate, popped off the top with a quick flick of his multitool, and reached inside. Some of the water inside sloshed over the edge as he raked his hand across the coral—

"*Damn*," he grunted, yanking his hand out of the crate.

"What is it?" Terese asked tensely.

"I forgot the bloody coral lives in salt water," Morse said wryly as he gripped his hand. "Stings like—never mind." He unclasped his hand and showed us the bright red line of oozing blood. "Okay, let's see how this works. Depending on how long it takes for the polyps to find their way to my brain and join with the Modhran colony, we may need to tailor the size of the scratch a bit."

I shook my head as I started my watch's timer. "You are absolutely the most reckless lunatic I've ever worked with," I told him.

"Coming from a former Westali, that means so much," Morse said dryly. He peered at his scratch one more time, then dropped his arm to his side. "Well, what are we standing around for?" he demanded. "There's work to be done. Let's get to it."

Yandro to Earth was about a nine-and-a-half-hour trip, a short enough run for us to do via tender. But I'd had enough of tenders, and I was way behind on my sleep, and the idea of getting to lie down in a real bed in a secure and semi-private Quadrail compartment was too good to pass up.

Besides, the way our group was growing, a tender would have been uncomfortably crowded. Morse and Terese were coming with us, of course, with Morse having volunteered to be Terese's escort and protector on the torchliner trip from the Tube back to Earth. Terese and Rebekah both insisted that Rebekah be allowed to accompany us as well, so that the two girls could have a few last hours together.

And then there were Sam and Carl. The two defenders didn't say anything, but I knew full well what would happen if I tried to leave without them.

I also knew what would happen if I tried to crowd them into a tender with the rest of us. For one thing, I would have to sit and look at their dot-patterned globes the whole way back to Terra Station. For another, I'd caught Morse throwing thoughtful looks in the defenders' direction, and I knew that somewhere down the line he would be asking me about them. I didn't want that happening in an open car with everyone else listening in.

So when all the coral and Melding members were loaded, and the transports and torchyachts safely on their way, the rest of us piled into the tender and I told Bayta to take us around the edge of the system to the main Yandro station.

From the way *Isantra* Yleli had talked I'd assumed the Shonkla-raa or their agents had scattered themselves among every Quadrail station between Sibbrava and Terra, plus probably a few more beyond it. In a place like Homshil, with upward of a thousand beings moving around at any given time, we'd never have spotted the presence of such agents. At Yandro, though, a loiterer would stick out like a giraffe at a polar bear convention.

I didn't see Riijkhan as being that blatantly obvious, and so wasn't surprised to find the station deserted when we arrived. There were two hours until the regular train, and we spent most of the time in the station's lone gift-and-packaged-food shop, browsing the selection under the watchful and hopeful eye of a bored-looking Human clerk.

The train that pulled in again had only one double compartment left. I put Terese and Rebekah in one side, with Bayta on the other. I unashamedly called dibs on the other bed in Bayta's half, leaving Morse to rough it in the first-class coach car.

I expected both defenders to try crowding into the compartment with Bayta and me. But that clearly wasn't practical, so Sam moved in with us while Carl stayed outside. I wondered if he would go to ground somewhere in the service areas of the dining car, or whether he would simply spend the next few hours wandering the train looking for trouble.

I was too tired to really care. Locking the compartment door, I stretched out on the bed, and as the train pulled out of the station and headed for New Tigris I fell asleep.

I was working through a particularly eerie dream when I was startled awake by a sharp shake of my shoulder.

I snapped my eyes open. Bayta was standing over me, her face tight. Behind her, Rebekah and Terese were clinging tightly to each other. "What is it?" I demanded, swinging my legs over the edge of the bed and sitting up. A quick glance out the display window showed we were in Terra Station, and my inner ear told me we were slowing down as we headed for the passenger area.

"Agent Morse says there are walkers out there," Bayta said tensely. "Nearly a hundred of them."

"A *hundred*?" I echoed, taking another look through the window. The platforms were reasonably crowded by Terra Station standards, but there couldn't be more than a hundred and fifty people out there. For a hundred of them to be Modhran walkers—

I looked back at Bayta, a sinking feeling in my stomach. "It's a trap," I said.

"Yes," she said quietly. "And there's no way out."

TWENTY-SEVEN :

For a long moment my sleep-fogged brain skidded like a train on iced tracks. Then the mental wheels caught again. "Don't stop," I said, getting to my feet. "Whoever's driving this thing, tell him to just keep going."

"I already tried," Bayta said. "The schedule says to stop at Terra. So we're stopping."

I bit back a curse. Damn passive Spiders and their damn rigid adherence to the rules.

Unless— "You," I said, jabbing a finger at the defender as he stood silently behind Terese and Rebekah. "Countermand the schedule, or the standing order, or whatever it takes. Keep us moving."

"I cannot," he said. "The slowdown procedure has already been started. It cannot be stopped."

"What are we going to do?" Terese demanded, her voice half angry, half pleading. "You said we'd be safe. You said you'd keep us safe."

"Shh," Rebekah soothed, reaching up to touch Terese's cheek. "It'll be all right," she said quietly. "He'll get us through."

But for all her comforting words, her face was as pale as Terese's. And for the moment, I had to agree with them. Stepping over to the window, I gave the station a long, careful look.

For once, the walkers arrayed against us were easy to identify. They were lined up along the platform our train was headed for, three deep and as stiff as soldiers on parade. Standing in a more spaced-out row a few meters behind the lines, looking like armchair generals who are eager to go to war but don't want to get too close to the actual fighting, were four Fillies dressed in the upper-class clothing favored by the *santra* class. Clearly, they knew we were aboard this particular train.

"Where did they all come from?" Bayta murmured from beside me. "And so many of them are Humans, too."

"They're a pickup squad," I told her. "Look at their clothes—most of them are second- or third-class passengers. I'm guessing our friends out there pulled Morse's trick: get hold of some coral, wait until they know we're on the way, then grab everyone in sight and start scratching."

"But how could they have known we'd be on this train?" Bayta asked with helpless chagrin. "I watched at New Tigris. No one got off our train, and no one already in the station sent any messages. I had the Spiders check."

"They knew because Riijkhan's started being cute," I growled. "They have an agent aboard who must have signaled someone in the station. It didn't have to be anything elaborate—a piece of red paper in one of the windows or something equally simple. Then, since they knew we'd watch for someone to send a message, the watcher in the station *didn't* send one. In this case, the lack of a message was the signal that we were on the way."

There was a movement behind me, and I turned as Rebekah stepped to the door and opened it, just in time to let Morse slip into the compartment. "I hope you've got one bloody good plan," he said.

"Working on it," I told him, giving the rest of the station a quick scan. There were other small clumps of people wandering around out there whom the Shonkla-raa apparently hadn't bothered to recruit. Some were looking curiously at the walker formation, probably wondering who the celebrity was who was arriving, but most were pretty much ignoring us. Late arrivals, I tentatively identified them, who the Shonkla-raa had decided couldn't be turned into walkers in time to be of any use to them.

And scattered haphazardly throughout the station, standing as rigid as ice carvings, was the local contingent of Spiders.

The Shonkla-raa had the whole place locked down,

all right. But we still had one weapon in our arsenal. "What's the activation range on the *kwi*?" I asked Bayta. "How close do you have to be to keep it working?"

"A couple of meters," she said. "Five or six at the most. But the minute I go out there I'll be frozen like everyone else."

"That's why you won't be going out there," I said, thinking hard. "We *can* keep the train's doors closed, right?"

"Yes," Bayta said. "That's done internally. I've already given the order."

"Order number two: as soon as we've stopped, try to get us moving again," I said. "I don't suppose the Shonkla-raa have overlooked that possibility, but we might as well try. If it works, we just keep going until we find a station that's clear of them, or a siding big enough for us to pull into."

"We can try," Bayta said doubtfully.

"If that doesn't work—" I turned away from the window and gestured to Morse. "Get down to the compartment nearest the car's door and clear out whoever's inside. I don't care how, just do it."

"Right." Morse hit the door release and disappeared back out into the corridor.

"Sam, get Carl back here," I ordered the defender. "Where is he, by the way?"

"In the dining car service area," Sam said.

"Good," I said. "Have him stop by the bar car on his way and grab as many big bottles of the most flammable alcoholic liquor you've got aboard. The higher the proof, the better. If there's any *skinski* flambé fluid, grab that, too."

"We going to set the train on fire?" Terese asked.

"Not the train, no," I told her. "You girls start tearing apart some strips of flammable cloth—a proper Molotov cocktail needs a proper fuse."

"How are we going to get them out there?" Rebekah asked, her voice tight but controlled as she pulled two of her lightweight shirts from her carrybag and handed one to Terese. She was, I suspected, probably trying hard not to think about the actual, gritty consequences of deliberately setting a whole bunch of people on fire.

"She's right," Terese said, her breath edging toward the fast and shallow as she started tearing the shirt apart. "The minute you open the door, they'll have us."

"That's why all of you will be in the compartment Morse is getting for us," I told her. "Close enough for Bayta to activate the *kwi*, but behind enough sound-proofing that none of you should get enough command tone for it to be a problem. It'll just be Sam, Carl, and me out there."

"But they're Spiders," Terese protested. "The minute they hear the Fillies they'll be frozen."

I smiled tightly. "Exactly. Hang on to those shirts, and let's see if Morse has our new quarters ready."

The train was just rolling to a stop as we headed down the corridor toward the front of the car. Along the way we passed an eager-eyed Tra'ho hurrying in the opposite direction, her multiple sets of earrings jangling as she all but ran us down.

Morse was waiting by the open door of the compartment beside the car door. "I told her the *grafft'a* singer Mov Tree'es was preparing to make a musical dit-rec and needed a few Tra'ho'seej to fill in for some of the background line who hadn't shown up," he said as we came up. "What's the plan?"

"As soon as the rest of my squad shows up—ah; there he is," I interrupted myself as the vestibule door at the rear of the car opened and Carl appeared with a dozen bottles cradled in his folded legs. "You and I will put together a few Molotov cocktails, then I'll stay out here while all the rest of you seal yourselves into the compartment. Bayta, why aren't we moving?"

"As soon as we stopped some of the walkers wedged themselves into the engine's wheels and drive mechanisms," she said tightly.

Terese inhaled sharply. "Oh, no," she breathed. "They didn't—?"

"No, no, of course not," Bayta assured her quickly. "That's why we're still stopped."

Morse grunted. "They *are* already dead, you know," he said darkly as he took one of Carl's collection of bottles and pulled out the stopper. "The Shonkla-raa aren't going to let any of them live."

"That doesn't mean we have to be a direct party to their murders," I pointed out as I took another of the bottles and gave the rest of the assortment a quick look. Carl hadn't found any flambé fluid, which burned a lot hotter than alcohol, but he'd put together a selection of Halkan rotgut that ranged from a hundred twenty to a hundred thirty proof. Not perfect, but it would have to do. "Besides, I'm guessing that grinding a bunch of bodies into the wheelworks would probably damage something and lock us down solid."

"Yes, it probably would," Bayta confirmed, a shiver running through her as she took one of the bottles from Carl and starting working on it, watching me closely to see how I was putting the bomb together. "How many do we need?"

Abruptly, there was a loud thud and the car seemed to shake. "What was that?" Terese gasped.

"They're trying to push us over," Rebekah said.

Morse grunted. "Good luck with that," he said. "Just as well Compton scrapped the idea of coming the whole way by tender. One of *those* they might have been able to knock over."

"Six of them ought to do it," I told Bayta as I started stuffing one of the cloth fuses into my bottle. "The plan is to—"

"Hold it," Morse cut me off. "They *can* hear us, remember."

"Only if they think to ask their walkers what I've got planned," I said. "Doesn't matter. The plan is to put a fire barrier on both sides of the door and then *kwi* as many of the walkers as I can as they charge at me up the middle. When the fires start dying down, I can feed them extra fuel straight from the other bottles."

"All while you're busy shooting people?" Terese asked tightly. "You planning on growing a few extra hands in the next two minutes?"

"I'm open to suggestions," I said as I finished one cocktail and started on the next. "You may have noticed my current lack of useful assistants. Unless you're volunteering?"

She took a deep breath. "Actually," she said, "yes, I am."

I looked up from my work, momentarily at a loss for words. Terese's face was pale and tense, but there was a stubborn determination there that, for once, wasn't in opposition to something I was trying to do. Hanging out with Rebekah had apparently been good for her. "I accept with thanks," I said. "Grab that bottle from Morse and come over here."

I positioned Sam and Carl in front of the outer door, their legs interlocked and braced against the walls and ceiling. I crouched behind them, *kwi* in one hand, lighter in the other, my six Molotov cocktails at the ready. Terese squatted behind me where she'd be at least a little protected, the other liquor bottles uncapped beside her.

"Okay," I said as yet another thud rocked the car. The Shonkla-raa weren't giving up easily. But then, it wasn't their own personal bodies that were being bruised and battered in the useless attack. "Everyone else, inside the compartment. When the door closes, Bayta, fire up the *kwi*. Five seconds after you do that, have the Spiders open this door. And *only* this door."

"Understood." She hesitated, as if wanting to say more but knowing there was no time. "Be careful."

"And take care of Terese," Rebekah added quietly.

Ten seconds later, the door slid shut behind them, and the *kwi* wrapped around my hand began its activation tingle. "Get ready, Terese," I said as I lit the fuses. "Here we go . . ."

And in front of me, the car door irised open.

The Shonkla-raa had been keeping track of our plans and progress, all right. The door was still opening when, with no sound other than that of the Shonkla-raa command tone that burst in through the open door, a wall of Human and alien flesh surged into the opening as the walkers tried to shove their way inside.

But for once, the Shonkla-raa's magic command tone was working against them. As Terese had already pointed out, the instant the door opened Sam and Carl froze solid, wedged in place and blocking the attack like a set of surrealistic prison bars.

And in that same instant I saw the Shonkla-raa's strategy.

He knew I had the *kwi*, and that I could instantly zap the people who were shoving against the defenders. The problem was that the physical driving force of the surge was coming from the walkers piled up at the rear of the crush, people who were being blocked from the *kwi*'s effects by the rest of the crowd in front of them.

I could reset the *kwi* for one of its three pain settings and try to distract the mind segment that way. But I'd seen Shonkla-raa drive their captive walkers through pain before, and I doubted even my highest setting would stop them. Simply knocking out the front line would be even less useful. The crowd pressing behind them would continue to shove their unconscious bodies forward against the barrier, turning them from active attackers into passive battering rams.

Which left me only one option.

Maybe the Shonkla-raa out there thought I would shy away from the prospect of torching fellow Humans. If so, they'd severely underestimated my resolve. Clenching my teeth, I scooped up one of my Molotov cocktails and lobbed it through the interlocked Spider legs toward the rear of the mob.

A normal glass whiskey bottle would simply have thudded against head or torso and dropped clattering onto the ground. But Quadrail bottles were deliberately designed to be useless as an impact weapon. Instead of thudding into the close-packed people back there, the bottle's flimsy plastic split across its tear lines, scattering the alcohol and burning fuse across the crowd.

My second and third firebombs were in the air before the first one ignited.

Group pain shared through a group mind was one thing. Individual pain—real, live, and immediate—was something else entirely. The forward surge against my barrier seemed to hesitate as I sent my fourth and fifth bombs sailing into the crowd to explode into their own patches of fire.

With a normal mob, under normal circumstances, I would be hearing multiple screams of agony by now. But not this mob. Not these circumstances. Under Shonkla-raa rule the standing order was apparently not to speak unless spoken to. The shock front wavered, then pressed ahead even as the blue-edged flames danced across the hair and shoulders of those behind them.

Over the whistle of the command tone, I heard a sort of gurgling sob. Like the Shonkla-raa, Terese also hadn't expected me to be willing to do whatever needed to be done. But there were no words of reproof or horror, and that single sob was all I heard, and even as I threw my last Molotov cocktail I saw her move two of the uncapped bottles forward into my reach.

But for the moment I wouldn't need them. The attack had hesitated at my second and third bombs. Now, as my sixth detonated into flame, the entire crowd wavered, then drew back a little as the pain flooding the mind segment briefly overrode even the Shonkla-raa's control over it. They only moved a little, not more than half a meter and for no more than a couple of seconds before their new masters regained control and forced them back under their telepathic whip.

But that half meter was all I needed. With the forward pressure from the rear of the crowd no longer pressing the front line against the train and my defender barrier, I leveled the *kwi* at our attackers and squeezed the trigger.

My first target's knees buckled, dropping him into a heap on the platform. I held down the trigger, sweeping the *kwi* back and forth across the line, collapsing them like legs of an overloaded table.

The Shonkla-raa tried to surge them forward again, trying furiously to regain the initiative. But they were too late. With the front line down, the stacks of unconscious bodies had become an impediment to further forward movement, slowing the advance still farther and giving me that much more time to mow them down. If the Fillies were stupid enough or determined enough to keep at it, they would quickly run out of troops.

Unfortunately, they were neither. I'd just started on the third row, with maybe twenty out of the hundred walkers down for the count, when the rest abruptly scattered to the rear and to both sides. I managed to nail three more of them as they ran, and then they were out of range or my line of fire.

I took a deep breath, instantly regretting it as the distant stink of burned clothing and flesh assailed my nostrils. Now that the crowd had dispersed I had a clear view of the burn victims I'd created, lying or writhing on the platform with wisps of smoke curling up from their smoldering bodies. I fired a *kwi* blast into each of them, to at least give them the temporary respite of unconsciousness.

"Clever, Compton," a Filly voice called. "But surely you realize it's all futile. You don't truly think you can hold out against us forever, do you?"

"I don't have to hold out nearly that long," I called back. "Just until the next express train coming through here sees us, figures out something's wrong, and sends an alert to the orbiting transfer station out there. There's a whole contingent of Human soldiers aboard who'd love the chance for a little exercise."

"And will they come into a Quadrail station willing to shoot everyone in sight, including their own people and visiting non-Humans?" the Shonkla-raa countered.

"An interesting question," I agreed. "Shall we find out?"

For a moment the other was silent. I listened to the persistent and increasingly annoying command tone as I peered back and forth through my barrier, trying to figure out where all the walkers had disappeared to. But they'd all gone to ground somewhere out of sight. Only the four Shonkla-raa were still visible, still standing in their generals' line, out of range of my *kwi*.

But if I could get out there and close some of that distance before they could get their walkers close to me . . .

"Your words demonstrate true Shonkla-raa spirit," the spokesman said. "But I do not believe your strength of will is of the same magnitude."

"I just firebombed a dozen of my own people," I reminded him.

"I grant your willingness to wound or kill Humans you do not know," the Shonkla-raa said. "But what about friends and allies? Are you willing to sacrifice them, as well?"

I snorted under my breath. "I think you may be missing the point of why I'm sitting here in this doorway."

"I do not refer to those allies aboard the Quadrail," he said. "I refer to *these* allies." He shouted something in an unfamiliar Fili dialect.

"What's he talking about?" Terese murmured in my ear.

"I don't know," I said, frowning as two Humans and a fifth Filly appeared through the door of one of the cafés. They headed across the line of platforms toward us, and I saw now that the Shonkla-raa was pushing the

Humans ahead of him with his hands wrapped snugly around the backs of their necks.

"Who are they?" Terese asked.

"Can't tell yet," I told her. But both men definitely seemed familiar. They continued forward, the Humans' faces slowly coming into focus—

I caught my breath. One of the men was UN director Biret Losutu. The other was my former employer Larry Cecil Hardin.

I stared at them, a sudden sinking feeling in the pit of my stomach. Losutu, the one man on Earth who knew enough about this war and had the authority to recruit the army I needed. If the Shonkla-raa murdered him, that would be it for any and all help from my own people.

Larry Hardin, the high-profile industrialist whom I'd blackmailed out of a trillion dollars and who would gladly see me twisting in the wind. If the Shonkla-raa murdered *him*, it would be a race as to whether the Shonkla-raa or Hardin's own security force got to me first.

"I don't think either of those are what I'd call a friend or an ally," I called out to the Shonkla-raa, forcing my voice to stay calm and detached. "You got anything else?"

"I offer you a trade," the newcomer called as he brought Losutu and Hardin to a halt, again staying well out of *kwi* range. "These two Human males for the female Terese German."

Behind me, Terese gripped my arm tightly. "Sorry," I called back. "Ms. German and her baby aren't for sale."

"Then we will kill the males," the Shonkla-raa said, his voice darkening. "And then we will kill all the other innocents in the station. And all for nothing, because no help will come from your transfer station. Not ever."

The knot in my stomach tightened another turn. "You don't seriously expect me to believe you've taken over the whole transfer station."

"And you think we could not?" He gave a contemptuous whinny. "Perhaps someday. This day we content ourselves with controlling the Spiders, who in turn control the docking hatchways. No help will arrive, for no help can enter the station."

I grimaced. I'd hoped he wouldn't realize that. "Except that unlike your Quadrail stations, *ours* have manual overrides," I said, trying one final bluff.

"They do not," the Shonkla-raa said flatly. "I make the offer again: Terese German for these two males."

"Compton!" Losutu called. "Don't—" He broke off with a strangled gurgle.

"What are we going to do?" Terese asked tensely.

I chewed at my lip. Unfortunately, the Shonkla-raa was right. We were trapped here, with no hope of help from Earth or the Spiders, facing five Shonkla-raa and probably seventy-five or more functional walkers. No matter what kind of defenses we were able to cobble together, sooner or later they would find a way through or else would overwhelm us with sheer numbers.

There was nothing more I could do in here except stall for time. Out there, though, I might find a weakness I could exploit. "Counteroffer," I called. "You release the two males, forget about Ms. German, and you can have me."

Terese's grip on my arm tightened. "Do you then consider yourself worth as much as the female?" the Shonkla-raa called.

"*Osantra* Riijkhan seemed to think so," I said. "He offered to give the whole Terran Confederation a get-out-of-tyranny-free card if I came over to your side."

"Is that what you offer in exchange for these Humans?"

"I'm offering to leave the train in exchange for them being allowed to join my friends in here," I said. "Whether I'll actually work for you is a different negotiation for a different day."

There was another pause. Then, below the whistling

of the command tone I caught the low murmur of hurried conversation in that same Fili dialect. They knew I was up to something, and were probably trying to decide whether the risk of me springing some trap was worth getting me out of the train.

Terese was clearly thinking along the same lines. "You can't leave us," she murmured. "If you do, they'll get us. All of us."

"Don't worry," I said, wishing I had an iota of reason for her not to. If the Shonkla-raa still hoped they could turn me, I might have enough time to find the weakness I was hoping for.

If they'd decided I wasn't worth any more of their effort, I'd be dead thirty seconds after I stepped out onto the platform.

"We accept your offer," the Shonkla-raa holding Losutu and Hardin called, switching back to English. "Open your barrier and come out."

I took a deep breath. This was, I knew, very possibly the last stupid mistake I would ever make. But stupid or not, it was the only chance we had. "You'll have to drop your command tone for a minute," I called back. "The Spiders are wedged in the doorway. I can't move them— they'll need to be mobile enough to move themselves."

There was another silence. "Shonkla-raa?" I prompted. "Come on, read the logic. You want me out there, you'll have to drop the tone."

"You will leave the Spiders and exit from a different door."

"The Spiders have been ordered to keep the other doors closed," I said. "Bayta can't override them from the compartment here."

"Then she may leave the compartment."

"When hell freezes over," I retorted. "It's this door, or none at all. Now shut off the damn command tone."

The Shonkla-raa snarled something I couldn't hear. "You will have ten seconds," he said, his voice low and dark.

"I'll try," I said. "But they're pretty well wedged."

"You will have ten seconds."

Abruptly, the command tone stopped, leaving a sort of auditory afterimage ringing in my ears. "You heard him," I said, tapping Sam's globe. "Or maybe you didn't. Whatever. Come on, time to untangle yourselves."

And then, to my surprise, the tingling of the *kwi* wrapped around my hand stopped.

I threw a reflexive glance at the wall of the compartment beside me. Surely Bayta wouldn't have deactivated the weapon now, with the defenders about to move out of the door and us at our most vulnerable. Had something happened to her?

Apparently not. A fraction of a second later, with the usual tingle, the *kwi* came back on.

And then went off again. And then on, and then off, and then on and then off. I lifted my hand, peering closely at the weapon, wondering if the thing was finally starting to fall apart. That would be just perfect, for us to lose our single best weapon right when we needed it most—

I frowned. The *kwi* wasn't just sputtering. It was sputtering in a pattern. A bit clumsy and amateurish, but a pattern nonetheless. A pattern that Bayta didn't know, but was probably being dictated to her by someone else in the compartment.

Someone like, say, a EuroUnion Security Service agent who'd probably been teased the entire week he and his fellow trainees were learning the aptly named Morse code.

And the message itself—

McMicking here.

The message began to repeat. Casually, I lowered my hand again, my heart thudding with new hope. Hope, and a bit of embarrassment. Of course McMicking was here—Larry Hardin was here, and McMicking was his chief troubleshooter. It only made sense that McMicking would be here with him.

And with that, we now had a genuine chance. The

Spiders obviously knew about McMicking, and it was only because of the Shonkla-raa tone freezing out their system that they hadn't been able to pass that information on to Bayta until now.

The Spiders knew, and now we knew. More importantly, the Shonkla-raa *didn't* know.

Of course, the Spiders probably didn't know what McMicking's plan was, and I sure as hell didn't. But whatever it was, there might be a way to help it along a little.

"Here's the plan," I said quietly to Terese. "Go to the compartment and tell Bayta—"

I broke off as the Shonkla-raa tone resumed, again freezing the defenders in place. "Not done," I called, peering out through the tangle of Spider legs. "I need more time."

"You have had all you need," he called back.

"You want me out there or not?" I countered. "If you do, I'm going to need more time."

The Filly's mouth moved as he muttered something under his breath. "Ten more seconds."

The tone again shut off. "Go back to the compartment and tell Bayta I'm going to try to get to the engine," I told Terese as I continued helping the defenders untangle themselves. "I'll pull out as many of the walkers as I can from the wheels and drive mechanism. With luck, I'll get enough of them clear that she'll be able to get the train moving again before the Shonkla-raa can react."

"But what about you?" Terese asked. "We can't just leave you here."

"Don't worry about me," I said. "They want me alive, remember? You just focus on getting yourself and the rest of the train out of here and going for help. Bayta will know how and where to do that."

Outside, the tone again resumed. "And take this with you," I added, handing her the *kwi*. On the platform, out of Bayta's range, the weapon would be useless to me, and I had no intention of letting the Shonkla-raa get hold of it. "Go," I ordered, giving her a little push.

Her face was screwed up halfway to tears, but she gave a jerky nod and hurried back to the compartment. I waited until the door had closed behind her, then pulled the refrozen defenders out of the way. Taking a deep breath, I stepped outside, standing still until I felt the slight movement of air that meant the car door had irised shut behind me.

"Welcome, Frank Compton," the Shonkla-raa holding Losutu and Hardin called, and there was no mistaking the malicious satisfaction in his voice. "We have waited for this moment for a long time. A long, long time."

TWENTY-EIGHT :

"Have you, now," I said, trying to sound casual and suave, the way a proper dit-rec detective would sound under these circumstances. "It's so nice to bring happiness into people's lives." I started toward him and his hostages.

And two steps later, I abruptly spun to my left and broke into a flat-out sprint.

Only to discover a double line of walkers already standing between me and the engine.

I slowed to a halt again, letting my lip twist as I looked back at the Shonkla-raa. "I seem to have been anticipated," I said lamely.

"Did you really think such an obvious attack point would escape our notice?" the Shonkla-raa asked contemptuously. "Look also at the train cars behind you."

I turned. About thirty of the walkers who'd retreated in that direction in the face of my earlier *kwi* attack were standing alertly alongside the compartment car, ready to counter any move I might make in that direction. The rest of the group, another fifteen or twenty of them, had wedged themselves into the wheels of the compartment car and the first-class coach car behind it. "You see," the Shonkla-raa continued. "Even had you reached the engine, your efforts would have been futile."

"I suppose," I said, letting just enough chagrin make it into my voice to sound like I was stifling a whole lot more.

And trying very hard not to smile.

Because my impromptu gambit had actually worked. In an effort to counter the ridiculous plan I'd spun for Terese, the Shonkla-raa had now made twenty percent of their remaining force unavailable for a quick response.

I looked up at the window of our appropriated cabin, making sure to keep the same stifled chagrin on my face. Bayta and Morse were gazing out at me, Bayta's face tense, Morse's that of a poker player who's just put all his chips into the pot but has no idea what his hole card is.

And then, as I started to look away, something else caught my eye. In the compartment next to theirs a large piece of paper covered with alien writing was being pulled away from the window, and I caught a glimpse of another of the scrawny Fillies who'd been dogging our trail ever since at least Venidra Carvo.

So that was how the Shonkla-raa out here had been apprised of my charge-the-engine plan. I let a little more chagrin into my expression, just in case the Filly or anyone else in that compartment was also watching.

I heard the sound of footsteps over the noise of the command tone, and turned as half a dozen of the walkers who'd been blocking my path to the engine came up to me. My official reception committee, apparently. The two in front, a Jurian diplomat and a pudgy Human wearing a banker's scarf with a half-open courier's briefcase still slung across his chest, took my wrists and turned me toward Losutu and Hardin and their Shonkla-raa keeper. "Okay, I'm here," I called. "You can let them go now."

"In good time," the Shonkla-raa called back. The Juri and Human gave simultaneous tugs on my wrists and we headed across the platform, the other four walkers following close behind us.

I glanced around the station as we walked. The non-walkers who'd been watching bemusedly from afar when this whole thing started had vanished, probably cowering in disbelief and horror in the cafés and gift shops, wondering what in hell was going on.

There was no sign of McMicking. Wherever the others had gone to ground, he'd apparently gone with them.

The Spiders, in contrast, were still standing where they'd been when our train pulled in, just as frozen and useless as before. A pity, I thought, that Bayta hadn't been able to do something with them when the command tone was off. But then, she'd only had a pair of ten-second intervals to work with, and I doubted the Shonkla-raa would have missed any sort of concerted action. Even if Bayta had found anything that the permanently nonviolent creatures could actually do for us.

And then, something caught my eye. The Spiders were indeed still where they'd been standing. But their postures had subtly changed. Every one of them was now standing on only six of their seven legs, with the seventh leg folded up beneath their domes.

And all of those folded legs were pointed off to my left.

Casually, I let my gaze wander in that direction. The Spiders were pointing toward a pair of drudge Spiders about a hundred meters away along the axis of the station from where Losutu and Hardin were standing. The drudges were also perched on six legs, leaning toward each other in unstable-looking poses, their unused legs pointed downward toward a partially open service access airlock.

The implication was clear. It also made no sense.

Because the airlock didn't actually go anywhere. Not unless there was a maintenance skiff attached to the other side. Even if there was, we would have no way of getting into it. We would need a Spider to close the air-lock's upper hatch and open the lower one, and thanks to the Shonkla-raa all the Spiders were temporarily out of service. All we could do, even assuming I could free the hostages and get to the airlock ahead of the Shonkla-raa, would be to stand there in the pit and wait for the walkers to stroll over and pull us out again.

But the signs were too clear to be misinterpreted. Clearly, Bayta wanted me to go there.

I squared my shoulders. She'd trusted me often enough during our time together. Now it was my turn.

The Shonkla-raa was still gripping his hostages' necks when my escort and I arrived. "Okay, I've made good on my half of the bargain," I said. "Your turn."

"In good time," the Shonkla-raa said, eyeing me curiously. His nose blaze, I saw now, had the same sort of slanted lines through it that I'd also seen on *Osantra* Riijkhan. Coincidence? Or were the Shonkla-raa blaze-coding their field commanders?

"That's what you said about seventy meters ago," I reminded him, nodding over my shoulder toward the train. "You've got me. Let them go."

"You are not what I expected," Slant Nose continued. "A hero of the Humans should be taller." He cocked his head. "He should also have a longer nose."

"Now you're just being ridiculous," I growled. "You never intended to let them go, did you?"

"A hero of the Humans also requires proper motivation if he is to cooperate with his new masters," Slant Nose said. "I have no intention of allowing this mission to fail as have others." His blaze darkened. "Nor will I allow the deaths of my comrades to go unavenged."

My throat tightened. So it was going to be a quick death after all. "*Osantra* Riijkhan won't like it if I arrive in damaged condition," I warned, trying to stall for time. Where the *hell* was McMicking?

"Even *Osantra* Riijkhan does not obtain everything he desires," Slant Nose countered. Behind me, one of the men from my escort detached himself from the group and stepped in front of me. His hand dipped into the banker's briefcase and pulled out a mite Spider, its slender legs sticking out rigidly from its fist-sized globe.

And in a single smooth motion, the man turned and jammed the Spider into Slant Nose's neck, burying the stiffened legs in the other's oversized throat.

Without a word, or even a dying gurgle, the Shonklaraa dropped to the ground.

I had just enough time to let my mouth drop open in surprise when the man spun back around and dropped my two handlers with quick jabs to the Juri's throat and the Human's solar plexus. "You can thank me later," McMicking said, deftly snatching the briefcase from around the banker's neck and shoulder as he fell. "Everyone—to the café. We'll make our stand there."

"No," I said, spinning around as the three remaining walkers in my escort—or rather, their distant Shonklaraa controllers—broke free from their shock and attacked. I dropped one with a side kick to the knee, evaded another's arms as he tried to throw a bear hug around me, then jabbed him in the ribs and then behind his ear. The third gave a sudden whimper and staggered backward, clutching at a pale red liquid that had suddenly appeared on his face.

"Here," McMicking said, thrusting a bright yellow restaurant condiment squeeze bottle into my hand. "Why not the café?"

"We go by those two drudges," I said, pointing. Back by the train, the line of walkers broke into a concerted charge toward us.

"You heard the man," McMicking said, giving the still goggling Losutu and Hardin a shove each. "*Move* it."

"Come on," Losutu said. He slapped Hardin's shoulder for emphasis, and the two men took off, running as if all of hell was after them.

Which, in a very real sense, it was.

"Nice timing, as always," I said to McMicking as we watched the approaching wave of walkers. I felt a flicker of satisfaction as I watched the ones jammed into the train's wheels struggling madly to extricate themselves so that they could join in the party. "Any other useful items in your bag of tricks?"

"One or two," McMicking said, reaching into the briefcase and pulling out a familiar set of nunchakus. "Here—Fayr let me keep this as a souvenir."

"Amazing the sort of things that end up in a banker's briefcase," I commented, taking the nunchakus and tucking one of the sticks in ready position under my arm. Even with a weapon, I was going to have my work cut out for me.

And not just with the walkers, either. The four remaining Shonkla-raa were on the move too, their layered tunics flapping in the breeze as they charged toward us.

"No one ever said it was the banker's briefcase," McMicking pointed out. "I just slipped it over his neck in the crowd and the Shonkla-raa came to the correctly wrong conclusion. They really do need to learn to ask the right questions."

"And to take an occasional roll call?"

"And to work out the bugs in their overlapping chain of command structure," McMicking agreed. "With five of them giving orders to different groups of walkers, I figured I could slip into the group without anyone noticing. Go easy on that squeeze bottle, by the way—that's chili sauce, full strength, courtesy of the station gift shop. You want to put the walkers out of action, not blind them outright."

"Right," I said, glancing back at Hardin and Losutu. "You think they've got enough of a lead yet?"

"Give it another couple of seconds," McMicking said. "Our long-nosed friends are nearly through the crowd."

They were, too, I saw, their legs pumping hard as they caught up to the walkers' leading shock front. I half expected the Shonkla-raa to simply charge straight through the crowd in their wrath, scattering Humans and aliens to all sides.

But even in their fury at McMicking and me they weren't stupid enough to waste allies that way. The line of running walkers opened up smoothly in front of each of the Shonkla-raa in response to their telepathic orders, letting the faster Fillies through. "I hope you're not expecting them to run themselves too ragged to whistle their happy little tune," I warned.

"Not exactly," McMicking said. "What's over there with the drudges?"

"An open service hatchway," I told him. "What we do once we're there, I haven't a clue."

He grunted. "Well, the Spiders have already proved themselves useful today," he said. "I'm willing to see what else they've come up with. Okay, here we go. Your job is to take out anyone still standing."

I frowned. *Still standing*?

And as the four Shonkla-raa closed to within five meters, McMicking thrust the open banker's briefcase toward them, sending a clattering wave of hundreds of clear plastic marble-sized spheres bouncing and rolling across the floor toward them.

The Shonkla-raa didn't have a chance. They hit the rolling hazards at a dead run, their feet flying as the ground suddenly slid out from under them. Three of the Fillies went down instantly, slamming hard onto torsos and backs, the impact sending more of the marbles scooting off in all directions. The fourth was fighting to stay upright when my nunchaku slammed across the side of his head, putting him down with the others.

Behind the sprawled Shonkla-raa, the incoming wave of walkers hit the marbles, and Humans and Juriani and Halkas joined the Fillies in twisting and thudding helplessly to the ground.

And then, even as I aimed my nunchaku toward the next Shonkla-raa in line, he rose half up onto his hands and screamed.

It was a scream unlike any I'd ever heard from a Filly, loud and ululating and enraged, and it froze me in my tracks as effectively as the thunderclap from a stun grenade. With a supreme effort I shook off the paralyzing effects and raised my nunchaku again—

The blow went wide as McMicking grabbed my arm. "Time to go," he snapped, shooting a healthy glob of chili sauce from his own squeeze bottle into the Filly's eyes. "More company coming."

I looked over at the station buildings as I abandoned my attack and headed after McMicking. Pouring out of the café and gift shops were more Fillies, at least two dozen of them, all heading our way.

The next time you come after me, I'd told the late *Usantra* Wandek at Proteus Station, *you'd better bring all of you.*

Someday, I really should stop delivering challenges like that.

"I hope," McMicking called over his shoulder, "that the Spiders have one hell of an ace up their sleeves."

"Me, too," I said grimly, my heart sinking as I quickly reassessed the situation. The drudges, I'd already noted, were about a hundred meters away. Losutu and Hardin had covered over half that distance, and even though they were slower than McMicking and me they would make it to the access hatchway well before either what was left of the line of walkers or the new wave of Shonkla-raa. The timing for McMicking and me was a little iffier, but unless the Shonkla-raa were significantly faster than the standard Filly—which they very well could be—we ought to make it all right.

Which still left the question of what we were going to do once we got there.

We'd covered about half the distance, and Losutu and Hardin had reached the drudges and were slowing to a somewhat uncertain stop, when the wind in my face suddenly disappeared.

I frowned as I realized the strangeness of that. The wind was caused by me running through the air. I was still running. How could the wind stop?

I was still trying to figure it out when the wind started up again.

Only now it was blowing against the *back* of my head. As if I'd unknowingly started running backward, or as if the station air itself was on the move.

And with a horrified jolt, I understood.

Shifting my attention from the drudges and hatchway, I peered down the long axis of the station. In the distance, nearly masked by the Coreline's own coruscating multi-colored light show, I could see the faint ring of flashing red warning lights around the far end of the station.

The Spiders had opened the atmosphere barrier.

"McMicking!" I called.

"I know," he called back. "Save your breath for running."

I grimaced as the wind at my back began to intensify. Save my breath for running, and for survival.

I don't know when the Shonkla-raa figured it out. Probably not long after I did. Possibly even before. But as the wind started to edge toward gale strength I heard the command tone filling the station becoming fainter. Not just from the rapidly thinning atmosphere, but also because the Shonkla-raa also recognized the need to conserve air and were alternating the command tone among them, each Filly whistling for only a few seconds at a time before passing it on to the next.

Losutu and Hardin were still standing by the open hatchway as McMicking and I ran up to them. "The air!" Losutu barked frantically, the words almost inaudible in the turbulent wind blowing against him. He jabbed a finger at the end of the station.

"We know," McMicking shouted back. "Get into the airlock—now."

"There are air tanks down there," I added.

It took another half second for that to penetrate. Then Losutu's face brightened with sudden hope, and he grabbed Hardin's arm and jumped them both through the hatchway.

"Hang on," I called as McMicking started to follow, my eyes on the frozen drudges looming over us. Up close, they looked even more precariously balanced than they had from a distance, leaning over the airlock hatchway as if they'd been turned to statues just as they were about to fall in. . . .

On impulse, I jumped up beneath one, grabbing one of the inward-leaning legs at the top of my arc. A second later, I landed with a thud beside a startled Losutu as the drudge crashed down across the hatchway above me, its tangled legs neatly blocking half of the airlock opening.

McMicking was nothing if not a fast learner. I'd barely recovered my balance when he landed a couple of meters away from me, bringing the other drudge down across the rest of the gap. "We need to tether them!" he called.

"First things first," I said, looking around the airlock. My vision was dancing with flickering white spots, a telltale sign that I was within seconds of blacking out from oxygen deprivation. I spotted a row of oxygen tanks along one wall and hurried over to the first one in line.

The valve was screwed on tight, and for a moment I thought I was going to die right there with my hand still on the valve. But then it came free, and a flood of cold, dry, delicious air blew across my face.

"Over here," I called to the others, taking a few more deep breaths and then moving to the next tank in line and opening it. "I don't see any masks—you'll have to just stick your faces into the flow."

"And go easy," McMicking warned as he maneuvered Hardin and Losutu into the twin streams I'd set up. "We don't know how much we've got, or how long we'll need it. Compton?"

"Right." I took a couple more breaths, then crossed to where McMicking was unhooking a coil of safety line from one of the other walls. I took one end and jumped up to thread it over two of the drudge's legs.

And twitched my arm violently away as a Filly hand darted through one of the gaps and tried to grab me.

I dropped back to the floor, crouching down as a second hand jabbed toward me. Across the airlock, I saw that McMicking had the other end of the coil looped around the other drudge's legs and was tying it to a large lock ring fastened to the wall.

Or rather, trying to tie it. His hands, I noticed suddenly, were fumbling uncertainly with the line.

There was a blast of air in my ear, and I turned to see Losutu coming toward me, one of the oxygen tanks in his arms with the nozzle pointed toward me. I took two quick breaths and jerked my thumb toward McMicking. Losutu nodded and headed toward the other, and I bent to the task of fastening my end of the line to another of the lock rings. I finished it and turned around.

And stiffened. McMicking was lying on the floor, unmoving, the oxygen tank near him but spraying its air uselessly in the wrong direction. Losutu was hanging just beneath the drudge, fighting weakly against the Filly hand that had reached through another of the gaps and was holding him by his neck.

Two seconds later, I was at McMicking's side, crouching low in case there were more Shonkla-raa out there still conscious enough to go fishing for Humans. I rolled the oxygen tank over, positioning it so that it was spraying its air supply toward McMicking. Standing up again, I pulled the squeeze bottle of chili sauce from my pocket, aimed as best I could, and sent a stream of the fiery liquid squarely into the Shonkla-raa's face.

There would probably have been a bellow of pain if the other had had enough air to bellow with. The hand around Losutu's throat slackened, but before I could pull it free it tightened again.

Grimacing, I gave the Shonkla-raa's face another squirt of sauce. This time, the hand didn't even twitch.

There was another stream of air at the back of my head. I turned to find Hardin coming up behind me, the other oxygen tank hissing toward me.

And as I inhaled the splotchy white spots out of my vision, he slapped the grip of a long, narrow-bladed screwdriver into my hand.

I turned, and with a silent snarl I jabbed the tip of the screwdriver with all my strength into the back of the Shonkla-raa's wrist. With a violent spasm, the hand finally opened, dropping Losutu to the floor.

I tried to catch him. But the lack of air had dulled my speed and sapped my strength, and the best I could do was partially break his fall. He landed heavily beside the tank that was slowly reviving McMicking. I motioned Hardin to get down beside him, then finished tying off the tether line.

Not that the Shonkla-raa were likely to be coming in after us. Not now. The Shonkla-raa I'd stabbed was lying across the drudge's legs, his bloodied arm still hanging limply through the opening. He was dead, or close enough. So presumably were the rest of his colleagues.

So was Losutu.

We were huddled together on the floor, one of us dead, the rest of us barely alive, pressed close around the second to last of the airlock's oxygen tanks, when the Spiders finally came for us.

TWENTY-NINE :

"I understand," Morse said quietly from beside me, "that the whole thing's being filed under the heading of a tragic accident."

I nodded silently as I gazed across the station at the rows of bodies, and the grim-faced soldiers and medics from the transfer station carrying the stretchers to the shuttle hatchways.

Two hundred and fifty-six dead. Five survivors, aside from McMicking, Hardin, and me, all of them in critical condition. The Quadrail schedule crashed, with ever-growing disruptive ripples flowing out across the galaxy in both transportation and the critical area of interstellar messages and other communication.

An accident.

"What about the passengers on the train?" I asked. "Are they saying anything?"

"Nothing of interest," Morse said. "Bayta was able to get all the display windows opaqued before anyone saw anything."

I nodded. "Small favors."

He nodded back. "Bloody small."

For another minute we stood in silence, watching the grisly cleanup duty. The Shonkla-raa bodies, not surprisingly, had all been spirited away by the Spiders before emergency teams had even been called. Under other circumstances, I reflected, such subterfuge would have been futile, given how many witnesses had seen them.

In this case, most of those witnesses were already dead, and the rest of us weren't talking.

"Is Bayta still with Losutu?" I asked.

"Yes, I think so," Morse said. "The others are down the hall, keeping Hardin company while the Cohn aerator cleans out his lungs. Looks like most of the damage is repairable."

"Good to hear," I said. I didn't have any particular

affection for the man, but we'd lost enough people for one day.

"Yes," Morse said. He hesitated. "McMicking is also telling him everything about the Shonkla-raa."

I grimaced. But there was no way we were going to hide this one under the rug. Not from Hardin. "I trust he made it clear that Hardin needs to keep all this secret?"

"Very clear," Morse said. "Under pain of death, actually."

"Which probably doesn't mean much to Hardin."

"Coming from McMicking?" Morse smiled tightly. "More than you might think." He nodded toward the medical center. "Go on over, if you'd like. I can handle any last-minute questions Colonel Savali might have."

"Thanks," I said. I took a deep breath, wincing at the brief stab of pain in my lungs and ribs, and headed toward the medical center.

Sam and Carl, naturally, were right behind me.

In any normal disaster of this magnitude, a medical facility this size would have been swamped. Here, with barely enough survivors to fill a vacationers' travel van, the place was eerily empty.

Losutu's body had been put on the bed in one of the treatment rooms, laid out almost as if he was lying in state. Seated in a chair beside him, gazing expressionlessly into space, was Bayta.

Pulling another chair over, I sat down beside her, trying to ignore the two defenders as they tapped off into the corner behind us. "Hi," I said quietly.

She didn't answer. I reached over and took her hand. It was cold, and felt as lifeless as the body in front of us. I thought of telling her it was okay, or that we'd won, or any of a hundred different inane platitudes.

Instead, I just held her hand and kept quiet.

I don't know how long we sat there. Probably no more than five minutes. Finally, she stirred. "Two hundred and fifty-six innocent people," she said softly. "I killed them, Frank. I opened the atmosphere barriers, and I killed them."

"You had no other choice," I reminded her gently.

"Didn't I?" she asked. "I keep thinking there must have been something else I could have done."

"Every soldier who's ever been in combat has had those doubts," I told her. "Once it's all over, when you're out of the heat of battle and the need for split-second decisions, you always think back and wonder what you could have done differently. Sometimes those thoughts are legitimate, and you realize too late that doing something else would have changed the outcome. But usually they're not."

I nodded toward the wall and the station beyond it. "For whatever it's worth, I've been out of the heat of battle for over four hours now, and I still can't see anything else you could have done. Nothing that wouldn't have gotten all of us killed and still not saved any of the lives that were lost. I can't think of anything McMicking, Morse, or I could have done, either."

"So you're saying I shouldn't worry about the cost? That the cost was inevitable?"

"The cost was determined by the Shonkla-raa, not you," I said firmly. "It was defined the minute they chose this time and place for their attack. It's like the terror wars—an enemy who uses innocent civilians as shields has already decreed that some of those civilians will be killed. If you're going to fight someone like that, you either have to accept that there's going to be heavy collateral damage, or you have to capitulate. Those are your only choices."

She sighed. "It was still my idea. My plan. I can't just brush all those deaths aside."

"I wouldn't want you to," I said. "They were people, and they deserve our honor and respect. Part of that respect is to minimize such deaths wherever you can. The other part is to make sure they died for a reason, that their lives were given so that others might live. In this case, those others are going to number in the billions."

"Will they?" Bayta asked, the last word almost a sob. "We haven't stopped them, Frank. Not today, not any other time we've tried. They just keep coming and coming. Sooner or later, they're going to win."

"No, they aren't," I said, reaching into my pocket. "Because—"

I broke off. There were footsteps coming toward our door. Shifting my hand to a different pocket, I got a grip on the *kwi*.

The door opened, and McMicking and Hardin walked in. "Yes, they're here," McMicking called to someone still out in the hallway.

"Hail the conquering hero," Hardin said with only a hint of sarcasm. His eyes flicked to the two defenders, then came back to me. "How are you holding up?"

"A little lung and ear damage," I said as Rebekah and Terese walked in and joined the party. "Nothing a layered QuixHeal regimen won't solve. You?"

"My lung damage sounds a little more serious than yours, but the doctor said I'll be all right," he told me. "McMicking tells me you've been fighting these Shonkla-raa bastards and their allies ever since you left my employ. He also tells me you were hoping to get Director Losutu to help you raise a private army."

"You offering to take his place?" I asked.

"I may be," Hardin said. "I didn't know Losutu well, but I respected the man." Almost reluctantly, I thought, his eyes drifted to Losutu's body. "Besides which, the damn horse-faces had the same thing planned for me. He and I both got identical messages, seven days ago, asking us to come up here and meet with a high-ranking *usantra* about some big deal they were thinking about offering Earth and Hardin Industries."

"Fortunately, I returned from my own trip a few hours before the meeting was to take place," McMicking put in. "I lasered a message to Earth before leaving the station, just as a matter of routine, and when they lasered back that Mr. Hardin was on his way to meet with some Filiaelians I decided I'd better stick around."

"Good thing you did, too," I said.

"So you're still going with this army thing?" Terese asked hesitantly. "I mean . . . you really think an Earth army can fight them?"

I took a deep breath, looking at each of their faces in turn. It was time, I knew. It was finally time. "No, we're not doing the army plan anymore," I said. "Not after what happened here today. Bayta's right—we can't beat them this way. "

"Sure we can," Hardin said. "We just need—"

"*No*, we *can't*," I said bluntly. "Furthermore, I'm not going to subject the people of the Confederation to any more of this kind of butchery."

"So we're just giving up?" Terese demanded.

"Not at all," I said. "We can't fight them, so we're going to isolate them."

"How?" McMicking asked.

"There are three super-express lines between this side of the galaxy and the Filly side," I said. "Plus probably a couple hundred local lines linking their worlds with the Shorshic Congregate. I propose we destroy every one of those links, starting with the super-express Tubes."

"Frank?" Bayta murmured tensely. "Do you really want to be talking about this?"

"She's right," Hardin seconded. "We *need* the Quadrail, Compton. We need the commerce, the transportation—"

"And we'll keep all that," I cut him off. "All we're going to lose is the Filiaelian Assembly. The Shonkla-raa are Fillies? Fine—let the Fillies deal with them."

"Supposing we agree in principle," McMicking said, eyeing me closely. "How would you do that?"

I hesitated. If Bayta hadn't liked the first part of my speech, she was going to absolutely hate this part. "I know where there's a group of warships," I said, lowering my voice. "*Big* warships, leftovers from the first Shonkla-raa war sixteen hundred years ago. We'll activate one of them, fly it out to the super-express Tubes, and blow them up."

"Wait a minute," Hardin said, straightening up a bit. "There are starships out there? *Real* starships, that travel faster than light and everything?"

"Not on their own, no," I said. "But I'm told there's a way to piggyback with Quadrail travel. I think we need to fly in synch with one of the trains, only on the other side of the Tube wall—something like that. Don't worry, we've got time to figure it out."

"Where are these ships located?" Rebekah asked, her expression a mix of cautious trust plus outright disbelief that I would ever talk about such things out loud. It was probably the same expression Bayta was wearing right now. Not that I dared to look.

"That's where we start getting clever," I told her. "They're buried near a place called Proteus."

"*Proteus*?" Terese asked, her eyes widening. "Proteus *Station*? The place we just got chased out of?"

"Actually, no," I said. "But I'm hoping that's what the Shonkla-raa will think."

Terese shot a bewildered look at Rebekah. "I don't get it."

I sighed. "Look. The word about the ships is bound to get out. The Modhri will know about them—he has to; we're going to need his help in tracking the Shonkla-raa's movements—and sooner or later the Shonkla-raa will grab a walker and ask him what I'm planning."

A look of comprehension blossomed on Rebekah's face. "And he'll say the warships are near Proteus."

"Exactly," I said. "We know the Shonkla-raa are really sloppy about asking the right questions. With luck, they'll jump to the conclusion Terese just did and scramble to meet us at Proteus Station. By the time they realize their mistake, we'll be on our way to cutting them off from the rest of the galaxy forever."

"Where are the ships actually located?" Hardin asked.

"On a world called Veerstu, in the Nemuti FarReach," I said. "Not too far from a place called the Ten Mesas."

"Excellent," Hardin said briskly. "I have some interests in the FarReach. I should be able to get the people we need in there without attracting attention."

I frowned. "What people?"

"Were you planning to fly this warship around all by yourself?" Hardin asked. "I, on the other hand, have whole battalions of pilots, navigators, and engineers."

"Of course—why didn't I think of that?" I said sarcastically. "And their licenses for ancient Shonkla-raa spacecraft are current?"

Hardin's lip twitched. "I hadn't thought about that," he admitted.

"Fortunately, we should be able to give them a head start," I said, taking Bayta's hand. "Bayta's studied the Shonkla-raa language. She can at least teach your pilots how to read the controls and gauges."

Bayta stirred, and I sensed her getting ready to protest that she wouldn't know ancient Shonkla-raa if it took out ad space on her eyelids. I squeezed her hand warningly, and she remained silent.

"But it will take a while for them to slog through all of it," I continued. "Eight weeks, maybe a little more."

"Two months is a hell of a long time in warfare," Hardin pointed out. "Are we expecting the Shonkla-raa to just sit on their hands while we're off deciphering their hieroglyphics?"

"Yes, actually, we are," I said. "Because while Bayta's playing language professor, I'll be sending a message to *Osantra* Riijkhan offering to reopen negotiations for me to go over to their side."

Hardin snorted. "You really think he'll buy that?"

"Why not?" I said. "He's already offered protection for the Confederation in return for my services. After today's object lesson, it would only make sense that I might be reconsidering his offer."

"That's an easy enough game to play as long as you can stay on Earth," McMicking pointed out. "What happens if he wants to meet with you somewhere else, where we can't protect you?"

"We'll cross that bridge when we get to it," I said. "Are we agreed, then?"

There was a moment of silence. "There are a lot of details we haven't touched on," Hardin said. "But we've got time to work those out. Fine. Hardin Industries is in."

McMicking half lifted a hand. "So am I."

"You're part of Hardin Industries," Hardin reminded him dryly. He cocked an eyebrow at me. "So are you, Compton, if you want to be."

"You mean reinstatement?" I shook my head. "Thanks, but it's bad enough I have to work with a man who employs people like our friend from the super-express. I don't think I could handle being on the actual payroll."

Hardin hissed out an impatient sigh. "I already told McMicking, Compton. Now I'll tell you. He was working entirely alone. *Yes*, he was working for me; and *yes*, I had him on a very loose leash. Too loose, as it turned out. But as you may recall, I gave *you* the same freedom when *you* worked for me."

"Leashes aside, you're also the one who created his neat little bag of tricks," I reminded him.

"And you should be damn glad I did," he countered. "Those bouncy marbles McMicking used against the Shonkla-raa out there? They came onto the Tube as protective bubble wrap."

I frowned at McMicking. "*Bubble* wrap?"

"Two-centimeter-diameter air-filled plastic spheres set between two thin sheets of plastic," he confirmed. "The stuff looks and acts just like normal protective wrap, except that the spheres are three-hundred-kilo test weight. Pull the two enclosing sheets apart, and the spheres drop out, ready to use."

"Very neat," I said.

"The point is that I may have equipped the bastard,

but I never authorized his plan," Hardin said. "That was all him."

"Fine," I said. "*My* point is that I'm not working for Hardin Industries anymore. I'll work *with* you, but not for you."

Hardin grimaced, but nodded. "Fair enough," he said. "Would you be willing to at least accept a ride back to Earth? My torchyacht is faster than anything you could rent at the transfer station, and a lot more secure."

"That one I'll be more than happy to accept," I assured him. "Why don't you and McMicking go find Morse and see if he can talk Colonel Savali into letting us leave the station. Terese, you and Rebekah might as well go with them. We'll be along in a minute."

"Right," McMicking said before anyone could object. "Mr. Hardin?"

"Just make it fast," Hardin warned me as he headed toward the door. "I'm suddenly not liking this place very much."

"We'll be right there," I promised.

They filed out, the door closing again behind them. "You do realize," Bayta said into the silence, "that I don't know enough ancient Shonkla-raa to teach a fifteen-minute class."

"That's okay," I said. "I wasn't going to have them spend more than fifteen minutes on it anyway."

She frowned. "Then why an eight-week delay?"

"Two reasons," I said. "First, there *is* an actual course of study I want Hardin's people to take. And second, we need to give the fleeing rats a place to flee to."

"Which fleeing rats?"

"All of them," I said. Reaching into my pocket, I pulled out the data chip I'd been about to show her before McMicking and the others interrupted. "The thing that's been nagging at me the whole time was *why* they chose Terra Station for this confrontation, and why they made it so big. Why in the world would they risk this kind of exposure in a full-blown battlefield assault?"

I handed her the data chip. "So while Morse and I were taking a breather from all the official questioning, I slipped over to the message center to see if the Spiders had anything for me."

Bayta fingered the chip, making no move to pull out her reader. "And?"

"It's my version of the same news the Shonkla-raa must have gotten before we arrived," I said. "A report from *Logra* Emikai saying that the Shonkla-raa gene-manipulation facilities aboard Proteus Station have been completely destroyed."

Bayta's eyes widened. "Already?"

"Already," I confirmed. "And when I say completely I mean down to the last DNA molecule. He planned it well, and was able to bring in some of his old friends to assist. That, plus the intel the Modhri provided him, let them launch a single coordinated raid and take down everything." I tapped the chip. "And there's more. Emikai and Director *Usantra* Nstroo were able to find enough proof of the Shonkla-raa activities that a quiet alarm has now been sent out across the entire Assembly. Within weeks, months at the most, the Shonkla-raa are going to be hunted down and captured."

"Or killed," Bayta murmured.

"That's up to the Fillies," I said. "The point is that with their handy genetic assembly line on Proteus up in smoke, there aren't going to be any new Shonkla-raa anytime soon. With their hoped-for future numbers wiped out, and with my well-established knack for thinning their current ranks, they apparently decided I needed to be taken out, one way or another, no matter what the cost. Hence, today's desperate gamble."

Bayta gazed down at the data chip in her hand. "So what you're doing now is baiting them," she said. "You've set up a plan you don't intend to carry out, hoping they'll now come to you." She looked at me, her face pale. "And kill you."

I sighed. "For whatever it's worth, I don't like this any better than you do," I said. "But like you said, we need to get them out into the open." I shrugged. "This was the best bait I could think of."

Bayta took a deep breath. "I just hope you're right."

"Aren't I always?" I countered, trying for a levity I didn't feel. "Ready?"

She braced herself, and I could tell she was dreading the thought of walking the gauntlet of dead bodies out there. "Ready," she said, standing up and handing me back the data chip. "I never liked this war, Frank. But now, I'm starting to hate it."

"No one who's in the middle of a war likes it, Bayta," I said, gently stroking the back of her neck. "But it'll be over soon."

She shivered. "Or at least, our part will be."

I swallowed. "Yes," I agreed. "It will."

We were standing on the platform, waiting while Morse used his EuroUnion Security Service badge to persuade Savali to let us leave the station, when I saw the scrawny Filly from our ill-fated train emerge from the message center. I watched as he turned his back on us and headed toward one of the trains heading toward the Bellidosh Estates-General.

The message I'd sent Riijkhan had gotten through.

And with that, the last of my cards had been played. All that was left was to play out the hand, and see how those cards stacked up against everyone else's.

To see whether we would live or die.

Across the platform, the Shonkla-raa agent boarded his train. Distantly, I wondered if I'd ever see him again.

THIRTY :

The torchyacht trip to Earth was as fast and secure as Hardin had promised it would be. We held endless discussions about strategy and tactics, but what impressed me most was that Hardin's cuisine was the best I'd tasted since we'd left Ambassador ChoDar's Peerage car back at Venidra Carvo.

We landed at Hardin's private spaceport on Long Island late at night, where by prearrangement a heavier than usual contingent of his security force was waiting to meet us. There we said our last farewells to Terese before she, Rebekah, Morse, and a security team left in one of Hardin's air transports to take her on the last leg of her long and tangled journey home.

Even now, after all we'd been through together, she wouldn't talk to Bayta or me about her home and family, or even where home actually was. But I didn't press the point. For one thing, I figured she'd earned a little respect, which for her translated into whatever bits of privacy she could scrape together.

For another, I already knew who and where her family was.

The rest of us boarded another transport and headed in the opposite direction to Hardin's western Idaho estate, where his main security force training center was also located. The two hundred men and women McMicking had requested were already assembled, and after a short night's sleep we got to work.

Eight weeks later, we were ready.

"The teams will leave on the schedule you've been given," McMicking said to the group on our final evening. "Once you reach the Tube, each group of twenty riding on a particular Quadrail will split into pairs. Let me remind you that while you'll all be in the same car or two, each traveling pair is to remain strictly detached from all the others except in a declared emergency situation. Any such declaration will be made by squad leaders, who will determine the proper response and how much pair interaction will be required. Clear?"

Two hundred heads bobbed in silent acknowledgment. "ESS Agent Morse will be going out with the first team," McMicking continued. "He and his team will collect the gear and weapons, which will be shipped separately to the Veerstu transfer station. They'll proceed to the Proteus jump-off point, assess conditions, and bring in the other teams as they arrive. Once you're all assembled, he'll guide you to the actual target area."

He gestured to Bayta and me. "Given the enemy attention we're expecting Compton to draw along the way, he, Bayta, and I will be the last three to arrive, hopefully several hours after the rest of you are in position. If all goes well, we should be assembled, on the ground, and ready to move thirty-eight and a half days from now. Questions?"

This time, none of the heads moved. "All right," McMicking said, turning to me. "Any last words of wisdom, Compton?"

"Just don't try to take over your torchliners," I said. "Everyone knows what rotten passengers pilots make." It was a poor joke, but a few of them smiled politely anyway. "Aside from that, watch yourselves, remember that the Shonkla-raa have non-Shonkla-raa agents who can be almost as troublesome as they are, and keep in mind that Mr. Hardin's tech people went to a lot of trouble creating your weapons and equipment. Treat it carefully and use it well."

"The first transport leaves at oh-three-thirty tomorrow," McMicking said. "Good luck, and we'll see you on Veerstu. Dismissed."

With a rustling of cloth and a muted clattering of chairs the men and women stood up and filed silently from the room. "Well, that's that," McMicking said as we watched them leave. "Any recent word from Riij-khan? I haven't had time to check the message log lately."

"I got one yesterday," I told him. "I'd mentioned in my last note that I was concerned about the mobs that would come after me if I helped them take over the galaxy, so he's now upped his offer to immunity for the Confederation *and* a personal fiefdom for me anywhere in the galaxy I'd like."

"Thoughtful of him," McMicking said. "You have any particular place in mind?"

"I was thinking about Modhra II," I said. "Nice view, out of the way of the average mob, and there's all that under-ice scuba diving available for recreation."

"And maybe a little Modhran coral still left?"

"Could be," I said. "This particular message came from Jurskala, by the way, so he's apparently been traveling again."

"Interesting," McMicking said thoughtfully. "I wonder what he's doing there."

"Probably looking to build himself an entourage," I said. "He's still pressing for me to let him come to Earth for a face-to-face, and he's certainly not going to find a preassembled army of walkers here that he can use."

"Maybe you should tell him that Terese and Rebekah have gone off to Bellis or Misfar or somewhere," McMicking suggested. "See if he's still so hot to come to Earth if they're not here."

"No good—he'd know I'm lying," I said. "He's bound to have a permanent spy nest in Terra Station by now."

"Maybe," McMicking said. "Speaking of Rebekah and Terese, what's the word on them?"

"I talked to Rebekah this morning," Bayta said. "Terese's father is still very upset that Dr. Aronobal reneged on her promise to heal Terese's genetic disorders. Rebekah heard him tell his chief medical director yesterday that he's never working with Filiaelians again."

"I suppose we can count that as a small victory," Mc-

Micking said. "But there are others out there with a handle on that kind of treatment. Maybe he can find someone else who can fix her."

"He *is* trying to interest a Shorshic team in the project." Bayta hesitated. "The big question right now is whether she's healthy enough to bring the baby to term. Rebekah said that, under the circumstances, he's now pressuring her to end the pregnancy."

I thought back to Terese's attempt, back on Venidra Carvo, to do just that. "What are Terese's thoughts?"

"It's strange," Bayta said. "Three months ago, she would have jumped at the offer. But now, she's not so sure. The baby's moving and kicking, and all. *And* she's got Rebekah there, who also has another life inside her."

McMicking grunted. "Not exactly the same thing."

"I know," Bayta said. "But from Terese's point of view it makes them almost kindred spirits. She trusts Rebekah, I think more than she trusts anyone else in the world."

"Considering her opinion of all the rest of us, that wouldn't be very hard," I said.

"Don't be cynical," Bayta reproved me mildly. "In fact, Rebekah said Terese *did* ask about us the other day. Both of us. Rebekah told her we were still busy training Mr. Hardin's team, but that we would come see her as soon as we were able. She *does* like us, Frank."

"You, she likes," I said. "Me, she probably just misses being snide to. Still, it's a service I'm glad to provide. Maybe we can sneak over for a quick visit before we leave."

"I think she'd like that," Bayta said. "Aside from Rebekah, we're the only ones she can really talk to about her baby."

"I gather she hasn't told her family the truth about him?" McMicking asked.

"Rebekah didn't think she has," Bayta said. "Knowing Terese, I'd have to agree."

"It's not like it's that big a deal," I pointed out. "I'd

bet money that the Shonkla-raa coded his telepathy to work only with them, and once they're out of the picture the kid's extra wiring will be pretty useless. Like having a talent for some art form that doesn't exist." I looked at McMicking. "That answer your question?"

"And then some," he said. "I'd like to go back to that bit about the Shonkla-raa having spies in Terra Station. If they do, they may spot Morse as he leaves with Team One. Do you think I should take them instead?"

"Isn't it a little late to change that?" Bayta asked.

"Not really," I said. "But I don't think we should. It makes much more sense for you to come with us. Besides, I'm sure the ESS issues their agents some sort of Junior Disguise Kit. Morse is probably dying to play with it."

"I'll tell him you said that," McMicking promised. "Better yet, I'll tell him it came from Rick to Major Strasser. His attempts at a German accent are always so amusing."

"I'll have to drop in for a show someday," I said dryly.

"You'll enjoy every minute of it," McMicking assured me. "Well, I've got a few last-minute details to work out, then it's off to bed. You going to see Morse and the first team off?"

"I thought I would, yes," I said.

"Good," he said. "I'll see you then." With a nod to each of us, and a quick glance at the two defenders standing at their usual respectful distance, he turned and strode across the room to the door.

"I suppose we'd better do likewise," I told Bayta as I collected my papers and other gear. "I have a feeling this slow-motion infiltration is going to drive me nuts, though. I wish we could send everyone in at the same time and be done with it."

"You know we can't," Bayta said. "Aside from everything else, you're way more subtle than that."

"I suppose," I conceded. "Sometimes it's hell being me."

She took my hand. "It'll work, Frank," she said quietly.

"I know," I said. It was bad form, I remembered reading somewhere, for a commander to express doubts and fears in front of his troops. "It's just that . . ."

"Shh," she said softly. Letting go of my hand, she stepped closer and wrapped her arms around me.

For a long minute we held each other. And then, through the doubts swirling around my brain an old, almost forgotten memory flicked back to mind. Something the first Chahwyn Elder I'd ever met had said as he related the history behind the Chahwyn, the Modhri, and the Quadrail system.

I will admit that we began to wonder if there was still any hope for us, or whether we and the galaxy had instead begun the long dark path to defeat, he'd said. *And then, thirty years ago, you Humans burst upon the scene.*

Maybe his words had been prophetic. Maybe he'd just been trying to flatter me into staying on their payroll.

But suddenly, I realized he was right. We were the unknown quantity, the big bright-orange monkey wrench in the Shonkla-raa's carefully planned grand scheme to once again dominate the galaxy. If anyone could stop them, it was going to be Bayta, me, and the men and women who'd been sitting in this room tonight.

Two thousand years ago, the original Shonkla-raa had ignored Earth because we hadn't been telepathic enough for easy conquest and they'd been too lazy to use the old-fashioned brute-force approach on us.

It was time we showed them just how big a mistake that had been.

I took a deep breath, inhaling the subtle scent of the woman in my arms, and with that some of the swirling demons faded away. "Come on," I murmured, gently disengaging from our hug. "We need to be up early if we're going to see Morse off. We should get some sleep."

"Yes," she agreed. She hesitated, then leaned close and kissed me. "We should."

I was lying alone on my bed, staring at the ceiling with Sam and Carl standing their silent watch over me, when my alarm signaled that it was time to get up.

The schedule McMicking and I had worked out had the various twenty-man groups dribbling out into the Quadrails over a ten-day period, with Bayta, McMicking, and me bringing up the rear. Right on time, a day after the last group left Terra Station, the three of us boarded our train and headed out to join them.

Recent events had understandably given me a somewhat paranoid view of Quadrail travel. But as we rolled along at our brisk light-year per minute, somewhat to my surprise, nothing happened.

Not just nothing threatening, but *nothing*. No Shonklaraa stared at me from across the bar or dining car, no suspicious-looking Juriani or Halkas lurked around corners or paced back and forth in front of our compartment doors, no one tried to pass me messages. Best of all, no one aboard died a strange or violent death. Even the scrawny Fillies I'd grown accustomed to seeing everywhere we went were conspicuous by their absence. It was as if the Shonkla-raa had been genuinely taken in by my ridiculously transparent long-distance correspondence with Riijkhan, and were waiting patiently at Jurskala for us to come to an agreement.

I didn't believe it for a minute. Neither did Bayta. Neither, presumably, did McMicking, though I was careful not to approach him closely enough to actually ask. Wrapped inside his new face and identity, he was my last and best wild card, and I had no intention of doing anything to compromise that.

Bayta and I had traveled this route before, over a year ago, back when the Modhri had been chasing down the last of a group of sculptures which, when properly assembled in groups of three, became highly deadly weapons. As a bonus, those weapons were also undetectable by the Spiders' sophisticated Tube sensor arrays. We'd won that particular battle, and while we'd destroyed most of the weapons, I knew there were probably a few of the components still buried under the dirt in the Ten Mesas region of Veerstu.

I couldn't help thinking that, with our other weapons and equipment waiting for us on that same world, it would have been awfully nice to have an undetectable weapon in hand right now. Something that, unlike the *kwi*, I didn't need Bayta or a functioning Spider to activate for me.

We changed trains at Homshil, and as we crossed the platform we passed by a Juri at a candied flower stand who was also surreptitiously giving every passing walker a scratch from the Melding coral he had hidden in his cold-water storage tank. Serious scratches, too, from the one instance I saw, the kind that would put enough polyps into the walker's bloodstream to influence the original Modhran colony within an hour or two.

Bayta and I stopped to buy a sample of the vendor's wares. The Modhri told us that three days earlier there had been two Shonkla-raa in the station, who had spent a few hours watching the trains come and go before leaving on a train headed in the same direction as we were. Bayta checked with the stationmaster and learned they'd bought tickets for Ghonsilya, a three-day journey past the Trivsdal stop where we would be switching to the Claremiado Loop and heading into Nemuti territory.

Of course, having tickets for Ghonsilya didn't mean the Shonkla-raa would actually be getting off there. It would be trivial for them to change tickets somewhere along the way, someplace where they thought they might not be as noticeable. We thanked the Modhri and moved on, and I made a mental note to keep an eye out as we got close to Trivsdal.

From Homshil we passed through Jurskala, the source

of the messages I was still getting from Riijkhan about our pending deal. None of the walkers in the station had spotted him, though, or seen any other Shonkla-raa for at least a week.

Two days beyond Jurskala was Ian-apof, and a change to one of the lines that passed along the edge of the Nemuti FarReach and into the Tra'hok Unity. Two days after that we reached Trivsdal and switched one last time, this time to the Claremiado Loop.

Four days later, we arrived at the Veerstu Quadrail station.

The entry procedure was quick and efficient, and if the Nemuti manning the customs desks were surprised by the unusually high number of Humans that had been coming to their world over the past couple of weeks they hid their bemusement well.

Or maybe that avenue of curiosity was simply being overshadowed by the novelty of having a pair of Spiders on the passenger side of the station. Usually, the only Spiders aboard were those picking up or dropping off the lockboxes or handling other sensitive or secured cargo.

In fact, the situation was unprecedented enough that they were initially at a loss on how exactly to proceed. Sam and Carl obviously had no IDs or other official documents, and at first the station director wasn't going to let them through. I finally had to declare them as part of my luggage, a solution that didn't exactly thrill the director and probably irritated the defenders themselves.

But finally we were through.

The lockboxes where McMicking and I had stored our guns had been delivered. With my Glock once again snugged beneath my jacket and his Beretta under his, we headed for the torchyacht rental desk.

Along the way, we picked up the special equipment that the Spiders had been quietly holding for us at the station.

It was a five-day trip from the transfer station to the planet itself. We spent most of our time checking our gear, discussing the plan and last-minute thoughts that each of us had had, and otherwise just preparing ourselves for the upcoming task.

Bayta and I also spent a lot of time together. McMicking was perceptive enough to give us as much privacy as he could in the somewhat cramped quarters. Sam and Carl, naturally, didn't.

Veerstu had only two spaceports that could handle torchships. The last time Bayta and I had taken this trip we'd tried to mask our destination by landing at the port farthest from the Ten Mesas region. Now, with the long procession of human travelers making subterfuge largely moot, we chose the closer one instead. We rented an aircar, loaded everything aboard, and headed out. Two hours short of our destination, we put down in a secluded area and changed into our desert camo outfits, heavy-duty jumpsuits with thin armor plates already sewn into pockets around the torso and groin areas. With another few kilos' worth of gun belts and weapons vests loaded on top of that, we were ready.

Five minutes later, with our final task complete, we were once again in the air.

The Ten Mesas was a group of large rock formations, up to two kilometers long each, that rose up from the Veerstu desert amid a sea of smaller buttes, rock spines, and occasional clusters of vegetation, the whole thing overlaid by a light dusting of feathery, waist-high brown grass. Three of the mesas were of particular interest: a bit over two kilometers long, each one rose more or less gradually to a sudden and startling ten-meter-tall spike at one end. The Ten Mesas were the premier tourist attraction of the region, as desert tourist attractions went, with those particular three garnering most of the appreciation and photos.

What the tourists didn't know, but Bayta and I did, was that they weren't simple rock formations. They were, instead, the hidden resting place of three ancient Shonkla-raa warships.

The ten-meter spikes were the clue that had finally tipped me off when Bayta and I had first been here. Cozying the main body of a huge ship right up against the Thread would be risky; cozying the end of a ten-meter spike, not nearly so much.

I thought about the ships as we flew across the Veerstu landscape. They'd obviously been there since before the Shonkla-raa were destroyed sixteen hundred years ago, presumably stashed away as part of some military strategy the slavemasters had never gotten a chance to use. Sixteen hundred years was a long time, and the question on everyone's mind was almost certainly whether or not they still worked.

For me, the question wasn't even worth pondering. The Lynx/Viper/Hawk trinary weapons that the Modhri had been digging up the last time we were here were from that same era, and they had certainly been functional. So were the handful of *kwis* the Chahwyn had found. I had no doubt that the warships were just as functional. And even more deadly.

Bayta had wanted to destroy the ships as soon as she learned about them. I had talked her out of it, warning that letting the Modhri even suspect their existence might prove fatal somewhere down the line.

Now, because of me, the Modhri knew about the ships. Now, also because of me, the entire future of the galaxy was resting on a knife's edge.

A couple of hours before sundown, we reached the Ten Mesas.

The last time we'd been here, the Modhri had had a full-blown archaeological dig set up in the middle of the area, complete with dozens of tents of various sizes, paths with nighttime guide lights, sanitation facilities, and lots of ground vehicles. After we chased them out, I'd expected the Nemuti would move in and dismantle the facility.

Only they hadn't. If anything, the encampment was bigger and more elaborate than ever. Apparently, I'd overestimated the value of the Ten Mesas as a pristine tourist destination.

I was bringing us around in a leisurely curve to the west when I spotted the tunnel that had been dug into the western slope of the southernmost warship's burial mound.

Bayta spotted it the same time I did. "Frank?" she asked, pointing.

"I see it," I said, trying to make out the details through the shimmer from the low sunlight on the field of swaying brown grass. "McMicking?"

"Got it," he said, and I glanced over my shoulder to see that he'd already pulled out his rifle scope and was peering through it. "Looks Human-sized, as opposed to vehicles or rolling carts. Wood or ceramic framing, probably the latter. Floor appears to be dirt."

"How far does it go?" I asked.

"Three or four meters at least," McMicking said. "That's as far in as I can see."

I frowned. The plan had been for the team to play it coy, create something that looked like a staging area, and try to draw the attention of the enemy, who were surely on Veerstu and aware of their presence by now. The idea had *not* been to give the enemy any inkling that the warships were right here in the Ten Mesas region, and *especially* not that they were buried under the mesas themselves.

Had the Shonkla-raa already made their move? I'd expected Riijkhan to at least wait until Bayta and I arrived. "Is anyone moving out there?" I asked.

There was a soft click as McMicking switched the scope to infrared. "Got a foxhole sentry line," he said. "Heat shields ready but not deployed."

"Any signs of visitors?"

"Nothing showing outside the perimeter," he said. "Could be hiding behind the mesas we didn't pass."

"Maybe," I said, the uneasy feeling growing stronger. I would have sworn we'd anticipated all of the Shonkla-raa's possible gambits. Was there one we'd missed? "What about the tents?"

"Afternoon deserts are hard to read," McMicking said. "But it looks like only a few of the smaller ones are occupied, again mostly around the perimeter. Most of the heat's coming from the two big tents in the middle."

I exhaled loudly. That could be the Hardin team, the Shonkla-raa, the Hardin team plus Shonkla-raa prisoners, or the Shonkla-raa plus Hardin team prisoners. With all the heat confusion out there, and my strict order to maintain radio silence, there was no way to find out which except to go in and take a look for ourselves. "Okay," I said as I straightened out of my curve and started us inward. "Let's go see what we've got."

A few Humans appeared from the outer tents as we neared the encampment, shading their eyes as they watched our approach. As we passed the outer perimeter three men emerged from the two large tents: Morse and two of the team leaders. The team leaders, like the others we could see, had stripped down to their armored jumpsuits. Morse, like us, was in full gear, complete with vest and gun belt.

He spotted us against the low sun and lifted his own rifle scope to his eye. I waved through the windshield, and he lowered the scope and pointed to an open spot beside the spot where he and the team leaders were standing. Giving the distant mesa to the east one final look, I brought the aircar in and set it down.

Morse came over as I popped the door, the two team leaders beside him. "Welcome to Proteus," Morse greeted me, his voice slurred a little.

"Thank you," I said, frowning. Morse's cheeks seemed to be sagging, and there was something odd about his eyes and voice.

But there was no sign of the Shonkla-raa command tone. Could the strain on his face be due to the heat?

It was only as Morse's hand dropped to his Beretta that I noticed the small earpiece nestled in his left ear. His ear, and the ears of the two men beside him. "Mc-Micking!" I snapped, snatching out my Glock.

I was bringing the weapon to bear on Morse when the tent door behind him opened and a stream of jumpsuited men and woman strode out into the sunlight, all of them moving in the same rigid lockstep. "You wish to shoot them?" Morse asked, his voice still slurred. "Please—indulge yourself. They're all unarmed." In an almost leisurely manner he drew his gun and pointed it at the sky. "Or shoot me. I won't even shoot back."

I sighed. How the *hell* had the Shonkla-raa pulled this one off? "You know, I really thought you'd at least wait until I got here," I commented.

Morse lowered his gun and twitched it to the side. "Outside, all of you," he ordered. His eyes flicked to the two defenders hunched down in the rear of the aircar. "The Spiders too."

"Bayta, give them the order," I said grimly, holstering the Glock and popping my restraints. "McMicking, just play it cool."

"One at a time," Morse said, lowering his Beretta again. "You first, Compton."

I climbed out onto the sand. The desert air was shimmering with heat, and I could feel sweat popping out all over my skin as the two team leaders silently relieved me of my vest and gun belt. Morse ordered me to the front of the aircar, then gestured to McMicking.

A minute later McMicking was standing beside me, his own arsenal also confiscated. Bayta was next, and then Morse watched closely as she directed Sam and Carl outside and sent them to the rear of the vehicle. "What happens next?" I asked when we were all finally lined up where Morse wanted us.

Morse shook his head. "You are indeed a fool, Compton—"

"—if you have not already guessed," a new voice finished the sentence from behind Morse.

And the door of the big tent opened again and *Osantra* Riijkhan stepped into view.

"But don't worry," he continued as he walked toward us, four more Fillies filing out of the tent behind him. "We want you and your companions alive."

His eyes glittered with malice and anticipation. "For the present."

THIRTY-ONE :

"A well-conceived plan," Riijkhan said approvingly as he came to a halt a couple of meters behind Morse. The four other Shonkla-raa took up positions behind him as another silent stream of men and women poured from the tent. They and the original dozen whom Morse had invited me to shoot gathered themselves into two groups, one on either side of the Fillies. "Well-conceived, and subtly executed," Riijkhan continued. "You first spin this tale of a great prize waiting at Proteus Station, thinking we will perhaps be too hasty to dig deeper into the words. Then you send out your team of pilots, a few at a time, in hopes of reaching the true location while we hurriedly gather our forces at Ilat Dumar Covrey."

He gestured toward Morse. "Did you truly think we wouldn't notice the presence of Agent Morse as he left Terra Station?"

"It was a calculated risk," I said evenly, nodding at the newly minted Modhran walkers behind him. "I see I should have taken the lesson of your last attack more seriously."

"Ah, and therein lies the true genius of your plan," Riijkhan said. "A subtle and layered plan, indeed. Because you *did* anticipate that Morse might be noticed.

You also anticipated that we would still have Modhran coral we could use against you."

One of the team leaders beside Morse lifted his hand. "The skin coating was brilliant," Riijkhan continued, as the other showed me a callused but otherwise unmarked palm. "A thin layer of carefully tailored poison that would be driven into the wound made by a coral scratch, thus killing any polyps so introduced. Not only would such a sheath protect your pilots from all such attacks, but the attacks themselves would betray ourselves or our agents to them."

I felt my throat tighten. Naturally, once Morse and the others had been taken, the Shonkla-raa would have easily been able to dig out all the various layers of my plan.

Only how in hell had Riijkhan managed to take them in the first place? Hardin's medical techs, and the Modhri himself, had assured me that the skin coating would work. "Yes, you've been very clever," I said. "But I can't help noticing that aside from Morse none of them are carrying any weapons. Worried about another slave revolt like the one that killed off your forebears?"

Riijkhan's blaze darkened a couple of shades. Apparently, he didn't like hearing about unpleasant subjects. I might be able to use that. "Focus on the future, Compton," he said stiffly. "Not the past."

I took a deep breath. I still had a hole card, I reminded myself firmly. Maybe two of them.

Out of the corner of my eye, I caught the glint of sunlight off Carl's metal globe. Maybe even three of them.

But before I could play them, I needed Riijkhan to come a little closer.

"How about I just concentrate on the present?" I suggested. "Such as my former teammates here. Are you grooming them to be a future army? Or are you picking up where *Usantra* Wandek left off?"

Riijkhan snorted. "Slander not the dead, but *Usantra* Wandek's plan was wasted effort," he said. "Why spend time creating future slaves when a touch of Modhran coral can create the same slaves today?"

"I don't mean Wandek's supposed plan," I corrected. "I mean his *real* plan."

Riijkhan took a step closer to me. "You know nothing about *Usantra* Wandek's plans."

"On the contrary," I said, noting his reaction with interest. Were Wandek and, by extension, Proteus Station just two more unpleasant subjects that he didn't want to hear about? Or was this something he didn't want me talking about for some other reason entirely? "You see, I made the effort to find out why he picked Terese German," I went on. "Once I did that, everything else just fell together." I gestured to one of the Shonkla-raa behind Riijkhan. "Did you know Wandek was planning to betray you?"

The Filly stirred, and I saw his blaze darken. "You will not speak—"

He broke off at Riijkhan's upstretched hand. "Explain," Riijkhan ordered.

"Terese German is actually Terese von Archenholz," I said. "She's the daughter—well, the unhappy, estranged daughter, anyway; they don't see much of each other these days—of Martin von Archenholz, founder and head of Hands Across the Stars. That's an organization in Zurich that brings in non-Human medical experts to treat diseases we don't yet have a handle on, particularly children's diseases. Wandek's idea was to clear up Terese's genetic ailments in hopes of leveraging that success to a presumably grateful Daddy and get him to push for a permanent Filiaelian medical presence on Earth. Once he had that, Wandek would have a free hand to cure lots of children and turn them into future telepaths." I cocked my head. "And into Junior Shonkla-raa."

Riijkhan's eyes flicked to Bayta, then back to me. "Impossible."

"Not at all," I assured him. "Your throats were originally designed that way so you could sing better. Humans already have all the necessary vocal apparatus—no obvious modifications would be needed. And a Human Shonkla-raa is something none of you would ever anticipate. With Wandek pulling our telepathic strings, we'd be the perfect weapons to throw down your leaders so he could set himself up in their place."

Riijkhan took another step forward. "You lie," he said. "*Usantra* Wandek would never commit treason."

"But the interesting part," I said, ignoring his protest, "is how *you* were also very keen on letting Earth off the hook in the coming conquest. Does that mean you were already secretly working with him?"

Riijkhan drew himself up. "I cannot rebel against the Shonkla-raa leader," he intoned. "I *am* the Shonkla-raa leader."

"Really," I said. I'd actually suspected that for some time now. "Ascended to the throne on *Usantra* Wandek's death, did you? I guess our activities on Proteus weren't a total loss, at least for you." I gestured to the Humans standing behind him. "Especially since it left Wandek's Human telepathy techniques free for you to take full advantage of."

Riijkhan gazed hard at me, and I could sense his uncertainty. Maybe he'd only recently been declared leader and still wasn't comfortable with the title. Maybe he'd declared it unilaterally.

Or maybe he suspected I was goading him for a reason. "*Usantra* Wandek's experiments are not at play here," he said. "It was Dr. Aronobal's idea. She had noted—"

"The *late* Dr. Aronobal, you mean?" I interrupted. "I'm assuming she died with the rest of your Proteus contingent when *Logra* Emikai took the place down. I hope my old friend *Isantra* Kordiss gave a good showing of himself before he died."

Riijkhan's blaze darkened. "You speak too much, Compton," he warned quietly. This time, he took two steps forward, coming to a halt beside Morse.

"I'm sorry you have such trouble with the truth," I said.

"The *truth* is that Emikai was lucky," Riijkhan growled. "The other truth is that you and your schemes are pathetically weak."

"Actually, the truth is—well, we'll get back to that," I said. "You were talking about Dr. Aronobal and her clever ideas."

Again, Riijkhan seemed to measure me. "She noted your interest in the super-express train's air filtration system," he said. "She realized that while a Spider air system would eventually filter out all particulate matter, for a time that matter would remain suspended in the air."

Beside me, Bayta caught her breath. "You made an *aerosol spray* of Modhran coral?"

"Of Modhran polyps," Riijkhan corrected, his eyes again flicking to her before coming back to me. "From original Modhran coral, naturally, without the disagreeable effects inherent in the Melding variety. With careful positioning and timing of the sprays, we were able to take control of each group of Humans as they neared the Veerstu station."

I grimaced. So that was how he'd bypassed the team's tricked-out skin. That approach hadn't even occurred to me. "Which is why there weren't any walkers hanging around the platform when we got to Veerstu," I said. "You made sure to clear them all out each time a team came through so that they couldn't tip off the rest of the mind about what had happened."

"What about the other passengers in those cars?" McMicking asked.

Riijkhan looked him up and down. "You're McMicking," he said. "Compton's chief enforcement officer. Perhaps later I'll measure you against single combat."

"I'll look forward to it," McMicking said. "What about the other passengers?"

"Not all of those in the cars were affected," Riijkhan said. "Those who had inhaled enough polyps to become true Modhran Eyes exited the train with us at Veerstu."

"And?"

Riijkhan cocked his head and looked at Morse. There was a silent order, I gathered, to Morse's Modhran colony— "They were killed," Morse said, a bitter edge in his slurred voice. "The Shonkla-raa made me kill them."

I felt my throat tighten. Even knowing it was coming, the revelation was still like a kick in the gut. Beside me, Bayta stirred, but didn't speak. "You're not to blame," I told the Modhri. "The guilt is with those who gave the order."

"Compton, I—" Once again, Morse stopped in mid-sentence.

"You know, that's really annoying," I told Riijkhan, forcing calmness into my voice. I was trying to make him mad. I couldn't afford to get mad myself. "You need to let your slaves speak every once in a while."

"There are few occasions when I wish to hear them," Riijkhan said evenly. "As to the rest—" He pointed at the earphone in Morse's ear. "Transmission devices don't work inside the Tube, so there the command tone must be delivered directly. Here, and in all places where we'll someday rule, the tone can be delivered from a distance."

"Though as you say, that won't work aboard the Quadrails," I said. "I'm guessing you're going to get pretty tired of singing those same damn notes for days or weeks on end."

Riijkhan snorted. "Foolish Human. Do you think we don't know the truth? We will gut the Tube, just as you threatened to do, and sweep away the Spiders and trains into the vacuum of space. Then we will once again ride the Starpath in all its power and splendor."

He lifted his focus to the mesa rising behind us. "Magnificent, aren't they?" he murmured. "Three warships from the days of our empire. And these are only the beginning." He looked back at me. "Soon we shall have a fleet—a hundred fleets—and will bring down our hand to crush all the inferior races of the galaxy."

"That's going to be a bit awkward for you," I suggested

mildly, "given that it's these inferior races who'll be crewing your fleets for you." I nodded to his four companions. "You don't really think a party of five can run a ship that size, do you?"

"You really don't understand, do you?" Riijkhan asked, openly gloating now. "We've known about these ships for a long time. Ever since you spoke of them at Terra Station, in fact. While you wasted precious time schooling your pilots in the Shonkla-raa language, we gathered our forces here."

"Yes, I can see that," I said mockingly as I looked around the tents and the empty desert beyond. "You'd better hope I did a good job teaching my inferior-race team how to fly your ships."

"We will need very little of your help," Riijkhan assured me. "I was told by *Isantra* Kordiss that you laid a challenge before *Usantra* Wandek before you fled *Kuzyatru* Station: that the next time he came for you, he should bring all the Shonkla-raa."

"Well, throwing yourselves at me piecemeal sure isn't doing a hell of a lot," I pointed out. "So, what, is this it?"

"This is it," Riijkhan said, eyeing me speculatively. "Is that the news you're waiting for?"

I frowned. It was indeed what I was waiting for. Only he wasn't supposed to know that. Had one of my hole cards suddenly become a deuce?

But it was too late to stop now. "All of you except the ones who died at Proteus, of course," I said. "Did I mention, by the way, that that wasn't just luck, or even just *Logra* Emikai's skill? The fact is, we had a spy in your organization. *Isantra* Kordiss himself was reporting to us."

Riijkhan's blaze turned a deep chocolate brown. "Slander not the dead," he snarled. He pushed past Morse and strode toward me, his hands stiffening into Shonkla-raa knives.

Finally. "And if you find *that* truth unsettling," I continued, raising my voice, "wait until you hear how the original Shonkla-raa actually came to be."

And across at the end of the aircar, Sam and Carl abruptly came to life and started along the side of the aircar directly toward Riijkhan and me.

Or rather, toward me. I was the one, after all, whom the Chahwyn Elder had ordered them to kill if I started to speak of the forbidden subject.

But Riijkhan didn't know that. As far as he knew, the defenders were heading toward *him*, probably with murder on their minds.

And his reaction was exactly what I'd hoped it would be. Spinning to face his approaching attackers, he opened his mouth and whistled the command tone.

The defenders froze in place, and I felt Bayta stiffen beside me as she also came under their spell. Riijkhan started to turn back toward me, his tone still ringing through the air, a baleful look in his eye.

And then, Sam started moving again.

He moved slowly, like someone wading against a spring-thaw river current. But he was moving nevertheless. Riijkhan spun back around toward the Spiders, his blaze paling, as Carl stirred and also resumed his advance. A moment of stunned disbelief later, the other four Shonkla-raa opened up with command tones of their own, adding their voices to Riijkhan's and raising the volume to a head-splitting level.

And with all eyes on the defenders, I dropped into a crouch and reached under the edge of the aircar for one of the flashless stun grenades McMicking and I had concealed under the vehicle's entire rim before we'd started the last leg of our trip. In a single motion I rose back to my feet, squeezed the trigger, and hurled it high above the army of Humans standing silently behind Riijkhan. Then, squeezing my eyes tightly closed in case this one wasn't as flashless as the ones Hardin's techs had demonstrated back on Earth, I pressed my palms hard against my ears.

With a thunderclap that eclipsed even the Shonkla-raa control tone, the grenade detonated, temporarily deafening everyone within a thirty-meter radius.

And as Minnario had proved back on Proteus Station, if a walker's Modhran colony couldn't hear the command tone, the Shonkla-raa power was broken. Riijkhan was fighting to regain his balance from the grenade's effect when Hardin's team, themselves not exactly steady on their feet, staggered into a charge.

They did their best, and with another thirty seconds they might have pulled it off. But Riijkhan hadn't been lying about not being alone. The echoes of the stun blast were still caroming off the Ten Mesas when the doors of both big tents were flung open and a horde of Shonkla-raa came charging out, a hundred strong at least, slamming into the rear of the unsteady Human charge and throwing the men and women aside like combat dummies.

And with the Shonkla-raa finally out in the open, it was time to play my final card.

My comm had been taken along with my gun belt. But Morse still had his. As Riijkhan grabbed Morse's Beretta and wrenched it from his hand, I ducked past the Shonkla-raa's side and snatched Morse's comm from its holder. "*Dies irae!*" I shouted into it, dodging back as Riijkhan slashed his hand toward me. I made it back to Bayta and pulled her down into a crouch beside the air-car. "*Dies irae!*" I shouted again.

Nothing happened.

I raised the comm again, my eyes flicking away from the melee around me long enough to confirm that all of the comm's settings were correct. "*Dies irae!*" I tried one more time. "Fayr—*now*!"

But there was still nothing. And with a sinking feeling, I realized that my Belldic sharpshooters weren't going to be saving the day.

It was too late anyway. The last of the Humans were down, lying motionless or twitching in the desert dust, and with the command tone once again filling the air Sam and Carl had also ground again to a halt, their metal legs stiff and glistening in the afternoon sun.

Riijkhan turned toward me, Morse's gun still gripped in his hand. Swallowing, I rose back to my feet. There were times, I reflected distantly, when making the enemy mad maybe wasn't such a good idea. "All right," I said. "What now?"

Riijkhan didn't reply, and for a heart-thudding moment I thought he was going to shoot me right then and there. But as we stood facing each other, the downed men and women began rising slowly to their feet. They stood motionless, pain and frustration simmering in their faces.

Their hearing was coming back, and with that the brief window of opportunity had passed. Once again, the Humans and their Modhran colonies had become Shonkla-raa slaves.

"Did you truly think we wouldn't notice your Belldic ally and his commando squad?" Riijkhan asked. Instead of the anger I'd expected, his voice merely held a sort of detached curiosity. "They, too, were carefully infected with Modhran polyps on their journey here."

"I guess I should have anticipated that," I conceded. "Are they even still alive?"

"Of course," Riijkhan said, sounding surprised at the question. "As are they," he added, waving a hand behind him at the unmoving Humans once more standing at attention. "One does not kill one's soldiers without need or cause."

"I suppose not," I murmured.

"In addition, as you said earlier, we may require the aid of a few of them to operate the ship." He raised his hand, frowning at the gun he was holding as if just noticing it was still there. I tensed, but he merely handed the weapon behind him to Morse, who silently holstered it. "Now that your last hope has been proved futile, I trust you're ready to cooperate?"

I frowned. "Cooperate how?"

For the first time he actually looked embarrassed. "We've found one of the entrances to the warship," he said. "But we haven't been able to open it."

I raised my eyebrows. "You're kidding. Your own ship has locked you out?"

"Hardly," he growled. "If necessary, we'll blast it open. But we'd prefer not to cause unnecessary damage."

"And you think I know how to open the door for you?" I asked. "Or would consider doing so even if I did know?"

"You're an uncommonly intelligent Human," Riijkhan said. "And your companion is a daughter of one of the ancient races. Together, I think it possible that you'll find the solution."

"And if we don't?"

"Then you will die," he said, the complete lack of emotion in his tone somehow more chilling than any of his earlier anger had been. "Slowly, of course, and in agony."

"Of course," I said. "And if we do?"

His blaze lightened a bit. "If you do?"

"What do we get if we open the door?" I clarified. "We get to live, of course—that one's obvious. But for a job this important you'll need to throw something else into the pot."

"I've already said we can blast the door open."

"Wrecking who knows what in the process," I reminded him. "Come on, *Osantra* Riijkhan—you were ready to hand over the whole Terran Confederation if I cooperated with you. Surely you can spare a little loose change on this one."

His eyes were steady on me. "What do you want?"

I pointed at my battered team standing unmoving in the sun. "Them."

Riijkhan seemed taken aback. "What?"

"You heard me," I said. "They all get to leave with

Bayta and me after we open the door for you. Unharmed, of course, and you pledge not to come after us."

"Impossible," Riijkhan said firmly. "But I offer a counterproposal."

I nodded. "I'm listening."

"Since they are clearly of value to you," Riijkhan said, "I offer to kill one for each hour you fail to open the warship. Beginning with him." He leveled a finger toward Morse. "The first hour begins now."

I looked at Morse. His face was silently contorted, the face of a man who wants desperately to say something. "Let him speak," I said.

Riijkhan shrugged slightly— "Don't do it," Morse gasped. "Let the bast—"

His mouth clamped shut again. "He's spoken his word," Riijkhan said. "Do I need again to speak mine?"

For a long moment I gazed into Morse's eyes. He'd hated me once. Probably still did. And I'd never really liked him, either.

I sighed. "Fine," I said, taking Bayta's arm. "Show me this damn door."

Riijkhan loaded us into one of the larger ground vehicles: Bayta, Morse, five of the other Shonkla-raa, Mc-Micking, Riijkhan himself, and me. Sam and Carl, their legs securely chained, they hauled away into one of the big tents.

Somewhere along the line, once he had a spare moment or two, Riijkhan would probably order their dissection.

Considering that the Shonkla-raa had known about the warships for only a few weeks, they'd done an impressive amount of work. The tunnel went straight into the mesa, cutting first through a meter or so of dirt and then boring through solid rock. Forty meters in, it had finally struck an old but still smooth wall of metal.

At that point, the tunnel branched off in both directions, widening at various points along the way, here and there climbing up the side of the hull as the Fillies had dug along an interesting set of markings or a promising groove. In a few places alcoves had been dug out of the rock beside the ship, where small machine shops or equipment storage had been set up. One of the alcoves we passed contained a collection of recovered artifacts, and I spotted a couple each of the small Lynx, Hawk, and Viper sculptures that had given Bayta and me such trouble our last time here. A string of lights glowed down from the ceiling, and a six-centimeter pipe running around the upper edge hissed out a continual flow of fresh air.

And amid the dust and light and rumble of activity, the whole damn place was filled to the brim with Shonklaraa.

I'd thought the hundred Fillies who'd suddenly appeared in reaction to my stun grenade attack had been impressive. But there had to be at least twice that number here in the warren, digging at the tunnel faces or examining the hull or working to coax more artifacts from the rocky ground. Three of the aliens were crammed into another of the alcoves, crooning their command tone softly into an impressively large radio transmitter.

On the ride over, with the advantage of hindsight, I'd been regretting not having simply rammed one of the big tents with our aircar on our way in, wondering if I might have been lucky enough to take out the command-tone transmitter that still held the Hardin team hostage. Now, with the advantage of even more hindsight, I was just as glad I hadn't tried it.

"Nothing like a really good group project to draw people together," I commented to Riijkhan as we walked along the left-hand branch of the tunnel. "Are you really all here? Or was that just a ploy to egg me into calling Fayr down on you?"

"Of course we're all here," he said. "This is the culmination of our dreams."

"Ah," I said. "Besides which, with your Proteus base gone and the rest of the Filiaelian Assembly hunting you like fresh game, this is as good a place as any to lie low?"

He didn't answer. Fifty meters later, we reached the door.

It was considerably bigger than any of us, taller and wider, implying it was probably a cargo or vehicle hatchway. There were eight small openings set into the hull on either side, evenly spaced from eye level to waist level. Some of them were covered with metal mesh, while others were little more than deep, irregular-edged dimples in the metal.

There was no handle, keyhole, touchpad, or anything else that suggested an opening mechanism. Or at least nothing recognizable as such. "There," Riijkhan said, jabbing a finger at it. "And your first hour is now half over."

Under normal circumstances, I would have stalled for a while, just to make it look good. But I was pretty sure Riijkhan meant what he said about the hourly executions. "Was that a collection of artifacts I saw back there?" I asked.

"It was."

"Have someone bring me one of everything," I said. "I think I can have this open for you in a few minutes."

Riijkhan's eyes flicked to Morse, who turned and headed back toward the artifact alcove. "We've already tried each of them in each of the openings," he warned. "None of them is a key."

"I know," I said. "While we wait, how about giving us a peek at your plans? Since you're going to kill all of us anyway, you really have nothing to lose."

"We may not kill *you*," Riijkhan said. "I still hope to find a way to persuade you to our side. If we do, Bayta will naturally also live."

"As a guarantee of my cooperation."

"Yes," Riijkhan said. "As to the others, we'll soon see if we need any of them to help control this ship. Those who aren't needed, as you say, will be eliminated."

"I thought you didn't like wasting troops."

"I don't," Riijkhan said. "But your demonstration earlier has also reminded me that it's dangerous to be overdependent on slaves."

"Seems to me that leaves you between the proverbial rock and hard place," I said. "Unless you expect more Shonkla-raa to rise spontaneously from the ground, your current crowd is pretty much it."

"Not from the ground." He tapped the metal hull beside us. "From here. Once the ship is activated and freed from its nest, we will have the necessary time, resources, and freedom of movement to re-create the *Kuzyatru* Station facilities that were destroyed by the traitor Emikai. Once we're fully operational, we'll send word back to the Assembly. From there, thousands of Filiaelians will rise up and join us, eager to take back what was once ours."

"Impressive," I murmured. "Hitler would be proud."

"Who?"

I shook my head. "Never mind."

Morse returned, a tray of artifacts in his hands. Among them, as I'd hoped, were a Lynx, a Viper, and a Hawk, the three components of the ancient Shonkla-raa trinary weapon. "Good," I said briskly. "Bring them here, and let's see what we've got."

Morse started forward, then abruptly stopped. "A moment," Riijkhan said, eyeing me closely. "Modhri: are any of these devices weapons?"

I held my breath. But Riijkhan had phrased the question just loosely enough. "No," Morse said.

Riijkhan nodded, and Morse started forward.

And again stopped. "Can any combination form a weapon?" Riijkhan added.

Morse seemed to wilt a little. "Yes."

Riijkhan eyed me, his blaze darkening. "Fine," I said with a sigh. "I just need the Viper."

"What is it?" Riijkhan asked suspiciously. "What does it do?"

"It's a power source," I explained. "I don't think the door's locked. I think it's just not powered up."

"And you can do that from out here?"

"I don't know," I said with strained patience. "Give me the Viper, and we'll find out together."

Riijkhan whinnied a snort. But Morse had, after all, already confirmed that none of the artifacts by itself was a weapon. At Riijkhan's silent command he set the tray down, picked out the Viper from the collection, and walked over to me.

I took it from him, an eerie feeling creeping up my back. The Viper was a power source, just as I'd told Riijkhan.

What I *hadn't* told him was that under the proper circumstances it could also explode violently. Circumstances that included an injured, pain-racked, or highly stressed Modhri.

Which meant that I held the final solution in my hands.

It wasn't a pleasant solution. Certainly not the one I would have chosen. But it was the best we were going to get. Normally, a Viper explosion was reasonably contained, but here inside a tunnel system I guessed it had a fair chance of bringing the whole wall of rock down on top of the working Shonkla-raa. If it managed to also take out the command-tone transmission station, Hardin's team back in the compound would suddenly be freed from Shonkla-raa control. If they were able to take out the remaining Fillies fast enough, and if Riijkhan was telling the truth about the entire Shonkla-raa contingent being here, we could eliminate the threat right here and now.

All it would cost would be Morse, McMicking, Bayta, and me. Heavy collateral damage, indeed.

But the only other choice was capitulation.

I braced myself. "Okay," I said to Riijkhan. "I need you to release the Modhri."

Riijkhan's blaze darkened. "Why?"

"Because this gadget was apparently designed and intended for Modhran use," I told him. "It therefore needs the Modhri to telepathically activate it."

"Very well," Riijkhan said. "I will give the order."

I locked eyes with Morse and gave a little nod. He couldn't nod back, but in his eyes I could see that he and the Modhri understood. He took the Viper and slid its irregular end into the opening that matched its shape. Stepping close to Bayta, I surreptitiously took her hand.

And with a grinding like sand in teeth, the door began to move, backing away ponderously into the hull. It receded about a meter, until the inner edge of the hull itself was visible. Then, just as ponderously, the door moved sideways, sliding into a pocket to the side and revealing a faintly lit corridor beyond. For a moment there was a small breeze as the air pressures between the ship and the tunnel equalized, and I caught the scent of dust and lubricants and old metal.

The door stopped, the breeze faded away, and Morse pulled the Viper from the receptacle.

And we were still alive. All of us.

I looked at Morse. Surely he'd understood what I'd been telling him to do with the Viper. He gazed back, his eyes trapped inside a body that was no longer his.

And with a sinking feeling, I understood.

Riijkhan had called it, way back on the super-express. The Modhri wasn't on my side. Not anymore.

I took a deep breath. "There you go," I murmured to Riijkhan, gesturing to the opening. "Help yourself."

Riijkhan drew himself up, murmuring something under his breath in Fili, and beckoned to one of the Shonkla-raa who'd come running up at the sound of the door's opening. {Inform the herders to gather the slaves and bring them here,} he ordered.

{The Humans only?} the other Shonkla-raa asked.

{Humans and Bellidos both,} Riijkhan said. {And bring all the *Psika* sculptures that have been found, as well. We may require them for power.}

{I obey.} The Shonkla-raa stepped back and pulled out his comm.

Riijkhan turned back to me. "Help ourselves, you say?" he said. "No, Compton, I'm not so selfish. Your people will have the honor of walking before us down the path that leads to our final victory."

I felt my stomach tighten. "Before they die?"

"Yes," he said softly. "Before they die."

THIRTY-TWO :

I'd suspected Riijkhan's grandiose offer hadn't been driven by magnanimity, or even by some strange nod toward future history. But it wasn't until the line of Humans and Bellidos began to file through the hatchway under Shonkla-raa supervision that I realized just how low Riijkhan's motivations really were.

No matter how good the ship looked, it was very, very old. Old electronics and power sources had a tendency to decay over time, and depending on how much power was running through a given system such decay could be lethal.

So the slaves would go first. They would be the ones to turn on lights and power systems, and along the way to also trigger any faults or short-circuits or pressurized chemical tank failures. They would take the risks and die so their masters could live.

Riijkhan went in on the third wave, taking Bayta, McMicking, Morse, and me with him. We didn't go far, ending up in what looked like a control/monitor room about twenty meters in from the hatchway. The leading edge of Humans and Shonkla-raa had already come by, and had used one of the Vipers to power up the banks of monitors arranged across two of the walls. Most of the screens showed large rooms, though their details could only be vaguely made out in the dim lighting that was still the norm across most of the ship. A couple of the screens also showed wide corridors, and one of them showed the hatchway through which Humans, Bellidos, and Fillies were still streaming. Four of the Shonkla-raa had seated themselves in the chairs at the control board and were gazing intently at the rows of controls or cautiously manipulating dials and keys.

"Probably a security office," McMicking said, nodding toward the board. "You see those holsters on each of the chairs? Just about the right size for extra sidearms."

"Looks like a rifle rack over there, too," I agreed, nodding toward an empty rack behind the desks.

"Shouldn't a security office also have a set of floor plans?" Bayta asked. "I don't see anything like that."

"It's probably all computerized," I said. "Or else it's supposed to be displayed over there," I added, pointing to the blank side wall.

The words were barely out of my mouth when one of the Shonkla-raa did something to his controls, and the deck plans popped up right where I was pointing. I got a glimpse of a maze of corridors and rooms before the view shifted to another deck with an entirely different maze. That one lasted a couple of seconds and was replaced by another, then by another, and another. Most of the decks, I noted, had one or two bright red spots in various places, usually in one of the larger rooms. About the time the tenth deck came along, I tentatively concluded the dots were the locations of the monitor cameras.

Finally, the series ended. {Excellent,} Riijkhan said. While I'd been busy gawking at the deck plans, I saw now, he'd been recording the whole sequence on his reader. {The monitor locations will indicate the most important rooms. We'll begin with those.}

{There are sixty of them,} one of the Shonkla-raa at the board reported. {Approximately one for each six of us. How do you wish to proceed?}

{You four will remain here,} Riijkhan ordered. {Divide the rest into sixty search teams, one for each location.}

{And the slaves?}

{Distribute them among the teams,} Riijkhan said. {Instruct each team to make certain one or more of their slaves travels at the front. The slaves will also take the lead in all activation procedures, especially those involving the *Psika* sculptures.}

{I obey.} The Shonkla-raa pulled out a comm and began speaking into it.

Riijkhan turned back to me. "It won't be long now," he said. "Are you hungry? I could send for food if you'd like."

"I'm fine, thanks," I said.

"I'd like something," Bayta said suddenly. "And something to drink, too."

"Of course," Riijkhan said. Now that he was about to get everything his evil little heart desired, he was all courtesy and goodwill. He pulled out his comm and gave the order.

I looked at Bayta. She couldn't really be wanting to eat, not under these circumstances. She held my eyes for a moment, and then nodded her head microscopically across the room toward Morse. Frowning, I looked casually over at him.

He was standing as rigid and emotionless as ever . . . but as I ran my eyes up and down him I saw that his right forefinger was moving. Not much, barely a quiver, probably the only freedom of movement he'd been able to find within the Shonkla-raa orders.

But it wasn't random or nervous movement. The finger was twitching rhythmically, deliberately, tapping out code. Tapping out a single word, repeated over and over.

Stall.

"Fine," I said with a sigh. "If you're ordering out for Bayta anyway, I suppose I'll have something, too. McMicking? Morse?"

"Morse has already eaten," Riijkhan said. "And McMicking may not wish to weigh himself down."

"I agree," McMicking agreed evenly.

I felt my eyes narrow. "What's that supposed to mean?"

"I may yet need you, Compton," Riijkhan said. "You've proved your value today, and there may be other small matters on which I'll wish your advice. Bayta, as we both know, I'll need to control you. Morse's training also makes him of unusual value as one of my soldiers."

His eyes glittered as he looked at McMicking. "McMicking, though, I don't need."

A shiver ran up my back. I'd hoped Riijkhan had forgotten about his casual offer of single combat with McMicking. "So make him one of your soldiers, too," I said, a small part of my brain noting the incredible irony of me even suggesting such a thing. "You must still have some Modhran coral around."

"*Isantra* Yleli was a loyal member of my force," Riijkhan said. "So were the others of his group. McMicking killed them."

"McMicking had nothing to do with Yleli's death," I insisted.

"No matter," Riijkhan said. "He's killed other Shonkla-raa. I'm curious to see his fighting technique."

"It's mostly just subterfuge and tricks," McMicking said. "I'll probably be a disappointment to you."

"Do you refuse, then?"

"Not at all," McMicking assured him. "Whenever you feel ready."

For a moment they gazed at each other, Riijkhan looking like a tightly coiled spring, McMicking looking preternaturally calm. The room had become very quiet, I noticed, not just because everyone had stopped talking but also because the sounds of men and Bellidos and

Shonkla-raa in the corridor outside had faded away. A movement caught my eye, and I looked up at one of the hallway monitors to see a cluster of Fillies and their slaves walking briskly past on their way to their target room.

I looked at Morse. *Almost*, his twitching finger spelled out. *Almost.* "There is one problem with this," I spoke up. "If you kill McMicking now, *Osantra* Riijkhan—or if he kills you, for that matter—one of you will never get to hear why I wasn't surprised that you knew about these ships. Because I *did* know you were going to be told about them. In fact, I was counting on it."

Riijkhan gave a snort. "You seek to stall," he said. "You hope to save the life of your friend."

"No, my friend is going to die today," I said softly. "And you're going to die with him. Because I know who your agent was, the agent you had planted on us. I also know that you lied to me earlier. *Usantra* Wandek's plan wasn't to overthrow the Shonkla-raa leadership. He had something much more subtle in mind."

Reluctantly, Riijkhan finally turned to face me. "Then tell me, since you're so eager to do so," he growled. "What in fact was this subtle plan?"

There was more movement on the monitors, and I looked up to see a couple of the screens grow brighter as the Humans handling the Vipers powered up the rooms' main lighting. "You were right about the pointlessness of creating Human slaves through telepathic manipulation," I said, looking back at Riijkhan. "But there's no point in trying to make them Shonkla-raa shock troops, either. We may have the voice to control the Modhri, but we don't have the muscle to take down Filiaelian or Shorshian warriors."

"Then what use *did* he see in you?" Riijkhan asked.

"You see, you slipped up, *Osantra* Riijkhan," I said. "Just a little, but enough. Back when you first tried to recruit me, you said that Humans would be given free run of the galaxy, and that we would be roaming wherever we wished."

I smiled tightly at him. "We were going to be your secret police, weren't we? We were going to roam, all right, roam around the galaxy watching for slave revolts or other dangers to the Shonkla-raa master race."

For a moment Riijkhan was silent. "I was right," he said at last. "You're indeed very clever."

"All it took was knowing how you think," I said. "You would never offer to leave Earth alone unless you had some better use planned for us. Your big throats are a dead giveaway. But Human spies would be completely anonymous, drifting casually along among all the rest of the ordinary tourists and businessmen, completely undetectable until they suddenly commandeered a group of Modhran walkers."

I lifted a finger. "But Wandek knew he could only risk giving Human agents that kind of power if he had rock-solid control over them. Hence, the telepathy experiments and Wandek's plan to set up a genetic farm with Martin von Archenholz on Earth."

"So you reach the truth," Riijkhan said. "But you reach it too late."

I shook my head. "You aren't paying attention. I'm not just coming to this conclusion *now*. I already said I've been on to you since Venidra Carvo. Because your spy was Terese von Archenholz's unborn child, whose partially developed auditory apparatus was nevertheless capable of picking up muffled conversations going on near his mother. Your receivers of those relayed conversations were the scrawny little Fillies, whose physique is presumably a side effect of the genetic manipulation that made them able to link telepathically with properly prepared Humans."

The four Shonkla-raa at the desks, I saw, had abandoned their own work and were listening intently to the conversation. "That's why you always had one of them dogging our trail," I continued. "That's also why, whenever there was any kind of confrontation between us, the scrawny ones were never around. They were always stuck in their compartments, as close as they could get to Terese, hoping to get something useful."

"Not always," Riijkhan corrected, his voice unnaturally soft. "On Venidra Carvo one of them joined our encirclement attack."

"Because he was already on the scene, and because you needed everyone you could get to make the encirclement look real," I said. "And I'm quite sure you knew at the time what a horrendous risk it was, given his value and knowing that he was the one we'd probably charge through on our way out of the circle. But you had no choice. He was on the scene because he'd been ordered to stay near Terese, and you needed to create a big, obvious threat in order to move us over to her before her attempt to poison herself robbed you of your inside man."

"And so you spoke of these ships at Terra Station, knowing we would learn of them," Riijkhan said, a growing edge to his voice. "You sought to draw all of us here, then set up an ambush with your Humans and your Bellidos allies."

"Exactly," I said. "The ships were the bait. You were the catch. And it worked."

"Did it?" Riijkhan waved a hand. "Your ambush has failed. We remain in full control of the ship and the situation. How do you then speak as if we have failed?"

"Because you have," I said. "You're not in control of the ships. You're not in control of anything." I looked at Morse. *Now*, his tapping finger confirmed. "I believe Agent Morse has something to say."

Riijkhan looked at Morse. "He will remain silent."

"Fine," I said, shrugging. "If you want to die without even knowing why, go ahead."

Riijkhan flashed a look at me— "Compton," Morse said, his voice gasping a little as the control over his mouth was suddenly released. "Thank you."

I felt my throat tighten. But as I'd told Bayta, the cost was always set by the aggressors. There was nothing we could do now but pay it. "You're welcome," I said.

"For what do you thank him?" Riijkhan demanded.

"For his trust," Morse said, his eyes still on me. "For his friendship. For the chance to see the leaves on the tree, if only for a brief time." His eyes rested momentarily on Bayta, then returned to me. "You will watch over the rest?"

"Yes," I promised, my thoughts flashing back to the scene at the warship door, and the sudden revelation I'd had there.

No, the Modhri was no longer on my side. Instead, I was now on his. With the failure of my plans, he had taken charge.

Don't ever ask me to do that, the Modhri had said when I'd once dared to suggest that he order part of a mind segment to die. But he hadn't said it because he wasn't willing. He'd said it because he must have suspected even then that it might come to this, and he didn't want even a hint of that thought floating around where the Shonkla-raa could pluck it from his mind or infer it from my words.

He had taken charge, and was about to make the ultimate sacrifice.

And when the mind segment died, the Shonkla-raa control over his hosts would vanish.

"And you were right," Morse added with a small smile. "It was indeed the beginning of a beautiful friendship."

"And it still is," I said quietly. "Good-bye, Modhri."

I don't think it was until that moment that Riijkhan suddenly got it. {Attack!} he shouted, and leaped toward Morse.

He never made it. McMicking was ready, stepping between them and dropping into combat stance. Riijkhan snarled something and jabbed a knife hand viciously toward him. McMicking dodged the blow, flashing a side kick into Riijkhan's abdomen. Riijkhan jolted back with the impact, then slashed another blow toward his opponent. Again, McMicking dodged, but this time he didn't dodge quite far enough. The clawed fingers caught him across the forehead, gashing a line of bright red and knocking him out of the way.

Just as Morse fired three thudwumper rounds from his Beretta into Riijkhan's chest.

The four Shonkla-raa at the control board were already in motion. But it was too late for them, too. I snatched one of my jumpsuit's armor plates from its pocket, snapped it in half and pulled the pieces apart, then hurled them in a diverging pattern toward one of the Fillies. He was watching them go past on either side of him, no doubt wondering at my incredibly inept marksmanship, when the nearly invisible connecting wire sliced through his neck. The second Shonkla-raa died in exactly the same bloody way as McMicking's wire bolo cut his throat, as well. The third was starting around the edge of the control board when McMicking broke open another plate from his jumpsuit, plucked out the throwing knife created as the metal shattered along its preset fracture lines, and hurled it squarely into one of the Shonkla-raa's nerve centers. He was howling in blinding agony when my own knife put an end to the pain, and to him.

The fourth was racing desperately toward McMicking when Morse fired two more thudwumpers into him. He sprawled onto his face on the deck, sending a splash of blood in all directions, and lay still. Taking a deep breath, I looked up at the monitors, wondering even now if it had all been for nothing.

It hadn't. All across the ship, in every room where the isolated groups of would-be conquerors and their newly freed slaves had gathered, the Shonkla-raa were fighting for their lives.

And they were losing. The Hardin security force—not the Hardin pilots and navigators that I'd carefully led

Riijkhan to expect, but McMicking's best combat experts—had had eight weeks of intensive training in the new and undetectable weapons the techs had created and hidden in their jumpsuits. Fayr and his commandos had no such exotic weaponry, but they had their own highly honed combat training plus the intimate knowledge of Shonkla-raa physiology that we'd obtained from Yleli and his late companions aboard the Homshil train.

Five minutes later, it was all over.

Almost.

"Frank," Bayta murmured, touching my arm, her eyes on Riijkhan. "He's still alive."

I looked down. Riijkhan's breathing was fast and shallow, and the thudwumper holes in his chest were still oozing blood. But his eyes were open, and he was gazing up at me with disbelief and hatred. "Any last words?" I asked, crouching down beside him.

His hand twitched, as if he was hoping for one last shot at me. But the strength necessary for an attack was long gone. "No?" I asked. "In that case, I have a few. You made two mistakes, *Osantra* Riijkhan. You and the rest of the Shonkla-raa. Your first mistake was in focusing exclusively on what *I* was planning, and never even considering the possibility that the Modhri might have plans of his own."

I looked up at the monitors and the dead and dying Shonkla-raa. "Your second mistake was a philosophical one," I said softly. "You understood masters and slaves and non-slaves. But you never understood freedom. That's what people will fight for. That's what they'll die for."

There was a gurgle from below me, and I looked down to see Riijkhan's eyes close again. "I suppose we should put an end to it," I said, standing up again. "Morse?"

"No," Morse said flatly.

I looked over at him. He was standing off to the side, his Beretta still gripped in his hand, staring down at the dying Shonkla-raa. "No?" I asked carefully.

"No," he repeated, looking up at me.

And as I gazed at his face, I understood. The Modhri, once Morse's silent puppeteer, had emerged hesitantly from the shadows to become his ally and, eventually, his friend. A closer friend even than he'd been to me. "Because if you don't shoot it'll take longer?" I asked.

A small, pitiless smile touched the corners of Morse's mouth. "And because it'll hurt more," he said grimly. "Let him die on his own."

And we did.

THIRTY-THREE :

The victory had been costly. Sixty of our two hundred men and women had been injured, along with nine of Fayr's thirty commandos. Twenty-one Humans and twelve Bellidos also lay dead. More lives, I reflected bitterly, for me to add to my conscience.

But the lives hadn't been given in vain. The Shonkla-raa, all of them, were dead.

And the galaxy was once again safe. At least, for now.

"We'll need to send the defenders back to the Tube as soon as possible," Bayta said as she and I wearily headed through the now silent tunnel toward the parked vehicles that had brought us here. It was night outside, and I could feel the cool desert air flowing in across our legs. "They'll be able to organize special transport for the wounded once everyone's able to travel." She hesitated. "We'll need to deal with the bodies, as well."

"McMicking and Fayr will probably want to handle that personally," I told her. "They can laser whatever requests they have up to the station, and from there to Earth and whoever's been backing Fayr's group."

"All right." Bayta paused. "I never thought the Modhri would be willing to do something like that."

"I was rather surprised myself," I admitted. "The

Modhri as a whole won't be affected much, of course. But it's still very impressive that an entire mind segment would be willing to sacrifice himself for us."

"Because he understood freedom," she said quietly.

"Yes," I agreed. "The big question now is whether or not he understands responsibility."

Bayta hunched her shoulders uncomfortably. "You mean whether he'll be willing to eliminate the colonies inside people who don't want them?"

"That's part of it," I said. "He may also have trouble with some of his more far-flung mind segments who may resist these changes."

Bayta gave a small almost-laugh. "You make it sound like he's heading for a civil war."

"That *is* a very weird image, all right," I agreed. "But it may not be all that far off."

"He'll come out of it all right," Bayta assured me. "And I think he'll be all right with his colonies, too. Agent Morse is already talking about going back to Yandro to get another colony for himself, and some of the Hardin Industries people were saying the same thing. They seemed to like the kind of instant communication and information access they could get from their symbionts."

"Their *symbionts*?" I asked, frowning. "I thought Riijkhan used the older version of Modhran coral on them."

"He did," Bayta said. "But Agent Morse's hybrid colony was able to influence the rest of the mind segment into creating the same relationship with the others that he and his colony already had."

"I didn't know a Melding colony was strong enough to do that," I said. "In that case, scratch my concerns about the far-flung Modhran colonies. That solves a lot of problems right there."

"Yes," Bayta said. "I'm mostly relieved that we won't have to worry about the Elders creating more defenders."

"Amen to that," I agreed. "Like I told the Elder at Yandro, I like the Spiders and Quadrail just the way they are."

"And the Elders, too?" Bayta asked, her voice suddenly a little odd. "Do you like them? Even when they try to kill you?"

I threw a sideways look at her. "What are you talking about?" I asked cautiously.

"You don't need to deny it," she said. "I was right there, this afternoon, when you offered to tell *Osantra* Riijkhan about the Shonkla-raa origins. I saw the reaction of the defenders, moving toward you even though I'd ordered them to stand still. And I also saw they were so intent on silencing you that they continued moving even over the first few seconds of the command tone. That implies whatever you were about to say was a secret they very much wanted kept hidden."

She took a deep breath. "Which can only mean that it was the Chahwyn. They were the ones who created the first Shonkla-raa."

I grimaced. So there it was. The Elder had promised me death if I told their secret. And now Bayta knew it. There was no way they weren't going to jump to the wrong conclusion on that one. "You never heard that," I told her firmly. "Not from me, not from anyone. You weren't supposed to ever know that."

She shook her head. "You've trained me too well," she murmured. "I see things now. I hear things. I understand things."

"And sometimes all that cleverness is a damn curse," I said harshly. "If the Chahwyn find out you know—"

"They won't find out," she said firmly. "Not until it's too late for them to do anything."

I felt my pulse suddenly speed up. "What do you mean, too late? Bayta, you're not—?" Impulsively, I stopped short and grabbed her shoulders, turning her around to face me. "Bayta, what are you saying?"

"I'm not going back to them," she said, her eyes smoldering with a cold fire. "They've manipulated us, over and over again. They've schemed and lied—they've especially lied. And now I find out they created not just one, but *both* of the threats who've killed so many people? The threats we've been risking our lives all this time to fight?"

"They were forced to create the Modhri," I reminded her. "As for the Shonkla-raa, it probably seemed like a good idea at the time."

"It doesn't matter," Bayta said. "I'm tired of it—I'm tired of *them*. I'm finished, Frank. I want to go someplace where I won't have to deal with them anymore."

"Such as?"

"I was thinking about Yandro," she said. "Most of the Melding is there, or will be soon. They'll be helping to nurture and teach the Modhran segment-prime. Maybe they can find something I could do to help."

"Ah," I said. "I don't suppose you'd consider coming to Earth instead?"

She shrugged. "I don't know. What would I do on Earth?"

I let go of her shoulders and took her hands. "Be with me," I said.

She gazed at me, her mouth dropping open a little. "You mean . . . you still want me with you? Even now that it's all over?"

"Especially now that it's all over," I said. "I don't have a lot to offer you, Bayta, with the Chahwyn about to cancel my stipend and my handy little first-class Quad-rail pass. Maybe I'll take Hardin up on his offer—he's obviously got some loose cannons on his payroll, and McMicking can't smoke out all of them by himself. But whatever I end up doing, I'd like you to be a part of it."

Her eyes glistened with sudden tears. "Even though I'm not Human?"

"Human and Chahwyn are just labels," I said. "What's important is that you're Bayta. The whole package is the person I've been working with." I braced myself. Two years of fighting and battling and denying even the word, let alone the thought— "The whole package is the one I've kind of grown to love."

It was a long kiss, a deep kiss, a satisfying kiss. And when it ended I felt as if the weight of the universe had finally been lifted from my shoulders.

Because it was finally over. The Shonkla-raa were defeated, the Quadrail wasn't about to be changed forever for the worse, and the Modhri . . . the Modhri would find his own way.

From the far end of the tunnel, I heard footsteps approaching. "We'd better go," I said, taking Bayta's arm and starting toward the exit again. "Under the circumstances, we probably shouldn't send Sam and Carl back to the Tube *quite* as quickly as we'd planned. We don't want the Chahwyn getting even a hint that we both know their deepest, darkest secret. Not until we're well beyond their reach."

"That's okay—we don't need the defenders to be physically there," Bayta assured me. "We can laser up our medical requests, then make any final arrangements in person once we reach the station." She paused. "And on the way back to Earth . . . ?"

"Yes?" I said cautiously.

"Do you think we could find a dit-rec of *Casablanca*?" she asked. "I'd really like to hear this story you keep talking about."

ABOUT THE AUTHOR

Timothy Zahn is the author of more than forty original science fiction novels, including the popular Cobra and Blackcollar series. His recent works include the previous Quadrail novels, *Night Train to Rigel, The Third Lynx, Odd Girl Out,* and *The Domino Pattern,* such stand-alone SF novels as *Angelmass, Manta's Gift, The Green and the Gray,* and the Dragonback young adult adventures *Dragon and Thief,* an A.L.A. Best Book for Young Adults, *Dragon and Soldier, Dragon and Slave, Dragon and Herdsman, Dragon and Judge,* and *Dragon and Liberator.* He has had many short works published in the major SF magazines, including "Cascade Point," which won the Hugo Award for best novella. Among his other works are the bestselling Star Wars® novel *Heir to the Empire,* the Hand of Thrawn duology, and the recent *Choices of One,* as well as other Star Wars® novels, and *Terminator Salvation: From the Ashes.* He lives in Oregon.

Contact him at www.facebook.com/TimothyZahn.

TOR

Voted
#1 Science Fiction Publisher
25 Years in a Row

by the *Locus* Readers' Poll

———•———

Please join us at the website below
for more information about this
author and other science fiction,
fantasy, and horror selections, and to
sign up for our monthly newsletter!